PRAISE FOR CYNTHIA EDEN
AND HER NOVELS . . .

BROKEN

"Cynthia Eden's *Broken* is what romantic suspense is supposed to be—fast, furious, and very sexy!"
Karen Rose, *New York Times* bestselling author

"Sexy, mysterious, and full of
heart-pounding suspense!"
Laura Kaye, *New York Times* bestselling author

"I dare you not to love a Cynthia Eden book!"
Larissa Ione, *New York Times* bestselling author

"Fast-paced, smart, sexy and emotionally
wrenching—everything I love about
a Cynthia Eden book!"
HelenKay Dimon

"Cynthia Eden writes smart, sexy and
gripping suspense. Hang on tight while

By Cynthia Eden

The LOST Series
BROKEN
TWISTED
SHATTERED
TORN
TAKEN

Coming Soon

WRECKED

ATTENTION: ORGANIZATIONS AND CORPORATIONS
HarperCollins books may be purchased for educational, business, or sales promotional use. For information, please e-mail the Special Markets Department at SPsales@harpercollins.com.

CYNTHIA EDEN

TAKEN

AVONBOOKS

An Imprint of HarperCollinsPublishers

This is a work of fiction. Names, characters, places, and incidents are products of the author's imagination or are used fictitiously and are not to be construed as real. Any resemblance to actual events, locales, organizations, or persons, living or dead, is entirely coincidental.

Excerpt from *Wrecked* copyright © 2017 by Cindy Roussos.

TAKEN. Copyright © 2016 by Cindy Roussos. All rights reserved. Printed in the United States of America. No part of this book may be used or reproduced in any manner whatsoever without written permission except in the case of brief quotations embodied in critical articles and reviews. For information, address HarperCollins Publishers, 195 Broadway, New York, NY 10007.

First Avon Books mass market printing: December 2016

ISBN 978-0-06243747-1

Avon Trademark Reg. U.S. Pat. Off. and in Other Countries, Marca Registrada, Hecho en U.S.A.
Avon, Avon Books, and the Avon logo are trademarks of HarperCollins Publishers.
HarperCollins® is a registered trademark of HarperCollins Publishers.

16 17 18 19   QGM   10 9 8 7 6 5 4 3 2 1

If you purchased this book without a cover, you should be aware that this book is stolen property. It was reported as "unsold and destroyed" to the publisher, and neither the author nor the publisher has received any payment for this "stripped book."

Quite simply, this book is for my readers—my wonderful, amazing readers.

Thank you so much for your support. Happy reading.

ACKNOWLEDGMENTS

I NEED TO START BY FIRST THANKING THE TALENTED staff at Avon. It is an absolute pleasure to work with you all!

I'd also like to thank my lovely and sharp agent Laura for her always spot-on insight.

I am having so much fun writing the LOST books, and I sure hope readers keep enjoying the stories. More twists and turns are on the way . . . and some familiar characters are about to appear again.

PROLOGUE

BAILEY JONES DIDN'T WANT TO DIE. NOT TIED UP, tortured, and all alone in that damn little shack. She couldn't feel her fingers. That should have scared her—that terrible numbness—but she was long past the point of being afraid. She was mad now. So fucking angry—why had this happened? Why her? And, why, *why* wouldn't the jerk who held her just let her go?

Her face slid over the rough wooden floor of the cabin. She yanked at the rope that held her wrists, but it wouldn't give. She was sure she'd been bleeding from her wrists earlier, but had that stopped? Or maybe she was still bleeding—from her wrists or from the slashes on her body. Bailey didn't know if the wounds still trickled blood.

She only knew . . . she'd been in that cabin for nearly three days. Light had come and gone, spilling through the window. Her lips were busted and raw, and her throat was sore—scratched from screaming and bone dry because the bastard who'd taken her had only given her the tiniest sips of water. And no food, no food at all. No bathroom.

Just pain.

She inched across the floor, moving like a worm. If she could just get across the room, she'd be able to get out of the door. If she could get to that door, she could escape.

Her captor had made a mistake. After his last time using that knife on her . . . he'd thought that she passed out. Bailey had learned fast with that freak. He only liked to hurt her if she was awake. If she was unconscious . . . well, there must not be any damn fun in the act for him. He liked to see her suffer. Liked to make her beg.

Eleven slices of his knife . . . he'd been counting. He'd stopped after eleven, his breathing heaving, his body shaking. And when he stopped . . .

I just pretended to pass out. And that freak in the ski mask stormed out of the room. In his haste, he'd left the door open. Oh, hell, yes, he'd left the door open. She'd gotten off the bed, fallen onto the floor—and now— she *was* getting out of this place. Her rage gave her the energy to keep moving. She'd get to the door. Get out and . . .

Her shirt snagged on a nail. Bailey froze. She hadn't even seen that nail, but when she moved her body, she felt the head of it—round and big—sticking up from the floor. Her breath heaved in and out of her lungs as excitement pumped through her blood. Bailey twisted her body and put the ropes that bound her wrists against the nail top. She jerked and sawed, moving as frantically as she could. Her breath kept rushing out in too-hard pants, burning her lips and making her tongue feel even more swollen in her mouth.

I'll get out. I'll get away.

For the first twenty-four hours, she'd thought she was trapped in a nightmare. That there was some mistake. She couldn't have woken up, tied and gagged in a dirty cabin. There couldn't have been some sick freak in a black ski mask who kept coming at her, slicing with his knife and laughing while she screamed. *None* of that could be happening, not to her.

Not . . . her.

She'd seen the stories on TV in the last few weeks. About women who'd vanished in the mountains of North Carolina. Their stories had been tragic. Their families pitiful as they begged for clues. She'd watched them and felt sympathy. Sorrow. But . . .

Those women had been strangers. Because things like *this* . . . stuff like this only happened to people you didn't know. Unfortunate people you saw on the news.

Not me. This can't happen to me.

But it had.

And I don't have any family to beg for me. No desperate parents to plead for my return . . . I lost them long ago.

Bailey was very much afraid she'd be losing her own life in that small cabin.

One minute, she'd been heading out of her Wednesday-night freshman history class at the local college. It had been the last class she had to teach before spring break. She'd been at her car, her keys gripped tightly in her hand, and then—

Then he hit me. Took me. I woke up in hell.

The ropes around her wrists gave way. Bailey choked out a sob as feeling surged back to her fingers—pain.

Burning white-hot pain. But as soon as that sob slipped from her mouth, she immediately bit her lower lip, terror clawing at her. Blood dripped down her chin from her busted lip.

Had he heard her cry?

Would he come back?

Bailey's whole body went tense as she waited. Waited. She heard the creak of footsteps, a sound that had her heart squeezing.

He's coming. He heard me. He's . . .

A scream seemed to echo all around Bailey. A woman's scream. Loud and long and desperate. Full of pain.

Bailey bit down harder on her bottom lip. She wasn't the one making that scream. Someone else was. Dear God, that freak in the ski mask had someone else in the cabin.

I'm not alone. He took another victim.

And when he'd stopped having his fun with Bailey, when she'd played possum with him, he'd turned his attention to that someone else.

Bailey jerked upright. Her fingers were slow and fumbling as she fought to free her ankles from the rope that bound them.

The scream died away.

She broke her nails on the rope. Jammed fingers that weren't working right.

Another scream—

And the rope gave way. Bailey immediately jumped to her feet and tried to stride forward, but her legs collapsed beneath her. She crawled then, dragging herself toward the door. She had to get to that other woman. Had to help her. Bailey grabbed the door, prying it open a little more with her right hand. Every breath she took seemed incredibly loud to her, and she was afraid he would hear her.

I guess I'm not over the fear, after all. Maybe I'll never be over it.

A peek in the hallway showed two other doors. One was shut. One open.

The screams were coming from behind the shut door. *He's in there with her.*

Bailey rose again, shakily. She kept a hand on the wall as she inched toward the closed door. She had to find a weapon. Had to get something to use against that bastard.

Another scream had her wanting to cover her ears. It was so loud.

"Help me! Please, help me!" the woman yelled. Begged. Pleaded. *"Please, dear God, someone help me!"*

And then Bailey heard the laughter. That taunting, snickering laughter that the bastard had made when he drove his knife into her. At that sickening sound, Bailey stopped thinking—a primitive instinct took over her body. She lurched forward and threw open the door. "Leave her alone!" Bailey bellowed.

His back was to her. A woman was on the bed in front of him. A knife was in his hand. A bloody knife. The same knife he'd so gleefully used on Bailey.

"Coming to save her?" he whispered, his back still to Bailey. When he spoke, he always whispered. "Ah, Bailey . . . is that what you're doing? Coming to help her?"

The woman on the bed didn't move.

Bailey lunged at him. She didn't have a weapon, and there was nothing in that room to use. No lamps. No tables. The only furniture was the old bed—the woman was on that bed. So Bailey attacked with her body. She went straight for him with a guttural cry.

He turned toward her, slicing with his knife, but Bailey didn't stop. The slice went right across her left arm. She barreled into him, crashing hard, and they both fell.

The knife slid from his hand, sliding across the wooden floor.

"Beautiful bitch," he rasped at her. "I'll make you pay . . ."

She was on top of him, and Bailey kneed him, as hard as she could. When he howled, she smiled, stretching her bloody lips. She was so glad he was the one who got to enjoy some pain.

But then he hit her, driving his fist right at her cheek. She fell back, her body rolling across the floor.

And footsteps thudded in that little room. The woman on the bed—she'd gotten up and she was running for the door. She hadn't been tied up like Bailey. She moved quickly, easily. Bailey saw her long dark hair, her pale limbs, the blue of her shirt as it flashed by—

"Wait," Bailey gasped out, the word a weak croak. "Don't—"

Leave me.

For an instant, the woman turned back toward her. Hope burst inside of Bailey. Yes—

The woman ran out of the room. Didn't look back again.

He was laughing again. Her abductor. Her killer?

"Trying to stop me . . ." he whispered. "Oh, sweet Bailey, I'll teach you . . ."

His hands went around her neck. Gloved, covered hands. She felt the leather against her skin. Oddly soft. So soft as he began to choke her.

"I can do this until you pass out . . ."

"H-h . . ." She was trying to say *help,* trying to call that woman back, but she couldn't get the word out. Not with his hands so tight around her.

"Then I'll tie you up again. I'll sharpen my knife . . . get it so that it can slice right through your skin . . ."

From the corner of her eye, Bailey saw the glint of the knife he'd dropped. Her right hand stretched for it. The knife was close. So very close . . .

"Still glad you tried to save her? Was she worth *your* life?"

The other woman had gotten away. Bailey couldn't hear her footsteps any longer.

"I'll take care of you," he promised as black dots danced in front of her eyes. *"And her."*

The knife. It was right there. She just had to reach it . . .

He squeezed harder. No air. No hope. No damn knife.

She couldn't reach it. But Bailey's right hand flew up toward him, and with the last of her strength, she ripped the mask off his face.

He stared down at her, as shock widened his eyes.

"No, Bailey . . . *no* . . ." And he almost seemed sad . . . as he kept choking the life right out of her.

BAILEY'S EYES FLEW open. She sucked in a desperate gulp of air; one, then another. Another. Her lungs burned and she coughed and choked.

I'm alive. I'm still alive.

Her hands flew out, and she touched—dirt. The

scent of dank earth filled her nostrils and she sat up fast, feeling pain cut through her—her arms, her stomach, and—

Dirt is all around me. Her grabbing hands closed around the soft soil, and when Bailey looked up, she saw the glitter of stars above her. A thousand freaking stars. *I'm not in the cabin any longer.*

But she didn't remember escaping. Didn't remember getting away from that bastard. He'd been choking her. The other woman had run, but Bailey hadn't. He'd caught her.

And . . . he'd tossed her into a hole? She sat up, but couldn't reach the top. Too deep. Bailey tried to stand, but her legs wouldn't hold her up, and when she grabbed at the sides of the hole again, the dirt just rained down on her.

Dogs were barking. She heard the sound distantly, and fear pulsed through her. Were those his dogs? Was this another game? Were the dogs going to attack her?

Bailey put her hand over her mouth so she wouldn't make a sound. She tasted the dirt that was on her fingers. Her tongue was so thick and swollen in her mouth. The nightmare wouldn't stop. Everything just kept getting worse and worse.

The barking was louder. Closer. The dogs were going to get her. Would they rip her apart? Bite and tear into her skin?

She curled into a ball in the middle of the hole, trying to make herself as small as possible. If she didn't move, if she didn't make a sound, maybe the dogs would leave her alone. They'd go away, and then she'd find some way out of there. She'd escape.

The other woman . . . where did she go? What happened to her?

But the dogs weren't going away. They were getting louder and louder. So close.

"Something's over here!" a man shouted. "Dirt. Oh, hell! A pile of it! Could be a body!"

Her head lifted.

"Get the lights!" Another voice. Another man. "Follow the dogs!"

The dogs . . .

Maybe they weren't there to hurt her. Maybe they were there to find her. Maybe the other woman . . . maybe she'd gotten away and sent help back to Bailey.

"H-help . . ." she whispered.

No . . . no sound had come from her lips. She'd tried to whisper but couldn't. Her throat was too raw. Her mouth too dry.

The lights were flashing over her hole. Not *in* the hole, but flying over the top of it. People were up there. She needed them to look down at her.

"H-help . . ." Another voiceless whisper. Inside, she was screaming. Roaring for help. But she couldn't talk. She tried to stand up again, but her body wasn't listening to her, not anymore. Too long without water? Without food? Too much blood loss?

Her hands curled around fists of dirt. *Look down here. Look at me. Look!*

A bright light hit her, falling straight into her face. It blinded her and she turned away.

"She's—she's alive! We've got a live one here!" Excitement burned in that voice—a voice with a heavy southern accent—and then a man was there before her. He'd jumped into the hole, and he was reaching for her.

She flinched away.

"It's okay," he told her quickly. "I'm a deputy. Deputy Wyatt Bliss. You're safe . . . we're gonna take care of you."

Bailey wanted to believe him.

More lights fell on her. So bright. She looked up and she saw the shadowy figures of other people—men and women. They surrounded the top of her hole now.

"Can you tell me your name?" He took his coat off, held it out to her. Was it cold? Was she supposed to take the coat?

Her teeth were chattering, but she hadn't noticed the cold, not until then.

She didn't take the coat. She didn't think her fingers would work and just keeping her eyes open was a serious effort.

"Your name, miss," he continued, that drawling voice of his careful now, sympathetic. "Can you tell it to me?"

"B-B . . ." *Bailey.* But she couldn't talk. Just that sad croak was all she could manage.

His flashlight fell to her neck. Whatever he saw there made him swear.

But then others were jumping down into the hole. Some men with flashlights. They were in the hole with her and they lifted her out. Someone carried her a few steps forward and then—then she was on some kind of gurney. Bailey craned her head and looked back. There were so many lights out there then, and the dogs were nearby, whining.

She saw her hole. Big and wide and deep. And a giant

pile of dirt was beside it. A shovel lay forgotten on the ground.

Was that my grave?

"It's okay." It was a woman's voice. Bailey jerked at that voice and at the soft hand that touched her shoulder. "You're safe."

She didn't feel safe.

"I'm an EMT," the woman continued. "And I'll . . . I'll get you taken care of, just . . ." The woman's voice trailed away. "Is all that blood yours?"

Bailey looked down at her body. Her shirt was soaked. Stained red, she saw in the light. Red and dirty. But was all the blood hers? *I think so.* Bailey nodded.

The scent of ash drifted to her. Ash and fire. *What's burning?* Her head turned as she was loaded into the back of an ambulance. She saw the fire in that instant, big and red as it burned so hot and bright. But . . . was that the cabin? Her prison? Was that what burned like hell right then?

"The fire brought the deputies in," the woman said, her blond hair in a bun near her nape. "It helped us find you." The ambulance's back doors slammed closed. "We found the other bodies first . . ."

No, no . . .

"And then you."

A man was in the back of the ambulance, too. Another EMT. He had red hair and freckles across his nose. He gave her a reassuring smile. "You're safe."

So she kept being told. *But I'm not. I'm not safe.* She needed to tell them about the other woman. They had to find her.

She grabbed for the redheaded man's hand. Held tight.

"What is it?" he asked, frowning at her. "Tell me where it hurts."

Bailey hurt everywhere, but this wasn't about her pain. "Wo . . . man . . ." She mouthed the words because she just couldn't speak.

His blue eyes narrowed on her lips.

"Wo . . . man . . ." She mouthed them again as her whole body began to shake. "Another . . . vic . . . vic . . . tim . . ."

His eyes became saucers. "Another victim was alive?"

She nodded.

"He had another victim with you?"

Once more, she nodded.

"Christ!" He lunged away from her and shoved open the ambulance's back door. "Keep those dogs searching! There's another woman out there!"

Bailey's head sagged back. She'd done it. They would find the other woman. She'd be safe, too.

They'd find her.

The ambulance's sirens screamed.

And Bailey closed her eyes.

CHAPTER ONE

SHE HAD GOTTEN AWAY. SURVIVED A SERIAL KILLer's brutal attack.

Asher Young couldn't take his gaze off the gorgeous woman who sat—her body perfectly still—at the conference table. He froze just inside the doorway, sure as hell never expecting for his new client to be *her*.

Bailey Jones. Bailey Fucking Jones. He knew who she was, of course. Pretty much everyone in the United States knew about Bailey.

Gorgeous Bailey. With her strawberry blond hair, her high cheekbones, and her warm, golden skin.

Bailey . . .

She got away.

For weeks, her face had been splashed in the news. Clips of her had been broadcast on every TV show. Her story had been in every paper.

Ex–prom queen. Golden girl. Grad student. Abducted. Tortured. Left in hole that would have been her own grave . . .

But she'd lived.

She was the only victim to have survived the brutal reign of the killer known as the Death Angel.

Bailey wasn't looking at him. He'd frozen in the doorway like some kind of dumbass, and she hadn't even glanced at him. She wasn't staring at anyone. Her hands were folded in her lap—all nice and neat—and her slender neck was bent as if she were lost in deep thought.

Asher had no fucking clue why she was in Atlanta's LOST office. Sure, the job of the Last Option Search Team was to find the missing, but Bailey—she *wasn't* missing. She'd been gone for days before she'd been discovered in the North Carolina mountains. She was alive. She was safe. She was *definitely* not in need of their services.

So what in the hell was she doing there?

Asher's gaze cut toward his boss, and friend, Gabe Spencer. LOST was Gabe's baby—his buddy had opened this business after Gabe's sister had vanished. Gabe had found Amy, but too late.

Too fucking late.

Gabe's blue eyes had narrowed on their would-be client. His fingers were lightly tapping on the edge of the conference table, and Asher could see the sympathy in his stare as Gabe focused on Bailey. When they'd been working together as SEALs, Asher never would have pegged Gabe for the kind of guy who had a soft touch. But Gabe's expression sure said he was worried about the delicate woman who sat hunched at the table.

Not that Asher blamed the guy. Because there was sure as hell something about Bailey that was pulling at Asher's own protective instincts.

You know she's a victim. A survivor.

"Thanks for joining us," Gabe said quietly as he glanced Asher's way. Gabe inclined his head toward Asher as he added, "I want you to meet our new client, Bailey Jones."

She jerked at the sound of her name, and her head lifted. She looked at him—finally looked—and her eyes were the same insane green that he'd seen on TV. So bright and bold. But . . .

There was fear in Bailey's gaze, so much fear that every muscle in his body stiffened.

They were at LOST headquarters, up on the top floor of a secure facility. LOST agents were all over the place. There was no reason at all for her to fear.

I don't want her afraid.

That was one of his many issues. Women shouldn't be afraid. Not ever.

Bailey rose quickly, and the wheels of her chair squeaked as it slid back.

"Hello," she said, her voice low, husky. Sexy.

Asher strode toward her. He saw her shoulders straighten as he drew nearer, and he offered his hand to her. "Ma'am." Even he heard the Texas drawl in his voice. "Nice to meet you."

Those seriously gorgeous green eyes of hers blinked, and then they seemed to sharpen on him. Her gaze traveled slowly over his face as she took his hand.

Damn but her skin was soft. His was callused to hell and back, a side effect of his workout routine. *Once a SEAL, always a SEAL.* Even though he wasn't active duty any longer, he still trained the same way. He wanted to be ready for anything his new life as a civilian—as a LOST agent—might throw his way.

As he stood there, her scent seemed to slide around him. A sweet scent; light. Feminine. Lavender?

"Asher will be the lead on your case," Gabe said briskly. A little too briskly.

Shit. Just how long was I holding her hand? Why am I being such a dumbass with her?

Her gaze had traveled over Asher's face, lingered just a bit on his chin. No doubt, she was looking at the scar he carried. The white line that slid under his chin was a reminder to him—monsters were fucking everywhere. And people needed to be ready to fight them.

She pulled her hand from his and tugged down the long sleeve of her shirt. The sleeve had already been long, though, sliding far past her wrist. "I appreciate your help," Bailey said, her voice still husky. He hadn't realized she'd sound that way.

Too sexy.

Yes, everyone knew that Bailey Jones was attractive. Gorgeous. That was one of the reasons the news crews had run her face again and again and again. But there was a whole hell of a lot more to her than just a pretty face. If all the stories he'd read were true, the woman had a spine of steel.

Not a victim. *Survivor.* And that made her even hotter.

But why was she at LOST? Since Gabe had just said Asher was the lead on her case . . . *I should probably figure out what is happening here, fast.*

Gabe sat down and Bailey followed suit. Once more, those chair wheels rolled softly.

Asher cast a quick, questioning glance toward Gabe, and then he sat down—right next to Bailey. Again, she stiffened, just the slightest bit, and then seemed to force herself to relax.

Gabe cleared his throat. "You're familiar with Bailey's case already."

Because he was so close to her, Asher saw Bailey's hands twisting nervously in her lap. "Yes. I'm familiar." *She'd been abducted, held for days, tortured. Then the asshole started to bury her alive. Only something happened. A fire erupted in the killer's cabin and he got himself trapped in there. He died in the flames. And those flames . . . they brought help to Bailey.*

Bailey released a ragged breath. "Everyone thinks it's over. I get that—six months have passed. Six long months. It *should* be over."

His brows lowered as he studied her.

"It's not."

Asher just waited. He sure wished she'd look at him again and—

Her head turned toward him, her strawberry blond hair sliding over her shoulders. Her long lashes swept up as Bailey's gaze zeroed in on him. "There's another victim."

"What?" Shock ripped through him.

"The cops . . . they said I must have imagined her. I *didn't*. She was there that night. I saw her. I heard her. He had another woman out there—and she was *not* one of those poor women he'd already killed and buried." Now her words came faster, but they were still soft. A little raspy. "I saw all of their pictures. The police identified all of the remains in those graves. *She* wasn't there."

He cast a quick glance over at Gabe. Gabe was always

very particular about the cases he took at LOST. If the boss had already agreed to help her . . .

Then Bailey said something that made Gabe take notice.

"I'm not crazy," Bailey said.

His stare shot back to her. "I never said you were," Asher told her carefully. *Crazy* wasn't a label that he liked to throw around, not with his past.

Red stained her cheeks. "The authorities didn't believe me. And the shrink I've been seeing . . . he didn't believe me, either. Said I made her up in some kind of effort to gain control—to make the whole ordeal seem like less of a nightmare." Her hands stopped twisting. "That's bullshit," Bailey said bluntly, still holding his stare. "I know I went through hell, but I also know I wasn't alone there. Another woman was in that cabin with me. He *had* someone else there."

Okay. Asher rolled back his shoulders as he considered her words. "Like you said, ma'am, six months have passed since that fire."

Her lips pressed together.

"The property has been searched thoroughly. Cadaver dogs went over the entire place." She had to know all of this. "If there was another body—"

"She got away," Bailey said.

His eyes widened.

"I—I helped her get away."

This shit definitely hadn't made the news.

"I got away . . . no, I got out of my ropes. I was going to slip out of the cabin, but I heard her screaming. I couldn't just leave her there . . ." She licked her lips. "So I rushed into the other room. I hit him. *She* got away. I saw her run past me when he had me on the floor." Her hand rose to her throat, but Bailey seemed to catch herself, and her hand dropped back to her lap. "She was my height, a little thinner than me, maybe by ten or fifteen pounds. Caucasian, with long black hair."

Silence.

He wanted to see Gabe's expression, but for the life of him, Asher couldn't look away from her green gaze.

"I'm not making her up," Bailey said doggedly. "She was *real*. And I have to know what happened to her."

Now he was seeing where LOST fit into the equation.

"I'm not crazy," Bailey said again. "She was there, and I want you to help me find her. The sheriff in the area—he won't do anything. The authorities found the killer's body in that cabin, and as far as they are concerned, the case is closed." She gave a hard shake of her head. "It's not closed. *She was there.*"

There was so much intensity in her voice. So much certainty in her face. Yeah, okay, now he understood why Gabe had agreed to take the case. *I believe what she's saying, too.* Her emotions were too real, too raw to be denied.

"Bailey wants us to find that missing victim," Gabe said.

Right.

"And she wants to go into the field with the agent who will be leading the case."

What? A civilian in the field? Asher started to shake his head.

"I'm going," Bailey said flatly. "That was part of the deal. I am going to be involved in the investigation. I *need* to be involved."

Now that sounded like one real bad deal to him, but he wasn't the boss.

The boss was Gabe, and the guy was nodding. Hell. Asher inclined his head toward Bailey. "Fine. But when we're in the field, just remember to follow orders, got it?" Because he didn't want to do anything that might put her at risk. Her safety would be priority one. Finding the missing woman—if she was out there—that would be priority two.

For an instant, a ghost of a smile tilted Bailey's full lips. "Sounds as if you were in the military."

Some habits are definitely dying hard. "Yes, ma'am," he told her. Her smile had made her eyes go lighter, pushing away some of the shadows. He wished all the shadows would leave her gaze.

There was a light knock at the door, and a moment later, Gabe's assistant appeared. "I've got the paperwork ready," she said.

"Great." Gabe waved her in and then nodded toward their new client. "Bailey, you can stay in here while you fill out the forms. Asher and I need to talk outside."

Bailey nodded. Her smile had vanished, too fast. Asher wished her smile had lingered longer.

Asher followed Gabe out of the conference room, and, yeah, maybe he looked back a time or two, just to make sure that Bailey was okay.

Gabe jerked the conference door shut, stopping him from taking a third look back at Bailey. "Be very careful with her," Gabe warned.

Asher's brows rose.

"I've got a contact at the sheriff's office up in Brevard, North Carolina . . . I called their office as soon as she appeared. There was *no* sign to indicate another victim was in the cabin with Bailey. Deputies searched, but they turned up jack shit." His voice was a low whisper. "And there are a few people up there who think that Bailey's captivity took too much of a toll on her. That she might be . . . having a breakdown."

Anger hummed beneath Asher's skin. "You heard the woman . . . she's not crazy."

"She was stabbed eleven times, strangled, and left in a hole to die. That shit would make anyone crazy." Gabe yanked a hand through his hair.

"If you think she's crazy, then why take her case?"

"Because when I looked in her eyes, shit . . . I wanted to help her. She's been through hell, and maybe we can give her the closure she needs."

"You don't think there was another victim . . ."

"I think I want you heading up to the mountains with her. I want you searching that area and looking at what is left of that crime scene. If you find a lead for us, if this pans out, then I will move heaven and earth to find that other woman."

"Just me? No other team members?" Usually the LOST agents worked with a partner.

"Not yet." Gabe dropped his hand. "I'll get Wade to pull all the missing persons' reports from NamUs and see if we have any hits that match up with the description Bailey gave us. It's possible there *was* another victim there, and when she got away, she never looked back."

She just left Bailey? With that killer?

"See what you can find out in the field." Gabe

glanced toward the shut conference door. "Like I said, that woman in there needs closure, and we can give it to her."

Asher thought she needed a hell of a lot more than just closure. But they'd start there.

"Your first solo trip with LOST," Gabe murmured as he lifted his brows. "You ready for this?"

He thought of Bailey's gaze. Of her fear. "Hell, yes, I am."

BAILEY MADE SURE her steps were slow and steady as she headed toward the elevator. Now that the big meeting was over, she was almost shaky with relief. She'd done it. Actually made it to LOST and convinced them to take her case.

She'd fought like crazy to get the sheriff and his deputies to listen to her back home. They'd pitied her. They'd looked sadly at her. They'd told her to see her shrink *again*. But they hadn't helped her.

And with the way things were going lately, the fear that she had . . .

Something has to change.

Her life was a wreck; she knew it. She'd withdrawn from pretty much everyone around her. Before the abduction, she'd had . . . well, not a *lot* of friends, but at least a few who were close to her. Now, she couldn't stand to be near them. They tried to talk to her as if everything were normal, they'd told her to move on . . .

I can't.

She'd tried, though, dammit. A month after her kidnapping, she'd even tried to go back to work. She'd gone onto the college campus, headed in to teach her history class, and as she'd stood up at the podium, staring at the students, she'd just been aware of the . . . whispers. The pity. The stares that wouldn't stop.

Bailey had broken out into a cold sweat. She'd barely made it through the lecture, and then, when the class was over, she'd been violently ill in her office.

She'd gotten damn lucky. A new position had come open at the college—or maybe her boss had just pitied her, too, and he'd moved folks around so that the job became available. But now, she didn't have to lecture in person. She could still teach the history classes she loved, but they were online these days.

No stares. No whispers. No pity.

She hated pity. Almost as much as she hated the fear that still held her in its too-tight grip.

But I'm breaking free now. I've got LOST on my side. Bailey jabbed her index finger into the button on the elevator's panel. The doors opened as if on cue, and she hurried inside. Her breath released in a low rush as the doors began to close. Bailey finally let her shoulders sag. She could stop pretending just for a moment and finally—

A man's hand slid between the closing doors, activating the sensors and causing the mirrored doors to immediately reopen.

Dark eyes. Dark hair. Dangerous. Deadly.

Asher Young.

All of the air in the elevator seemed to disappear. She took a step back automatically, and her shoulders pumped up against the mirrored wall behind her.

His hard jaw tightened even more. "I don't want you to fear me."

Too bad. These days, I fear everyone and everything.
She couldn't remember the last night she'd slept without waking up in a cold sweat, and every little sound she heard had her jumping.

She'd even started to feel as if she were being watched. Even in her home with its new top-of-the-line security system, she couldn't feel safe.

Maybe I won't ever feel safe. That would be another gift that the Death Angel had left her.

Carefully, she pulled down the sleeves of her shirt. She hated all of her scars. *More twisted gifts to always mark me.*

Asher stepped fully into the elevator and he hit the button that would take them down to the parking garage. When the doors closed, oh, jeez, the elevator immediately felt even smaller. Or maybe he just seemed bigger.

She figured the guy had to be around six foot two or three, and he was all muscle. Wide shoulders. Powerful arms. *Built.* The kind of guy that would have drawn her stare before her abduction.

Before I became scared of everyone.

And she *hated* that fear. So much. The Death Angel was long gone, burning in hell. So why couldn't she get her life back together?

"You can trust me," Asher told her.

"Trust doesn't come easily for me," she replied. Actually, it didn't come at all for her. Not these days. Once, she'd looked out at the world and never seen any darkness. She'd trusted blindly, dumbly.

Not any longer.

Asher. She made herself look at him again. An intense guy. Handsome, in a rough way. Dark brown eyes, a strong Roman nose. His hair was thick and nearly jet black, a little long. The faintest hint of stubble covered his hard jaw and on his chin, her gaze was drawn to the white scar that slid over his skin.

A scar from a knife? Bailey thought so. After all, she'd become very familiar with the marks left after an attack from a knife.

The elevator dinged. The doors opened. More people slid inside and Asher stepped closer to her. She sucked in a quick breath and caught his scent—rich, masculine. His shoulder brushed against her arm, and Bailey flinched. *Dammit.* She hated it when she flinched. She hated the way she'd become.

LOST was located in a downtown Atlanta high-rise. There were plenty of other offices in the building, and the people in the elevator had come from those other offices. One guy—a blond in a dark suit—glanced back at her with a flirtatious smile.

She looked away from him. Flirting wasn't her thing, not these days. She wasn't even sure she remembered how to flirt.

But she could feel his gaze lingering on her. The drumming of her heartbeat filled her ears and she just wanted that elevator to move faster. How many floors were in the building? How many—

"Don't I know you?"

It was the blond. His voice was a little nasally, a little Upper New York. She'd always been good at pinning down accents.

Like Asher . . . he was from Texas. Probably somewhere near Dallas, and his drawl had rolled over her.

And the Death Angel, he'd been whispering so she hadn't been able to—

She slammed that memory shut in an instant.

The blond stepped closer. "I *do* know you."

Bailey shook her head and her shoulder pressed a bit harder to Asher. "No, we haven't met." She didn't know anyone in Atlanta. She'd grown up in North Carolina, gone to college there. *Nearly died there.* Sure, she'd visited Atlanta a few times over the years, but those trips had just been pit stops. She had no friends there. No family. *I don't have family anywhere, except in the cemetery.*

The elevator dinged again. A few people exited.

Not the blond. He stepped closer. "I've seen you on TV," he said, voice thickening with excitement. "You're—"

Asher's tanned hand pushed against the guy's chest. "This is your floor."

"What? No, it's not." The blond glared at Asher.

Asher moved in front of her. "Yeah, it's your fucking floor. So get your ass off here." He was a wall between her and the blond. Protective, fierce.

Scary.

Bailey wanted to run off that elevator, too. But she didn't. The blond grumbled and swore and then stormed away. Actually, *everyone* left that elevator—everyone but her and Asher. When the doors closed again, she released the breath she'd been holding.

Asher glanced back at her as the elevator began to descend. "That happen a lot?"

"People know my face. It's been on the TV plenty."

Even though she'd only given one interview. Just one. One interview had been enough to show her that the reporters were only interested in the blood and gore of her case. Sensationalism.

Her pain.

She'd also learned that when people saw her face and heard the news stories, it made them think they knew her. They didn't. No one knew all the secrets she was carrying around. She hoped they never did. "I keep thinking that if enough time passes, everyone will forget about me."

He was staring straight at her—so totally focused, *on me*. "I don't think anyone can forget you."

The elevator stopped moving. Finally. They were in the parking garage. He exited first and she hurried out after him. Her car was parked just a few rows over. Another few moments and she'd be safely inside. She still tensed whenever she went to her vehicle, because that was when the Death Angel had grabbed her. She'd been *at* her vehicle, ready to unlock it, and he'd appeared, a reflection in the glass. Big, strong, wearing that ski mask. She'd whirled to confront him—

Asher took her hand in his. "You're shaking."

This has got to stop.

"I'm just not used to being around so many people," Bailey said. Part truth, part lie. She had been avoiding crowds because guys like that blond—they *did* notice her. People whispered. *Just like my students whispered.* They stared. They made her feel like the freak in any room she entered. So she'd started staying home more. Hiding.

"You'll have to get used to being around me."

His fingers stroked over her knuckles. Heat surged through her, and the reaction was so sudden, so shocking, that she tried to jerk away from him.

He didn't let her go. "I'm one of the good guys, I swear it."

Is anyone good?

"I'll help you. But I don't want you flinching each time I'm near. I don't want you backing away from me."

She wasn't about to give the guy a promise she couldn't keep. So she changed the topic. "When are you coming to North Carolina?"

"We'll go by my place, and we'll leave tonight, if that's what you want."

Wait—what?

He smiled at her, and a dimple flashed in his cheek. Maybe not a dimple. Too strong and hard for that. A slash? "That's why I followed you to the elevator. No sense waiting. You wanted to hire LOST, and now you've got us. And I'm on the job starting right now."

His touch felt too good. Okay, so maybe she'd lived too much of the hermit life if she was responding this way to him. She hadn't dated anyone, hadn't even looked twice at a man since the nightmare began.

I had a boyfriend before that—a lover. But he didn't like what I became.

Royce had been fast to turn his back on Bailey. And after he'd left her there, all alone in that hospital, she'd pulled into herself.

Asher's hands slowly slid away from hers, but the warmth she'd felt from his touch lingered. "So follow me back to my place. I keep a travel bag ready there. Five, ten minutes, tops, and we can be on our way."

It was only about a three-and-a-half-hour drive back to her place but . . .

It was already getting close to nightfall.

"Or we can stay in town for the night." Asher shrugged. "Your choice."

"I—I haven't booked a room." And she didn't want him to know that she'd put every penny of her savings in a special fund just to pay for LOST. She didn't know how long the investigation would take, and she wanted to be careful with her money. *I need to find her, so I have to give all my money to this cause.*

"I'm sure we can find you a room," he said easily. "LOST can—"

"No, thank you." She would get home that night. They had time.

"Then let's go to my place." He spoke so carefully to her, but in the elevator when he'd confronted the blond guy, there hadn't been anything careful about him. He'd been all danger and menace. "No sense burning the daylight that we have."

She gave a brisk nod and headed for her car. He followed behind her, and when she lifted her keys, pushing the button to unlock the door, his reflection was in the glass of her window.

Same size. Big and strong, just like the Death Angel.

"You're shaking again," Asher pointed out.

She jerked open the car door and jumped inside. "I'll follow you." She tried to pull the door closed, but he caught the door with one hand and leaned toward her.

"Bailey Jones . . ." Asher said her name softly, as if tasting it on his tongue. "There are a few things you should know about me before we begin."

There are things you should know about me, too. But I'm not going to tell you . . . or you won't help me.

"First, you don't have to fear me. Part of my job at LOST—well, let's just say Gabe hired me on because he wanted a bit more muscle. Protection is my role. I'll keep you safe *and* track down any clues about that missing woman. On my watch, nothing will happen to you."

She nodded even though—

I don't believe you. There is no safety. I learned that.

"And second . . . you don't have to bullshit me."

Now she blinked in surprise.

He laughed, a deep, rough rumble of sound that Bailey found she liked to hear.

"You think I can't tell when you're wearing a mask? You've got yourself locked down tight, under careful control, don't you? But you don't have to do that with me. I'm not one of the North Carolina deputies. I'm not going to judge you. And I'm not some lame-ass reporter who wants to splash your story all over the world."

I wear a mask all the time now because something is wrong inside of me. It has been, ever since that fire. That hole. That hell.

"So let's put a no-bullshit rule in effect," he murmured.

Her hands curled around the steering wheel. "Liking rules, is that more of a military thing again?"

"Wanting to break rules . . . *that's* why I left the SEALs."

He'd been a SEAL? She turned to look up at him. "Is there a rule number three?"

"We'll get to that rule later . . ."

She started the vehicle. "I'll follow you to your place."

"Do you have any rules for me?"

Don't hurt me. Don't judge me. Don't pity me. Bailey cleared her throat. "I'm sure we can get to those rules later, too."

He slammed her door shut. Through the window, Bailey watched as he strode away—not to another car, but to a shiny, big monster of a motorcycle. He climbed on, revved the engine moments later, and that rumbling growl filled the parking garage.

Asher slid the helmet over his head—a black helmet with a dark visor that completely obscured his face. Her heart beat faster as she stared at him.

Dangerous.

That had been her first thought when she'd seen him in the conference room.

But he was on *her* side. Not a threat to her. He'd help her.

At least, that was what she hoped. Because if something didn't change soon, Bailey was afraid that the deputies would be right about her. Her shrink would be right.

I may go crazy.

THE WATCHER SANK deeper into his car as they left the parking garage. The camera was slick in his hands, wet from his sweat.

Bailey. Beautiful Bailey Jones. He'd followed her for so long, it was almost second nature for him now.

When she'd left North Carolina, he'd been curious to see where she was going.

Bailey didn't go far most days. She was too afraid. The big, bad survivor—now afraid of her own shadow.

But she'd surprised him today. She'd driven all the way to Atlanta. Hadn't even hesitated when she went in that high-rise building. She'd jumped on the elevator and vanished, staying inside for hours, and when she'd come back down . . .

Bailey had been with *him*. The guy who'd held her hands. Who'd spoken so softly with her. Who'd *laughed* while he talked to her.

Naughty Bailey, holding out on me. Letting me think you were such a good girl when all along, you had a lover in the wings.

The taillights from her vehicle had just disappeared as she headed around the curve that would take her out of the garage. Smiling now, he cranked his vehicle. Things were getting interesting with Bailey. Fucking finally.

He couldn't wait to see what happened next.

Come on, Bailey. Show me something good.

Or bad . . . something very, very bad.

CHAPTER TWO

"Y OU DIDN'T HAVE TO FOLLOW ME HERE," BAILEY said as she turned, standing on her small porch and gazing up at Asher. "You could have just stopped at the motel in town." They had driven nonstop for the last three and a half hours, heading down the dark roads that took them back to North Carolina. The mountains had passed her in a blur, and she'd kept a death grip on the wheel. All Bailey had wanted during that drive was to get home. To get away from the darkness that surrounded her.

They were in Brevard, a little town in Transylvania County, North Carolina. Her home—or rather, what had been her parents' home. After the attack, she'd fled to the safety of this little historical house in the middle of the picturesque town. Situated in the foothills of the Blue Ridge Mountains, Brevard was a place of incredible beauty.

And it was . . . safe now. The Death Angel wasn't taking victims anymore. She could be protected in her hometown. Or so she'd hoped.

"Part of the LOST package," Asher murmured. "Escort service to the door."

He was so close to her. If someone passed, they'd probably think she and Asher were lovers who'd gone out on a date.

Lovers. Right. She was sure she wasn't Asher's type. Royce had made it clear she wasn't anyone's type, not anymore.

"Bailey? Is something wrong?"

She shook her head. "Thank you for the escort," Bailey told him quietly. Unfortunately, everything she said was quiet these days. Another stark reminder. "You saw the motel in town when we passed through, right? You can get a room there."

"I can get a room there," he agreed easily, inclining his head toward her. "Sleep well, Bailey. I'll see you tomorrow, eight A.M."

She nodded because nothing would stop her from being ready the next morning.

I will get my life back.

He turned away and headed down the porch steps. His motorcycle waited just a few feet away.

"Asher!"

No, she hadn't meant to call out to him. Had she?

But he was looking back and her heart was racing and she tried to figure out what to say. "Why don't you come inside a few moments?" *Because I hate going into the house alone. Especially at night. When it's so dark like this . . . and . . .* "I'd like to talk to you more about the case." That sounded good. Even confident. Not desperate. She hoped.

"Okay." He rolled back his shoulders and strode toward her. That long, lazy stroll of his was really quite something. A stroll that didn't look at all hurried but somehow reminded her of a jungle cat. Closing in on prey.

She fumbled with her keys and unlocked the door. All three locks. Then she hurried toward the beeping alarm and typed the code. Asher followed behind her, his steps slow, and he barely walked into the little foyer before stopping. He'd come in just enough to shut the door behind him.

"You're forgetting rule number one," he said, voice careful.

Rule number—oh, right. *You don't have to fear me.*

"It's not you." She dropped her purse and keys on the table. "Nights are always hard for me." Bailey made herself face him.

A muscle jerked in his jaw.

"Can I—um, get you some coffee?" That was what people did, right? Normal people? They drank coffee?

"Not this late. Thanks."

Oh, crap. Yes, he probably actually *slept* at night. Good for him.

She waved toward her couch. "Why don't you have a seat?"

He headed for her, but didn't move toward the couch. He—

"Do you want me to search the house?"

She bit her lip because it was trying to tremble. And she gave a quick nod. Without another word, Asher vanished into her kitchen. As the minutes ticked past, she heard him exploring every room in the house. The kitchen, the den, the small home office. Her bedroom. The guest room . . .

"All clear." He was back, just a few steps away from her.

Her breath heaved out. "It's stupid, I know. To—to worry, but—"

"There's not a damn thing stupid about you." He tilted his head as he studied her. "But how about next time, you just tell me what you want. No bullshit, remember?"

Ah, rule number two.

Asher's expression was guarded as he said, "I want to hear the story, you know that."

The story. Her hell. "Doesn't everyone already know the story?"

"The basics. You were taken. Tortured. You got out alive."

Not really. "What else is there to know?"

His gaze seemed so very dark and deep. "I have to know everything, Bailey, if I'm going to work this case the right way. Every detail you have. Every memory. Big, small, scary—doesn't matter. I have to know them all."

Her arms wrapped around her stomach. "I thought LOST was getting copies of the police reports."

"Yeah, I'm sure Gabe will have copies waiting in my inbox—probably there now, and I'll read them all. But it's not the same as hearing the story directly from you."

So she had to go through all the gory details again, huh? Bailey opened her mouth to speak, but then her phone rang. The loud, long peal of sound seemed to echo in the house as she hurried to grab her bag. She pulled out the phone, but didn't recognize the number on the screen. Frowning, Bailey put the phone to her ear. "Hello?"

"You should've died."

"Who is this?"

Asher's head jerked toward her.

"Why did they take you out of that hole?"

"Stop calling me!" Bailey rasped as laughter filled the line. She disconnected the call, her fingers shaking. Bailey slammed the phone back on the table, wishing the stupid thing would shatter into a million pieces.

Asher lunged forward and caught her hand. "What is it?"

"Another stupid prank caller." Goose bumps had risen on her arms. "I've changed my number over and over, but the calls keep coming. Calls from reporters, from punk kids, from assholes who just want to jerk me around."

He looked at the phone. "Which category did that caller fall into?"

"I don't know. I don't care—"

The phone rang again. She saw the same number flash on the screen. The peal of the rings seemed even louder to her. "Just let it ring," Bailey said. "They'll stop calling—or, or I can just turn the phone off."

"How long have you been getting calls like this?"

"I've always gotten them. They started as soon as my picture hit the papers." It had been easy enough for folks to track her down. She'd deleted her social media pages, changed her number—like she'd told Asher, again and again—but it hadn't helped. Some people just got off on torturing others.

She knew that fact better than most.

The phone had stopped ringing.

"See?" Bailey forced a smile for him. "Just some asshole—"

The phone rang again. This time, Asher's fingers curled around it and he picked it up. *Same number on the screen.* A number she didn't know. One of the deputies had told her to write down all of her prank calls, but . . .

When she'd given him a list a while back, he'd never followed up with her.

Just kids. It will all stop soon enough. The attention will go away. That was what she kept thinking.

Only it hadn't stopped.

Asher swiped his finger over the phone's screen. "Who the fuck is this?" he demanded. He'd put the caller on the speaker.

A sharply indrawn breath filled the air. Then . . . silence.

"Don't call this damn number again, you got it?" Asher barked.

The line went dead.

Bailey licked her lips. "It's just a kid . . ." But *had* it sounded like a kid's voice? The words had been whispered, so Bailey couldn't be sure.

The Death Angel had always whispered.

Shit, no. She would not go there.

"The call came just moments after you turned on the lights here." His voice had gone low. Harsh. Deadly.

And he'd pulled out his phone, too. As she watched him, Asher called someone, she had no idea who, and barely a second later he said, "Wade? Yeah, man, it's Asher. I need a number and a phone tracked down right away." Then he rattled off the number that had just called her.

He was . . . tracing it? "It's some kid," Bailey whispered. That was what Deputy Wyatt Bliss had told her about the calls. *Bad pranks.* She was safe now. Some kid was messing with her, nothing more.

Asher glanced up at her. His gaze appeared furious. "The call came *way* too soon after you got back here and turned on the lights. I don't believe in coincidences like that."

If it wasn't a coincidence then . . .

Her phone started to ring again.

"The asshole is calling again," Asher snarled into his phone. "Trace the call, now, Wade. Triangulate the signal, get those techs to do whatever the hell they have to do—find that phone." He put his phone down but kept hers. He answered it by saying, "Asshole, you don't take a hint well, do you?" His finger tapped on the screen, turning on the speakerphone option once more.

"She should be dead . . ."

Asher's expression altered. In a flash, it seemed as if a stranger were standing before her. A cold, deadly stranger. "Why don't you walk up to the door, you son of a bitch," Asher invited, "and tell that shit to my face?"

Laughter. *"A new lover? Come to play?"*

Bailey backed up a step. That didn't sound like a kid, did it?

"I'm coming for you," Asher said softly. "This shit is stopping."

"Let's see you try."

And, once more, the line went dead.

But Asher just picked up his phone again. "You got the location?"

Bailey wasn't breathing. It was just a prank call. *Just a prank.* She got those, all the time. She got—

Asher lunged for her front door.

Okay, yes, that must mean he'd gotten the location from that Wade person. She ran after him. Asher jumped down the old wooden porch and he began running down the middle of the street. It was a dark street—her neighbors had long since gone to bed and no one else was out. Just her and Asher.

She hurried after him. He was in the road.

And . . .

Near the corner of her street, bright lights suddenly flashed on. Car lights. Lights that blinded her for a moment. She staggered to a stop, but Asher didn't. He kept running right for the vehicle.

Only that car was now going straight for him, too. The tires squealed as that vehicle shot forward, heading in a path straight for him—and her. *"Asher!"* Bailey screamed as she ran to get out of the road. *"Move!"*

And he did—with seconds to spare, he leapt out of the road and the car barreled past him. The scent of burning rubber filled Bailey's nose because that car—

It's turning toward me. She was on the sidewalk, but the car was careening toward her. Aiming for her. For an instant, the street lamp glinted off the hood ornament—a horse. *Mustang.* She staggered back, and the front bumper missed her by inches. Freaking inches.

She could feel the heat from the vehicle on her skin.

"Bailey!"

The car lurched and shot back down the road, its tires still squealing and its red taillights flashing.

"Bailey!" Asher grabbed her arms. "Are you all right?"

"He was outside," she whispered. "Right outside my house."

"Yeah, Wade triangulated the asshole's signal." His hold tightened on her. "I knew he had to be close . . . he waited to call until you were home. He waited *for* you."

Outside.

She just stared up at him. "That wasn't some kid, prank calling."

"Hell, no." He glared down the road. The car had vanished. "That was some sick asshole that I *am* going to find."

What if she'd come home alone? "We should call the sheriff's office." Right away. They needed to call and give the deputies a description of the car. Get them to put out an APB and find that jerk.

Outside. She hadn't been safe. Someone had been right outside of her home, waiting for her. Someone who'd said that she should have died.

Why did they take you out of that hole?

Dear God, the nightmare would never, ever end.

"WE WILL TAKE care of this situation," the deputy said, nodding as he stood in Bailey's doorway. "I've got an APB out now. You can rest assured we'll find the troublemaker."

"Troublemaker?" Asher snapped because no damn way had the guy just said that shit. "You're looking for a criminal. An asshole who called, and *threatened* Bailey, and then tried to run us both down."

The deputy—a guy who appeared close to Asher's

own age—narrowed his brown eyes. "How do you know the perp called her?" His blond hair was cut in a short military style.

"Because I got the phone signal triangulated. That's the reason I ran out after the guy. I realized he was right outside, watching Bailey." Asher's gaze cut to the right, where Bailey sat huddled on her couch. "That woman has been through hell, and she doesn't need to be jerked around by some new bastard."

"No," the deputy said softly, his eyes narrowing. "She doesn't." His head tilted as he studied Asher. "How about you take a walk outside with me?"

How about you do your damn job? But Asher gave a grim nod and followed the fellow onto the porch. He glanced back at Bailey, but she didn't seem to even notice they were stepping out.

The deputy—Deputy Wyatt Bliss—pulled the door shut behind him. "What are you to Bailey?"

"What?"

"I got your name." Wyatt made a show of looking down at his little notebook.

Yeah, you got my name because I gave it to you when I called to report that freak who was outside.

"Asher Young," Wyatt said. "But you're not a local, and I've never seen you with Bailey until this night. The same night that some—according to you—asshole appears and tries to run you both down."

Asher fisted his hands. "She's my client. I work for an organization called LOST. We—"

Wyatt's chin jerked up. "I've heard of LOST."

Yes, well, their group gained more and more attention with every solved case. The fact that in addition to solving cold cases they had helped to bring down serial killers? That had sure played well in the media.

"What I don't get," Wyatt continued, "is why Bailey would need you. I found her."

I found her. Had the deputy been aware of that possessive tone that he just took?

"She was in that hole," Wyatt continued darkly, "curled up into a ball. My light hit her, *I* got her out."

Definitely possessive. Was there something going on between the deputy and Bailey that Asher needed to know about?

"So why the hell . . ." Wyatt continued, "would she need you?"

The street was quiet. Another deputy had been there earlier, but Wyatt had sent him out, hopefully, to find the troublemaking asshole. *He wanted more than trouble.*

"She needs me," Asher said, aware that his voice had gone tight and hard, "because Bailey said there was another victim out there."

Even before Asher finished the sentence, Wyatt was already shaking his head.

"Bailey said the victim was a dark-haired woman who was also held by the Death Angel." With an effort, he kept his voice flat. "Bailey wants me to help find her. She wants LOST to find that victim."

Wyatt kept shaking his head. *That shit is annoying me.*

"You are wasting your time," Wyatt said. "There *was* no other woman." Frustration flashed on his face. "Don't you think I looked? I mean, hell, do you really believe I'd leave some poor woman out in the mountains? I *looked*. My whole team searched. Deputies from three counties searched! She wasn't there. There was no trace of her . . . *because Bailey just made her up*."

Bailey's front door opened and she stood there, the light from the house spilling down behind her. Making her look almost like an angel.

One who had fallen hard to hell.

She was dead silent, and Asher knew she had overheard the deputy's words.

Wyatt swore. "Bailey, you should go back inside. Obviously, tonight has strained you. We'll find the—"

"Troublemaker?" Asher supplied grimly. His hands had clenched into fists. Bailey was hurting because of that guy's words, and her pain pissed him off.

Women shouldn't hurt. Women shouldn't fear. He tended to overreact where women were concerned. He knew it, a fucking by-product of his own screwed-to-hell past. But there was no changing who he was.

What he was.

I'm trying to do the right thing at LOST. I can be more than just a trained killer.

Wyatt edged closer to Bailey. "Maybe it was just a reporter."

"Uh, yeah. In my experience," Asher said, "reporters don't usually threaten victims and then try to run people off the road. Not trying to tell you how to do your job or anything . . ." Yeah, actually, he was. "But you need to find that bastard and lock him up." *Before I find him for you.*

"The reporters keep hounding Bailey," Wyatt snapped

back. "I had to drag two off her property just last week. Always snapping pictures, demanding interviews. Freaking predators."

Bailey hadn't mentioned that reporters had been hounding her that badly. Asher's brows lowered.

"Lock your doors," Wyatt said, his voice softer as his fingers brushed down Bailey's arm.

Asher's narrowed gaze noted that touch.

"If anything happens to scare you, just remember, I'm only a few minutes away. Call me, and I'll come right over."

Bailey didn't look overly reassured, and, in that moment, Asher made a swift decision. "Don't worry, Deputy," he told him, voice still tight because the deputy was pissing him off. *Go out there. Find the damn perp! Stop touching Bailey.* "Part of the whole LOST service includes protection while I'm on the case." He paused. "I'll be staying with Bailey."

He had to give Bailey credit. Her expression didn't change and she didn't so much as flinch at that little bombshell. In fact, some of the tension seemed to leave her delicate shoulders.

"You . . . are?" Wyatt asked, his voice a bit strangled.

"Damn straight." He smiled. "So do call and update us when you catch that perp, will you? I'd sure like to have a little one-on-one chat with him." Asher would like ten minutes alone with him so he could teach the asshole some much-needed life lessons, but . . .

Wyatt's jaw hardened. "I'll be sure to keep you both updated on the case." He gave a tight nod to Bailey. "And I'll still be close." His voice softened a bit as he told her that.

Then the deputy turned and headed down her steps.

"I didn't make her up." Bailey's voice was low, but firm.

Wyatt froze on the second step.

"I know you think I did. I know the shrink thinks I did, but you're wrong. You weren't there. I was. I heard her screams. I. Saw. Her."

Wyatt glanced back at her.

Asher didn't say a word.

"Asher believes me. He's the first person in a long time who does."

Take that, Deputy.

"And we are going to find her. Because I am sick of hearing her screams every time that I close my eyes."

"Bailey . . ." Wyatt began.

Asher stepped between them. "Do keep us updated, Deputy," he told him briskly. "And we'll do the same for you."

Wyatt looked as if he wanted to say something else, but Asher figured enough had already been spoken. The guy's careless words had hurt Bailey, and that shit wasn't going to happen again. Asher kept his body between them, his legs braced apart, his hands loose at his sides, and after a tense moment, the deputy headed back to his patrol car.

Silence reigned on that porch until Wyatt drove away. Then . . .

"Since when are you staying here?"

Ah, it figured that would be the first thing she asked. Asher faced her. "If you want me to leave, say the word." Her call. Always. "But after what happened tonight, I would just feel better being close to you."

"And I'd feel better not being alone." She'd wrapped her arms around her waist again. He'd noticed that she did that—when she was afraid. Most people did it. A way of comforting themselves.

I can comfort her.

Shit. He needed to get a grip. Pronto. He knew how to be professional, despite the way he was reacting to her.

There was just something about her . . . something that made him want. Made him need.

Desire. Yes—hell, yes.

He needed to tread very carefully with her.

"So why don't you come back inside?" Bailey murmured. "You can use the guest room."

"I'll just get my bag." He headed to his motorcycle, grabbed his belongings from the saddlebags there, and followed Bailey back into the house. He watched her as she carefully set the alarm, and Asher noted the faint tremble in her fingertips. "You didn't tell me that reporters were harassing you."

"They'll stop," she said, her back to him and her gaze on the alarm panel. "Eventually. The Death Angel just grabbed all the headlines. I mean, when women start vanishing from the mountains and pictures of them . . . with new tattoos are sent to the police . . ."

That had been the thing about the Death Angel. He'd *wanted* the cops to know he had victims. So his MO had been very distinct. He'd take a victim, then . . . mark her.

He'd tattoo small, black wings onto her shoulder.

That was where the name Death Angel had come from. Some reporter—it was always the reporters—

had taken one look at the wings and thought of an angel. But because the wings were black and the women were dying . . .

Death Angel.

"That's another reason why no one believes me." Now she did turn toward him. "My picture was the last one sent to the authorities. Me, with the tattoo on my shoulder. The woman I saw—the dark-haired woman who screamed—no one ever got a picture of her. So Wyatt said that was further proof that she was never taken."

"Or maybe the Death Angel just didn't have a chance to mark her." Made sense to him.

Bailey nodded. "That's . . . that's what I thought, too. Or if he had marked her, he just hadn't sent the photo out yet."

There were questions he wanted to ask her—plenty damn more—but she looked so tired. Everything else he needed to say could wait until the morning.

Bailey slid by him and went into the guest room. The top of her head barely came to his chin. Her scent swept out to him.

Asher swallowed.

Then she was pulling back the covers on the guest bed. Turning on the lamp there. Plumping up the pillows—

He dropped his bag near the door and caught her hands. "Stop. You don't need to do anything else for me."

Her eyes were so wide and so green. He'd seen that color of green once before, during a brief stay in Ireland. The grass had been that color—a brilliant green that was nearly unreal. "You're helping me," Bailey said. "I want to—"

"You don't need to fix a bed for me." And her just being that close to him *and* a bed . . . Hell. *Control. Get it. Use it.* Asher looked down at her hands. Her sleeves had fallen back and his fingers were just above her wrists.

Her scarred wrists.

Bailey gave a quick gasp and tried to pull her hands free of his. Asher tightened his hold on her.

"Stop. Let go—"

At that whisper of *stop*, he immediately freed her.

Bailey jerked down those sleeves, hiding her scars once more.

"Not from a knife." The scars had been too jagged to come from a knife's sharp blade. "The ropes?" he guessed. The scars were wide, and they looked as if the cuts had gone deep.

"Y-yes."

"You kept twisting your wrists against the rope until you got free." Asher nodded, seeing it all too clearly in his mind. Her blood would have actually made it easier for her to escape. The blood would have made the bindings slippery.

"They were too tight." Her words were hollow. "I twisted and twisted but couldn't get free . . . not until I found the nail sticking up in the floor. I sawed the ropes with it until they broke."

And now she hid her scars. Like they were something she should be ashamed of. *Wrong.* "You're a fighter. You shouldn't hide the scars. They just show how strong you are."

Her head sagged forward. Her hair slid down, covering her face. "People see the scars and they whisper about them. I hate it when people talk about me."

Yeah, he hated asshole people, too. His hand lifted toward her, and he pushed a lock of her hair behind her ear. She tensed at his touch and her head slowly rose. "Other people can screw off," he told her bluntly. "What they say and do—that doesn't matter. The scars you carry show how strong you are. They show that you are a fighter. You didn't let him win. You're alive. You made it."

Her gaze searched his.

"You don't need to hide those scars from me. You don't need to hide anything from me."

He heard the slight catch of her breath. And he realized that he was caressing her cheek. *Dammit. She is a client, and I am about to cross a fucking line.* Asher forced himself to step back. "Thanks for the use of the guest room."

She hurried for the door. Then stopped, hesitating. "I'm glad you're here."

So am I, sweetheart. But . . . "Bailey."

Her head turned toward him.

"Is there anything going on between you and the deputy?" *I shouldn't have asked that question. What in the hell am I doing?* This was professional, just a case.

Just. A. Case.

"What?" She gave a little laugh, one that he liked because it was so sweet, almost musical. "Of course not."

He didn't think the deputy would have responded with such a fast *of course not.*

"Why do you even ask?" Bailey wanted to know.

Then she gave a bitter laugh. "Trust me, there's nothing going on with *anyone*."

His head cocked at those words. She was so freaking gorgeous. Every man who saw her probably wanted her . . .

Maybe she doesn't want them. He cleared his throat and said, "I just like to know where things stand."

She shook her head and—

"Actually, if we're talking about where we stand . . ." Asher knew he should stop while he was ahead—or at least, not too far behind—but his big mouth just kept going. "There's something I think you should know."

Now she turned toward him fully. He didn't move from his position near the bed. Did she realize this room smelled like her? The whole house seemed to carry that feminine, tempting scent of lavender.

"What's that?"

I want you. I look at you, and I ache. And I know you're a client and I'm supposed to keep my hands off you . . .

If he told her that shit, she'd probably fire him on the spot. The woman had been living through a living hell. The last thing she needed was his lust. *Do the job, Asher. Do the fucking job.*

So Asher yanked a hand over his face. "Just wanted you to know you don't have to be scared," he muttered. "I'll be here if you need me."

"Thanks, Asher."

"Ash," he told her. "My friends call me Ash."

She gave him a slow smile. Sexy as all hell. Then she slipped from the room. He heard the faint sound of her soft footsteps as she headed down the hallway. A moment later, her bedroom door closed softly.

Damn. His first big solo case, and he was about to screw things to hell and back because he kept getting a hard-on for the client. What. The. Actual. Fuck?

She'd mentioned seeing a shrink.

Asher shut the door to the guest room then yanked out his phone. He needed someone to ground him, and he needed it fast. So he called the one person he always counted on—

And his twin sister, Ana, picked up on the second ring.

"Tell me you aren't in trouble already," Ana said, her voice sounding a bit sleepy, and he knew he'd woken her up.

"Might be." He paced the confines of the room. "This case . . . this client . . . it's not what I expected."

"Nothing in life is." Ana's voice sounded more awake by the second. "You need me there?"

"Something happened tonight. A caller—some jerk who threatened her. When I went outside, the creep was in a car down the street. He came at me."

"What?"

"Local deputies are on the case, but I didn't exactly get blown away by them."

"You need me there." She was definite.

"Not yet. I'm going into the mountains with Bailey tomorrow. Let me see where the day takes us. See if I find anything—" He gave a grim laugh. "And let's see if the deputies manage to surprise me by actually locating that jerk."

Silence drifted over the line. Then Ana said, "Your voice sounds funny."

His hold tightened on the phone.

"What aren't you telling me?"

He turned to look out the window. Saw only darkness out there. "You think I could ever be . . . normal?" She was the *only* one he'd ever talk to about this.

"Asher." A brisk demand. "You are normal. Screw what any bozos told you—"

"You know I'm not." She knew all his secrets. All his pain. Better than anyone, she knew the rage he carried, too. A rage he'd tried to work out as a SEAL. A rage that never ended. "I'm sorry, Ana."

"No, don't. *Don't.* Don't go there again. What happened . . . you *know* it wasn't your fault. Stop it! Do you hear me?"

He heard her. But . . . "There's something about my client . . ."

Ana sucked in a sharp breath. "Asher?"

"I look at her, and I . . ." No. Just, no. "She's already been through enough." So she didn't need to take the devil to her bed.

The devil. That had been the nickname given to him by his SEAL team, with good reason.

"You're a good man," Ana told him.

No, he wasn't. Not really. Ana knew that.

"I'm glad you came to work at LOST," Ana said.

He smiled. "I did it because you dragged my ass there."

"Kicking and screaming," she agreed, "but . . . you belong there. We both do. I know we can help people. And if anyone understands going through hell, it's us."

He tried not to think of the past because it just made

his fury worse. But the past was always there, along with the knowledge that at just fourteen years old, he'd killed a man for the first time.

He just wished he'd been able to kill that bastard sooner.

"It's different than bounty hunting," Ana said with a quick laugh, "that's for sure."

Ana . . . small, petite Ana had been one of the toughest bounty hunters in the U.S. Gabe had lured her into joining LOST because the woman was truly a master tracker, and he'd wanted her as part of his team. Once Ana had been on board, then both Gabe and Ana had convinced Asher to come join LOST.

Different, yes.

"Different from being a SEAL, too, huh?" Ana murmured.

"Yes." Because as a SEAL, he hadn't spent time with victims. And maybe that was the issue. He wasn't used to seeing someone else's pain this way. All up-close and personal. And when he saw Bailey's pain . . . *I want to fucking stop it. By any means.*

"You always wanted to save the world."

No, he'd wanted to save Ana. He hadn't. He'd failed his sister.

Maybe, though, maybe he could help Bailey.

"If you change your mind and want backup, I'm there," Ana said.

She always was. "Night, sis."

"Night, Ash."

He hung up the phone. Asher turned off the lamp, stripped, and climbed into bed. For a moment, he just stared up at the ceiling. Bailey had said that she was tired of hearing the other woman's screams every time she closed her eyes.

Asher had understood exactly what she meant. Hell, yes, he had. Because he heard screams when he closed his eyes, too.

Only they were his own cries. The cries of a fourteen-year-old kid. They would always haunt him.

Let my sister go! Stop it! Stop, please! Don't hurt her.

His eyes closed. And he still heard the screams.

CHAPTER THREE

THE CABIN HAD BURNED FAST AND HARD. THE firefighters had been able to stop the blaze only at the end—keeping up one wall and some blackened boards.

Bailey stared at the cabin. Or rather, what was left of it. Hardly anything at all. She could only remember the interior of that place in rough flashes. The wooden floor. The nail sticking up. The creak of the door to her room—

"Probably not going to get much from that place," Asher said as he stared at the remains. He had on a pair of dark sunglasses, so she couldn't see his gaze. His expression was guarded. He'd been that way all morning—guarded, careful. He'd spoken to her—very, very politely—during the journey out to the cabin. During the night, something had changed with him, only she didn't know what it was.

She'd barely slept the night before. No big surprise. She often didn't sleep, but this time, it hadn't been nightmares keeping her up. Bailey had been thinking about him.

About how his touch made her heart race. How her

breasts had tightened and ached when his hand had caressed her cheek. She hadn't responded to a man in a very, very long time. She hadn't even been sure that she *could* respond. Like . . . maybe something had broken inside of her during the attack. Just shut off. Desire hadn't been part of her life, not in so very long.

But things seemed different with Asher. She'd just met the guy, yet her body seemed to be revving to life. She was far, far too sensitive to him. Too attuned. That couldn't be normal.

Or am I just getting desperate? Her gaze slid toward him. Did it matter? Maybe she should just be happy to feel something other than fear. Desire was a nice change for her.

"Lay out the scene for me," Asher said, his sharp voice jerking her back to reality. "Tell me what I should see here."

Hell. That's what I see—I see hell. Bailey stepped closer to the cabin. She could still smell the fire—or maybe that was just her imagination, remembering that night. "They found the body, well, the remains, in the back room." She pointed. He'd been in the room near that remaining wall. The Death Angel. The cops had never been able to identify his body, probably because there hadn't been enough *to* identify. She knew the crime scene team had found teeth, but no dental records had ever matched up with the killer.

The Death Angel had taken his true identity to the grave with him.

"Anything special about that room?"

Her tongue swiped over her lower lip. "I think . . . I think that was the room he had me in." Her head turned. "There was no electricity in the place. The guy had everything off the grid. Wyatt said that was one of the reasons why it was so hard to find the killer." He'd built the cabin on his own, used solar panels to get light, then brought in lanterns, too. He'd dug a well—done everything *on his own*. A perfect prison that no one had known about.

Not until it was too late.

"Tell me more about it."

She inched closer to the burned wreckage. "Not much to tell." Her fingers fluttered over an old, tattered line of yellow police tape. Then, giving in to a compulsion that filled her, she slipped under the tape and went into the place that had once been her prison. Her hiking boots crunched over the ash. "The room was small. Maybe ten feet long? No window. Only a—a bed for furniture." She'd stumbled over that part. She hated to remember being trapped in that bed. At first, he'd tied her hands to the old headboard. Her legs had been bound to the footboard. Then he'd used his knife . . .

But she'd struggled so hard when he'd been hurting her that she'd broken the headboard. He'd bound her hands together then, so tightly.

Her gaze slid to the scars on her wrists.

You shouldn't hide them.

Royce had been horrified by her scars. *You were perfect.* His words haunted her. *Were.* In his eyes, she'd seen that he didn't think she was so perfect any longer.

I never was perfect. It was always a lie. A great big lie.

She found herself walking toward the back of the cabin, going unerringly down what had *once* been a hallway, even though that corridor was long gone. Then she was there, standing in the blackened remains of *her* room, the wind blowing through her hair.

"Walk me back through the night you heard the other woman." Asher had followed behind her, his steps silent. "Show me what happened."

The bed had been to the right. Against the wall. She pointed. "I slid from the bed. Then I crawled to . . ." She moved, counting the steps. Bailey stopped and pointed at her feet. "Here. I used the nail to get free. It was sticking up out of the wooden floor." She hurried to the door. "He'd left the door unlocked, because I was tied up and he didn't think I would be any trouble."

"Guess he was wrong."

"Yes . . ." She advanced.

He followed.

"I was going to try and run out, but I heard her screams."

Help me!

She turned then, only—nothing was left of the other room. "The other woman was in here, on the bed. He was over her. I ran at him, hit him as hard as I could."

Asher was glancing around, bending down, touching the black soil—was it soil? Or remains of the old floor? Soot? She couldn't tell for certain. "When he grabbed me, she ran out."

Asher looked up at her.

"He choked me until I passed out, so I don't know if she came back. If he went after her or . . ." *Or if she kept running.*

Once more, Asher surveyed the scene around them. "I read the fire marshal's report last night."

"You did?"

"Had a little trouble sleeping," he murmured. "So I booted up my laptop. Gabe had sent me some files, so I just did a little reading." He rose, brushing off his hands. "The fire marshal thinks the blaze started here, in this room."

The other woman's prison.

"That's why the damage is so severe in this spot. Based on his findings, gasoline was poured all over the cabin. It wasn't some accident. He figured the Death Angel was trying to destroy evidence."

"But he wound up killing himself in the process." And she was glad.

"Probably didn't understand how fast the fire would burn. It spread out of control, and he found himself trapped."

"In a room with no window." She remembered that. There had been no window when she burst into that little room. No furniture—other than the bed.

"Will you show me where Deputy Bliss found you?"

My grave. "Y-yes." She quickened her steps as she left that blackened mess behind. Had the Death Angel screamed while he'd burned? Had he begged for help?

Like his victims had?

Thick brush and trees waited just thirty feet away. Some had been burned—pines were scorched, their trunks dead. The fire had taken them, too.

She slipped through the woods. There was a trail there now, one that hadn't existed before. The crime scene teams had made the trail when they came to dig up all the bodies. The dogs had been there, again and again as they searched for more remains. *Cadaver dogs.*

Asher was right behind her. She could practically feel him there. Strong. Silent.

Bailey turned to the left.

A line of graves. Well. That was what it had been, before.

The holes had been filled in since that terrible night. Probably because the sheriff had been afraid some dumb tourist would come up and fall in one. Right after the murders, a ton of folks had come out—to take pictures. To gawk at the graves.

Five graves. Four bodies had been recovered— and . . .

Me.

"My grave was the last one, over there, on the right." She pointed.

"It wasn't your grave."

Her gaze whipped up to him. She saw a muscle jerk in his jaw.

"Not your grave, Bailey." He seemed to be gritting out each word. "The bastard tried, but you are *alive*."

So why couldn't she feel that way? *Dead girl walking.* Yes, she'd started saying that about herself lately. Because it seemed all she was doing was just going through the motions. The Death Angel had taken something from her. She'd fought him, so long and hard, but in the end . . .

When she'd been in the ground. When the dirt had been falling on her as she tried to claw her way to freedom . . .

Maybe she had given up then. Or maybe she'd given up after . . . after she'd gotten out of the hospital, when she realized that the only people who seemed to care about her story . . . that would be the reporters who wanted to make money off her pain.

Her family was gone. The pain from her parents' death still haunted her.

Her lover had left her.

Her friends . . . being with the few who'd visited had just become harder and harder as more time passed. Their lives were normal. They wanted *her* to be normal, too. And she couldn't be.

Asher paced toward the graves. New, dark dirt marked them, barren of any grass.

"I think . . ." She cleared her throat and tried again. Like she could do much to make her voice stronger. Another scar from the Death Angel. "I think he was done with me, so he had my grave ready. He had another victim to play with—the dark-haired woman. He wasn't ready to kill her, so he didn't have a grave for her. Not yet."

Asher's hands were on his hips. His gaze was on the rugged terrain around them. The mountains. The trees. "It would be hard for her to get out of here on foot."

They'd driven forty-five minutes from her home, then hiked for six miles in order to get to the Death Angel's cabin.

"A woman scared, hurt, running desperate in the middle of the night . . ." Asher gave a low whistle. "There are some jagged cliffs up here. It would have been easy for her to fall."

"Wyatt and his team searched—they took out their dogs but . . ." Now she stared at the mountains, too. "I feared the same thing. Maybe she *is* still out here. Maybe she never made it out of the mountains."

Maybe she died out here and no one ever found her remains.

He surveyed the area. "You up for some more hiking?"

"I—"

"We'll go back to town first. Gather supplies. Then I'd like to spend some time out here, doing a better search of the area. We can get a map and you can show me the locations that the deputies searched. We'll eliminate those and we'll hit other targets that seem likely."

This was happening. She wasn't being brushed off. Wasn't being told she needed to move on with her life. *He believes me.* "Yes, yes." Bailey nodded briskly. "I'm definitely up for more hiking."

"We should come back before nightfall."

She hadn't been in the mountains at night, not since her attack. Goose bumps rose onto her arms.

"If we're here at night, we can see what she saw," Asher continued briskly. "It was night, she was desperate—if we come back at night, we might see lights— see *something* that she saw, and that can give us a potential lead."

Going out at night—yes, okay, it made sense. Bailey rubbed her sweaty palms on the front of her jeans. "I used to hike up here all the time. I knew nearly all of the trails."

"Then you'll be invaluable to me tonight."

Would she? Or would she turn into a basket case? *I won't. I'm not going to be this person anymore! I hate being like this.*

He strode toward her. Bailey felt her body stiffen.

She did that when most people got too close. A visceral reaction. *Don't attack. Don't hurt me!*

But Asher wasn't going to hurt her. Every time he touched her, he was infinitely careful.

Maybe *too* careful.

Only he didn't touch her this time. He stopped just a foot away from her. "There weren't any hits in NamUs."

She blinked.

"NamUs is—"

"I know what NamUs is." She'd pretty much become obsessed with the missing since her attack. Bailey was now well acquainted with the National Missing and Unidentified Persons System. Obsessively acquainted.

"One of my colleagues at LOST, Wade Monroe, he checked their missing persons' database and there weren't any missing women—not within two hundred miles of the area here—who matched the description you gave."

"Maybe she dyed her hair," Bailey blurted. "Or maybe she *was* from more than two hundred miles away." There were a dozen other *maybes* that she could throw at him. But before she could, he said—

"Maybe. Maybe that did happen." His head inclined toward her. "I just like to keep you updated."

Oh. Okay.

"Let's go back to the parking lot," Asher said. "We're burning daylight."

SHE'D COME BACK.

Funny. He hadn't expected that. Bailey Jones seemed to jump at her own shadow these days, yet she'd headed back out to the scene of the crime.

Interesting.

Definitely a story there. And if anyone was going to break the story, it would sure as hell be him. *Richard Spawn. Fucking ace reporter.* At least, that was how he saw himself. Soon enough, the rest of the world would, too. And Bailey—she was his ticket to notoriety.

He inched closer to her car. Locked, of course, because she didn't believe in making things easy on him.

But the motorcycle nearby . . . now that was interesting. And it wasn't as if you could lock up a motorcycle. Smiling, he closed in. His hand reached for the saddlebags on the right side of the bike.

When Asher cleared the trees and edged toward the parking lot that waited at the end of the trail, his body immediately went on high alert. There was some blond SOB with his hands all over Asher's ride. He didn't stop to shout some lame-ass warning at the guy.

He just attacked. Asher rushed forward, moving silently just as he'd been trained. Before the would-be thief even sensed him, Asher was right behind the man. He grabbed him, caught the guy's hands, and in seconds, Asher had the fellow on his knees, with his arms stretched tautly behind him.

"Ow!" the fellow yelled. "Son of a bitch—stop! Stop! You're breaking my arms!"

"Not yet," Asher assured him. "Make another move toward my bike, though, and we'll just see what happens."

"Assault!" The word was a desperate scream. "You can't do this to me!"

"And you can't shove your hands into my saddlebags and try to find something to steal, asshole."

Footsteps rushed behind him. "Asher!" Bailey sounded breathless. "Asher, I . . . know him."

She knew the dick who'd been robbing him? He cast her a quick, suspicious glance and saw that her eyes were locked on the man he held prisoner. Her green gaze shot fury at the fellow.

"He's a reporter, one of the guys that Wyatt had to haul off my property two weeks ago."

His would-be thief was a snooping reporter who'd tailed them and then decided to poke around for a story? Yeah, sounded right.

Asher didn't have the best history with reporters. Like Bailey, he knew some could—and would—sensationalize the hell out of stories, no matter who got hurt.

Even kids.

"Let me go!" The reporter was yelling and struggling and if he kept moving like that . . .

"Do you *want* a broken arm?" Asher asked him.

The guy stilled. His body stopped moving, anyway. His mouth didn't. "You are in so much trouble," he blustered. "I'll call the authorities. I'll splash your face on the news. I am Richard Spawn. *Richard Spawn.* I will own you before I am done. I am—"

"A dick, right," Asher drawled. "I heard you the first time."

The guy sputtered.

Bailey gave a quick, sharp laugh. Damn but he loved that sound.

Taking his time, Asher let go of Dick—Richard. Richard Who-the-Hell-Ever he'd said he was.

The guy sprang to his feet and made a show of flexing his wrists and stretching his arms. Asher rolled his eyes. "No permanent damage. I knew exactly what I was doing."

The reporter immediately leapt for a black bag that waited on the ground, less than two feet away. He yanked out a camera and started snapping pictures. "The Death Angel's victim has a dark new lover . . . *one with a temper.*"

"This dumbass isn't serious?" Asher glanced at Bailey, a grim smile on his lips.

But his smile faded when he saw her face. There was no humor there. She'd gone pale, and her eyes were stark.

Fuck this. Asher stepped in front of her. "Stop taking the photos."

"Ha! I'm a reporter—"

"Then report, don't take photos." The fact that the guy was doing both jobs himself told Asher he wasn't looking at a man who worked for one of the more reputable news sources. *Tabloid much?*

But Dick wasn't lowering the camera.

"I warned you." Asher grabbed the camera in a flash. Dick yelled.

Asher held tight to his new prize.

"No way." Dick glared at him. "That is *my* property. Give it back."

Asher swept his gaze over the reporter. About five foot ten, lean, wiry. Blond hair that swept back from his high forehand. Pale hands. Twitchy hands.

"Did you follow us up here?" Asher's gaze slid toward the right, to the only other vehicle in that small lot at the trailhead. There were many lots like that one in the area, always located close to a trail entrance. Convenient spots for hikers to park while they explored. Such graveled parking lots dotted the North Carolina terrain.

"What?" Dick's gaze was on his precious camera. "How the hell dare you say that? I've been staying away from her, just like the good deputy ordered." His eyes rose as he smirked at Bailey. "Thought he was the love interest, so now things are picking up—"

A growl slipped from Asher. "So . . . to be clear . . ." he began as he tilted his head and still held on to the digital camera. "You're a piece of shit?"

Dick's jaw dropped.

"That your ride?" Asher asked him, glancing over at the Jeep. "Notice it's a rental. You don't happen to own a Mustang, do you?"

The guy glared. "What I own is none of your business! And I didn't follow her! I just came up here for some shots. They were for a piece I'm working on. It's pure coincidence that we're all here at the same time."

"Liar," Bailey muttered.

Dick shrugged. "Can't prove that."

Asher really didn't like that guy. "Why were you messing with my bike?"

"I wasn't messing with anything! I was just looking! I admire motorcycles, that's all. I was just looking at the damn bike."

Right. Like Asher believed that.

"I want my camera back. Give it to me, or I'll press charges. I swear I will."

Asher glanced down at his hand.

"Give it to him," Bailey said. "What does another picture matter?"

Asher stepped toward Dick. Leaning in close to him, he said, "I don't want to see you around Bailey again."

Dick snatched the camera from him. "Oh, like I'm supposed to be scared of the big, bad new lover who's chasing after Bailey."

You should be scared. Some people just didn't understand the basic facts of life.

Dick snapped a few more pictures, but then he hauled ass out of that place real quick. When he drove his Jeep away from the small lot, gravel flew in his wake.

With his hand on his hip, Asher watched him go.

"I'm sorry," Bailey said. "Getting my picture tossed on the web and on the news is one thing. But you didn't sign on to have your face splashed everywhere with mine."

"Don't worry about it." What worried Asher was the fact that jerks like Dick had been plaguing Bailey. Could that reporter have been outside her place last night? Looking to scare her so that he could get a new story?

Or was it another dumbass who'd formed some kind of obsession after seeing her on TV? Unfortunately, since he'd been working at LOST, Asher had become all too aware of the dark obsessions that some people had.

Obsessions that left them fixated on their victims. Desperate to see them, to touch them. To have them. At any cost.

"I *do* worry about it," she said, her words hard. "And I'm sorry. It's not fair to have your life broadcast for everyone, just because you're helping me."

He stepped toward her. Lifted his hand. Made himself stop. The urge to touch her was always too strong.

What was up with that? "You don't have to be sorry. Trust me, I want to be doing this job." He wanted to help *her.* "Now let's get back to town. We'll get our gear, check in with the deputy, and then do more recon work out here tonight."

She nodded, but still seemed to hesitate.

"Bailey?"

Her gaze was on the graveled road that led to the small parking lot. The reporter was long gone. But Asher was sure the guy would be back. Parasites like him never gave up easily.

"Bailey?" He kept his voice low, easy. "Are you all right?"

She glanced back at him, and her brilliant green stare was like a punch straight to his gut. Seriously, her eyes should come with some kind of warning label because when he looked into them . . .

"You're doing more for me than you have to do."

He shook his head, not understanding.

But Bailey gave that little laugh he rather loved and said, "You are. I think we both know that getting your life exposed to some reporter is going above and beyond the call of duty."

He eased closer to her. The woman was freaking pulling him in like some kind of magnet. Every word, every whisper—she had no clue what she was doing.

Professional. Keep it—

"Do you go so far for every client that you have?"

He cleared his throat and made sure to keep his hands at his sides. *Not touching her.* "LOST gives all for our clients. If we take a case, we're in until the end." That was Gabe's philosophy. During his training period at

LOST, Asher had come to understand just how dedicated the group was to finding the missing. Cops, the FBI—everyone else had given up on the missing who found their way onto LOST's radar.

Someone had to believe there was hope those missing would be found.

"Oh," Bailey whispered. And the lady almost sounded . . . what? Disappointed?

He cocked his head to the side.

"It's good that you give every client so much attention," she murmured, but she wasn't looking him directly in the eyes, not any longer.

She turned toward her car.

"Bullshit."

Bailey threw a questioning glance over his shoulder.

"I'm bullshitting you." So he'd bare this truth for her. "You're different."

Her lips parted. Those gorgeous lips that he should not be staring at so hard. "I'm sorry," Asher muttered. And he was sorry. "You didn't ask for this but . . . there is something about you. It makes me want to do more for you. Makes me want to do *anything* to chase those shadows from your eyes."

He heard her sharply indrawn breath. Hell, they were alone now so he might as well lay all the cards on the table. Maybe he should call someone else in to work with her. Maybe Ana . . . "I want you."

Shock washed over her face. "What?"

"Yeah, fuck, I'm sorry." He raked a hand through his hair and paced away from her. His movements were quick and jerky and he was making a serious clusterfuck of this situation. He just wasn't used to dealing with a woman like her. And he sure wasn't used to looking at a woman and just—wanting. Wanting so badly that he was losing his cool and his control was cracking more minute by minute. "But I . . . hell, I thought you should know."

"Know that . . . you want me." She was definitely sounding dazed. Shocked. But not furious, so that was something. But maybe the fury was about to come.

"Yes," he gritted out and he waited for her to erupt. To call him an asshole. To tell him that she was *not* paying LOST so that some jerk like him would lust after her.

But she didn't. She just kept staring at him in surprise, her eyes wide.

"I'm sure every man you meet wants you." How could they not?

She closed her mouth. Looked away. "I wouldn't know. I—I haven't exactly been looking for a lover."

I said the wrong thing. Did the wrong thing. Shit. After all she'd been through, of course, she didn't want this—*me.* "I won't do anything," he told her, voice grating. "I'm not going to pressure you for *anything.* Look, I know I overstepped. I just—I needed to tell you—"

"Why won't you do anything?"

Now his mouth dropped open in shock.

"Is it because of what happened to me?" Now anger flashed across her face. "Because I'm some victim? Too delicate to handle a lover?"

"What? Shit, *no.* That's not it at all." She'd just said she hadn't been looking—

"Then what is it?"

Okay, now he didn't know what was happening. "You aren't telling me to go to hell."

She blew out a hard breath. "Good of you to notice."

His lips almost twitched at that.

"Why won't you do anything?" Bailey asked him again.

Holy fuck . . . "You *want* me to do something?" Now he was moving even closer to her. He couldn't help it—his hand lifted and curled around her cheek. Her skin was so incredibly soft.

"I—" She broke off. "Maybe."

Okay, that wasn't the resounding *I want you* that he'd suddenly—probably foolishly—wished to hear.

"I haven't been with a lover since before the abduction."

Every muscle in his body stiffened.

"I haven't wanted to be," she continued and her cheeks flushed.

She was baring her soul to him. And he couldn't move.

"But then I met you," Bailey continued in that sexy voice that made his control quake. "And I started to . . . feel again. To want. To wonder . . . what it would be like, to be with you." She shook her head. "Is it wrong?"

Nothing would be wrong between them. He'd decided it. Right then. Right there.

"I'm not damaged," Bailey said.

"Hell, no, you're not."

"No matter what he said," she murmured.

"What dumbass said that?" He would happily beat the hell out of the fool.

But her gaze cut away from his.

His fingers lightly caressed her cheek. "You are *not* damaged. To be clear, you're the sexiest woman that I've ever met."

Her lips trembled. He wanted those lips, under his.

Wrong place. Wrong time.

"I wanted you to know how I felt," he continued, "because if you didn't want to work with me, I can get another LOST agent out here."

Now her gaze flew back to his. "I don't want anyone else."

Oh, baby, but those words are music to my fucking ears. Now, if only she'd meant that in the way his overactive body took it.

"I want you . . . on the case."

Right. Case. Check.

"And . . ." Her hands suddenly rose and pressed against the front of his shirt. "I don't know if I can do anything else. If I can even want . . ."

He waited, but she didn't say more.

If I can even want . . . He needed to back the hell off, right now. It had only been six months since her attack. She probably needed far more time. Far more care. He was a blundering bastard and—

"May I kiss you, Asher?"

You can do anything you want to me. "Yes."

Her cheeks had flushed. She inched closer to him. Her hands lifted, and he saw that her fingers were shaking. He wanted to take those fingers in his and hold them tightly, but he didn't want to scare her. This was her moment. No, her test. He realized exactly what it was.

She'd kiss him, and maybe nothing would happen

for her. Maybe she'd back away. Tell him to stick to business.

And if that happened . . . *I will.*

This was for her. Her body brushed against his as Bailey leaned up on her tiptoes. Her shaking fingers curled around his shoulders, pulling him closer.

She hesitated.

"It's okay," he told her gruffly. "You don't have to—"

She kissed him. Softly. Lightly. Quickly. A fast kiss, then she pulled back. She stared up at him, eyes wide, and her expression stark.

"Sweetheart . . ." he began, feeling his chest ache.

And she kissed him again. Not so fast. Her lips lingered on his. Caressed. Explored. He let her lead the kiss, every step of the way. He'd hated the fear he'd seen flash in her eyes.

If Bailey needed to find out if she could want a man again . . .

Use me, baby. Use me as long as you want.

As she kissed him, a shiver seemed to skate over Bailey and her lips parted. Her tongue snaked out, touched his mouth, sent the desire he felt for her raging even hotter within him.

His cock was hard, desire beat in his blood, but he kept his hands at his sides. His hands fisted as she explored his mouth. As the need built for him. *And for her. I hope it's building for her.*

Want me. Come on, baby. Want me as much as I want you.

Then he felt the light bite of her nails on him. Her body pressed more to his. And Bailey gave a low moan in her throat.

In that moment, he fought the urge to take the kiss further. To plunder with his mouth.

Her lips moved lightly against his. The soft stroke of her tongue had his cock jerking against his fly. But this moment wasn't about him. There was no doubt that he wanted her.

No fucking doubt at all.

Slowly, Bailey pulled back. Her lips were red and swollen.

Asher's heartbeat drummed in his ears. "Do you?" he asked her, voice rasping.

Do you want me?

Her long lashes lifted and her green gaze caught his. She didn't have to answer him—he read the answer in her eyes.

No matter what some dumbass had told her, Bailey wasn't damaged. Not by a long shot.

But she hadn't answered him. She backed away and put her fingers to her lips.

He watched her. Asher could still *taste* her, and he wanted more.

Hell, if Gabe found out what he'd just done . . .

Her fingers balled into a fist. "I think it's time to go back now."

Oh, hell. He'd scared her or hurt her or done something wrong. As he watched, Bailey turned away and he tried to figure out what he could say to fix this mess. She'd taken just a few steps when she glanced back. "Asher?"

The way she said his name . . .

You are working a case, asshole! And she's probably

about to tell your sorry self to take a hike. He cleared his throat. "Yeah, Bailey?"

"I do want you." She seemed surprised by her own words. "The problem is . . . I don't know what to do next."

Baby, I know.

"I'm scared."

"Don't be afraid of me. I swear, I would never hurt you." He'd sooner cut off his own hands than ever hurt her or any woman. That just wasn't in him.

"It's not you I'm afraid of." Her smile threatened to break his heart. "It's me." Then she headed for her car without another word.

Asher stood there a few moments, watching her.

Then she drove away.

HANNAH FINCH ADJUSTED her pack and stared out at the woods around her. Her first solo trek. Her asshole of an ex-boyfriend had told her going backcountry camping for four days would be too much for her. That she wasn't meant to rough it. That the first time she had to pee on a tree, she'd balk.

He had it all wrong. The truth was . . . she hadn't been *meant* to stay with an arrogant ass.

She had her water. She had her food. She had her tent and her supplies—her pack was all ready to go, all 32.4 pounds of it. She'd mapped out her trail, and this weekend was going to be all about her.

A smile stretched across her face as she advanced. Her boots hugged her feet perfectly. No amateur mistakes from her—she'd broken in those babies long before the hike. Her car was parked and locked at the parking lot below, the one that waited right at the tip of her trail.

She was going to see waterfalls, going to hike to the top of a glorious peak, and she was going to reconnect with nature. Screw technology. This was *her* time.

Hannah whistled as she walked. The temperature was perfect. The air smelled great. The leaves were starting to turn colors—absolutely gorgeous. This trip was so going to kick ass.

Her eyes closed as she walked and she just soaked it in. Nature. Freaking awesome.

THERE WERE PEOPLE in the world who believed that everything happened for a reason. There was no chance. No happy coincidence.

Every single thing that occurred was meant to be.

So when he caught a glimpse of the woman walking on the trail, her red hair glinting in the sunlight, he understood that *she* was meant to be—meant to be his.

Her whistle reached him. Some happy, silly little tune. She was walking easily, her backpack secured well as she walked. She was still pretty close to the parking lot—just starting her journey.

Alone.

When the Death Angel had been hunting, no one had hiked alone. Not men. Not women. Everyone had been extra vigilant. But the Death Angel was long gone, and people thought life was safe in those North Carolina mountains.

They'd all forgotten the terror that came before.

Perhaps it was time for everyone to start remembering.

The woman with the red hair disappeared as she headed farther on the trail. Her whistling carried back to him.

And he smiled. Then he began to follow her.

CHAPTER FOUR

DEPUTY WYATT BLISS WAS SITTING ON BAIley's porch when she returned home. She slammed her car door shut, frowning at him. It was just after lunchtime, and the guy didn't normally just appear on her doorstep.

When he saw her, Wyatt rose and headed toward her. "Found the car from last night," he said.

Her eyes widened. "Seriously? You caught the guy?"

The growl of a motorcycle's engine reached her ears. She looked back and saw that Asher had turned onto her street.

"Figured he'd be right behind you," Wyatt muttered. "Did some digging on *him,* too. Not real sure I like what I found."

"What?" Bailey shook her head. "You checked out Asher? But he's with LOST—"

"Right. A *civilian* group. He's not law enforcement, and with you inviting the guy right into your house, I wanted to learn more about him." His lips thinned. "Like I said, I didn't like what I found."

The motorcycle's growls had faded into silence. From the corner of her eye, she saw Asher push down the kickstand on his bike, then his hands curled around the helmet that covered his face.

"The guy's got a bad past, Bailey. You need to watch him."

"He's *helping* me."

"Then maybe *you* should have checked him out more before you hired the man."

Now he was pissing her off. She was tired of everyone telling her what she *should* do. It had been the same way after she got out of that freaking hole. The blame—it had been there. From the few friends who'd dropped by her hospital room. From her boyfriend. Telling her she *should* have been more careful. That she should have paid more attention to her surroundings.

Like—what? She'd been responsible for all the twisted shit that came her way?

"Maybe *you* should just tell me what you found out about the driver who tried to run us down last night," Bailey snapped back.

Surprise flashed on Wyatt's face. "Bailey?"

Asher had closed in. The guy had moved with that lethal, predatory grace of his. When he took a step, he didn't make so much as a rustle of sound. Was that a SEAL thing? And, really how bad could he be? *He was a SEAL.* Didn't that mean he'd been busy protecting and serving his country?

"You found the creep who was here last night?" Asher asked. His arm brushed against Bailey's.

She didn't flinch away. Actually, she was finding that she liked it when Asher touched her.

She liked him.

Maybe because he didn't constantly look at her as if she were some damaged doll. He looked at her, saw her scars and told her—

Don't hide them.

She'd been hiding so much of herself for the last six months. Maybe it was time to stop.

I was a fighter. I got out of those woods.

Time for that woman to come back, and not remain the scared shell she'd been for so long. Time for her to feel something more than fear.

Asher makes me feel desire. When I touch him, it's like I'm coming alive again. So she kept wanting to touch him, more and more. To feel . . . more and more.

"I found the car," Wyatt said carefully. "Turned out the Mustang was stolen a few days ago. And whoever took it decided to ditch the ride at a gas station just outside of Brevard this morning. Looks like the car was wiped down—no prints that we could see."

A knot formed in Bailey's stomach. "Stealing a car? Wiping it down? That all sounds . . ." Her voice trailed away. *It sounds like it isn't some punk kid. But then, as soon as the guy aimed at us last night, I knew it was something else . . .*

"I think you need to be extra cautious," Wyatt said, concern darkening his face. "There are an awful lot of weirdos in this world, and if someone saw you too much on TV—"

"And got fixated on you," Asher interrupted starkly.

"It just might not be safe," Wyatt said, his lips curving down in a small frown. "I've got my men searching the area. And I'll have a patrol coming through your neighborhood, just to make sure that you're all right."

Wyatt was a deputy, yes, but the guy was actually in line to take over for the sheriff. Technically, he already did all the work that was supposed to fall on the sheriff's shoulders because Sheriff Johnson was two steps away from retirement, and taking care of day-to-day business in the county wasn't exactly high on his priority list anymore.

Bailey knew that Sheriff Johnson blamed himself for the Death Angel's kills. Kills that had all happened in Johnson's jurisdiction. Under his watch. She wasn't sure if retirement was his plan . . . or if he'd just been caught drinking too many times and the guy was being forced out of office now.

Either way, Wyatt would soon be running things.

"I didn't like it when those reporters kept nosing around," Wyatt continued. "And now . . . with some guy stealing a car and making threatening phone calls . . ." He stopped, looking helpless.

"Bailey isn't alone," Asher said in that deep, rumbling voice of his. "I'll be at her side, and you can rest assured I won't let anyone near her."

That was—she exhaled slowly—*nice*. Nice that he had her back that way. "Speaking of reporters," Bailey murmured. "When we were in the woods this morning, at the crime scene, we saw Richard Spawn. The guy was messing around with Asher's motorcycle."

Wyatt's eyes turned to slits. "What the hell were you doing out there?"

She blinked. "Excuse me?" Had he missed what she said about the motorcycle?

But Wyatt stepped forward and caught her hands in his.

"You need to stay away from that place. Shit, Bailey, move on. Don't go back out there digging up ghosts. It's not good for you. You *know* what the shrink said. You should let go or you won't ever be able to get your life back."

He was doing it again. Looking at her like she was some beaten victim. Telling her all the things she *should* do.

"Uh, yeah, about letting go," Asher drawled before she could say anything. "How about you do me a favor, Deputy, and *you* let the lady go? Now."

Wyatt looked down at his hold on Bailey's wrists and he seemed surprised. He immediately yanked his hands back and jerked away. "Sorry."

Asher moved his body, not completely blocking her view of the deputy but making himself a nice, sturdy barricade between her and Wyatt. "If Bailey wants to dig up ghosts—if she wants to dig up freaking graves—then she's going to do it," he said bluntly. "And I'll be right there, helping her do that shit."

Her shoulders straightened.

But, if anything, Wyatt just appeared angrier. His gaze cut to her. "Bailey, you need to know . . . straight up, this man is a killer."

"What?" Shock rocked through her. He seriously hadn't just said that. Had he?

"Deputy . . ." The hard snap was a warning from Asher.

"He was a SEAL." Wyatt wasn't backing down. "What do you *think* he was doing on those missions? I tried to dig into the mission case files, but they were classified, every single one of them. But the training he had—he was trained to kill. Quickly, efficiently."

Her hands had balled into fists. "He was trained to protect. He was protecting our country."

"Bailey . . ."

"Stop it." She threw the words at him because she was done. "Stop talking down to me. Stop trying to *order* my life. I hired Asher. I *like* him. And, no, I don't believe for one moment that he is some kind of threat to me." He couldn't be because when she was with him—she felt safe. She didn't feel that way with anyone else. She couldn't let her guard down with anyone else.

He's the first man I can look at and actually want in a very long time.

She didn't feel the need to pretend with him. He saw her, just as she was.

Don't hide your scars. She didn't want to hide anything from him. With Asher, she wanted to be completely open.

"You carry a gun," Bailey pointed out to Wyatt. "And *you* were trained, too. But I don't call you a killer and I never will."

His gaze blazed at her. "I'm trying to tell you that you're making a mistake—"

"Going to LOST was the best decision I've made in a very long time. Now, if you'll excuse me, I need to get my backpack ready." But when she stepped forward, he was in her way, blocking her path. "Excuse me." Only those weren't nice words from her—they were an order. *Excuse me . . .* with an implied *get the fuck out of my way.*

"Your backpack?" Wyatt seemed to be sweating. "You're not going back out there—tell me you're not."

He was pushing her too much. "I'm going back there. Asher and I want to search the area some more to see if we can find any sign of the woman I saw."

"She was never there!"

And something splintered—just cracked apart inside of her. *"Yes, she was!"* Her words were a shout of fury. As much of a shout as she could manage. "I'm not crazy—I never have been! That woman was there, and I'm not going to forget her. I can't."

Wyatt stumbled back a step. "We searched those woods. The dogs searched—"

"There are a lot of woods up there," Asher said quietly. "A whole lot of ground to cover."

Wyatt raked a hand over his face. "Right, right, there is." His hand fell. "So how are the two of you supposed to magically find the victim—if there is one—"

"There is," Bailey said. *She is real.*

"How are you supposed to find her up there?" Wyatt demanded.

Bailey saw Asher flash a cold, hard smile at the deputy. Rather like a shark's grin. "We'll try our damnedest. *Trying,* that's what we are going to do."

Bailey wasn't going to listen to Wyatt anymore. She brushed past him and hurried up the steps.

"Bailey!" Wyatt called after her. "Stop! You don't *know* this guy—"

Bailey didn't stop. She did know Asher and she wasn't going to listen to Wyatt hurl his insults, not any longer. Things were changing for her. No more "poor Bailey Jones . . ."

It was time for her to take her life back. She'd realized that fact when she stood there with Asher, staring at those five graves. Four women didn't have lives any longer. They were gone.

But she had a chance. She couldn't let the Death Angel rob her of anything, not anymore.

My life. My rules.

Time to get back the woman she'd been.

Bailey Jones is coming home.

THE FRONT DOOR slammed closed behind Bailey, and the deputy—he stared at the door with a gaping mouth and shocked eyes.

Asher sighed, drawing the deputy's focus back to him. "Yeah, so . . . it's not going to happen."

"What?" Wyatt Bliss looked confused.

So Asher decided to clarify for him. "You. Bailey. Whatever little dream you had stirring in your head— it's not going down. Better just give it up now."

"Listen, you—"

"No, you listen." He stalked toward the deputy. "She wanted you to hear her. She wanted you to help, and you turned a blind eye. For months." *Idiot.* "I'm here now, and I'll make sure that she gets the help—that she gets *anything*—she needs."

"You want to fuck her."

Asher's eyes widened. Someone had certainly gone straight for the punch. At least he'd been more— delicate? Maybe. *Screw it.* "So do you."

If the deputy's eyes narrowed any more, the guy wouldn't be able to see. "She's a *victim*. She needs care. She needs—"

"Bailey is the only one who knows what she needs." But he'd learned that she wanted him. And Asher wasn't about to let this bozo with a badge try to come between him and Bailey.

"You think she needs you? Wants you? She's not at that damn point, asshole. She needs care. Protection. She can't get into some kind of relationship now."

Asher sighed. "There you go again. Thinking *you* know what she needs." His lips twisted. "That's why you're shit out of luck, man. You don't tell a woman what she needs or what she wants. You let her figure that out for herself."

Wyatt surged forward, nearly standing toe to toe with Asher. "You think you're something damn special, don't you?"

Asher carefully considered the question, then nodded. "Most days, yeah, I do." He gave the guy a grim smile. "Thanks for noticing, Deputy."

The deputy growled back at him. "I *know* you."

"I doubt that." *Just as I doubt that you know Bailey.*

"I dug into your past. So Uncle Sam kept your missions classified?" His face turned smug. "There was plenty more to find about you. I just had to look long and deep enough. Believe me. I did."

Anger burned in Asher's gut. "Shouldn't you have spent all that time looking for the jerk who tried to terrorize Bailey?"

"*I know what you did.* Awful young for a first kill, wasn't it?" The deputy raked him with a hard stare. "What does something like that do to a man? Does it twist you? Turn you into a monster? Is *that* why you took so many black ops missions? You got a dark side in you that just needs to come out?"

Asher breathed, real nice and easy. He wasn't letting this jerkoff get to him. The days of rage taking over and him throwing his fists at dumbasses were long gone. *Mostly.* "If you read up on my past, then you know everything I did was justified."

"You were in and out of juvie after that. Trouble, left and right. Trouble until you got sent off into the military—"

"I volunteered," Asher clarified. *My choice.* Because he'd known he was on the wrong path, and he'd wanted to change.

"You're not what she needs right now."

"Back to that, are we?" Asher murmured. Someone was sure obsessed with what Bailey needed. "How about we let Bailey decide?"

"I will tell her," Wyatt threatened. "I'll tell her everything about you."

Asher's brows rose. "Go right ahead. I don't hide my past. It's part of me, always will be."

Wyatt glared at him a moment longer, but then the deputy's phone rang, vibrating on his hip. He stepped back from Asher, looked down at the number on his phone's screen, and swore.

"Guess you better take that," Asher said.

Wyatt shot him another fuming glare but started marching for his car. As he left, Asher heard him say, "You know better than to call me now. What the hell do you want?"

The deputy climbed into his car, slamming the door shut behind him.

Asher tilted his head, studying the deputy. That was

a man who seemed to have a few secrets. Since Wyatt had been so determined to uncover his past . . .

Perhaps I'll see what secrets you carry, Deputy.

DEPUTY WYATT BLISS tightened his hold on his phone. "I am on duty today. This shit had better be important."

"It is," he was assured. "Remember that deal I offered you?"

He knew exactly who his annoying caller was. A reporter he *shouldn't* have been talking with—not at all. But when he'd been tossing Richard Spawn's ass out of Bailey's yard a few weeks ago, the reporter had made him an offer . . .

Talk to me about the case, and I can make it worth your while.

He'd never been on the take in his life. Always played the game true blue but . . .

Five thousand dollars. Just for information. You'll remain anonymous, I promise. And it's not like you'll be hurting anyone. Just giving me access to case files that connect to a dead man.

Where was the crime there?

So . . . he'd done it. Fucking hell, he'd made copies of all the files and given them to the reporter.

"I just wanted to let you know how much I've enjoyed our little relationship," Richard murmured.

It was hard to hear the bastard. In the mountain, cell service was a tricky bitch. Sometimes, it was perfect, even if you were in the woods. Other times, you could be in the middle of town and have nothing.

"If you get any more little . . . nuggets about Bailey or about the case, I do hope you'll pass them on to me."

For a minute, Wyatt thought about Asher Young. What he'd learned about that bastard.

"*Is* there something else?" Static crackled over the line.

"Fuck off," Wyatt snapped. "Don't call me again." He ended the call. Drove faster. He'd made a mistake with Spawn. A mistake that had *better* not come to light. If it did, he could kiss being sheriff good-bye.

What in the hell was I thinking?

Sweat dripped down his forehead. He'd fucked up. He'd just thought . . .

It won't hurt anyone. The case is closed. Those files don't matter.

It won't hurt anyone.

So why the hell did it feel so wrong?

THE WATERFALL WAS absolutely freaking gorgeous.

Hannah held on to her camera but dropped her pack as she headed closer to the cascading water. This area was everything that the travel guides had said—truly the land of waterfalls. They were *everywhere*. And this one was incredible. Spilling down from so high above, a rainbow sprouted at the waterfall's base. She edged closer, her feet dipping into the water because she wanted to get a great shot of this place.

But her boot skidded on the rocks. The algae there had made the rocks too slippery and she staggered, nearly going down. Hannah desperately tried to keep her camera up—

A man's hard hand locked around hers. He steadied her and stopped her stumbling fall toward the rocks. Spray from the waterfall fell onto her.

And him.

Her gaze flew to his. His eyes twinkled in a handsome face. And—

He smiled.

A killer smile.

"You should be more careful," he told her, still holding tightly to her hand. "A fall like that could really have hurt you."

She hadn't realized that he was there. Actually, she hadn't thought *anyone* was out there with her. Before she'd headed for the waterfall, Hannah had looked behind her because she'd thought she'd heard a twig snap. No one had been there.

"Thank you," she told him, making sure to keep her voice flat. Sure, he was a good-looking guy, but she was out in the wilderness, by herself, and suddenly, the memory of all those terrible news stories flashed through her mind.

Death Angel.

He was dead, though; everyone knew that. She was safe.

But I still know better than to flirt with a stranger out here.

"Let me help you to steadier ground," he murmured, flashing that smile again. Such a friendly smile. One that said, *I'm safe.*

She eased off the rocks and back onto dry land.

And he let go of her hand.

Hannah swallowed. "I should put the camera back in my pack." She bent toward the pack, then stopped, realizing that the man who stood just a few feet away—he didn't have a pack with him. "You . . . you live around here?" She knew cabins dotted the area, so maybe he was staying in one of them. Not her style. This trip was all about roughing it for her.

Hannah tucked the camera inside her bag. And maybe . . . maybe her fingers slid toward the pepper spray she'd packed, just as a precaution.

Behind her, he laughed. "No, not me. I just parked down the way at the trailhead. Heard that if you hiked up about two miles, you could see one of the most beautiful waterfalls that God ever created."

She glanced back at him. He looked a bit embarrassed as he added, "Though I should have planned ahead and at least grabbed the water bottle from my car. Guess you can tell I'm a first timer at this, huh?"

Her shoulders relaxed a bit. "Don't feel so bad. It's my first time out here, too." *He's not the Death Angel. Every man you meet isn't a killer.* Despite what her mother had always told her about strangers. Instead of reaching for her pepper spray, Hannah pulled out her bottle of water. "Want some?"

His gaze darted to her water. "Nah, I can't take a lady's water. Wouldn't be the right thing to do."

She was warming up to the guy. "You saved me from a bad fall. It's the least I can do." A smile tilted her lips as she headed toward him, the bottle offered in her outstretched hand. "Go ahead. I insist."

He took the bottle. His fingers slid over hers. "Thanks."

And she'd done her good deed for the day. A good deed, for a handsome hero.

"You out here all alone?" he asked her.

At that question, some of that warm, safe glow she'd

started to feel vanished. No matter how cute he might be, she wasn't going to spill that, yes, she was hiking by herself. Did she look like an idiot? "No, my friends are circling back to join me," she lied. "They were scouting ahead."

He nodded. "Beautiful area. Maybe they'll find some more falls for you to photo."

She hadn't managed to photo *this* waterfall yet.

"Better get going back to my car. Nice to meet you, Ms. . . . ?"

"Hannah." She only gave her first name. "Just Hannah."

He offered her the water back. "Thanks for the drink." His fingers touched the side of his forehead in a little salute. "Hope you and your friends have a good time out here."

She nodded. Her hold tightened on the water bottle as she watched him walk away. A few moments later, he disappeared behind the trees. Her breath expelled in a long, relieved rush.

Just a nice stranger. Someone else here to see the killer view. Get a grip, woman.

She put the water back in her pack and pulled out her camera. She was going to get these shots, and she was going to be one hell of a lot more careful about it this time. The water poured down from the falls, and the rainbow seemed ever bolder and more brilliant. She inched closer to the water, making sure *not* to get on those rocks . . .

Snap. Zoom. Snap. So she wasn't some kind of award-winning photographer. These pictures were still awesome. She'd put them on her wall and always remember *her* weekend. The time she got to break loose and just—

"Liar." The whisper came from right behind her.

Hannah yelled and jerked around, but something hit her. *He* hit her, slamming his fist into the side of her face. She fell back, tripping and sliding, and when she went down, her temple crashed into the side of those sharp rocks. Pain exploded in her head and for a moment, everything around her went dark.

I can't pass out. I can't.

She blinked, blearily, and he was crouched above her. That same harmless smile was on his face. *I'm safe.*

"You don't have any friends coming." He had picked up her camera. He started snapping pictures, of her. "I've been watching you. I know you're all alone. Poor Hannah. Poor, lying Hannah."

Her head wasn't just hurting, it seemed to be splitting open, and nausea rolled in her stomach. Bile built in her throat and she heaved.

He laughed and snapped more pictures. "Easier than I thought." His teeth flashed with that wide grin. "Told you . . . the rocks were dangerous. Now you've gone and had a terrible fall."

Her hands flew out. She managed to grab one of those rocks, she lifted it toward him, wanting to bash in *his* head.

But he caught her wrist. Squeezed it hard—so hard she thought her wrist might shatter. Maybe it *had* shattered.

The rock fell.

"You're going to help me, Hannah," he told her. "You're going to help make sure that everyone remembers."

"H-help!" Hannah tried to scream. But the cry didn't seem loud enough. The falls were thundering behind her. They were loud. Maybe that was why she hadn't heard him come back up behind her.

The falls . . .

He'd put down her camera and now he lifted her up against him.

"H-help . . ."

Smiling, he slammed her back down—hard—and the back of her head pounded into the rocks.

CHAPTER FIVE

ONCE UPON A TIME, BAILEY HAD LOVED TO camp. She'd grown up with the mountains as her backyard. Heading into the Blue Ridge Mountains, hunting waterfalls—those had been her favorite pastimes growing up. She'd spent countless hours out there with her parents.

Now she was breaking out into a cold sweat as she pulled on the backpack and walked away from her car. Her teeth were chattering, even though it was plenty warm out there. The heat of summer had faded, but fall was only whispering in the air. The leaves would turn soon, and the area would be gorgeous.

Too bad she didn't see the beauty of the place. Fear stopped that. The thick, hard fear that was nearly choking her. And if the knots in her stomach got much worse . . . *I'll be vomiting all over Asher.*

"You okay?" Asher asked as he marched closer to her.

He didn't look nervous. She doubted it was possible for him to appear anything but ruggedly capable and ready.

"If you're not up to this . . ."

"I am." She absolutely would not back down. Bailey took a moment to needlessly adjust the straps of her backpack and to suck in a deep, bracing breath. "I'm fine, don't worry about me." She wasn't going to crumble apart on him.

This was good for her, being out here. Her shrink, Dr. Leigh, would probably say that she was confronting her fears or some crap like that. Taking her life back.

You need to see that the monster isn't out there any longer, Bailey. He's gone. You have control of your life again. Those had been her shrink's words at their last appointment. An appointment over a month ago. Bailey hadn't been back.

Mostly because she couldn't rid herself of the notion that the shrink was wrong. The monster *was* out there. Waiting.

"We should hike toward the remains of the cabin." Asher had turned away from her as he spoke. "When night falls, I want to be able to see exactly what our missing woman might have witnessed. If you're trapped in the dark, human instinct is to go toward the first light that you see."

"There aren't any other cabins close by."

"Distances are deceptive at night. Maybe she saw a light and thought it was closer than it really was. Could be she got herself lost."

She fell into step beside him as they headed away from the lot. They'd only packed enough gear and supplies for two nights. Asher was carrying her tent, a two-person tent, and she wasn't even going to think about the fact that they'd be sharing that little space later.

At least, she wasn't going to think about it too much.

They started on the trail that would take them to that charred shell of a cabin. Asher led the way and she was glad. That way, he couldn't see her expression as they trekked out.

He had a pack, too. An extra one that she'd had at her place. He'd insisted on carrying all the food and shouldering as many of the supplies as possible. The guy didn't show any signs of strain as he hiked. In fact, she was having to hurry a bit in order to keep up with him.

Birds chirped overhead, and the leaves around her were starting to turn into brilliant fall shades. Orange. Red. Fall had always been her favorite time to hit the trails, and she even had a favorite waterfall that she liked to visit just a few miles to the east . . .

"May I ask you a few more questions?" His voice drifted back to her. "About that night?"

She'd figured this part would come, sooner or later.

"I read through all the files," Asher continued. "And one thing nags at me."

One thing?

"You said you pulled off his ski mask."

Her hands clenched into fists, and for a second, Bailey could imagine the feel of that soft cloth beneath her hands. "I did."

"So what did he look like? There was no description of the attacker in the files I got."

A lump had risen in her throat. She had to swallow a few times before she could say, "There was. A description, I mean. He was about your height. Muscled. Solid. Caucasian."

"Those are all facts you learn *without* taking off his mask. What did his face look like, Bailey? When you ripped off the mask . . ." He kept walking ahead of her. The sun was dipping into the sky. "What did he look like?"

Her eyes squeezed shut. "I don't know." She wished that she did. Whenever she tried to see him in her mind, her head seemed to splinter. A terrible pain burst in her temples. And there was just . . . nothing. Darkness where a face should be.

"Bailey . . ."

"I don't, okay?" Now she was snapping at him; so what? Her eyes opened and she glared at his bouncing pack. "You think I haven't tried to remember. I can see my hand—reaching for that black ski mask. I can feel it beneath my fingers. But when I try to picture him, I can't." Her laughter was bitter. "Probably because he was trying to choke the life out of me at the time and everything around me was going dark. Maybe I *never* saw his face at all. He was busy crushing my windpipe and giving me this lovely new voice that I have." Sarcasm was heavy in said voice.

Asher stopped hiking. He turned toward her. His face was such a mixture of emotions—surprise. Rage.

"Didn't realize it?" Most people didn't. "This isn't the voice I had pre-attack. I can barely get it above this level." And even though she was straining to speak as clearly as possible, her voice still sounded husky and low to her ears. "The docs said that I'm lucky to be able to speak at all because of the pressure he applied. That's why I couldn't call out when Wyatt and the other deputies finally came to me. The Death Angel had taken my voice away."

A muscle jerked along Asher's jaw. "It's a good thing the bastard is dead."

But it was too bad that he kept haunting her.

"I wish I could remember. Every single day, I wish that I could see his face. But I can't. There's no face to go with the monster in my mind." She wet her lips and saw his gaze follow that nervous movement. Another habit—thanks to her captivity, she'd been so freaking dehydrated. She found herself still feeling that way. Dr. Leigh had said it was some kind of shadow after-effect. Whatever. "We should keep going," she said, trying to sound brisk. She didn't want a pity party. So, yes, her voice was broken. Her body was scarred. The last thing she needed was for Asher to start looking at her like some poor little victim, especially when she liked it when he looked at her with desire in his eyes.

"You want to lead the way?" Asher asked her. "You know this area better than I do."

"Sure." She adjusted the straps on her bag and brushed past him. The man always felt so incredibly warm. His heat seemed to reach out to her, and Bailey was so tempted to reach right back to him.

What would he do, she wondered, if she did stop? If she put her hands around his shoulders. If she rose onto her toes and kissed him?

It had been so long since she'd known passion with a man. He was the first to make her desire again.

But . . .

Bailey didn't stop. She walked past him, her gaze

straight ahead. Her pace remained steady as she made her way back to that hell site, and all too soon, she was there at the cabin—what was left of it, anyway—and the sun was setting just over the mountain, bathing the whole area in a reddish gold light.

"What now?" Bailey asked as she turned to look around.

"Now, we wait. Once the darkness comes, then we'll see just what our missing victim saw."

But what if they saw nothing at all?

HANNAH'S EYES FLEW open and terror immediately burst through her. *He hurt me. He attacked me!*

She wasn't at the waterfall any longer. She was tied, lying facedown, and trapped on some smelly old bed. Her hands were secured to the headboard and her feet were bound together at the ankles. The rough rope bit into her skin.

Reddish sunlight trickled through a dirty window and her head craned toward it. "Help!" Hannah yelled. "Someone . . . *help me!*"

That crazy jerk at the waterfall had kidnapped her. And her head—jeez, her head hurt so much. She remembered falling and slamming into the rocks, but she had no clue what had occurred after that. How far had they traveled? *Where* had they traveled to?

"Help!" She screamed at the top of her lungs, her throat hurting from the effort and her head throbbing in pain. Hannah yanked on the ropes, but they wouldn't give. This couldn't happen to her. It *shouldn't* happen to her. *"He—"*

A door squeaked. Such a faint sound, but it immediately cut through her cry. For an instant, Hannah didn't even breathe.

Then she heard the creak of the floor. Her head twisted on the bed, and she saw his black boots . . . coming closer to her.

And—*snap.*

He had her camera. He was still taking pictures of her, the sick jerk.

Snap.

Snap.

"Come on, now," he murmured. "Don't you want to smile for the camera?"

An animalistic growl burst from her, and she bucked on the bed, desperate to get free. But the ropes just ground tighter into her wrists and her breasts scraped across the rough covering on the bed.

My breasts scraped across . . .

Hannah froze. Until that moment, she hadn't realized that he'd taken her clothes away. She'd been preoccupied by her pain and the fear. She'd been desperate to get help and she hadn't even realized that he'd stripped her.

What else did he do to me? How long was I out?

His fingers trailed over her shoulder and she flinched. He laughed.

Snap. The camera's flash had gone off that time, blinding her for an instant.

"These will be so good," he murmured. "Just what I need."

Her mouth was bone dry. "Please," Hannah whispered. "Let me go. I won't tell anyone about you."

He put down the camera.

Hannah sucked in a deep breath, relieved. Maybe that was all he needed to hear. Maybe—

He reached under the bed and pulled out a knife. A long, gleaming knife with a curving blade. "I've heard this is the best knife to use if you're skinning deer. You're not a deer but . . ."

She whimpered.

"*I need people to know about me,*" he told her as he ran the blade of that knife over her left shoulder blade. "I need everyone to remember. You'll help me do that."

Wait—so he wanted her to talk? She could do that. "L-let me go," Hannah said, frantic, "and I'll tell them anything you want! I'll make sure everyone always remembers, I'll—"

The knife jabbed into her side.

"Of course you'll tell them. Your body will tell them everything they need to know."

When the knife slid out of her, Hannah screamed again.

BAILEY JUMPED TO her feet, her heart racing in her chest. "Did you hear that?"

Asher turned toward her.

"I think I just heard a woman screaming." Her whole body had gone onto high alert. She strained, trying to see if she could hear the cry again, but there was only silence. Bailey waited, waited . . .

Asher touched her arm. "Are you sure you're okay, being out here?"

Her gaze snapped up to his. What was he saying? That she was imagining things? Going crazy? "I *heard* a woman screaming."

"Tonight . . . or in your memories?" His dark gaze slid away from her as he focused on the blackened remains of the cabin. "I'm sure plenty of women screamed at this place."

Too bad no one was ever around to hear our cries. "He . . . he reinforced the walls," Bailey recalled. "When he built the cabin, he did it then. He told me I could scream as loud as I wanted, and no one would ever hear me. He bragged . . . about those walls."

"Charming bastard."

There had been nothing charming about him.

Goose bumps rose on her arms. "I was sure I heard a woman screaming." The cry had been fast and desperate, fading away almost instantly.

Asher didn't speak for a few moments. He seemed to turn and sweep the area with his gaze. The sunlight had faded away, vanishing into the night. Night always came so fast in the mountains, and the darkness brought the cold with it.

"Let's go to the front of the cabin," he said.

She nodded and headed to what *would* have been the front entrance to the cabin. Bailey sucked in a deep breath and her gaze slid over the mountain and the trees. She didn't see any light. She didn't—

There.

For an instant, her heart actually seemed to stop because there *was* a light out there. It seemed to be in a line straight across from the Death Angel's cabin. The glow gleamed like a candle in the darkness. "Asher . . ."

"Yeah, I see it, too." He pulled out his headlamp. She'd packed her own at her house, but Bailey had been impressed to see him pull one out of his saddlebags.

She was getting the impression that Asher was the kind of guy who was prepared for anything.

Her eyes narrowed as she stared at that light. "How far away is it?" The night was so deceptive, and that little light was incredibly faint.

"Probably at least four miles, maybe five." His voice was grim. "Won't know for certain until we start hiking."

And in the mountains, Bailey knew it would probably take at least an hour just to hike two miles. Or at least, that was what it had taken her in the past. *And I was hiking in the daytime then, my trail clearly visible.*

"Let's wait a bit," Asher advised. "Make sure there aren't any other possible locations for us to scout."

More lights. Right. She swallowed and tried to grab on to her patience. When she'd first seen that light, Bailey had wanted to run wildly toward it.

Is that how she felt, too?

"Want to mark the location, though," Asher added. "In case that light goes dark. We'll be heading due west."

She shifted from her right foot to her left. Inside her boots, her toes curled nervously. Darkness was all around them. That one light was the only bit of hope she saw.

But Bailey waited . . .

HE STARED DOWN at his prey, his whole body shaking. Talk about an incredible fucking rush. Her blood had sprayed onto him, onto the wall. Every freaking where.

She'd been helpless. His to control totally. And he had.

She wasn't crying any longer. Not screaming or begging. She barely seemed to breathe. Soon enough, he knew she'd stop that, too.

His hold tightened on the camera. He'd have to wipe that down, ever so carefully, before he dropped it off. But first . . .

Smiling, he lifted the camera to his eye and snapped another picture.

After all, he had to make certain that everyone understood just how very serious he was.

The Death Angel wasn't gone. He wasn't supposed to be forgotten or laughed about.

He was real, he was strong, and he was going to make certain that everyone remembered what it was like to fear.

Especially you, Bailey.

Because he knew exactly who he'd be targeting next. This girl . . . she'd just been the warm-up.

Bailey Jones would be his main attraction.

One more picture, and then he turned away from Hannah. He'd wait until she was good and cold, and then he'd dump her. But for now, he had to clean his ass up.

And he had a delivery to make.

THEY'D BEEN HIKING for an hour when the light vanished.

One moment, it was there, the only beacon they had out in the woods, and in the next instant, it winked out. Bailey had been in the lead, walking—okay, nearly running—toward her goal, but when the light disappeared, she stopped.

Asher's hand curled around her shoulders. "You okay?"

No, no, she was far from okay. And she *knew* this could be nothing more than a wild goose chase. Them, heading into the mountains in the night, searching for a needle in a haystack . . .

Or a light in the dark.

"They must have gone to sleep," she whispered. *They.* The people who controlled the light. What if it was just campers? Someone who'd turned on a lantern for a bit? People who hadn't even *been* in that area when the Death Angel had burned that long-ago night.

I could have Asher out here for nothing.

"If they've gone to sleep, then we can wake their asses up," Asher said simply.

Automatically, she glanced back at him. Her headlamp hit him in the face, and his eyes squinted closed. "Sorry," she muttered, adjusting that light. "I just . . . this could be a waste."

"Could be." But he didn't sound overly concerned about that option.

She turned around, began walking determinedly forward. *Due west.* "The light could mean nothing. We both know that." It was easy to say the cold, hard truth when she wasn't looking at him. "So why are you out here with me?"

"Um . . . because you hired me?"

So that means you have to put up with my crazy ideas? Crazy . . . like finding a victim everyone else believes isn't real.

"I'm out here," he said, continuing before she could reply, "because I don't think we're going after some camper's light. That light we saw was too big, too strong. It was from a cabin, *not* a tent. It was steady, unwavering. And I want to meet the owner of the cabin up here—the cabin that was damn close to the Death Angel's hideout. Because, if we could see that owner's place at night, then it sure as hell stands to reason that—whoever this guy actually is—he saw the lights come on from—"

"From the Death Angel's cabin," she finished, the words tumbling out and her steps moving even faster.

I asked Wyatt if he interviewed any cabin owners in the area. He'd told me that the nearest person he spoke with was over twenty miles away from the Death Angel's place.

More and more people were going off the grid these days. Perhaps Wyatt hadn't even realized that this guy *had* been out there.

There was so much land out there. Lots of hikers slipped into the entrances to the Pisgah National Forest or the DuPont State Forest. They could hike for hours—*days*—there. Public and private land were side by side in so many areas up in the mountains. She knew there had been a real pissing match that went on with the FBI and the local authorities because of all the land-control issues. As if their territorial arguments had helped anything.

Women still died. And the killer . . .

"I'd like to know"—Asher's deep, rumbling voice flowed around her—"just what the owner of our mystery cabin may have seen while he or she was up here. All those long winter nights . . ."

Because the Death Angel had taken most of his victims during the winter. The cold isolation of the mountains had worked to his advantage—no tourists had been hiking during that time, so he was unlikely to have been disturbed.

"The Death Angel had to use a fire for warmth. There must have been smoke coming from his place. Our mystery owner had to see *something*."

If we can see him . . . then he should have seen us.

Her doubts slid to the back of her mind. Yes, there was a damn good reason why they were out trekking in the night, and she wouldn't second-guess herself again. It was her shrink, it was Wyatt—it was all the people who kept telling her that she was confused. She'd let them get to her.

Not again.

Not freaking again. The ground inclined beneath her feet and Bailey pushed forward, going fast, and when she saw a rough, heavy stone overhang to her right, she sidestepped it easily. Her boots moved carefully and—the toe of her boot hit a clump of dirt that was hollow. The buzzing started almost instantly and then she saw the small, swarming wasps flying up toward her light.

Yellow jackets. Oh, shit, she'd forgotten about them—and about just how bad they could be in the fall when their nests were full. That hollow chunk of earth she'd hit with her boot must have been their home. She gasped as one stung her, a sharp jab that burned her hand, and Bailey jerked back.

"Bailey!" Asher cried out her name.

But her boots had already slipped. Dirt and rocks rolled beneath her feet and Bailey's body tumbled to the right, twisting and tumbling down the incline. Only it wasn't the small incline that she expected. *Not so small at all.* Bushes and twigs hit against her face and arms and when her body finally stopped tumbling, she was in a hole.

Deep. Dark.

She'd lost her headlamp.

Her hands flew out, but she couldn't touch the surface of that hole. Her feet were in water—a stream?—and her fingers sank into the dank earth around her.

A grave. I'm in a grave again and I can't get out. I can't—

"Bailey!"

A light hit her in the face. Asher's light.

Her hands pressed to the dirt around her.

"It's okay," he said, speaking slowly, easily. "I'm here. Everything is all right. You're in some kind of riverbed. Mostly dry from the look of things." He leaned down and offered his hand to her. "I'll get you out." Again, his voice was so easy and calm.

Her drumming heartbeat shook her chest. She could smell that dank earth. Just like before. Trapped in a hole, that smell, pain . . .

No, it's not before. It's not the same. Get a damn grip.

Her hands reached for his.

"Good job, sweetheart," he murmured. "I've got you."

He lifted her up, as if she didn't weigh anything, and a moment later she was on the ground beside him. Bailey started to pull away—

"Are you hurt? Shit, but you just scared the hell out of me."

She'd scared him? Bailey had thought it would take a whole lot more than her tumble to scare the SEAL.

"Yellow jackets." She'd nearly forgotten the sting to her hand. "One stung me, and I—I just lost my balance." *I freaked the hell out.*

He was still holding her.

He was—

Kissing her. Deep and hard and wild. He pulled her closer, lifted her up against him, and seemed to devour her mouth.

Desire ignited within her. Bailey didn't want to think about why she shouldn't be kissing him back. There were too many reasons to pull away from his embrace.

And only one reason to stay close. *I want him.*

His mouth lifted a bare inch from hers. "I can't have you hurt. I couldn't reach you—don't ever do that shit to me again."

Then he kissed her once more. Kissed her with that wild fury that she was coming to crave. Their bodies were pressed together, and she could feel his growing arousal shoving against her. Asher was such a big guy, strong and powerful, but she wasn't scared in his arms.

He made her feel safe. And she hadn't felt safe, not like that, not this way, in so very long.

Over six months.

Her tongue licked over his lower lip then slid into his mouth. When he gave a low growl, heat spread through her. She liked that animalistic sound. It made her feel sexy. She was doing that—turning him on that much. So much that Asher was literally growling with desire.

Me, with my scars. Me, with my weaknesses. Me.

A shudder worked along the length of his body. Slowly, he eased back, but his hands stayed curled around her shoulders. Her lashes lifted as she stared up at him.

"You know I want you."

Did he have any idea how sexy his voice was? That rumble cut right through her.

"Will I get to have you, sweet Bailey Jones? When we're out of these woods, will you still kiss me like that?"

Don't be afraid. Not any longer. Not of him. "When we're out of these woods," she said, "I'll do a whole lot more than kiss you."

"Bailey . . ."

No other man had ever said her name quite that way. With so much raw hunger.

She stepped back, breaking his hold on her. "But for now, we need to get to that cabin." Before she took another inglorious tumble off the side of the mountain.

Or before she gave in to the urge to strip him and just take the pleasure she wanted. Right there.

What better way to banish the ghosts that haunt me?

"The cabin," he agreed, voice still rumbling. "Let's get the fuck there." He bent and picked up his headlamp. She didn't even know when he'd taken that off, and hell, how was she supposed to find hers? When the yellow jackets had swarmed, she'd lost it in her tumble.

But . . . Asher put his headlamp on her head. "No, I—"

"I can see plenty," he told her. "And I'll be right with you every step of the way."

Those words warmed her. She liked having him with her, liked having a partner who believed her.

They headed back up the incline, making sure to avoid the yellow jackets that still swarmed. They hiked in silence, but for every step that she took, Bailey was hyperaware of Asher.

Her body was so tuned to him. When had that happened? They'd just met, yet she ached for him. In the woods. With yellow jackets flying around them. With dirt beneath her nails. With sweat slickening her shirt.

She ached.

Never let it be said that I have good timing.

In fact, she pretty much had shit timing.

They didn't speak again, not until they left the thicker bushes and entered a narrow clearing, one that led them to a small wooden cabin. It just sat there, its windows dark. Its porch sagging. For all the world, it looked as if the place had been abandoned for years.

But there was a light on here before. I know there was. I saw it.

It didn't look as if the owner of that cabin was sleeping inside. It didn't look as if there was an owner. Just a place that had been forgotten. When they crept closer to the cabin, her borrowed headlamp hit the front window—a spiderweb-like crack slid across the glass.

"Is this the right place?" Bailey asked him quietly. Maybe they'd gone in the wrong direction after she fell. Or maybe there was another cabin, farther over.

Asher went straight to the front door. He lifted his hand, banging against it. Once, twice . . .

There was no sound from inside.

A dirt drive led to the cabin. Her light shone on that dirt and she saw the clear impression of tires. Someone *had* been there before, but no vehicle was around now. "No one's home," Bailey said, frustration beating inside of her. They'd come all this way and they hadn't—

"Help . . ."

Bailey's head whipped back toward the cabin. "I *heard* that." A rough call, desperate, but real.

"Yeah," Asher said grimly. "So the hell did I."

She rushed up the porch toward him.

Asher lifted his leg and he kicked in the door. The wood went flying inward, chunks breaking off as part of the door shattered.

"Hello?" Asher yelled. "Who's here? Where are you?"

Bailey rushed in after him. Her head turned to the right, then the left. Her light bobbed, showing the empty interior of the cabin. Cobwebs were everywhere and dust had settled heavily on the floor. *But I see footprints in the dust. Heavy, big prints.* From a man's boots?

"Help . . . please . . ."

That weak cry was coming from down the little hallway. Bailey flew past Asher, running desperately toward that cry. Her light fell on a door at the end of that hallway and she shoved it open.

Tied. Bleeding. Dying . . .

Her headlamp illuminated the woman on the bed. A woman who was on her stomach, with her hands stretched high above her head, bound to the bed. Her ankles were bound together, too, and there was blood— everywhere.

On the walls. On the bed. On the window.

"Dear God . . ."

"Help . . ." the woman rasped.

Bailey rushed to her. She sank to her knees beside the bed and her fingers immediately went for the ropes that bound that woman's wrists.

And Asher was there, putting his hands on the woman's deepest wounds, trying to stop that terrible blood flow. She'd been stabbed. Again and again. Bailey knew those marks.

He stabbed me, too.

But the knife wounds weren't the only thing familiar to her. The woman's clothes had been stripped away and there, on her upper left shoulder, her attacker had left *his* mark.

Black angel wings. Small, but distinct.

He gave me those wings, too.

"It's going to be all right, ma'am," Asher was saying to the woman. "We'll get help out here. An airlift. We'll get you to a hospital."

Bailey couldn't get the ropes free. They were so tight around the woman's wrists. *They're cutting into her. She'll have scars on her wrists, just like I do.*

No, no, this couldn't be happening again. The Death Angel was in hell. He wasn't still alive. He couldn't be out in the mountains, still hunting. Still killing.

It wasn't possible. He'd died in the fire. The fire that had brought help to her.

"Put your hands here, Bailey!" Asher's sharp words had her hands flying down to cover one of the gaping wounds on the woman's side. "Hold her tight. Put pressure down, hard." His hand flew out, and she saw that he'd taken a knife from his boot. The sharp edge of that knife gleamed and she tensed, but Asher just cut right through the ropes that bound the woman's hands, then her feet.

Then he was back with Bailey. One of his strong hands covered another gushing wound that the poor woman had, a wound near her spine, and with his other hand, he gripped his phone to his ear. Into that phone, he barked, "Ana, dammit, I need you. Triangulate my signal. Get an emergency team out here right away. A woman's been attacked. We have to get her to a hospital, now!"

The woman's eyes were closed. Her lips parted but . . . *I don't think she's breathing.* "Asher . . ."

He dropped his phone. "Fuck me."

The woman was still. The old bed was soaked with her blood.

"No!" Asher snarled. "Don't do this. Stay here! Fight, dammit, *fight!*"

But Bailey was afraid the woman couldn't fight, not anymore.

Her gaze locked on the black angel wings that rested on the still woman's shoulder.

The redheaded woman wasn't asking for help any longer. She wasn't even breathing.

The Death Angel had claimed another victim.

CHAPTER SIX

S HE HADN'T SURVIVED.

Asher stood a distance away from the cabin, watching as the victim's remains were removed. The place was a circus right then—a helicopter had rushed in less than twenty minutes after his frantic telephone call, but it had been twenty minutes too late.

I knew it was too late. The instant I saw her on that bed, I knew. There'd been far too much blood loss. The woman's killer had inflicted maximum damage on her, then he'd just walked away.

Deputies and other law enforcement personnel had flocked to the scene. Of course, Deputy Wyatt Bliss had been leading the charge, and when he'd gotten a look at the woman's body—and the mark left on her shoulder—there had been no missing the shock on his face.

But then the deputy had ordered that Bailey be put in the back of a patrol car, secured, for her protection. And he'd demanded then a deputy keep Asher company. *Guarding my ass, as if I'm the bad guy.*

So Asher had stood in the dark, watching the teams sweep in. He had to give Wyatt credit; the guy was like a drill sergeant as he oversaw the scene. Evidence was being carefully collected—bagged and tagged left and right. These weren't small-town idiots—these were men and women trying to do their best to stop a killer.

His respect for the deputy kicked up, but then . . .

"You." Wyatt pointed at Asher. The whole scene was lit up now—lights on at the cabin, lights blaring from the patrol cars. Lights everyplace. Wyatt marched toward him. "How the hell did you know how to find this cabin?" Suspicion laced his words.

Asher rolled his eyes. "Right. I'm your killer. Not like I have an alibi. Not like Bailey was with me every single moment of the night." So much for thinking the guy was organized and had his shit together—

Wyatt grabbed his shirt front. *"She should never have been out here with you! You put her in danger!"*

Around them, the voices of the other deputies and first responders stopped.

Asher looked down at the hands fisting in his shirt. "I think you need to take a real deep breath, Deputy," he said, aware that his Texas drawl had just gotten a little more pronounced. Ana always said that was a sign his temper was about to rage out of control. "And you need to get your hands off me. Bailey and I are the ones who found the victim. If we *hadn't* been out here, that poor woman's body could have stayed in that cabin for God knows how long."

Wyatt let him go, snarling.

Asher straightened his shirt. "Good choice there, buddy."

The deputy's hands were tight balls at his sides.

"We found the woman because we went back to the

spot where *you* found Bailey. We wanted to see just what that missing victim—"

"There was no other victim that night! Bailey imagined her."

Asher's back teeth locked. "We disagree on that."

Wyatt surged toward him.

Asher kept his body relaxed. If the guy swung at him—deputy or no deputy—Asher would be hitting back. "We went back to the scene," he said flatly. "We looked out into the night—trying to see what the victim would have seen if she was running away. A woman, hurt, frantic, if she'd seen a light, I figured she would have run to it."

Wyatt didn't speak.

So Asher kept talking. "Bailey and I saw a light. We followed it. Before we got here, it shut off, but we kept going. We found this place. Saw fresh tire tracks— tracks that I sure hope you and your *team* haven't destroyed." Though he had very little hope of that shit now. "Then we heard the woman in there crying out for help. I busted down the door and we found her."

"And the killer? The guy who stabbed her? You never saw him?" Wyatt pressed.

Asher shook his head. "Like I said, we only saw tire tracks. He was long gone before we pulled up here."

And Wyatt took another step toward him.

Bring it, you bast—

"You saw the wings on her shoulder," Wyatt whispered. "I know you did. Tell *no one* about those, got it? Not until I figure out what in the hell is happening. If we've got some copycat on the loose up here . . ." He shook his head grimly. "Dammit, the folks in this area are still recovering." His head turned and Asher saw he was staring at the patrol car that waited to the left, the car that Bailey was huddled inside of. "We can't take another madman hunting up in these mountains."

Too bad. Because it sure as hell looked as if they had one on their hands.

His gaze locked on the patrol car—on Bailey. She was in the front passenger seat, and, as he watched, she shoved open the door and jumped out. She rushed toward them. "Asher—"

A young deputy stepped into her path. "No, ma'am. No. You have to wait in the car. I'm sorry."

"No, I don't," Bailey gritted out. "I'm not some prisoner." She sidestepped around the guy but he reached out his hand, curling his fingers in a quick grip around her wrist.

Asher tensed. "You better tell your man to stand the hell down." *Before I make him stand down.*

"Ben! Let her go!"

Bailey jerked away from Ben and she marched toward Bliss and Asher. "What is happening here?" Her frantic gaze locked on Wyatt. "It's not him. It *can't* be him. You—you found his remains . . ."

From what Asher knew, not a whole lot of remains had been left after that fire.

"It's not the Death Angel," Wyatt assured her. He curled his hand around her shoulder. Once more, his voice was low, not carrying away from their little group. "My money is on a copycat, but don't worry, I am going to stop him. I *will* find him."

A shiver slid over Bailey's body. "I heard her scream for help."

Asher swore.

"I heard her scream before we even started trekking to this cabin. Sound can . . . it can carry so easily in the mountains." She looked back over her shoulder at the cabin and its blazing lights. "I should have moved faster. If we'd gotten here sooner . . ."

"Then you might be dead, too," Wyatt said, voice cold and hard and brutal.

Bailey flinched away from him.

"You need to go home, Bailey." Wyatt's hold on her tightened. *That asshole touches her far too much.* "Go home, lock your doors, and get some sleep. Don't come back to these woods. Let me do my job. Let my team take care of this mess."

Mess? *Try clusterfuck.* They had a sadistic killer on the loose. It wasn't some spilled freaking milk that had to be wiped up. A woman was dead.

The last time a killer had hunted up there, five women had been tortured before Wyatt and his team had managed to stop him. *At least five.* If there was a missing victim, that put the total up to six. *Six women.*

So excuse the hell out of me if I don't have a whole lot of faith in the deputy's team.

Asher didn't plan to keep this shit on the down low. He'd be calling in *his* team from LOST right away. Actually, after his frantic phone call to Ana, Asher suspected LOST backup was already en route.

"Ben will take you home," Wyatt said. "He'll make sure you get there safely. There's no sense in you hiking back through the woods tonight. Not when there's an old dirt drive that connects this place to the highway on the ridge. Ben will take—"

"I'm with Asher," Bailey said flatly. "I'm not going anyplace without him."

"Then Ben can take you *both* back," Wyatt gritted out.

"Ben can take us to my car," Bailey allowed. "But we'll get back home on our own."

Bliss finally took his hand off her shoulder. Seriously, *finally*. And the guy glared at Asher. "You make sure she's safe."

"Don't worry. I'm staying with her." *Every moment.*

"I want to help," Bailey said. She looked down at her hands. Oh, hell, they *both* had that woman's blood still on them. "I need to help her."

"You can't do anything here." Wyatt's words were flat. "This is my scene, my case. We're going to collect evidence and we are going to give that woman justice."

But Bailey didn't look convinced.

"Go home," Wyatt said. "And that's a damn order." Then he gave her a brisk nod and walked away, heading toward the cabin and the crime scene techs who were inside.

Ben lingered, looking uncomfortable and lost. What was Ben? All of twenty-one?

"It's happening again," Bailey said as she stared after Wyatt. "He knows it is. Same MO."

No, it wasn't exactly the same. Because they'd found the woman's body; she hadn't been buried like the others.

Like Bailey.

"Let's go home," he said, wanting her out of there. The woods were too vast; someone could be out there— watching them from the darkness right the hell then. He needed to figure out what was happening, but first . . .

Bailey. Bailey was his priority.

He looped his arm over her shoulders and led her toward the patrol car. Ben rushed behind them.

WYATT WATCHED BAILEY and Asher climb into the patrol car.

One problem solved, for the moment.

He turned and headed into the back room of that hell-forsaken cabin. It was a cabin he'd visited before, months back. Hell, he'd *told* Bailey that he'd searched, and this place? Yeah, it had been on his radar. And back then, when he'd come here . . . he'd found death waiting.

The old guy who owned the cabin had been dead. His body decomposing—the smell. *Shit. It was awful.* Because the guy had been dead there for so long. Dead, forgotten. ME had said he'd probably died of a heart attack, and if they hadn't been searching the area for the presumed missing victim, they might never have found him.

Wyatt had managed to keep the story about the old man's death from the media. They'd been too fixated still on all the blood and gore that had been left in the Death Angel's wake, and the old man had been given some peace.

And now this shit happened. Wyatt glanced around. Blood had soaked into the wood. Dripped on the dirty windowpane. "Looks like a freaking slaughter," he said, stomach twisting.

This couldn't be happening again. The sheriff would lose his shit.

Not in my county. This can't happen again.

As soon as word spread, the tourists would scatter. The locals would be afraid to go anyplace. They'd be right smack in the middle of a nightmare once more.

Once word spread . . .

"I want to make sure no one talks to reporters," he said to the men and women in that room with him. "This case needs to be locked down tight, understand? Until we know what we're dealing with, no media communication, got it?"

They nodded. He raked a hand over his face. That room was starting to smell. "I need to find out who owns this cabin." Had someone in the old guy's family inherited the place? Had it been sold? "And I need to know who that woman was." He pointed to the bed. He could just see a lock of her red hair, hair matted with blood. "Jesus Christ," Wyatt muttered. "I can't let this happen again." He turned away, bile rising within him.

I can't. I won't let it happen. He'd been the hero before. He could be that hero again. He would be.

The Death Angel is gone. This is some copycat. I'll show them all.

THE WATER FROM the shower pounded down on Bailey, like pinpricks against her skin. It was too hot. She should turn the shower off.

She didn't move.

Her gaze was on her hands. No blood coated her fingers any longer, but she swore she could still feel it.

That could have been me. I could have died. I didn't . . .

But she'd sure felt as if she'd been the walking dead for months. Instead of grabbing life, holding tight to it, she'd become a hermit, jumping at her own shadow.

This isn't me.

The woman who'd died that night, the woman with the long red hair, Bailey bet she would have given anything to live. To have a chance to laugh and love again.

I have a chance.

But Bailey spent most of her days and nights too afraid to take the chance.

"Bailey?"

Her head whipped up. The glass door of her shower had fogged up, so she couldn't see Asher, but—

"I just wanted to check on you. I knocked and when you didn't answer . . ." His words trailed away. "Sorry."

She lifted her hand and rubbed at the glass door, making a small spot so that she could see out. But Asher had already left her bathroom and closed the door behind him. For a moment, she just kept her hand pressed to the glass. Then her shoulders straightened. She yanked at the faucet, turning off the blast of water. Bailey stepped out of the shower, grabbing for the white towel nearby. She raked it over her skin and hair, then reached for her robe.

Taking a deep breath, Bailey didn't even bother glancing into the mirror to see how she looked. She just went after him. The lush carpeting in the hallway swallowed her footsteps. In moments, she was in the den. Asher was there, dressed in loose sweatpants and a tight black T-shirt that hugged his wide shoulders. His dark hair was wet, and his gaze was focused out of the wide picture window as he stared into the night. This moment was important. For the two of them . . . this moment could change everything.

I won't be afraid. Not again.

Dr. Paul Leigh sat in his office, tapping away at his computer. He accessed one patient file after the other, smiling at the progress he'd made.

So much progress.

He clicked on the keyboard, and opened the file for the patient who'd challenged him the most.

Bailey Jones.

His smile dimmed a bit. Bailey hadn't come in to see him for quite some time, and that just wasn't acceptable. There was still work to be done.

She'd made enormous progress. Confronted her demons and her guilt head-on . . . the *most* impressive patient he'd had in that respect.

But we aren't finished. Not yet.

Because Bailey persisted in thinking that someone else was out there, another victim. *She just needs to listen to me.*

Paul shut down his computer. Collected his files. A few moments later, he was riding down in the elevator. The building was deserted—he was the only one who enjoyed late-night work sessions there, so he had the elevator all to himself.

His phone rang. Paul pulled it out, frowning down at the screen. *What does he want now?*

He answered, his voice curt. "Look, you want to talk, then you can call me at a *normal* hour—"

But the man just laughed. "Normal? Like that shit applies to us?"

The elevator doors opened with a faint ding.

"Better stay tuned to the news, Doc."

"Why?"

"Because some big stories are coming . . . big . . .

things aren't going to stay quiet much longer. You had a chance . . ."

A chance? A chance to do what?

"Now it's my turn . . ." The line went dead.

Paul walked into the cavernous parking lot, aware that he'd started to sweat.

"ASHER . . ."

His shoulders stiffened when he heard Bailey's voice. "Sorry about . . . *that*. I just got worried about you. But I shouldn't have just . . . barged in." What in the hell had he been thinking? "It won't happen again."

"People seem to worry about me a lot. The shrink I see worries that I'll have a breakdown."

He glanced back at her. She wore only a dark blue robe, one that skimmed down to the middle of her thighs. "You won't."

She took a step toward him. "Wyatt worries I'll crumble under the pressure from the press."

"Not you." Asher was adamant. He didn't think she'd ever crumble.

"My ex-lover Royce worried I'd never be the same. That I would never get past what happened to me." Another step. She was so close to him now.

"You *will*. And that guy sounds like a dick."

"He was a dick." Her hands were in the deep pockets of her robe. "But do you want to know what I worry about?"

Instantly, he was reaching to curl his hands over her arms. "You don't need to worry. I'll stay here all night." The last thing he wanted was for her to fear anything. But after finding that body, shit, he knew all of her

worst memories—memories of the Death Angel—
must be flooding back to her.

She gave a hard shake of her head. "I worry about
losing *me*."

"Bailey—"

"I'm not this scared, timid person. This woman who
is afraid to touch life. Afraid to let go and have fun.
Afraid to take pleasure and enjoy herself. Afraid to
laugh and . . ." Her voice broke. "He took something
from me that night. When his hands were around my
neck and I couldn't get free. When he dumped me in
that grave and left me to die."

His chest burned as he listened to her speak.

"The woman that Wyatt pulled out of the grave? She
wasn't me. She was afraid of everything. She woke up
at night, shaking and crying." Her long lashes swept
down, covering her eyes. "She still does that, and I am
sick of it. I am sick of the fear. I want my life back. I
want me back."

He wasn't staring at a timid woman who'd had everything taken from her. When he looked at Bailey,
he saw strength. Perseverance. Courage. That was the
same thing that everyone saw; didn't she get that? Why
did she think the public had become so obsessed with
her? Bailey Jones was the hero. The woman who had
survived a madman's attack. The only known survivor.

"So it's time for me." Those lashes lifted, revealing the green gaze that always seemed to gut him. So
bright. So gorgeous. Unforgettable. As long as he lived,
he would never be able to erase the memory of Bailey's
eyes from his mind.

"And it's time for us," she whispered.

Then Bailey shrugged his hands off her body and she let the robe drop.

Fuck me. I won't ever forget a single inch of her.

She stood there before him, her body completely exposed, and she was beautiful. Perfect. Full, pink-tipped breasts. A flat stomach. Hips that curved and made his mouth water. Sexy as all hell. Long legs that stretched and stretched.

And her sex. Shaved. Bare. His fingers were already reaching to touch her but he clenched his fists. "Bailey . . ." Her name was torn from him. "Be sure . . ."

She put her hand on his shoulder. "I am sure. Sure I want you to make love to me. I don't know that I've ever been more *sure* about anything in my life."

"I'm not . . ." *The gentlest of lovers.* He liked hard and wild sex. The kind of dirty fucking that left him hollowed out. Making love? When had he ever done that? A woman like Bailey, she'd deserve that. All of those tender touches and soft caresses. She was made for things like that. He was already nearly shaking with the lust he felt for her. His control wouldn't last long.

I am not the man she needs. That knowledge went soul deep. *But there is no way in hell or heaven I can give her up.* Because she'd gotten to him . . . Bailey with her gorgeous eyes. Bailey with her husky voice. Bailey with her spine of fucking steel.

His hand sank into the heavy curtain of her hair, still wet from her shower. He leaned over her and that delicious scent that was pure Bailey Jones wrapped around him. His dick shoved at the front of his sweats. "Sweetheart, I will try my damn best to be careful with you."

She rose onto her toes. Braced herself against him. He bent toward her and Bailey's perfect little white teeth closed on his lower lip and she gave him a sensual nip.

Fuck.

"Who said . . ." Bailey whispered against his mouth, "that I wanted you to be careful?"

No, she didn't know what she was asking for. She'd said *make love*. Not fuck like animals. She—

"I haven't been with anyone since before the attack. I haven't wanted anyone . . . only you."

His body shuddered. Did she have any idea just what she was doing to him?

"I want to do this your way, Asher. Show me what you like. Because I'm ready for everything you can give to me."

Oh, sweetheart, be careful what you say.

She nipped his lower lip once more and arousal had his dick jerking eagerly toward her. In an instant, Asher took control. He drove his tongue past her lips and tasted the wine of her mouth. And sure enough, he felt drunk on her. He kissed her deeper and harder and loved the faint moan that built in her throat.

But it wasn't enough. She was naked and he needed to touch her. Every single inch of her.

I have to make Bailey enjoy this. Have to make her want me again and again.

Because he already knew that was the way he would want her, endlessly.

So his hands locked around her waist. He lifted her

up—she was too damn light. He kept kissing her as he walked and Bailey wrapped her legs around him, putting her sex right over his surging cock. His hands tightened on her waist, and her tight little nipples stabbed against his chest. He'd be tasting those nipples, he'd feel them beneath his tongue, and he'd make her go wild while he licked her into a frenzy.

So many things that he wanted to do with his beautiful Bailey . . .

He made it to her bedroom. He rather considered that a minor miracle. Asher flipped on the lights because he didn't want her hiding from him. When he took her, he wanted to see her, every single moment.

Asher put her on the side of the bed, positioning her body so that her legs dangled over the edge. A quick frown pulled at her face as she said, "Asher, what—"

He pushed her legs apart and her delicate, pink sex waited. In the next moment, his mouth was on her. He *needed* to taste her. The craving controlled him, and he licked and kissed, sucked and tasted, as she sank her hands into his hair and moaned.

He wanted her to come this way. With his tongue on her sex and her hips surging toward his mouth. The first time should be this way. Then he'd know she had her pleasure. Know that she was ready for the deep thrust of his cock into her core.

She was moaning again, her breath coming in quick pants. Those wild sounds were driving him mad. His hands rose up and his fingers closed around her breasts, stroking her nipples, squeezing them, flicking the tight little peaks with his fingers.

"Asher!"

She came against his mouth. He looked up and she was so fucking sexy. Her face flushed, her eyes went even greener, and her whole body shivered beneath him.

Perfect.

Another long lick, and he was on his feet. It took five seconds too long to realize that he was just wearing his sweats and that his wallet—and his condom—weren't close by. "Don't move," he gritted out then he strode for the door.

"Asher—wait! What are you doing?"

He didn't stop. His cock was so erect the damn thing hurt. He marched straight for the guest room and grabbed his wallet and the condom that he was freaking glad as all hell to possess. And he headed back for Bailey.

But he froze in her doorway.

Bailey had grabbed the bedcovers and pulled them over her body. She'd pushed up in the bed and her hair was a tangle around her—sensual as fuck. But her shoulders were hunched and her cheeks too red.

"I told you not to move."

Her head whipped up. "You also ran out of the room right after—" She broke off and that flush deepened on her skin.

Not a flush from sensual release. From embarrassment. That wasn't going to work, not for him and not for her. When it came to her body, when it came to the things he'd *do* to her body, she should never be embarrassed.

"I left right after you came against my mouth," Asher finished.

She lifted the bedcovers a bit higher, making sure

that her gorgeous breasts were covered. "Fine, yes, after that. You *bolted*."

He lifted up the condom. "Trust me, sweetheart, I was coming right back."

"You . . . oh. Right. Condom."

He tore open that foil packet. "I thought I told you not to move."

"Giving orders . . . is that the SEAL thing again?"

A hard smile curved his lips as he stalked back to her. He put the condom packet down on the bed and leaned over her, bracing his hands on either side of her body. "You don't need to cover up. Thought we'd already established that. I freaking love your body."

"Asher . . ."

He caught the covers with his fingers and pulled them away. "I think you have the best breasts that I've ever seen." Full and round, thrusting toward him with those tight tips. He just had to lean forward and put his mouth on her.

And when he did, she gave that breathy moan that now addicted him.

Taking his time, even though every instinct he possessed screamed for him to take *her*, Asher kissed his way to her other breast. And he lingered a moment on the thin, white scar that sliced into her chest.

She trembled beneath his mouth.

Then he was kissing her other breast. Licking. Sucking. And Bailey's hands were tight around his shoulders as she pulled him closer. Good. Because closer to her was exactly where he wanted to be.

His fingers trailed over her stomach. He could feel the raised marks that had been left by the Death Angel.

Those marks pissed him off. No one should ever hurt her. To think of some bastard cutting into her skin . . .

"You make me feel so good," Bailey whispered. Her sensual words were the best temptation he'd ever heard.

"Sweetheart, I'll make you feel even better," he promised.

Her lashes swept up. Her gaze held his. "I'll make you feel the same way." Then her fingers were reaching for him. She shoved down his sweatpants and his cock—overeager bastard that he was—sprang toward her. Bailey didn't hesitate. She was still on the bed, he stood at the edge, and she leaned forward and put her mouth on him.

Fuck, fuck, fuck. Asher's eyes nearly rolled back into his head. Okay, maybe they *did* roll back. Her mouth was so wicked hot and her little tongue was about to lick him straight into oblivion.

Only there was one problem with that. When he blasted into oblivion, he wanted to be *in* her. His hands closed around her shoulders and—carefully—he pushed her back onto the bed.

"Asher, I want—"

"I need to fuck you." His words were guttural.

She smiled. "Then what are you waiting for?"

He had the condom on in about two seconds. He tossed his shirt toward the wall because he wanted to feel her against his skin, and then Asher climbed into the bed. Her legs parted and a dull drumming filled his ears. He didn't put his hands on her. If he had, he knew he would have touched her too hard. Held her too tightly. So he slammed his hands onto the bed on either side of her body.

She reached for his cock. She positioned him at the entrance to her body, and when she arched her hips toward him, Asher thrust deep and hard into her.

She lost her breath, he heard the choked gasp, and Asher damn near lost his mind. She was tight and hot and wet, and when he pulled out—and thrust back in again—her sex clamped greedily around him. Her legs curled around his hips. Her nails sank into his sides and she pulled him closer. Her breathy cries urged him on and the bed shuddered beneath him as he drove them both toward release with a wild frenzy of thrusts.

He wasn't holding back with her. He couldn't. Asher was too far gone for anything but a lust-crazed mating. She was so soft. So warm. No, *hot*. His climax bore down on him, but Asher wanted her to come again first. He *had* to make it good for Bailey.

He wanted to fucking ruin her for all other men. Maybe that made him a selfish bastard, but he didn't really give a shit. He wanted her to always remember him and the pleasure that he could give to her.

Asher changed the angle of his hips, making sure that when he thrust down, his cock slid over her clit. Her nails dug into him, harder and rougher now, and he growled his pleasure because she felt so fantastic.

Then she stiffened beneath him. Her green gaze seemed to go blind as she stared up at him, and her sex squeezed him so tight, fast contractions around his cock that drove him straight into—

Oblivion.

He erupted into her, pouring out his release on a wave that seemed never-ending. And he kissed her, drinking in her pleasure as he came, as *she* came. His thundering heartbeat filled his ears and her softness surrounded him.

Best sex of my life. He knew it with utter certainty. *Best fucking ever.*

He kept thrusting into her, determined to ride out the last bit of pleasure. His mouth slowly lifted from hers as he peered down at her.

Her eyes gleamed, and her smile made his heart ache. "I think you were worth waiting for," Bailey murmured.

He knew she sure as hell had been.

And I feel just like that . . . like I've been waiting too long . . . for her.

HE SAW THE lights turn out in Bailey's house. He'd been watching her. Seeing her too easily through the curtains.

Bailey Jones hadn't been alone in her bedroom. No doubt about it, she was definitely fucking the new guy in her life. Interesting. She'd played the innocent for months. The too-good-to-touch routine had gnawed at his insides.

He was glad she'd dropped the act.

But he wasn't thrilled about the new player on the scene. Especially since he didn't know much about the bastard. While he'd been waiting for those lights to shut off—*and for them to fucking finish*—he'd taken down the license number on the motorcycle that waited in Bailey's drive. Soon enough, he'd know plenty about that guy.

Soon enough, this little town would be on fire again, and he'd be right there, ready to see it all go down in a blaze of glory.

Careful now, he eased toward her porch. He'd wanted to leave his little present earlier, but he'd been delayed.

Bailey was a necessary piece in this game—the best possible pawn to use. He left his present on her doorstep and made sure to get the hell out of there as fast as he could.

You never knew when a nosy-ass neighbor might show up to send things to hell.

He hurried away from Bailey's house, sticking to the shadows, and when he was clear, he jumped into his vehicle.

A smile curved his lips. Poor Bailey. She thought she'd escaped the death that waited for her.

She had no idea her world was about to be ripped apart.

There was a reason you were taken before.

And there would be a reason when she was taken again.

CHAPTER SEVEN

THE SUNLIGHT POURED THROUGH THE CURTAINS, falling onto the bed and rousing Asher from sleep. He blinked blearily and glanced around.

He'd stayed the night with Bailey. Stayed in her bed.

His body stiffened as that realization dawned because when it came to lovers, he generally had one rule—*don't get close. And sure as hell don't stay the night.*

With his past, he just couldn't afford to make that mistake. So he took his pleasure, and he made damn sure his partner found hers, too. But staying in bed, sleeping with a lover—being that close to someone all night?

Not an option. He had nightmares, fucking terrors from his past, that usually barely let him catch a whole hour's worth of uninterrupted sleep. And when he did wake up—his SEAL training took over. He could be rough, dangerous—a threat.

There had been one lover, just one before, that he'd slipped up with. He'd been a teen back then, and he hadn't realized just how dangerous he could be.

But the fear in his lover's eyes had changed that.

When he'd shaken the nightmare, come to his senses and realized what he'd almost done—

I swore I would never take a chance like that again.

Yet here he was. In bed with Bailey. With the woman he *never* wanted to hurt. Bailey—Bailey who mattered to him, more than any of the other lovers ever had.

I won't screw up like this again. I'll be more careful. He was just real lucky nothing had happened last night. He would *never* ever want to hurt her. He would never want her to look at him with fear in her gaze.

As things stood, Bailey looked at him like he was some kind of hero, and yeah, he was getting off on that shit. He liked the way he felt when she looked at him that way.

I like who I can be, with her.

Asher started to ease from beneath the covers. Maybe he'd go make her breakfast or do some nice shit like that. Women were supposed to enjoy that, right? He'd never made breakfast for a lover, not a single time in his life. Mostly because of that whole never-stay-the-night rule, but he wanted to do something good for her. He wanted—

Bailey shifted a bit in her sleep, and the white sheet dipped away from her shoulder, revealing the black tattoo on her skin.

For an instant, Asher was sure that the world stopped spinning. His heart stopped beating. His breath froze in his lungs.

Fury iced his whole body.

The wings were delicate, intricate. Not like a fairy's, but stronger, wider. Angel wings. A permanent mark that graced Bailey's skin. *The Death Angel.*

The bastard's MO was carved into Asher's brain and he sucked in a deep gulp of air as his gaze stayed fixated on that tattoo.

He took his victims. Twenty-four hours later, the authorities would get a picture.

The picture would always be of the victim's upper body and face. Her naked shoulder. Her new tattoo.

Each image fired off a massive manhunt, but despite the desperate searches, those victims hadn't been found. None of them . . . until Bailey.

And then everyone realized what had happened to the others. Buried in graves, tossed away in the mountains. Turned into angels by the man who'd taken them.

His hand reached out toward her. He was almost touching that tattoo but . . .

Asher stopped. Instead of his fingers skimming over her skin, his head bent and he pressed a quick kiss to the tattoo. It wasn't a mark left by the bastard who'd taken her. He refused to think of it that way. It was a sign of Bailey's strength.

He slipped out of the bedroom and made sure to close the door as quietly as possible behind him.

As SOON AS the door shut behind Asher, Bailey's eyelids opened. She'd been awake when he kissed her shoulder, but she hadn't moved. Mostly because if she'd moved, then she would've needed to talk to him.

He might have asked questions about her tattoo.

Might have talked to her about last night.

Might have said what they'd done had been a mistake.

It wasn't. Being with Asher was exactly what I needed.

She still needed him.

Bailey pushed away the covers and padded to her bathroom. Still naked, she stared at herself in the mirror. In the harsh light of day, there was no missing the scars on her body. The slash marks that would always be there. Eleven of them. They'd faded a lot in the last six months. Not red and angry any longer, but thin, white raised lines on her flesh.

She turned and peered over her shoulder.

And there . . . darkness. Two wings on her right shoulder, spaced barely an inch apart. She hadn't even realized the Death Angel had put that tat there—she sure didn't remember getting it. When she'd woken— tied up in that cabin—her whole body had hurt. The sunburn sting of a new tattoo hadn't registered on her mind. She'd actually seen it for the first time when she'd been in the hospital. Bailey had made her unsteady way to the bathroom. She'd stared at her sunken eyes and bruised skin in the mirror—horror filling her. Then she'd turned away from her reflection. Her too-big hospital gown had slid down her shoulder. She'd glanced back at the mirror, almost helplessly—

And seen it. The tattoo.

The reporters always asked her about it. Asked if she hated it. Asked if she'd be getting it removed.

They didn't understand. That tattoo was part of her now. And, unlike the scars . . . *I like it.* But most people didn't get that. They couldn't understand how she looked at the tat and didn't feel immediate revulsion.

But . . . she did.

Bailey showered and dressed, putting on jeans and

a light sweater. She even took the extra time to apply some blush and eye shadow.

I must seriously like this man.

She hadn't bothered with makeup since . . .

Royce? The day in the hospital when he'd looked at her as if she were a stranger and she'd been frantic to get her old self back again.

Bailey grabbed for her lipstick. A quick swipe over her mouth and she was done. Now if she could just have a conversation with Asher that didn't involve her stumbling and saying something that was way not Night After casual . . .

Straightening her shoulders, she headed out of the bathroom, out of her bedroom, and down the hallway toward him. As she approached, the scent of chocolate chip muffins teased her nose and had her stomach growling.

When she entered the kitchen, he was there. Hair tousled, eyes gleaming, a line of dark stubble coating his sexy jaw. He wore only a pair of dark sweatpants, the pants that she distinctly remembered shoving off him the night before. He had a plate of muffins waiting on her table and when Asher saw her, a slow smile curved his mouth.

She staggered to a stop, feeling that smile sweep straight through her. *That man is lethal.* She had never, ever seen anyone look so sexy.

And he'd *baked* her favorite breakfast ever. She had a serious chocolate weakness.

His smile stretched a bit more. "You had a dozen chocolate chip muffin packages in your pantry," he murmured, that drawl deep and toe-curling. "So it wasn't a hard stretch to realize they must be your breakfast of choice."

Her bare toes had definitely curled into the tiled floor of the kitchen. "I, um, yes. I like them. A lot." Her gaze dropped to the plate of muffins. "But you didn't have to bake them for me. That's not what I expected at all." Actually, Bailey had no clue what she *had* expected.

Not him. Never him.

Asher picked up a muffin and strolled toward her. "I like the unexpected."

Oh, damn.

He lifted the muffin to her lips. "Want a bite?"

She wanted a bite of him. It was as if some switch had been turned *on* inside of her during the night. She'd avoided sex, avoided all physical contact with men for months, and now her body was in some kind of over-drive.

I want him. Right there. In the kitchen. On the counter. On the table. Beside that plate of muffins.

And it was wrong. A woman was *dead*. Bailey knew she should be terrified—some jerk was out there copying the Death Angel. But instead of being overwhelmed with fear, she wanted to reach out and grab on to life with both hands.

I want to grab on to him with both hands.

But she didn't. After all, she had some control. Her lips parted and she took a bite of that muffin. The chocolate chips literally melted in her mouth and a moan slipped from her.

"I love that sound," Asher said.

Her gaze flew to his.

"Sexy as all hell." He lowered the muffin. "Especially when you make that moan and I'm *in* you."

Her cheeks flamed.

"Can I get a taste, too?"

He didn't wait for her to answer. His mouth took hers and she felt the soft sweep of his tongue over her lower lip. Bailey leaned into him even as her nipples tightened. *Just a kiss. Get a grip, woman! A kiss.*

He eased back, but didn't let her go. "Tastes good."

Wait, did he mean the chocolate or her?

Did he have any idea just how far out of her league all of this was?

"Want another bite?" He offered her the muffin.

She was about to devour him. "Asher . . ."

Her doorbell rang. The loud peal echoed through her house and Asher's brows shot up. She glanced at the clock on her stove. Barely past eight A.M. On a Sunday. Her stomach twisted. "Do you think it's Wyatt? That he's already learned something about the killer?"

Asher curled her fingers around the muffin as he pushed it into her hand. "Stay here. Let me see who it is."

Then he was gone. She downed the muffin fast, because she was *starving*. But Bailey didn't stay in the kitchen. After all, it was her home, her doorbell, her life.

So she rounded the corner to the little foyer just as Asher opened the front door . . .

"Who in the hell are you?" a rough male voice demanded. "And why the fuck aren't you dressed *while you're standing in my girlfriend's house?"*

Her lips parted in shock. Royce. Royce Donnelley.

She hadn't heard his voice in months, and she was sure not his girlfriend.

Before she could speak, Asher gave a low growl, a sound that made the hair on the nape of her neck stand up, and he braced his legs apart. A quick glance showed her that his hands were loose at his sides, but she had the feeling that he was readying himself for battle. "You're at the wrong house," Asher said flatly.

"No, I'm not!" Royce blasted back at him. Then he made the mistake of locking one hand around Asher's bare shoulder. He shoved Asher back. "You are. And you need to get the hell—"

It happened fast. Too fast. Later, she'd wonder about that insane quickness. But right then, she just saw Asher move in a quick blur. One instant Royce was shoving him, and in the next breath of time, Asher had slammed Royce into the nearby wall, face-first. The hand that had made the mistake of grabbing Asher was now held up high behind Royce's back, and Royce was yelling—

"Stop!" Bailey leapt forward and grabbed Asher's hand. "I know him. Just *stop*." Because she was afraid that Asher would break Royce's arm.

Asher's head turned toward her. He didn't let Royce go. "Who is he?" Flat. Cold. Just like his eyes.

Swallowing, she said, "Royce Donnelley. He's my—"

"Ex." Asher let him go. "The prick. Yeah, I read about him in your files. Dumbass bleached his hair blond and lost weight so I didn't recognize him at first."

Royce spun around. His blue eyes glittered with fury as he rolled back his shoulder and rubbed his wrist.

"I've been working out, *asshole*. Want to try coming at me again and see how that works for you?"

"Don't tempt me," Asher muttered.

"Oh, really?" Royce blasted. "How about—"

Bailey stepped between them. "You don't want to push Asher." She had no doubt that an ex-SEAL like Asher could kill or maim in an instant. And as for a tax accountant like Royce . . .

Not happening.

And Asher was right. Royce had changed his hair. There were blond highlights running through his thick mane. He still was handsome. Royce had the golden-boy looks down to a T. And since everyone had always told Bailey she was a golden girl . . .

We were together far too long. For no reason. Just because others said we were a good couple. That we were meant to be.

Such utter bull.

And everyone had been wrong. There was nothing golden about her.

Or about him.

"Asher." Royce spat the name in disgust. "So he's the new one, huh? Finally defrosted enough to—"

Asher went in for the attack. Bailey whipped around and her hands pressed against his chest. "Asher, *don't*."

"I'm just going to teach the dumbass some lessons," he said, not looking at her. His furious glare was locked completely on Royce. "Lesson one . . . *never, ever* say a word about Bailey when I'm near." He paused for the barest moment. "And even when I'm fucking not."

Royce made a quick leap for the door. Once he was

clear of the threshold, he turned back and made a show of straightening his polo shirt—it was already straight. "I was *worried* about you, Bailey. You know I have friends at the sheriff's office. One of those friends called me . . . tipped me off about what was happening and when I heard about that body . . . about the fact that *you* found her there last night . . ." Royce shuddered. "Like I said, I was worried. I came right over to check on you."

"She's fine," Asher snapped.

Royce's eyes widened. "If you believe that, you don't know her at all."

"I know her better than you'd think."

This whole scene was like something out of a nightmare. "Have they identified her? Wyatt and his team—do they know who the woman is?"

His lips thinned. "No, not yet. They hadn't even gotten the medical examiner in yet. Though I don't know why we need the guy. From what I was told, it's obvious the killer knifed her, again and again." His gaze swept over her body. "Just like he did you."

"It's *not* the same killer. It's not him." There was no way it could be. The Death Angel was little more than ash.

"Always thought it was too convenient," Royce said, nodding a bit. "That this guy somehow trapped himself in his own fire and was burned beyond recognition. I mean . . . what if that body wasn't the Death Angel's? What if it was just another victim? I told the sheriff he should have thought that, too. People should have listened to me." His chin notched up.

Her skin felt clammy. "The Death Angel never took male victims."

"Not that we know about." Now Royce appeared concerned, his anger fading. "The story never sat well with me. *Never.* I always thought there was more that happened that night. More you didn't tell me . . . or your shrink."

She could feel Asher's gaze on her. "I told everything."

"Did you?" Obviously, Royce didn't seem so sure. "I've been talking to a reporter who has a different take on all the Death Angel's crimes. Richard thinks—"

"Richard Spawn?" Asher demanded, cutting through the other man's words.

Royce nodded.

"Don't waste your time with him," Bailey said carefully. "He's slime. Just looking for the next big story."

And with this new murder, he'd have one.

Royce's eyelashes flickered. "Bailey . . ." His voice dropped. "I've thought about you so much over the last few months. I'd turn on the news, and there you'd be."

Not by choice.

"I made a mistake." Now he sounded cajoling. It was a voice she recognized—one Royce used when he really wanted to get something. Someone? "I know that now. Nothing was your fault. It was all me."

Asher gave another one of those low growls.

"You need to leave," Bailey said. She couldn't talk to him, not then. Not with Asher right behind her and her own anger growing with every moment that passed.

I wasted too much time with him. But then, she'd

always been told that she should be with Royce. That they were perfect together.

A perfect nightmare.

"Promise you'll talk with me soon. I mean, really talk." His right hand had curled around her door frame. "I need a chance to explain all the shit that was going down. A chance to prove I am better than you think."

The last thing she wanted was some kind of one-on-one chat with him, but if she could get him to leave . . . "Yes, fine, call me later. We'll set something up." *No, we won't.*

Relief flashed across his face, and he leaned forward as if he'd kiss her.

Her hands flew up and pressed to his chest. Was he really missing the furious six-foot-two male behind her? "Good-bye, Royce."

He nodded once, twice, and turned to leave. But then he stopped.

Seriously, again?

"You left this outside." Royce bent and picked up a camera that had been on her porch. "Noticed it when I rang the doorbell." He held the camera out to her. "Here you go."

Bailey didn't take it. "That's not mine."

"Isn't it?" Royce frowned at the camera. "Looks like the one you used to haul around everywhere, snapping your pics." His frown slid away. "Especially when you'd go hiking out to the waterfalls. You'd take a ton of photos, remember?"

Bailey had taken a step back. Her shoulders hit Asher. "That's not mine," she said again. She knew her camera—knew that it was in the bottom drawer of her dresser, collecting dust.

Why had someone left a camera on her doorstep? Had another reporter been nosing around again? Someone who'd run off because a neighbor had appeared?

It's an expensive camera. Royce is right. It does look a lot like mine, just a newer model. Someone wouldn't just run off and leave a camera like that.

He still held the camera out to her. Asher took it from him, holding it gingerly.

"Asher, wasn't it?" Royce murmured. "I'm sure we'll be seeing each other again, too."

"Count on it."

Royce's lip curled but he turned on his heel and hurried down the steps. Bailey didn't wait to watch him drive away. She had already shut the door, triple locked it, and turned to face Asher.

"That camera . . ."

He'd opened the side hatch. "A memory card is inside." He pulled it out and held up the blue card. "Let's see who owns it, shall we?"

Because if there were photos on the card, then maybe they could see that it did belong to a reporter or . . .

Bailey hurried past him and booted up her computer. She pulled out her office chair and turned to him with her palm out. He'd crowded into the little home office with her. Ever since the attack, that place had been her refuge. No more lecturing on campus. Now she only taught online history classes. Students saw her only via webcam and no one talked to her in person.

But things are changing now.

Asher put the memory card in her hand. Bailey sucked in a quick breath, then she inserted the card in the slot on the right side of her computer. A few clicks of the mouse later, and she had the images opening.

The first image showed a woman, smiling. A close-up shot, her hand was even still in the frame. She stood in front of a car, with a familiar trail sign in the background. The woman's long red hair was pulled back in a ponytail, but a few loose locks had slipped to hang near her face.

"Oh, my God," Bailey whispered. Because she knew that woman.

She'd watched her die last night.

Her breath hitched and Bailey hit the mouse again, harder. Faster. Again and again. Images flew up on the screen. The hiking path. Trees. The mountain in the distance. A waterfall.

The twisting waterfall that Bailey liked to visit. She knew that spot so well.

Her finger clicked the mouse again.

Asher was dead silent behind her.

This time, the image was blurry, out of focus. A nothing shot, as if the woman had dropped the camera or taken the picture by accident.

When she saw that shot, Bailey hesitated. She just couldn't make herself click the mouse again.

Asher's fingers curled over hers. He pressed down on the mouse.

Another waterfall image. Beautiful. Breathtaking. Bailey could see the rainbow at the bottom of the falls.

Asher clicked again. Another waterfall picture. Closer

now, as if the woman had zoomed in on the base of the falls and the rainbow.

His fingers moved against hers. Bailey's heart raced in her chest. *I don't want to see . . .*

This image was farther away, as if the photographer had panned out or backed away from the falls.

Asher's fingers moved again.

A new image loaded and a gasp was torn from Bailey.

The redheaded woman was on an old bed, bound, her hands stretched above her. Her head was turned to the side, her profile visible . . .

As visible as the black image of wings that had been etched onto her shoulder.

The killer had her.

This was . . . "This was her camera." Bailey words sounded hollow to her own ears. "How did her camera get on my doorstep?" And she clicked that mouse.

I have to see.

Blood. So much blood. Long gashes in the woman's body.

Bailey jumped to her feet, covering her mouth with her hand. "Call Wyatt. We have to call him *now*." She was shaking, unable to stop.

Asher hadn't answered her question about the camera, and he didn't have to. She knew the answer. The dead woman certainly hadn't brought the camera there.

The person who'd used the camera last—her *killer*—he'd brought it.

He came to my house. He was here while I slept.

Her gaze was on the dead woman. On her tattoo.

It is happening again. The nightmare is happening again.

THEY'D BEEN SEPARATED.

Asher glared at the closed door, wondering what the hell was going on. When he'd called Wyatt Bliss, a patrol car had quickly come to Bailey's house.

And they hauled our asses down to the sheriff's office.

Only Bailey had been taken one way, and Asher had been sent to another—with an armed guard. If that fresh-faced kid Ben counted as a guard.

Ben's hand kept nervously sliding toward his sidearm. The kid had better watch that shit. Asher's eyes narrowed on him.

The door flew open. Wyatt stood there, deep lines under his eyes and patches of stubble along his jaw. "Ben, give us a minute."

The younger man nearly ran out.

Wyatt shut the door behind him, then he stood there a moment, body tense.

Asher didn't speak. He'd long ago learned how to handle interrogations. The strategy was simple, really. You just waited out your prey.

Wyatt raked a hand over his face. "This shit can't be happening again."

It sure looked as if it was.

"Sheriff Johnson resigned. Effective as of six A.M. this morning. He just turned his back and left this county when I've got a victim in the morgue." His hand fell and his eyes locked on Asher. "That means I'm in charge. No time for a special election or any shit like that. I'm the next in line. This killer is *my* responsibility."

Then you need to find his ass before he strikes again.

The fact that the perp had come to Bailey's house, that he'd left that camera for her to find—Asher's guts were in knots. The killer was pulling Bailey into his web. Could be he was even targeting her as the next victim.

"I told the team last night to keep this case under wraps. That I did *not* want media attention." Disgust was thick in his voice. "Then I swear, the news was everywhere within an hour! Freaking social media . . . and dumb jerks here who can't follow an order!"

Asher just stared at him.

"Tell me that you saw something last night." Now Wyatt almost sounded beseeching. "When he was at Bailey's house . . . tell me you saw *something*. That you heard something. A car's engine. A voice. Give me something to go on here, man."

I was lost in Bailey. I couldn't see anything but her. Asher's back teeth ground together. "Bailey's ex, Royce, is the one who found the camera. He said it was on her doorstep. I have no clue when it was put down, just sometime after midnight." Because that was when they'd gotten back to Bailey's place, and the camera had *not* been there then. "Run it for prints. Maybe the bastard left evidence on it. DNA—"

"Already checking." Wyatt started to pace. "And I got an ID on our victim, the poor woman in those images. Hannah Finch, a twenty-two-year-old college student. Her car was exactly where she left it—right in front of that damn trail entrance shown in the photos. We ran her tag number, got a hit in the database. Got *her*." He paused in front of the small window—the only window in that little room. He gazed out at the parking lot. "Twenty-two. That's too young to die."

"Has your ME looked at her body?"

The new sheriff glanced over his shoulder, a frown pulling down his brows. "He's in with her now. You have to understand, we're a small operation out here. This county—"

"He needs to focus on her tattoo."

"What?"

"I saw the time stamp on those photos. She was taken and killed within hours." *Hannah Finch.* "But her tattoo wasn't red, wasn't scabbing. That's not the way that shit works."

Wyatt turned toward him.

"The Death Angel used black tattoo ink on his victims. I've seen the pictures he sent to law enforcement. The tats all looked fresh. You could tell they'd just been applied." And he also knew that was the way law enforcement had tried to track the guy. They'd run down every male tattoo artist in the area.

The FBI had been in on the hunt. One of their profilers had come in, told everyone who they were looking for as a perp.

White male, probably in his late twenties, early thirties. Fit, strong. He knows the area, so we could be looking at an avid hiker. An outdoorsman. There were no hesitation marks with the tattoo—the lines were precise, curving. He knows what he is doing. Look for an artist, a tattoo expert.

They'd tried to follow the ink back to the killer.

Only the trail hadn't worked for them.

"Either that tat is old," Asher said—*and why the hell would she get that particular mark on her skin? A serial killer's mark.* "Or something else is happening.

There is no way the image should look that good, not just a few hours after an inking."

Wyatt seemed to be weighing some kind of decision, but then he gave a nod. "You're right. You're fucking right, and we need to go look at her body." He headed for the door. "Come on."

Just—what? Asher rose slowly. "Thought I was some kind of suspect. Isn't that why you've kept me locked away in here?"

Wyatt stopped near the door, his back to Asher. "Let's be clear. I don't like you."

Good to know. Asher didn't exactly have the warm fuzzies for him, either.

"I think you're bad for Bailey, but right now"—he glanced Asher's way—"I also think you're her best shot at protection. You're better than my men, I realize that. When it comes to hunting, to fighting . . . they can't compare."

Asher tensed.

"So I kept you in here because I wanted to talk to you. I wanted to make sure you wouldn't cut and run, not until we catch this bastard. I *need* to know she's safe, and my department is going to be too stretched as it is."

Too stretched to provide Bailey with protection.

Wyatt's hands clenched, then opened. *Clenched.* "He left the camera on her doorstep. He could have brought it to the station. Could have left it in the cabin or even in Hannah's car. *He brought it to Bailey.* And I don't have to be some fancy FBI profiler to know why he did that."

No, none of them did. But Asher did know one damn fancy profiler that he *would* like to confer with on this case. Dr. Sarah Jacobs worked for LOST, and when it came to killers, she was always dead-on. He wanted Sarah to look at the case, to look at the profile that had been generated on the Death Angel before and see if she agreed with the FBI guy's assessment.

Or if she thought it was just bullshit. From what he'd learned about her in his time at LOST, Sarah had always been great at seeing the bullshit and calling it.

"She was the only one to live before. If this is some copycat or just some weird obsessed psycho who thinks he's finishing up the Death Angel's work, then we both know Bailey could be in danger."

Right. They should be clear about this. "I'm not planning to go anywhere." If Bailey needed protection, he'd give it to her. He'd be her shadow twenty-four seven. But what he didn't get was the guy's turnaround. Yesterday, Wyatt had been saying that Asher needed to get the hell away from Bailey and now . . . Asher's eyes narrowed on him. "You've been digging more into my past, haven't you?"

Wyatt's chin notched up. "So maybe I do have a few contacts in the government that decided to talk with me a bit more."

Hell.

"They backed you up," Wyatt admitted grudgingly. "Said in a firefight you were the one they'd want covering their asses."

Was that supposed to be a ringing endorsement? Asher didn't let his expression alter.

Wyatt blew out a frustrated breath. "So I want *you* covering Bailey's ass, got it? You're the protection that this killer won't see coming." His smile was grim. "As

I said before, I don't like you. I think you're dangerous, but it's a danger I *will* use in order to protect Bailey. She matters. Her life *matters*."

It sure did.

Asher nodded, accepting this uneasy alliance. "You said I could see the body?" He wished that Victoria Palmer was there with him—Viki was the forensic anthropologist that LOST had on staff, and the woman sure knew her dead bodies. If this case was over the local ME's paygrade, maybe Wyatt would be open to bringing her in.

"I said we should see that tat. If it's new, it'll show scabs, just like you said."

Asher didn't think it was new.

He followed Wyatt from that little room. The sheriff's station was buzzing with activity. Phones were ringing, deputies were rushing left and right and . . . "Where's Bailey?"

"My office. She's drinking coffee and eating doughnuts, and I have a man right outside." He pointed to the left.

Asher immediately headed in that direction. And the man guarding the door? Young Deputy Ben. Ben gulped when he saw Asher and hurriedly straightened.

"Kid, move," Asher ordered.

"Wait!" Wyatt called, grabbing his arm. "Bailey should stay in there until—"

Asher tossed him a frown. "Are you serious? Bailey is the one we need. You said it yourself. She's the only one to ever get away from the Death Angel." *Unless we count our mysterious missing victim.* And Asher wasn't counting her, not yet. "She's the one who knows him.

Knows these crimes. I want her to look at the victim. I want her to see the tat. Bailey can help us—she can look for things that we might miss." Because Bailey's perspective on the Death Angel was far more intimate than anyone else's. She'd been with him for days. She knew how he tortured his prey. How he enjoyed their pain.

She knows so much more than we do.

"I don't think she's strong enough to handle this," Wyatt said, voice tense.

Asher's brows shot up. "Hell, yes, she is." No doubt in his mind. "And if you think otherwise . . ." His words trailed away. *You don't understand her at all.*

"I can't have her breaking down on this case. You don't know what she was like before. I was there." Dark emotion shadowed Wyatt's face. "I saw her in the hospital. She wouldn't speak—"

"She couldn't! The guy had nearly crushed her larynx." Fury boiled within him as he remembered Bailey's soft confession of her ordeal. *He choked her until she passed out. Then dumped her in a grave.*

"She was nearly catatonic." Wyatt shook his head. "Her shrink—Dr. Leigh—he tried to help her, but she wasn't forthcoming with him. I mean, hell, Bailey is the one who *saw* the killer! By her own account, she ripped off his mask, but she can't remember him. Leigh said it was some kind of traumatic block. Some protective psychosis thing. Her mind shut down because she couldn't handle more. Whenever she tried to remember, she'd get splitting headaches. Physical pain. She'd just . . . shut down after that. *I don't want Bailey shutting down again.*"

This shrink . . . the guy kept being mentioned and Asher was getting damn curious about the fellow. *Someone I need to meet.* Or rather, someone he needed to investigate. He'd be doing that, ASAP. With some help from LOST.

"I don't think we should risk her," Wyatt continued doggedly. "She needs protecting. She needs—"

"Why don't we let Bailey decide what she needs?" And Asher strode around the eavesdropping young deputy and opened the office door.

Bailey immediately jumped to her feet—she'd been sitting in front of Wyatt's desk—and relief swept over her face. "Finally! I was afraid I'd be in here with the stale doughnuts all day." She hurried to Asher's side. "What's happening?"

"This isn't a good idea," Wyatt muttered from behind Asher.

Asher ignored him. "Do you want to help on this case?" he asked Bailey.

She bit her lower lip, then said, "Help? How?" Her gaze darted over to Wyatt. "How can I help?"

"You don't need to help," Wyatt said quickly. "You need to go home. Or maybe . . . you know, you could even take a little trip out of town with Asher to—"

"We're going to look at the body. We want a closer look at the tattoo on the victim's shoulder."

Bailey's hand rose and she started to touch her right shoulder, but then she stopped, seeming to catch herself.

"I think you can give Wyatt insight into this killer," Asher said. "But if you don't want to be involved, if you don't want—"

Her hand fell to her side. Her spine straightened. "I want to help. In *any* way that I can."

Yeah, he'd thought that Bailey would say that. Asher glanced back at Wyatt.

Wyatt swore. "If she breaks, it's on you," he warned Asher.

Jerk.

"I won't break," Bailey said. "Don't worry about that."

Asher almost smiled. He liked Bailey's bite.

BREAK DOWN, MY ASS. Bailey made sure to keep her head held high and her spine ramrod straight as she entered the morgue. So the place creeped her out. So she didn't like dead bodies. Who did?

The fact that she'd almost been buried alive once, yeah, that had soured her even more on the whole *death* thing, but she wasn't going to break. She *wouldn't* break.

The ME was an older guy, balding, with a slight paunch. He had classical music playing from a small radio on his desk, and he looked less than thrilled to see their trio in his workspace. *Workspace. Crypt. Seems like the same thing to me.*

"I haven't finished my work," the ME said, definitely sounding put out. "I'll be sure to send you my report just as soon as—"

"Don't worry, Dr. Moore," Wyatt cut in, voice curt, "we won't be here that long. We just need to see the body for a moment."

But Moore put his body between them and the victim. "You *cannot* touch her. That would compromise evidence!"

"I said *see*," Wyatt muttered. "Not touch. And this is important. We need to look at Hannah's tattoo, now."

"She doesn't have a tattoo," Moore said with a huff. He turned away from them and his gloved hands locked around the woman's body.

Hannah. On the way over, Asher had told her that the victim was named Hannah. A beautiful name.

Moore lifted Hannah up and his gloves swiped over her shoulder.

A shoulder that was . . . smudged?

"Just ink," he said. "Regular ink like you get out of a ballpoint pen. It had already smudged when she was brought in and put on my table."

"You were right," Wyatt said, nodding toward Asher. "Not the same. The Death Angel *always* permanently inked his girls."

Bailey's tattoo seemed to burn. Her eyes were on Hannah. Her gaze drifted over the woman's body. Stark white. Pale beyond belief.

The wounds from the knife were jagged tears in her flesh and—

"That's not right," Bailey whispered.

"Yeah, I know," Moore said as he carefully lowered the victim's body back to the table. "I know the Death Angel always used real tattoo ink. But this woman didn't get a tat. Someone drew on her, and those wings don't even look exactly like yours."

Bailey flinched.

His face flamed, as if he realized he'd just over-stepped. "I mean . . . I saw the pictures of yours. Of the other victims. The wings are close, but they aren't the same," he hurried to say. "Not as detailed. Not as curving. This guy had seen the pictures, too, obviously, but he wasn't as good of an artist as the Death Angel."

Her heartbeat thudded in her ears. "The Death Angel wasn't an artist. He was a twisted, sadistic killer. And this is—it's wrong."

She stepped closer to Hannah. "Her wounds are too jagged. The knife he used on me made a clean, deep cut. Her skin is sawed—" Nausea rose in her but she just sucked in a deep breath. *I won't break.* "The killer used a different kind of knife on her." *The killer . . . a black ski mask . . .*

Why can't I see the man beneath the mask? Why?

"Different knife," Wyatt said as he moved closer. "No tat. Different artist. Hell, yeah, I think it's clear we're looking at a copycat." He turned on his heel, heading for the door.

"I haven't finished my exam!" Moore called after him.

Wyatt glanced over his shoulder. "I've got the governor calling me. The freaking governor. He wants to make sure we didn't screw up down here before and let the Death Angel slip away. I need to let him know that we've just got a copycat up here. A guy that we *will* catch. And that the real Death Angel is dead and buried."

Just a copycat. Bailey didn't like those words. "What you have is a killer. A man who tortured Hannah just like—" *I was tortured.*

But Wyatt shook his head. "You saw the pics, too, Bailey. The time stamps. The killer only had her for a few hours. His whole MO is off. Hell, for all we know, this guy was just some bastard who had a personal grudge against Hannah. Maybe he wanted to eliminate her so he just set the whole thing up, hoping to make it look as if the Death Angel had struck again."

"But—"

"You can bet I'll be interviewing everyone in Hannah's life. And right now, I need to get on the phone with the governor and let the guy know that our state's most notorious killer *is* long gone, not still stalking the mountains." His gaze slid to Asher. "And you . . . Remember what you promised. Do *that* job, above all others."

Then he was gone. Hurrying out of there so he could call the governor.

Silence reigned for a moment, silence broken only by the soft *tick-tick-tick* of the clock in the ME's office.

"I need to get back to work," Moore finally said, his voice grating.

But Bailey wasn't done. "Have you determined how many times he stabbed her?"

"Not yet."

"Eleven. That was how many times he stabbed me." She remembered every single cut. "And he counted as he did it." She could hear his voice in her ear, that low whisper. "As if he had to do it. Eleven slices. They started small. Barely pricks of his blade. Then they got deeper and deeper."

Sympathy flashed on Moore's hard face. "The other victims . . . because of decomposition . . . the way he'd put them into the ground—" He cleared his throat. "It was impossible to tell exactly how many times he'd stabbed them."

"He stopped at eleven," she said. "When he came at me again, it was to choke the life out of me. I think that number, eleven, it mattered to him." But that had been a detail not released to the media. "I told two people about that," she managed to say. "Wyatt and my shrink, Dr. Paul Leigh. That wasn't a detail released to the media. It's something only the killer should know."

"I'll be sure to examine her carefully," Moore said, his voice subdued, softer now.

Bailey gave a jerky nod. She made herself look away from Hannah's body. So still and cold.

Asher caught her elbow and led her to the door. When they were outside, she gulped the air. Air that didn't taste like death and antiseptic. "I—I didn't break."

Asher smiled at her. "No, sweetheart, you sure as hell didn't."

She gave him a weak smile. "I just . . . I need a minute by myself, okay? Just a minute."

"Take whatever time you need."

She paced away from him, hugging herself. Asher watched her go. He kept his gaze on her. There was no way he'd be letting Bailey out of his sight. Asher pulled out his phone, dialed LOST, and had Gabe on the line in moments. "Need you to run a check on someone for me," he murmured softly. "Dr. Paul Leigh." Because that name was popping up far too much for him. "Do the typical work—financials, personal life—see if anything sticks out to you."

There was a long pause, then Gabe said, "You okay? You sound . . . different."

"The case is different," Asher replied quietly. "Far different than I expected." *Because Bailey is different.* "Get me that intel as soon as you can?" Bailey was coming back toward him. Asher ended the call and went to meet her.

CHAPTER EIGHT

ASHER LED BAILEY BACK TO THE SHERIFF'S STA-
tion. A deputy had picked them up from her
house, so they had to get a ride back to her
place. It would have been great to have his own set of
wheels, but that hadn't been an option earlier—

"Bailey!" The sharp cry of her name came as they
rounded the corner and headed toward the long, flat
building that served as the local sheriff's station. A
station that was blocked by a small crowd of men and
women. People with video cameras. Microphones.

Reporters.

Oh, hell. How had the story spread so fast?

"Bailey Jones!" A blonde woman rushed toward
them, leading the pack. "Is it true that the Death Angel
took another victim last night?"

Asher stepped in front of Bailey. "Ma'am, you need
to stand back," he told the reporter quietly.

She just motioned toward her cameraman to keep
rolling. "You found the body, didn't you, Bailey? Was
she alive? Did the victim speak to you before she died?"

"Asher . . . let's get out of here." Bailey had grabbed
hold of the back of his shirt.

"Bailey has *no* comment," Asher said, voice flat. "If you have questions about any case here, then I suggest that you speak with the local authorities."

To get Bailey out of there, they needed to walk straight through that throng. They'd get inside the sheriff's office and then get a ride to her house.

He put his arm around Bailey's shoulders and pulled her closer. "It's all right," he told her softly.

"Who is he, Bailey?" a male reporter with dark hair and a too-bright smile asked. "Is he protection that you've hired? A new boyfriend? How does Royce feel—"

"No comment," Bailey said, as she leaned in closer to Asher. "I have no comment at all."

"A woman died!" It was the blonde reporter again. "You—of all people—should have sympathy for her! Don't you want her killer stopped?"

The damn cameras were rolling.

Bailey stilled.

No, Bailey. Sweetheart, we have to keep going.

"Of course I want her killer stopped," Bailey said. "How can you even ask me that?" But she'd heard the stories before. She'd taken off his mask, she saw him . . .

But never identified him. So some folks believed she was protecting the bastard.

Some folks were idiots.

The reporter's blue eyes gleamed. "What were you doing in the mountains? Isn't it quite an odd coincidence that *you* found the victim?"

Asher tightened his hold on Bailey. "Come on." That crowd of reporters was just thickening around them.

"Why were you out there?" another shouted.

Beyond that throng, Asher could see Deputy Ben. He'd just rushed out of the sheriff's office. Wyatt was right behind him.

Wyatt looked pissed.

Join the club, buddy. Join the fucking club. But Asher fought to hold down his fury. The last thing he wanted to do was explode in front of those reporters. That would be a news story he didn't want.

"We were—" Bailey looked up at Asher. "We were hiking."

"So *he* was there, too?" the blonde asked. "After all this time, why did you decide to go back to that place? What did you think you were going to find out there?"

Silence.

All the reporters watched them avidly.

And, sidling up to that pack, Asher caught sight of Richard Spawn. The dick was grinning, a sly, arrogant curve of his lips.

"What were you looking for?" the blonde pushed again.

"Back away!" Wyatt called out. "Give my witness room. I will be issuing an official statement soon enough, but for now, rest assured that we are not dealing with the Death Angel."

The reporters immediately whipped around to face him and the questions exploded from them in rapid-fire succession . . .

Most of the reporters had turned toward him, anyway. Not Richard Spawn. He was still staring at Asher and Bailey.

"Come on," Asher said. Ben was motioning for them

to follow him to the right. A patrol car waited there. They could get in, get out of there, and—

Spawn stepped into their path.

He just wants an ass kicking.

"Bailey Jones!" Spawn shouted her name. Fucking shouted it when he was two feet from her. And Asher knew exactly why the guy had done that—every eye there immediately rolled back to them. "Bailey, do you know that your new lover is a killer?"

Shit. The guy sure liked to play for a crowd.

"Killed when he was just fourteen. Incredibly young, don't you think?" Richard went on, his eyes gleaming.

Asher knew the bastard had dug into his past. All those secrets were about to come tumbling out. No way would the pack of reporters overlook a juicy tidbit like this one. Within hours, his story would be spread far and wide.

Just like before.

Years had made the notoriety fade, but time could only make people forget. The crime could never be erased.

"Asher Young," Richard spat his name. "Didn't they have to lock you up following that attack? How the hell did the military ever accept *you* after that?"

Asher wanted to drive his fist into the guy's face, but . . .

He's baiting me. Looking for a reaction just like that one. And Asher wasn't going to give him the satisfaction of that shit. He'd get his payback, later. They wouldn't always have that audience.

So Asher just tightened his hold on Bailey and made his way closer to the patrol car.

But then . . .

Then the dick made the mistake of slamming his hand into Asher's chest. "I asked you a question." Spawn smirked at him. "Is it true you killed when you were fourteen years old?"

Asher looked down at the hand on his chest, then back up at Richard.

The other guy's eyes widened.

"Get your hand off me," Asher said simply. His voice was mild. Easy. But he knew his gaze would show his fury.

He didn't roar his fury.

He didn't make a sound when he attacked.

I didn't when I was fourteen. That bastard never saw me coming. I moved in and I sliced open his throat before he could even so much as utter my name.

His first kill, but not his last.

Spawn made his first smart move. He yanked his hand back. He grabbed for the bag that was slung around his neck. A camera bag.

"Ms. Jones?" Ben called. He had the back door of his patrol car open.

Bailey slid inside.

"Oh, Bailey?" Spawn called.

She glanced back.

"Smile for the camera," he murmured.

Snap.

Asher surged toward him.

"Asher, no! Just get in the car."

Everyone was taking pictures then. Filming them. This wasn't the time to take down that bastard. Asher sucked in a deep breath and climbed into the car. Ben slammed the door shut behind him.

The reporters' voices were muted now. Like the buzzing of bees.

"It was just like this," Bailey said, her eyes on the hands she'd twisted in her lap. "When I got out of the hospital. For days, weeks, they followed me *everywhere*."

Ben had jumped into the front seat. "That is one serious feeding frenzy out there."

And Asher suspected it would only get worse. Once word reached all the national news organizations about the attack last night . . .

Ben turned on the siren and the shrill scream had the reporters finally backing away. "I'll get you home safe, ma'am," Ben assured her as he cast a quick, reassuring glance Bailey's way. "Don't you worry."

But Asher knew Bailey was worried. About the killer. About the reporters. About—

Her gaze slid toward him. Then away.

About me.

Hell. Asher swallowed the heavy lump in his throat. "I can explain." He kept his voice low, not wanting the deputy to overhear this part.

"You don't have to," Bailey responded quickly. "Spawn is a liar. I know that. He loves to take a tiny kernel of truth and just twist it and distort it for his stories. I don't believe him. I know you aren't a killer."

But I am.

Her fingers were still twisting in her lap. "I know," she said again.

He caught her hands in his, stilling that restless movement. He saw Ben glance at them in the rearview mirror. "There are things I need to explain to you." Things that couldn't wait because he didn't want her to doubt him.

Worse, he didn't want Bailey fearing him. Not after last night.

She'd just told him that Spawn's words didn't matter, but he'd heard the hitch in her voice. And when she'd looked at him—ever so briefly—he'd seen the fear in her gaze.

"Bailey, look at me."

Her gaze always showed her emotions, so when he told this story, he needed to see exactly what she felt. *How* she felt, about him.

"I was taken when I was fourteen."

Her lashes fluttered. "What?"

"My twin sister and I were abducted." He could tell the story now without rage making the words tear out of him. Barely. "Two men broke into our house. They were high as all hell on drugs and looking for a fast score. They didn't know we were home or . . . or that our mother was." Remembering her would *always* hurt. "They shot her. Laughed when they did it—I can still remember them laughing."

"Dear God, Asher—"

His fingers tightened around hers. He hated this tale, but he had to get it out. For her. Because he knew Spawn and the other reporters would all be reporting their slants on his story later. He wanted her to hear *his* truth.

"They took us. Took us and planned to make my

father pay to get us back. They kept us in some run-down warehouse on the edge of town. They tied me to a chair and my sister—Ana—they put her there, too. They put her right across from me."

The siren was off now. The whole car seemed tense.

"They wanted fifty thousand dollars from my father. The trouble was . . . he didn't *have* fifty thousand. They were two high-as-fucking-kite drug dealers who hadn't even noticed that we lived in a lower-middle-class house. We didn't have fifty grand lying around, and the cops had found out about my mother's attack. They knew about our abduction. So the story hit the news and those guys *freaked*."

Her hands turned so that she was holding *him*.

"They took out their rage on us." He pulled his right hand from her and his index finger lightly traced the scar on his chin. "Actually, they started with me. A fast slice, but when they cut me, I didn't make a sound." Stupid, arrogant kid. "My mother had screamed and begged, and they still shot her. I wasn't going to make a sound. I wasn't going to let them hear me beg."

A tear slid down her cheek.

"And I think those assholes knew it. So they . . . they moved to my sister. They started cutting *her*. Saying that I was the one causing her pain. I was the one hurting her. If I'd been a better brother, I would have protected her. If I'd been a man, I would have saved my mother. Ana was screaming, and I was telling those bastards I would do *anything* if they would just let her go. I begged them to kill me. To let her live."

"Asher . . ."

"But they weren't going to let either of us go. I

knew that. When Ana passed out, they went to get high again. One of them came back just a few minutes later, ready to go at her once more. He was laughing. Smiling like a fucking idiot. He even stopped to sharpen his knife."

I wasn't going to let anyone hurt Ana again.

"But while they'd been gone, I dislocated my shoulder and got out of those ropes. The fool didn't even check me when he came back into the room. So I got up, I walked right behind him, and the bastard who was holding the sharp knife . . ." He exhaled on a long, low breath. "I used it on him." He'd sliced right across the other man's throat, making sure he couldn't scream a warning to their second abductor. "I killed," Asher said simply. "At fourteen."

"You were protecting your sister!"

Yes, he had been. He'd kill for Ana in an instant. He had, and he would again.

"You were protecting yourself!"

It wasn't that simple. He'd been enraged. There had been no way he was going to let those men go.

So I waited for the second man to come into the room. I knew he'd be there soon. I hid behind the door. And when he came in . . .

Asher cleared his throat. "I got Ana to a hospital. The police went back to that hellhole. The news swarmed on the story, just like they did with yours." The smile that curved his lips was bitter. "But there is always another story, waiting in the wings. Another monster who steals the public's attention. Soon enough, Ana and I were forgotten."

They'd been left to obscurity. Their father had never

been able to handle his guilt. He'd blamed himself for their mother's death, for not helping them—Asher sometimes believed his father had carried enough guilt for the whole damn world on his shoulders. And that guilt had taken him straight to the bottom of a bottle.

And, when Asher had been just eighteen, his father had died, driving his car straight into a utility pole. The guy's blood alcohol level had been sky-high at the time of the crash.

"You were a hero that day," Bailey said.

Asher shook his head. She had that so wrong. He'd been helpless that day. Desperate to save Ana and to stop her pain. He still had fucking nightmares about that. About her hurting, screaming for him to help, but . . .

I can't.

"I was a victim. And then I was a killer." He'd been both within a twenty-four-hour period. Twenty-four hours had completely changed his life.

The patrol car slowed. "We're, uh, here," Ben muttered. Then he looked back at them. Asher saw the wariness in the guy's gaze. *No need to be wary. I didn't even tell the good stuff. Like what I did to the second bastard who came in that room to hurt my sister.*

"No handles back here," Asher reminded the guy blandly. "Think you can let us out?"

Ben's face flushed and he fumbled before jumping out of the vehicle. A few moments later, he'd opened Bailey's door. Her hand slid from Asher as she left the car. He followed her, aware of a tightness in his muscles and a cold fury in his gut. *That fury is always there when I remember the past.*

A past he couldn't change. A past he couldn't outrun, though he'd certainly tried.

"You, ah, need anything else, Ms. Jones?" Ben asked carefully as he followed them to the porch.

Bailey gave him a quick, if distracted, smile. "No, but thank you for the ride home."

Ben lingered. "If anything happens, you'll call the station, right?"

"Right," she agreed, voice soft. "But I'm okay. Asher is with me."

When Ben cast a doubtful glance his way, Asher realized the guy didn't exactly consider his presence to be the best thing ever. Asher just stared back at him. A few uncomfortable moments later, the young deputy headed back to his car.

Bailey remained on the porch, not going inside, her hands now shoved into the pockets of her light coat. Her gaze followed the patrol car as it disappeared down the road. "Thank you for telling me about your past."

Oh, sweetheart, I didn't tell you everything. He couldn't. If he told her more, she wouldn't want him near her. She sure as hell wouldn't want him touching her. And Asher had discovered that he liked touching Bailey, liked it a great deal.

"You think the reporters are going to pull up your story again, don't you?" She moved toward the wooden railing on the porch.

"I think Spawn already has. I expect to see him blasting the news from every rooftop soon enough."

"I'm sorry." Her shoulders slumped. "I had no idea when I hired LOST—"

He went to her, curled his fingers around her shoulder, and turned Bailey to face him. "I'm a big boy," he said, flashing her a smile. "I can handle whatever crap they throw at me."

"What about your sister? I don't want them wrecking her life."

He thought of Ana, and his smile grew a bit more. "Ana can handle herself. Don't worry about that." She'd made it her mission in life to do so. Delicate, fragile-looking Ana . . . she'd become one of the fiercest bounty hunters in the U.S. The woman had tracked down—and taken in—some of the worst criminals out there. Hunting was her specialty. And she used her delicate looks to her advantage. Her prey never saw past her slow smile and her wide eyes . . . not until it was too late.

Of course, she wasn't tracking down criminals any longer. Ana worked with him, at LOST. Now she was hunting the missing.

And if I know her, she'll be here all too soon. A good thing. The way this case was going, Asher could use some backup. It would be nice to have someone else he trusted completely in this town.

"I . . . I don't want to hide, Asher." She turned to face him fully. "I know that is what Wyatt wants. And maybe it's even what I *should* do, but I'm tired of hiding. That's all I've done for the last six months."

He waited, knowing there was more to come.

"I hired you because I wanted to find that missing woman. I *still* want to find her. And that house last night—I think it's important. That cabin is a lead we have to use."

He'd been hoping Bailey would want to keep up the

search. But if she'd been ready to back away, hell, even if she wanted to pack up and get out of the city, he would have understood.

Running had never been his thing. Fighting—getting answers . . . *hell, yeah. Game the fuck on.*

"I'm sure Wyatt is already digging into property records to see who owns that place. But we can do our own investigating, too, right?"

To get intel like that . . . "All we need is a computer."

She nodded. "Then let's find out. I want to talk to the owner."

So did Asher. Because when someone died on *your* property, hell, yes, the owner tended to look real damn suspicious.

"No more hiding," Bailey said again.

And he nodded.

"THIS IS RIDICULOUS." The woman with the midnight black hair and golden skin glared at Wyatt even as her fingers tapped against the edge of his desk. "I'm brought into this office by armed deputies? Because why—my grandfather left me some old cabin in his will months ago?" Her lips tightened. "This is total bullshit."

His gaze moved from her tapping fingers up to her face. Her pale blue eyes were lined with dark shadow, making them appear even bigger. The edge of a black tattoo peeked from the top of her shirt, reaching up to curl around her neck. Was that a snake? Hard to tell for sure.

"You see something you like?" Her words held a definite edge.

Wyatt yanked his gaze back to her face. "You saw that pack of reporters outside."

She rolled her eyes. "Hard to miss them."

He walked around, taking his time, and propped his hip on the edge of his desk. The position put him over her, a stance of power. Yeah, he'd read up on that power stance BS a time or two. When he'd been an eager deputy looking to climb the ladder of success.

He wasn't so eager anymore, but he still used the tricks he'd learned.

"When was the last time you were at your grandfather's property?"

"Um, *never*?" But then she shook her head. "Okay, that's a total lie."

Good of her to admit it.

"I went out there a few weeks ago, actually. Hadn't been there in ages before that little trip, though. I'm not exactly the woodsy type." Her blood-red nails tapped again. "I just wanted to check around. I was going to put the place up for sale soon, so I figured I'd better make certain nothing of any value was up there."

So now if I find anything there that links back to you, you've very nicely and neatly explained it all away with a fairly recent visit.

"Why are you asking about that place, anyway?"

He was curious about her reaction to this reveal. "Because a woman was murdered in your cabin last night, Ms. Drake."

Carla Drake. It had been easy enough to find her—she had an art studio in nearby Asheville. He'd tracked down the property records for that cabin, found out

Carla had inherited the cabin after her grandfather died. She was his only heir. The unlucky lady who'd inherited an old, nearly forgotten cabin—a cabin that a killer had decided to use. *And that alone makes huge freaking red flags fly in my mind.* Did Carla know the killer? The copycat he was after? Wyatt was determined to find out.

At his words, her mouth parted in surprise and her eyes widened a bit more. "Sorry. Did you just say someone was killed up there?" Her fingers weren't tapping any longer.

"That's exactly what I said."

She sucked in a quick breath.

"The victim was a young woman named Hannah Finch. She went hiking and someone . . . a killer stabbed her in your cabin."

Carla shot to her feet. "You think I did it!" She looked frantically around the small office. "That's why I'm here—why you hauled me through that crowd of reporters! You think I'm some kind of killer?" Her voice rose with each word.

"Ms. Drake." Wyatt kept his own voice quiet and level. "Ms. Drake, calm down. I'm merely asking you a few questions. My job is to find the perp who killed Hannah, and to do that job, I have to talk with you." *I need to interrogate you because right now, hell, yes, I'm suspicious of you.*

She was pacing and *not* calming down. "I went there *once* in the last few weeks. Just like I said. I might have stayed a few hours, but that was it. I even contacted a real estate agent. I can give you her name, if you want." She paced faster. "Murdered. In *my* cabin? See, there's a reason why I don't like going into the mountains. Bad things happen up there." She shuddered. "Do you know how close that place is to the Death Angel's kill grounds? I mean, that shit just creeps me out."

"Actually, yes, I do know." He exhaled slowly as he revealed, "I was the one who found your grandfather's body."

"You did what?"

"We canvassed that area." Too many times to count. And Bailey had been so certain that another victim was out there. *I did believe her, at first. I went back . . . and discovered Jerome Drake's body.* "I went to your grandfather's cabin during the search and that's when . . . I found him." What had been left. They'd been lucky, though, no animals had gotten inside that cabin.

"We didn't exactly get along," Carla said, glancing down at her hands. Another tattoo slid around her wrist. "I was the wild child he never understood." A faint smile curved her lips. "And he was the old guy who couldn't stand it when I liked to have fun." Her eyes squeezed closed. "I hate that he died up there like that, all alone. I know you probably think I'm a really shitty person because I didn't go check on him . . ." She stopped. Shrugged. "Maybe I am a shitty person."

How was he supposed to respond to that? "I'm sorry for your loss." The words seemed wooden, but he needed to say them, right? That was the deal. And it was a good law enforcement technique, playing the sympathetic card. Gaining her trust.

But at his words, her eyes immediately flew back open. "Try saying it like you mean it next time. I've found that works better."

He blinked in surprise.

"I'm *sorry* about the woman who died."

She actually did sound as if she meant that.

"Some crazy bastard must have broken into the cabin. Probably realized it was—for all intents, I guess—abandoned."

Yeah, some crazy bastard. That was certainly possible.

She blew out a hard breath. "I don't know anything that can help you. I mean, feel free to search that property to your heart's content, and I hope you find some clues to help you figure out who that nut job is, but . . . I don't know what else to say." Her hands rose and fell in a helpless gesture.

Wyatt nodded. "We will be searching the property." He already had cadaver dogs on the way, just in case . . .

Just in case this turns into another nightmare.

"I'll have my deputy take you back home." Wyatt rose and headed toward her.

She stepped closer to him. "Did she suffer?"

His brows rose.

"That poor woman," Carla said with a sad sigh. "Did she suffer in that cabin? Did he . . . hurt her for a very long time? I read that the Death Angel did that. That he kept his prey and tortured them for hours. Days."

"We believe Hannah Finch was killed quickly." Not that it was much consolation. Wyatt was sure her last moments had been filled with terror and pain.

"I guess that's something." She rolled back her shoulders. "I'd like to say it's been a pleasure, Bliss, but, well, I'd be lying again."

"Do you lie a lot?"

She headed toward the door, her hips doing a little roll. "Only every chance I get." Then she was gone. He saw his deputy hurry toward her, probably ready to offer her a ride. He'd had Ben keep the roads hot that day.

Wyatt went to his window so he could watch the scene outside. Ben followed Carla and just when they were about to reach the patrol car, Richard Spawn reached out and touched Carla's shoulder.

That son of a bitch.

But when Carla turned to look at the reporter, a wide smile split her face. And she stopped . . .

And started talking.

What in the hell?

His hand pressed to the windowpane. The two of them sure looked cozy as all hell. Hardly what he expected, and those warning bells in his head chimed even louder—

"Um, Sheriff?"

A feminine voice came from behind him—like, right behind him. Wyatt whipped around, his hand automatically going toward his sidearm.

Then he saw her.

Dark hair. Heart-shaped face. Eyes so big and deep . . . brown but littered with brilliant specks of gold. Her lips were full, red, and a faint scar slid over her upper lip.

"You *are* the sheriff now, right? I mean, I thought I heard you got bumped up in the chain of command recently." She waved a delicate hand. "Something about the other guy cutting and running because he couldn't handle another case going to shit with him in charge?"

He'd never seen this woman in his life. Mostly because Wyatt didn't think a guy *could* forget a woman like her.

Has to be a reporter. "I'm not giving any comments on this story yet." That order had come straight from the governor. He was supposed to wait until Dr. Moore finished the autopsy, and *then* they'd see just what they wanted to reveal to the media.

Her brows—delicately shaped and as dark as her hair—arched. "How good for you."

He couldn't catch an accent with her words.

"But I'm not here for your comments. I'm here because my boss, Gabe Spencer, wanted to extend LOST's assistance to you on this investigation."

LOST. Oh, hell—

She offered a delicate hand to him. "My name is Ana Young, and I'm here to help you track down a killer."

CHAPTER NINE

WHEN BAILEY PUSHED OPEN THE DOOR OF the little art shop, the bell above her head gave a happy jingle. "Hello?" Bailey called out as she stepped inside. Asher followed in right behind her.

The scent of paint hit her. Paint and some other, deeper, stronger vapor that had her nose crinkling. Canvases were all around. Brushes. Open cans of paint. But that smell was so strong. Was it a paint cleaner? Remover? Or—

Bailey heard the fast pad of footsteps. "Sorry!" A woman with jet black hair and a wide smile hurried from the back of the shop. She wore a paint-splattered apron. "I was working on a new project in the back—"

"*You.*" Bailey stared at her, and the world seemed to stop.

The dark hair. The skin. The wide eyes. *Blue eyes.* Bailey hadn't remembered the shade of her eyes until then. *Pale blue.*

The woman's voice seemed to echo in her head. *Help me. Please, help me!*

"Me, what?" The dark-haired woman frowned at her,

then her gaze slid over Bailey's shoulder toward Asher. Her smile flashed again, flirtatiously. "Hello, there, handsome. In the mood to buy some art?"

Bailey stepped closer to the other woman. She wanted to grab her and shake her. *"I know you."*

The woman's brows shot up. "Well, then you have an advantage over me." She gave a light, tinkling laugh. "But feel free to look around my shop. If you see something you like—"

"You were there." Bailey was shaking. "You were in that cabin, screaming for help."

And the woman—Asher had said her name was Carla Drake—stumbled back a step. "Excuse me?" Her face paled.

"I remember you," Bailey said again. Her temples were pounding. Her stomach churning. Asher had researched property records online, and they'd discovered that *this* woman, this Carla Drake, owned the cabin. And that she owned this little art shop in Asheville, North Carolina. They'd gone there to question the woman about the cabin, but Bailey had never expected . . . "I knew you were real."

Carla shook her head. "Okay, I don't have time for crazy. You need to go." She pointed imperiously toward the door and Bailey saw the flash of the dark tattoo on her wrist. A butterfly? Yes, it was a butterfly with wide wings, dark and muted.

Asher's fingers curled around Bailey's shoulder. "You're sure it's her?"

Bailey stared at Carla. Yes, she got it—she couldn't remember the killer's face. So maybe he doubted that she remembered this woman, but she did.

Because she ran out.

She left me there. I saw her. I. Saw. Her.

Bailey's gaze slid from the butterfly tattoo back up to the woman's face. "I bet you have another tattoo, one on your right shoulder. Bet it looks just like mine."

And she saw it—the raw terror that flashed on Carla's face. *"Get. Out."* Her words were nearly a yell. "Get out or I will call the cops right now!"

"Call them," Asher dared her. "Because I think Sheriff Bliss would love to talk with you."

Carla shook her head frantically. "Don't do this. Don't do this to me." Her voice had gone ragged in an instant. "Please, I'm begging you."

Please, help me!

"Get out of my shop." Tears fell down Carla's cheeks. "Just get out and forget all about me."

Bailey knew with one hundred percent certainty that she was staring at the missing victim. And the woman was splintering apart before her eyes. "I—"

"Get out." A ragged whisper. More tears fell. "Just . . . leave."

Bailey didn't want to leave. She'd been thinking about this woman—having nightmares about her—for months. The victim wasn't some figment of her imagination. She was real. She was alive. She'd gotten away scot-free.

And left me.

Asher was a solid wall behind Bailey. So strong. So warm. She could really use his warmth right then because Bailey felt as if she were freezing on the inside. Abruptly, she turned away from the other woman, desperate to get out of there. "Asher, let's go."

"But—"

Bailey couldn't say more to him right then. She pushed toward the door.

And then she heard Asher's voice. Angry, rumbling, behind her. "Why did you leave her there? She tried to save you. You just—"

"Who do you think set the fire?" Carla rasped back as tears trickled down her cheeks. "And called the cops? That was *me*. I did everything I could that night, and, now, I just want to be left alone. *Alone*. I don't want this. Not any of it."

This. Bailey knew what she meant. The circus show that would come with the reporters. The mad media attention. The endless questions from the cops.

Bailey hadn't wanted it, either. She also hadn't wanted nightmares of a woman screaming for help.

She shoved open the door. The bell jingled. The sound was ridiculously happy. She rushed outside, her feet slapping against the sidewalk. Cars bustled by her on the street. The buildings rose up, but the mountains towered behind them. Bailey tried to suck in a deep breath. One, another. *Another*.

Her heart felt as if it were about to leap out of her chest.

She turned back and saw that Asher had followed her. He was pulling out his phone. Calling someone. "No!" She grabbed his hand, stopping that call. Because she knew just *who* he'd been calling.

Wyatt.

"The sheriff has to know." Asher was grim. "It's all related, Bailey. Every fucking thing. You think the killer just picked her cabin by chance? No, He knows who she is . . . and he sent her a message. The same way that he sent a message to you. He wants you both to know what he's doing. That he's out there."

Goose bumps covered her arms. "She just wants her life."

"And if she's going to keep living, she needs protection. The man who killed Hannah is still on the loose. Maybe he is just some copycat, but that doesn't mean he isn't incredibly dangerous. Incredibly fucking sick. He is fixated on you and Carla. He may think he has to finish the job that the Death Angel started. And to do that . . ."

Her gaze darted to the art shop. "He has to kill us." *No, no, no. I want to be safe. And Carla—she just wants her life. To be normal.*

"I'm calling the sheriff." His voice was flat. "He needs to know what's happening here."

She'd been so focused on finding the missing victim that Bailey hadn't stopped to consider—*what happens when I do find her?*

Now she knew. An image of Carla's tear-streaked face flashed through her mind. *I can remember her face so easily . . . why can't I remember his?*

RICHARD SPAWN SNAPPED a few more photos. Oh, but the plot was thickening nicely. He'd already sent in a story and some killer shots to his editor—those shots would be hitting the web any moment, and they'd air in the news blast that hit cable TV that night.

So fucking awesome.

A new kill had definitely livened things up in this town. Everyone was freaking the hell out. It was truly glorious to watch.

And speaking of watching . . .

He snapped another photo. Bailey and Asher were busy in front of the shop, so they hadn't noticed the black-haired beauty who'd slipped out the back. *Carla Drake, I see you.* She jumped in her car and hightailed it out of there as if she were running from the devil himself. As she flew out of that place, he saw that she had a phone to her ear, and she seemed to be speaking frantically to someone.

Asher and Bailey had no freaking clue what was happening. No, they didn't see her.

But I sure do.

He put his camera down on the passenger seat and cranked up his Jeep. He knew a big story when he saw one, and Carla Drake?

Hell, yes, she was newsworthy.

It was your cabin, Carla. You are in this mess up to your pretty neck.

He couldn't wait to make her a star.

ASHER SHOVED HIS phone back into his pocket. Bailey was too pale. Too pale by fucking far. He wanted to wrap his arms around her and hold her tight. But when he moved toward her, Bailey stiffened.

I don't know how to handle her.

"Bailey . . ." His voice came out too rough so he cleared his throat. "The sheriff wants us to keep Carla company until he arrives. Seems he already talked to her this morning and she stonewalled him, so he sure as hell has more questions for her now." And so did Asher. A whole lot of questions.

Carla said she set that fire. She said she called the police.

But Asher wasn't ready to believe her. Considering the woman had been covering up the truth about herself for months, he figured his mistrust was more than justified.

Bailey gave a brisk nod and squared her shoulders. She opened the art shop's door again.

The bell jingled.

The heavy odor inside the shop seemed even stronger than before. Paint fumes? The scent stung Asher's nose. Carla needed to crack a window in there. Ventilate the place better.

"Carla?" Bailey called out. "I'm sorry, but we have to talk. You could be in danger."

No response.

"The sheriff is coming over," Bailey said.

There was no quick rush of footsteps toward them.

"Carla?" Bailey edged closer to the back of the art shop. A big, colorful curtain separated the area at the rear. Bailey's fingers closed around that curtain and she pulled it back.

But Carla wasn't in the rear of the store. And the back door was cracked open, slightly ajar.

Hell. *She ran.*

Asher rushed forward and glanced outside. A small alley snaked behind the building and he raced down it. A quick turn to the right and he was in a parking lot— an empty lot.

Son of a bitch. Rookie mistake. Gabe was never going to let him live this one down at LOST. He'd let a woman's tears distract him, and she'd gotten away.

Forget Gabe. Ana would give him hell over this shit.

He yanked out his phone and called Wyatt. When

the new sheriff answered, Asher said, "Carla Drake bolted."

"Fuck me."

Exactly the way Asher felt.

"I'll get deputies searching for her now. And I'll send a team to the shop. I *need* to talk to her."

Yeah, like Asher didn't understand that. He wanted to talk to Carla a whole lot more, too. Asher knew what was happening. They had a runner. And unless they found Carla and stopped her . . . *she'll vanish.*

"I'll send your partner over there. Maybe she can help you figure out what the hell is happening."

My partner? The twist in his gut told him just who that would be, who *always* had his back. He hung up the phone and turned back toward the alley.

"Asher." Bailey stood there, her hands fisted at her sides. "There's something you need to see inside the shop."

Frowning, his steps quickened as he headed toward her. Bailey led the way back into the shop and he saw that she'd pulled the covering off two canvases in that back room.

And he repeated Wyatt's words. "Fuck me."

Because those images were blood-soaked. One canvas showed a woman on a bed, her long reddish blond hair matted with blood, her body showing the wounds from a knife's deep cut. She lay sprawled on the old, sagging bed, her eyes closed, seemingly dead.

"I think that's me," Bailey whispered.

Asher fucking did, too. Rage built and twisted in him, nearly choking him as he stared at the first painting. *You aren't dead, sweetheart. You got out.*

"Why would she paint that terrible image of me?" Bailey asked him.

Asher intended to find out just why the hell she'd done it. His gaze slid to the next image. This time, the shot was of a man—tall, with broad shoulders, and covered in darkness. A black ski mask—one that resembled a thick cloud more than anything else—hid his features. In his right hand, the man gripped a knife . . . a knife that dripped blood onto a wooden floor.

The killer.

The killer and the victim, a set of paintings that chilled Asher's blood.

And Carla Drake had stood there, ordering them out of her shop? Carla was hiding secrets, dark and twisted secrets, and Asher was determined to discover them all.

Bailey turned then, stumbling toward the front of the shop. He hurried after her. "Bailey—wait—"

But then his nose twitched. In the back, he'd smelled the thick scent of paint. Heavy. But . . .

But there was something else. Something that had been nagging at him all along.

Asher looked up. For just an instant, he swore that he saw someone upstairs. A black shadow, running along the balcony up there. Asher tensed to go up—

And then he heard a *whoosh*. Loud and distinct and he saw the flash of fire racing down the stairs. The flames seemed to follow a trail and the thick scent in that place suddenly made terrible sense.

"Bailey!"

She'd looked back. She was right at the door. Almost out. Almost free but she turned back toward him and when he saw the horror on her face, Asher knew that she understood, too.

He leapt toward her. Grabbed her and they flew out of the shop. Flew out even as the flames erupted behind them. But it wasn't just a surging fire, not anymore. It was a full-on detonation. The shop exploded and the glass from the windows flew outward.

Asher and Bailey hurtled toward the sidewalk. He covered her doing his damn best to shield her from the shards of flying glass. He felt the heat lance around his body, rolling right over him, and he yanked Bailey up, holding her tightly as he ran across the street with her in his arms. All around them, car alarms were shrieking, one right after the other. Men and women were running in the streets, shouting, ducking for cover.

And Asher held tight to Bailey. *She* was what mattered. And if they'd stayed inside that shop just a few minutes more . . .

We'd both be dead.

"What happened?" Bailey shook her head and stared up at him in shock. "It was . . . it was like a bomb just went off in there at the end."

Asher looked over at the wreckage.

Gone.

RICHARD PARKED HIS car a few feet away from Carla's. She'd gone to her house; not a very smart move. Her front door was slightly ajar. The woman must have hauled ass inside. What did she think she'd do? Get a bag together and get out of dodge?

Not happening.

Not until he got his story.

He killed the ignition and then he climbed out of his car. His fingers curled around his camera as he put one hip on his front fender and waited.

Five.

Four.

Three.

Two.

She ran out of her house, a big bag slung over her shoulder. He lifted the camera and snapped a picture. "Going somewhere?"

Carla froze.

She didn't flash him that fun, flirtatious smile—the smile she'd used down at the police station when she'd told him that *of course, I'll be happy to give you an interview. Just come by my shop today at three. You come by and I'll give you the scoop of a lifetime.*

He'd gone to her shop. And seen Bailey Jones.

Carla's jaw hardened. "You shouldn't be here."

He shrugged and took another picture. "Why not? I thought we had a meeting."

"At my *shop.* Not my house."

"But you weren't at the shop. Bailey Jones was. And I have to say . . . she seemed upset." His finger pressed down to take another picture.

"Stop doing that," Carla gritted out.

He grinned at her. "Can't. It's my job. And you'd be surprised by just how much these pictures go for."

She lunged forward, attempting to grab the camera, but this wasn't his first ball game. So he just lifted that camera high above his head and laughed. "No, baby, it doesn't work like that."

Her cheeks flamed red. "You don't know what you're doing."

"Oh, I have a pretty good idea. I'm about to break a major story. I mean, the pieces are all there—everything points to you being important. Deputy Do-Right called you in to his office and then, bam, right after that Bailey Jones pays you a personal visit. As fast as I can blink, you're running away from her, you're packing a bag, and you sure seem ready to head out of town . . ." He gave a low whistle, but kept his camera out of her reach. "In my experience, a woman runs because she's guilty or because she's scared. Which one are you?"

Her lips pressed together.

"Or are you both?"

"I don't have time for this." She tried to step around him. He just moved with her, blocking her path with his body.

"I suggest you make time. Because if you don't give me the interview you promised, well, then I'll just decide to put my *own* take on the story. I'll say what I *think* you did."

Her eyes flashed at him. "You're not a very nice person, are you, Spawn?"

"Never claimed to be."

"Good." She pressed her body close to his and he blinked in surprise at the seductive move. "That makes it easier to do this . . ." And he never even saw the knife coming. He just felt the hard slash of the blade as it cut into his abdomen. He staggered back from her, and his hands flew to his gushing wound.

A smile curved her lips as she held the knife in her hand.

"You crazy bitch!" His camera had crashed to the ground as he tried to stop the blood flow.

"I've been called worse," Carla said, that grin stretching a bit. "Don't worry, I didn't hit anything vital . . . I don't think."

He was bleeding like a stuck pig!

"Maybe that can be a lesson to you. Screw your damn stories! Leave people alone!" She scooped up his camera and ran toward her car.

Fucking insane bitch.

Carla looked back at him. "No one controls me, not anymore. You'd better remember that." Then she jumped into the car and the bitch left him there, *bleeding.* Too late, he tried to stagger after her. When she whipped her car back then spun it around, he realized that she would mow his ass down if he didn't move.

Crazy. Absolutely insane.

He jumped to the side but the vehicle still clipped his hip.

She will pay.

Her tires squealed as she drove away.

THE SMOKE BILLOWED in the air. Firefighters raced to battle the flames, and water shot at the blazing inferno.

It was a fire that lit up the whole night sky. A fire that burned hot and bright and wild and . . .

Just like last time.

The fire raged in a frenzy, just like the blaze Bailey had witnessed before. She'd climbed out of that grave and seen the flames. *The same.*

"What in the fuck happened here?" Wyatt demanded as he charged toward her. Bailey was sitting in the back of an ambulance, the doors open so she could watch the scene. The EMT had just finished with her and when Wyatt came storming up, the guy gave a little nod, indicating that she could go.

"Thanks," Bailey murmured to the EMT, then she hopped down. She had a few bruises and scrapes, but thanks to Asher, she'd been saved any serious injury.

"Bailey!" Wyatt put his hands around her shoulders. "What happened?"

"A fire," she told him flatly. "A really big one." Though she was sure he hadn't been able to miss it.

"Bailey . . ." he growled.

"Where's Asher?" a female voice asked. The question came from behind Wyatt, and his body blocked Bailey's view of the woman speaking.

Who is she?

So Bailey just pulled away from him and craned her head so she could see the mystery speaker.

A woman with dark hair—hair the same shade as Asher's. Her body was smaller than Bailey's, more delicate. She wore jeans and a battered jacket, and her narrowed gaze was on Bailey.

"Asher," the woman said again, more bite definitely in that name. "Where is he?"

Asher walked up behind the other woman, soot on his cheeks. "I'm right here, Ana. Don't worry."

Ana.

That was Asher's twin?

Ana whirled toward him and she grabbed him close in a tight hug. "Don't do this shit," Bailey heard Ana snap at him. "Don't make me come up to some insane blaze scene and *not* see you. That isn't cool, Ash. Not cool at all." She pushed him back. "And since when does a missing person's case turn into *this*, anyway?"

Wyatt closed in on Bailey once again. "I am still waiting to hear what happened. I gave orders to hold the woman here—Jesus Christ, please don't tell me she was inside when that building blew!"

"She wasn't," Asher said, voice curt. "But I think she planned for that building to go. The place was *rigged*. It wasn't some accident. Hell, look at the way it went—fast and hot. A fireball that destroyed everything."

Just like before.

Bailey could practically see those thoughts on Wyatt's face. He was thinking the same thing that she was.

But . . .

"I did see someone, right before it blew."

Wyatt's brows shot up.

"It looked like a man. W-wearing a black ski mask." She wrapped her arms around her stomach. "He was on the second floor of her art shop, and I saw him for just an instant. Asher was pretty much throwing me out of the shop—and saving my ass—so I didn't get to look longer."

Wyatt whirled toward Asher. "Did you see the guy, too?"

Asher hesitated a moment, then gave a grim nod. "Yes. I thought I did. A man, big, like she said. In black. But, hell, the guy would've only had seconds to get out."

Bailey hugged herself even harder. "But if he was the one who set the place to explode, I'm sure he would've had a way out. I mean, Carla was gone. She—"

"Could have set a timer before she split," Ana cut in

to say. "And that way, Carla would make sure that she got out of there all right."

Bailey wasn't sure what had happened. Not exactly. "The place smelled wrong the whole time we were there. Like . . . like . . ."

"Like an accelerant had already been poured everywhere," Asher finished. "And I think that's just what the hell happened. Wyatt, you said you pulled her into your office earlier?"

"Yes." Wyatt nodded. "But she told me jack shit."

"Doesn't matter." Asher was standing close to his sister. "You could've rattled her, made her think her secret was coming out. So she rushed back here and got ready to torch the place."

Only we arrived first. Bailey looked down at the scratches on her palms. She'd hit the cement pretty hard. "At the end, though, when I saw that guy . . . It was just a fire then, the flames racing. But the building just—it erupted after that."

"Maybe the flames reached the central explosion point." It was Ana who spoke now. "They followed the trail that had been left and then . . . boom. Everything was gone."

Bailey shivered. Shivered, when the flames were still burning.

"I need an APB on this woman," Wyatt said. He whirled away and called out for two nearby deputies.

Asher edged closer to Bailey. "You okay?"

"I'm alive. That's a major bonus." She licked her lips. "Thanks for saving me."

His hand lifted and his fingers brushed over her cheek. "Anytime, sweetheart."

Ana stiffened. "Uh, Ash . . ."

But Wyatt was already coming back. "Okay, I've got a team going to her house and word is spreading for everyone to be on the lookout for Carla Drake."

Bailey's gaze focused on the blaze. "She told us that *she* set the fire at the cabin."

"So she has a history of arson," Wyatt mumbled. "Great."

"No, no." Now Bailey was angry. And, yes, she was pissed at Carla but . . . "That fire saved my life out there at the cabin. It saved *her* life. She told us that she just wanted to be left alone, but I was the one who kept pushing. Maybe when you called her in to the station and then she saw me on her doorstep, maybe Carla realized her whole world was about to come tumbling down and she panicked. It *does* happen, you know. People panic."

But Asher shook his head. "That fire could have killed us both. That's not panic. That's premeditation. And what about the guy? Where does that asshole fit into things? Because it sure as shit looked like he let *her* leave, then he was the one who set the blaze, with us inside."

Bailey flinched. Yes, it had looked that way.

"An accomplice." Ana nodded. "Maybe a lover? Someone who knows her secret and is covering for her, too?"

"I think she would've needed to tell someone the truth." Bailey's gaze flickered to the smoke that rose in the sky. "Otherwise, keeping that inside . . ." *It would have hurt too much.*

"The mistake is that you want to think that she's like

you." Asher's face appeared almost angry. "A victim who survived. But you saw those canvases, too, Bailey."

"Uh, canvases?" Wyatt's voice rose with curiosity. "What canvases?"

She was still looking at the smoke. "There were paintings inside but . . . there won't be anything left of them now."

"A painting of Bailey, tied up on that bastard's bed, with stab wounds all over her." Asher's voice was chilling. "And a painting of that freak who took her—all decked out in his ski mask."

"The paintings just show that she was there, at the cabin," Bailey said as her gaze jerked toward him. "They confirm that other victim was Carla." *I was never crazy. And she was here—all along. So very close.*

Silence.

"I think you should take her home." Wyatt nodded toward Asher. "You both need to go get cleaned up and get out of here before the reporters start swarming again. This story is freaking exploding . . ."

Such a bad choice of words.

"I'll let you know when we have Carla in custody." Wyatt ran a hand through his hair. "You two just—try to play things low-key for a while, okay?"

The reporters had already arrived. Bailey saw them filming from across the street.

She knew exactly what would be showing on the six o'clock news that night.

Another death-defying adventure in the life of Bailey Jones.

"I'm going to stay here," Ana said, lifting her chin up

and seeming to square her shoulders. "I want to talk to the firefighters and try to figure out what sort of accelerant was used. I figure I can learn if we're dealing with an amateur or if there's a signature with this blaze."

A what now? Bailey's brows shot up.

But Asher just said, "Call me when you're done." He gave his sister another hug and because they were all standing so close, Bailey overheard Ana say . . .

"Be careful with her, Asher. Be very careful. There are risks . . . you know there are. Especially with someone like her."

Bailey actually took a step back, her mouth dropping open in shock. Had Asher's twin just warned him that Bailey was some kind of—of what? Villain? A threat? *Why in the world would he need to be careful with me?*

Asher looped his arm around Bailey's shoulders. As they walked away from the smoking scene, she couldn't help but stiffen beneath his touch. "You shouldn't be doing this."

His hold tightened as he brought her even closer. "Why not?"

She pointed to the reporters. "You're just giving them more fuel. Making them want to dig even harder into your life."

He laughed. *Laughed.* They were covered in bruises and soot and the guy dared to laugh in the middle of that chaos. "Let them dig. I told you before, I don't care."

They were near her car. Luckily, they'd parked it far enough down the road that it had been spared any major damage. Soot and ash just covered the exterior. He opened her door and she hesitated. "Your job is over."

A furrow appeared between his eyes.

"We found the missing victim. You did exactly what I hired you to do." Actually, he'd gone way above and beyond the call of duty by saving her life. And now she was wondering . . . was he going to leave? *Are we finished now?*

"My job isn't over." His words were almost a growl.

"But you don't—"

"Do you think I'm going to leave you while a killer is out there? Playing some crazy-ass game with you?" He gave a grim shake of his head. "That isn't who I am."

She climbed into the car. When he slammed her door shut, her fingers curled around the steering wheel. A few moments later, he was in the passenger seat. She should crank the vehicle. Get them out of there. But . . . "I don't want you to get killed." Because it hadn't just been her in that shop. He'd come far too close to burning. And if something happened to Asher . . . "I don't want you in danger."

But he laughed again. "Aw, sweetheart, danger is what I live for."

Her head turned toward him. "An adrenaline rush is one thing. Death is quite another."

His hand curled around the nape of her neck. He brought her head in closer to his. And he kissed her. Deep. Hard. Sensually. His tongue pushed past her lips and he tasted her, savored her. Aroused her.

"I don't plan for either of us to die," Asher rasped against her lips.

Good. Because that wasn't on her to-do list, either.

She drew in a deep breath, tasted him once more. Her hands were shaking when she started her car.

CARLA DRAKE HAD a death grip on the steering wheel. None of this shit should be happening. *None.*

She looked down at her knuckles and saw that asshole reporter's blood on her. "Shit!" She yanked back her hand and rubbed it over her shirt. She hadn't meant to stab him, but some primitive instinct had kicked in when he'd been threatening her, and she'd attacked.

So maybe she'd been dealing with some anger issues in the last six months. Wasn't she entitled? And it wasn't as if she could go talking to some shrink about what the hell was going on. That wasn't happening.

I just wanted to be left alone. Why couldn't they just leave me alone?

Only . . . it hadn't been *they*. It had been one woman. Only one knew about her.

Bailey Jones.

I left you alone, Bailey. You should have given me the same fucking courtesy. But, oh, no, the woman who hogged all the TV airtime had just had to go out and wreck things for Carla.

Carla braked at a red light.

Where do I go? What am I supposed to do now?

The cabin was out. Her house was out. The shop—ha! Hardly. If things had gone according to plan, the place should be a pile of ashes.

Her hand reached for the camera. So she'd stolen it. Hardly the worst act she'd ever committed in her life. Her fingers pushed on the side and she got the images to appear for her. She immediately deleted the shots of herself.

She frowned at the pictures of Bailey Jones and that

mystery guy. What had his name been? Ace? Allan? Something with an *A* . . .

Those two sure looked chummy in the photos on Spawn's camera. Like, lover chummy.

She swiped past those pics, curious now about what other shots the reporter might have taken.

A new image appeared. One that was outside of a house. Bailey's house because, yes, she knew where the other woman lived.

She pressed the button to look at more photos.

And . . .

"Oh, my God . . ."

A car horn honked behind her and Carla dropped the camera. It fell down to the floorboard even as her foot pressed down hard on the accelerator, flooring the car and making it surge forward.

Oh, my God . . .

Sweat slickened Carla's body as she tried to figure out just what the hell she should do. *If* she should do anything.

Or if she should just watch her own ass.

Save my own hide . . .

CHAPTER TEN

"So . . . THAT WAS YOUR SISTER?" BAILEY'S VOICE seemed guarded as Asher followed her into her house. She reset the alarm quickly and turned back toward him. "She seemed . . . um, nice?"

"Fuck. I didn't introduce you." Okay, so he was an idiot sometimes and he'd been distracted by the raging inferno that they'd barely escaped. "Yes, that was Ana. I figured she'd show up here after my call to her last night." It wasn't like he could phone and say he'd found a dying woman without Ana coming in like the cavalry she was.

Bailey's hands twisted in front of her. "I don't think she liked me very much."

"What?" He shook his head. "You're wrong. She's just—" *Reserved.* That was a serious understatement for his twin.

"I heard what she said to you. About being careful with me. That there were risks." Bailey's hands were still twisting. He'd come to recognize that nervous habit for a sign that Bailey was on edge. "Just what is it that she thinks I'm going to do?"

He stilled. That warning from Ana hadn't been about

Bailey, not at all. If anything, Ana had been telling Asher to be careful and not hurt *her*. Because Bailey was good and sweet and when Asher looked at her, he could practically see picket fences behind her.

Only he'd never been the picket-fence type.

My sister was telling me to watch my ass and not hurt you.

"I'm pretty sure," Asher said, trying to choose his words carefully, "that she realized I was . . . involved with you."

Her cheeks stained red. "What? It was just—just the once!"

But he wanted more. Asher frowned at her.

"Did you *tell* her?" Now she was horrified.

"Twins." He shrugged. "The woman knows me. She probably read my body language. She's good at that." Or she'd just noticed the frantic look in his eyes when he'd stared at Bailey. *Too close to losing her.* He'd never forget the fear he felt as he ran from that shop. Another few seconds. A hesitation that went too long . . .

"And she thinks I'm dangerous . . . somehow . . . to you?" Bailey glanced down at her hands. "Why?"

"That isn't what she thinks."

Bailey swallowed. He saw the delicate movement of her throat. "I need to go shower. Get this soot off so I can stop smelling like a fire. You can use the guest bath. We'll both probably feel a lot better in a few moments." She turned away from him, but stopped. "Thank you for saving me." Bailey glanced over her shoulder. Her gaze—*I'll never get used to that green shade*—found his. "And thank you for sticking around. It really means a lot to me."

She padded down the hallway.

Asher just stood there, frozen, searching for words that wouldn't come. *You mean a lot to me.* More than just some casual fling. His sister knew that he'd had plenty of lovers—lovers that were there for a fleeting time and then gone from his life. Because after the hell that he and Ana had endured, Asher had made one vow . . .

No one else will matter. No one else will matter so much that I die inside when that person is hurt. That I am willing to beg and kill and die to stop that person's pain. No one else can ever matter that much.

So he'd put up walls. He'd gone for casual sex. He'd frozen out all emotion.

And then he'd walked into a conference room and seen the infamous Bailey Jones standing there. He'd taken her hand in his. Heard her voice drift around him. Her scent had seduced him and then she'd smiled.

I am in so much fucking trouble.

Because his emotions weren't frozen any longer. They were burning as hot as that damn fire at the art shop. He was out of control—feeling too wild and rough and desperate. Desperate to stop anything bad from happening to her. Wild because he wanted her so much, but he wanted her his way . . .

No control.

No boundaries.

Nothing but pleasure.

"Hell." His breath heaved out as he marched away and pulled out his phone. Luckily, it had survived the hell of the day. He dialed Gabe and—

"Jesus Christ," Gabe snapped. "Do you know how

damn worried I was today? Thank fuck that Ana was on the scene and she updated me!"

"I'm glad you sent her in, too." He raked a hand through his hair. "Having Ana here . . . she's what I need." His sister would always watch his back. He had no doubt about that.

"I've been trying to reach you," Gabe blustered. "But I guess since you were battling *fire* you were a bit busy."

Serious damn understatement.

"We ran the check on the shrink."

Asher glanced down the hallway. Had Bailey turned on the shower yet? He didn't hear it.

"The guy got a big deposit in his bank account recently."

His muscles tightened. "What kind of deposit?"

"The kind you get when you sell someone out." Gabe's disgust was obvious. "A publishing house was listed on the check. Yeah, I got a copy—don't ask me how—"

Asher hadn't planned to ask him.

"Did some more digging and found out that good old Dr. Leigh is writing some kind of book on serial killers and their victims . . . convenient, don't you think?"

Asher didn't think it was convenient. He thought it was a fucking major betrayal of trust. *As if Bailey doesn't have enough pain.* "Knew I could count on you."

"Yeah, well, my advice is to *not* count on the shrink. Because he has to be violating about a hundred ethical codes if he *is* writing a book on Bailey. Find the guy—interrogate the hell out of him."

He would. But first . . . "I have to take care of something else. I'll check in soon." He put down the phone.

Turned and hurried down the hallway. Bailey had been betrayed again. She didn't deserve that.

She should never be hurt.

His steps quickened as he neared the shut door. He could hear the rush of water in the shower. She'd finally turned it on.

Was she already naked in there? And if he went in after her, would she kick his ass out? He hoped not because right then, he needed her.

No more betrayals. No more pain. Not for either of us.

His hands gripped the door frame. "Bailey." Her name came out as ragged whisper. He could do better than that shit, right? He could be charming. He could *try.* For her, he could do anything.

His hand lifted and he rapped against the door. "Bailey."

No answer. Maybe she couldn't hear him over the thunder of the shower. He'd done this before. Gone to this door. Knocked for her. She hadn't answered and he'd opened the door and seen her beautiful body.

He'd gotten so erect right then, so fast, he'd sworn all of the blood in his body had gone straight to his cock.

But he wasn't about to open that door again. No way. If she heard him, if she wanted him to come inside . . .

Her choice. Always . . . her. I won't add to her pain. Not ever.

He knocked again. "Bailey, I—"

This time, the door swung open. Bailey was there, with a white towel wrapped around her body. Her hair was still dry; she still had a small smudge of soot on her cheek and on her neck, so he knew she hadn't gotten in the shower, not yet.

His tongue felt too thick in his mouth and, once again, his cock was surging against the front of his jeans. *I should tell her about the shrink. I should—*

"Asher, what is it?"

She was so beautiful. Steam drifted in the air behind her. All he could think was that she looked like some kind of angel, standing in the clouds. An angel . . .

And I almost lost her.

"I was scared as all hell today." His confession came out rough and stumbling. "If anything had happened to you . . ."

Her brows rose. "You think I wasn't scared?" Her head tilted as she studied him. "You were *behind* me, every step of the way. You were the one taking the brunt of the fire. I was so afraid that you'd be the one to burn. That I'd look back and see flames running over your body. I—I couldn't handle that. I needed you to be safe, too."

"I never want you hurt." The words were nearly guttural as they came from him. Something was happening inside of Asher. He couldn't hold back. Maybe because she was too important. "I see the pain in your eyes, and it fucking cuts me apart. I hate it. I want to do anything I can to take it away. I want to protect you, every single moment."

"No one can be protected every moment." Her words were soft, almost sad.

And there it was again. His hand lifted and his knuckles softly stroked her cheek. "I wish I could take that away, too."

A furrow appeared between her eyes. "Your sadness. The ache that you try to keep hidden inside." But he knew it was there. "I wish I could make you happy. Give you good memories to replace all the bad ones."

Her lower lip trembled, but then she lifted her chin. "You think I don't feel the same way, with you?"

"Bailey . . ."

"You think I don't see your shadows, too? Your pain? Your sadness? Maybe, Asher, maybe we're just alike. Two lost souls, coming together. Rushing toward hell together." She paused. "Or maybe it's toward heaven. I'm not sure yet."

He was pretty sure. If Bailey was there, they were rushing toward heaven.

She exhaled on a long breath. "How about we take the pain away, *together?*"

He would do anything she wanted.

"Let's make more of those good memories. See how they can fight the dark ones."

His head moved in a quick nod.

"I need you, Asher." Then her hands rose and she unknotted the towel. It fell into a puddle at her feet. "I need you," Bailey said once more.

Like he had to be told twice. The woman *had* him. Asher stepped forward and his arms swept around her. He pulled her close and took her mouth. He tried to hold on to his control, but her nails dug into his bare shoulders and he liked that hard sting.

Then she took his lower lip and nibbled on it. A quick bite, then a sensual swipe with her tongue. A ragged groan broke from him.

"Oh, Asher . . ." She whispered this against his mouth. "You think I don't know what you really want?"

I don't want to scare you. I never want you to fear me.

"Give us what we *both* want," Bailey said. "Give us what we need. Let's race to paradise together, with nothing holding us back." She pushed against his shoulders, and he took an instinctive step back.

The better to watch her as she turned away and rolled her hips as she headed toward the shower.

Perfect ass. Perfect.

She stepped into the shower. The water poured over her, soaking her hair and then sliding over her breasts, her stomach, down to her sex.

He threw out a hand and grabbed on to the granite counter of her sink. "Bailey . . ." He should warn her.

"I'm on the pill," she told him. "And I'm clean. I already told you, I haven't been with anyone else in months."

No one except that asshole Royce.

But wait, was she saying . . .

"I'm clean, too," Asher managed. He'd never gone without protection before. Not with any other lover, but he sure wanted to be that way with her. Skin to skin. Sex to sex.

Bailey stared at him, desire bright in her gaze. "What are you waiting for?"

"I'll be . . . in control." He could hold on to his control. For her. He wouldn't be rough. He'd be—

"Why? That isn't how I want you." She smiled at him. "Don't you get it yet, Asher? I don't need you to hold back. I want everything you have."

Then she would get it.

He ditched his clothes and was in that shower with her in seconds. He pressed her back to the tiled wall and his fingers went straight to her sex even as his lips took hers. The water pounded on him, but it sure didn't do anything to cool him off. His fingers sank into her, thrusting knuckle deep, and she gave a quick gasp as she arched toward him.

"Asher!"

He liked the way she said his name, but he loved it when she screamed it.

He kissed a hot path down her neck. He used his teeth to give her a quick bite, a mark. His fingers kept pushing into her sex. Playing with her, readying her, and when he felt her delicate little muscles start to squeeze around him . . .

"Are you going to come for me, sweetheart?"

Her lashes lifted. Her breath rushed out in pants.

His thumb pushed down on her clit, he stroked her harder, working her desire into a frenzy with his touch.

"No, Asher!" Her hands clamped around his upper arms. "I want *you* in me."

"Trust me, I will be." But he pulled away from her delectable sex. For the moment. He wrapped his arms around her hips and lifted her up, holding her easily against the tile, and then he took her breast into his mouth. Her nipple was tight and sweet and he worked it with his tongue. The water crashed onto his back and he didn't care. All that mattered was her. He was fucking breathing her in because she was everything to him right then.

He kissed his way to her other breast. Her legs were around his hips, her tempting sex flush against his cock. He could push, could thrust, and he'd be in her. Tight and wet and driving him insane.

If he pushed . . .

His lips closed around her breast. He sucked hard even as he surged forward with his hips.

"Asher!"

Hell, yes, that was the scream he'd wanted. He withdrew, plunged in deep, but he made sure to slide right over her clit.

Come for me, sweetheart.

Withdraw. Thrust.

The water poured down on them.

Come for me.

He caught her arms. Pinned them to the cold tile. Steam was all around them. Her legs were locked around his hips. He wanted her to climax and squeeze him tighter with her sex. Wanted to feel those wild ripples of her release.

Withdraw. Thrust.

Come for me.

He kissed her neck again. Licked her. Felt her buck against him.

He drove into her, even harder than before. His control was holding by a thread . . .

And her climax hit. He saw her face flood with pleasure, saw her eyes seem to go blind. Contractions of her delicate inner muscles vibrated all along his cock and he locked his muscles, holding still as he enjoyed that fucking glorious ride.

When it was over, when her ragged breath steadied and she blinked up at him, he couldn't manage a smile. All he could say was, "Are you ready for more?"

She bit her lip.

No, I get to bite.

And he did. He caught her lip. Tugged. Enjoyed her quick gasp. "Are you ready?" he whispered.

She nodded.

His hands freed hers. Bailey didn't move her hands, though; she kept them up against the tile, on either side of her head. His fingers trailed down her body. Over her neck. Over her breasts. Over her tight nipples.

She jerked beneath his touch. "Sensitive . . ."

Good.

Down, down his hands went. He was still in her and he loved to see their bodies joined but . . .

Asher pulled out of her.

"Asher?"

He flipped her body around. "Put your hands back on the tile."

Her hands slapped against the tile.

"Trust me."

She looked back at him. "I do."

Yes, he thought that she did and it was damn humbling. *I won't ever betray your trust, Bailey.*

He could see the tattoo on her shoulder. Those dark wings. He put his mouth on the wings. Kissed her softly there.

Then he lifted her hips up, positioning her, controlling her completely, and he sank into her in one long, hard plunge. Instantly, he was balls deep in her hot core, feeling the aftershocks of her release once more as they squeezed his cock.

He held her hips, probably too tightly, probably bruising her, but his control was gone. He thrust into her, over and over, the slap of their flesh making him growl with raw need. More. Everything. He wanted to take every single thing that Bailey had to give.

And he wanted to give her so much pleasure in return that she would never, ever be the same.

Her hands had fisted against the wall. She shoved her hips back against him, the movement just making his lust burn darker. His right hand slid around her body. He stroked her. Loved working her with his fingers even as his cock drove into her again and again.

"Asher! I'm coming—again . . ." Her voice broke off as she trembled.

He didn't stop thrusting this time. Didn't go still. He took her and he went wild. There was no restraint. There was just the drive for release and when his climax hit him, he poured into her on a hot blast that seemed to surge from his fucking soul. It didn't end, just kept going, and he was wrung out, spent, so sated he thought he'd lost his damn mind.

And maybe he had lost it.

Sanity returned slowly. So slowly.

First he heard the roar of the shower. Then he felt the water on his back. Sharp pinpricks on his skin. He blinked open his eyes and the water droplets were sliding down his cheeks.

His body was bowed over Bailey's. He held her hip in a desperate grip, and he made his hand relax.

Fuck, one of his hands was still stroking her sex. Again and again, like it had a mind of its own.

My body is obsessed with hers.

Her head was tilted forward. Her forehead rested on the tile. Her shoulders were arched.

Once more, his gaze slid to that dark tattoo.

Not his angel. Mine.

He kissed that mark once more.

His fingers rose up her side, over her scars, and he slowly pulled out of her. Bailey gasped at the contact, and he froze, realizing he'd probably hurt her and—

"I don't want to stop," Bailey said, looking back at him. "I don't want to be done."

And Asher felt a hungry smile curve his lips. "Sweetheart, we aren't." He didn't think he could ever be done with her. He turned off the faucet. The roar of the water became a steady *drip-drip-drip*.

Bailey turned toward him.

His gaze raked over her and he said, "You are the most perfect woman I've ever seen."

Her hands came down then, sliding over her body, over the scars. "You don't have to lie to me."

Asher caught her hands. Stared straight into her eyes. "I'm not."

Her smile came, starting with a slow stretch of her lips. Moving ever so tentatively until that smile crept into her eyes, lighting them up and making them sparkle.

He wrapped a towel around her and picked her up into his arms, holding her against his chest. One of his arms was under her knee, and the other was behind her back. She laughed and hooked her elbow around his neck.

He loved her laughter.

Asher carried her out of the bathroom and put her just where he wanted her—in bed, with him.

And as they drifted to sleep, he realized he hadn't told her about the shrink. About the money in the guy's account. About someone else she *shouldn't* trust.

Soon enough, he'd have to tell her. Soon enough . . .

But for that moment, he just wanted her to have some peace.

ROYCE DONNELLEY TAPPED the top of the bar, indicating that he wanted another drink. It was still early—damn, only six o'clock? But he'd been hitting the drinks hard.

Ever since the run-in at Bailey's. That visit sure as shit hadn't gone the way he planned. The woman was freaking haunting him. Everywhere he turned . . .

"Bailey Jones narrowly escaped death today . . ."

His eyes squinted and Royce looked up at the TV. Sure the fuck enough, Bailey was there. Or rather, she was in the background and that Asher asshole was with her. The news footage showed the two of them huddling close near a burning building.

The bartender had turned around to stare at the TV. Everyone stared when the news was about Bailey.

I should have stayed with her. Fuck.

"What is happening in this town?" the reporter asked as the camera zoomed back in on him. "Is the Death Angel hunting again? And what about the man who saved Bailey today? Asher Young—"

"Is an asshole," Royce muttered.

"—is himself the survivor of an abduction. Only Asher didn't just escape, he killed the men who had taken him and his sister."

What the fuck?

Then a grainy clip filled the scene. Of some punk kid and his sister being taken into a hospital.

The bartender nodded. "Sounds like the guy is a real hero."

What. The. Hell. "Sounds like I still need my drink!" Royce snarled.

Then . . . then *she* appeared. A woman who smelled like brandy and who had on one tight-fitting black dress. She sat on the stool next to him. Glanced up at the TV, then turned away dismissively.

That's what I'm talking about.

She smiled at him, and, hey, she was pretty enough, so he smiled back.

Fuck you, Bailey Jones. I'm moving on.

"Make it two drinks," Royce ordered the bartender.

He stopped watching the news, turning to focus on the woman he planned to soon have naked. But the reporter's voice kept blasting . . .

"Sources are saying that Bailey Jones managed to track down another woman who escaped the Death Angel's clutches. That woman . . . Carla Drake . . . owned the shop that is now blazing behind me." A dramatic sigh. "I'm Dave Barren, reporting live, and I will continue to bring you updates on this dark and twisted story . . ."

Royce smiled. "What is a beautiful woman like you doing in a shit hole like this?"

She blushed.

CHAPTER ELEVEN

SOMEONE WAS KNOCKING AT HER DOOR.

Bailey heard the distant pounding and she cracked open one eye. Her room was dark, so she knew the sun had set, but she had no idea what time it actually was. After another toe-curling, knee-shaking, orgasm-inducing round of sex, she'd fallen into an exhausted sleep.

Um, on *top* of Asher.

"I swear . . ." His voice rumbled beneath her and she knew the pounding had woken him, too. The pounding and now the peal of her doorbell. "If that is your asshole ex again, I will kick his ass."

Bailey pushed up, her palms sinking into the mattress and her elbows locking as she stared down at him. "He's not worth an ass kicking." Royce was better just forgotten. She'd thought that he'd forgotten her, too, until he showed up on her doorstep.

Asher tensed beneath her. "He hurt you."

I needed him to be there for me. At the moment I needed him the most, he turned away. As if I wasn't good enough for him anymore.

The pounding came again. So did the ring of her doorbell. Someone was persistent.

"Better not be him," Asher murmured, then his hands settled around her hips and he very carefully lifted her off him. He yanked on a pair of jeans and started to head for the door.

Oh, wait, they'd played this routine before. Back when he'd thought she would just stay tucked away while he faced whatever trouble had come knocking.

I don't think so. In a flash, Bailey grabbed her robe and rushed past him.

"Bailey!"

She whirled back around to face him, her hands automatically going to her hips. "How about we *both* go see who is out there?" And a quick glance at her bedside clock showed her that it was barely past eight P.M. Still early; they'd just hit the bed too hard and collapsed.

Asher nodded, and he caught her hand in his. A few moments later, she had her eye pressed to the peephole. Surprise rocked through her when she saw the identity of her visitor.

"Definitely not an ex," she told Asher.

Bailey moved back, took a bracing breath, and squared her shoulders. "But apparently, I've got a shrink who pays house calls."

Asher's eyes widened as Bailey opened the door. "That's him?" And just like that—his voice had gone cold, sinister. "Been wanting to meet that dick, too," Asher muttered, voice carrying only to her ears. "Especially after what Gabe told me . . ."

"Bailey!" Dr. Paul Leigh hurriedly stepped over the

threshold and caught her hands in his. "My God, I saw the story on the news tonight and I had to rush over!"

Right. The news. She was rather glad she'd missed that segment.

"They found the missing victim." Paul squeezed her hands, his dark eyes somber. "They found her!"

"Well, actually . . ." Asher said, clearing his throat, "Bailey found her. Not the authorities. She's the only one who kept looking. Seems everyone else didn't believe her. Including you, Doc."

At least her shrink had the grace to flush. Grace, guilt, whatever. Bailey wasn't really sure why he was at her house. She hadn't gone in for a session with him in over a month. Mostly because the last time she'd visited his office, he'd told her that her continued talk of a missing victim was "delaying the healing process" and that she'd never be whole again until she let go of "the fictitious persona that you developed" to deal with her emotional stress.

In other words . . . he'd thought she had a breakdown and imagined the other woman, and he'd wanted her to move the hell on.

"I made a mistake," Paul said gravely.

Bailey pulled her hands from his. His grip had been a little too sweaty for her taste. *And this is so weird. I'm in my robe with my shrink at the door.*

In case there were reporters lurking outside, Bailey waved the shrink further in. Asher shut the door behind him.

"A very terrible mistake," Paul continued as he faced her. "And I need to offer you my deepest apologies."

"Um, thank you?" Yes, those words did sound like a

question. She tightened the robe's belt, feeling terribly exposed in front of him.

She supposed that some people would say Paul was attractive. He had dimples that flashed when he smiled. Dark eyes that could appear warm, concerned. His jaw was strong, and his thick hair was always swept back from his high forehead.

He was in his early thirties, fit, and she knew that he'd been in the area for all of his life. Well respected, trusted . . . yep, that was Dr. Paul Leigh.

He should have been able to help her. Everyone had said that, even Wyatt.

But he didn't help me.

"This changes everything." Paul nodded. "Your diagnosis, of course, will need to be altered. You probably need to unburden yourself now that you've come face to face with the victim. You'll want to talk through your feelings. Address any inner demons that you still have. I can treat both of you—you and Ms. Drake— and we can make real progress to—"

"Stop." Bailey held up her hand. Had he just said *address* her inner demons? Like she was going to sit down and talk with them?

And have therapy with Carla Drake?

He paused, his mouth still open.

"I'm not having some therapy session with Carla Drake." *She may have tried to kill me.* May have? Ha! "The authorities are looking for her now. Wasn't that on the news, too?"

Paul's mouth slowly closed. "They said she was a person of interest in their investigation, yes, but . . ."

"Are you writing a book?" Asher suddenly asked.

Paul took a step back. "Excuse me?"

Bailey blinked, confused. Why was Asher even saying—

"Writing a book," Asher snapped. "On Bailey. On the Death Angel."

"I—I don't know what you're talking about." Paul's gaze swept over him. What *could* have been anger flashed in his eyes.

He's mad at Asher? And where was Asher getting this book stuff?

"Really?" Asher's lips curled down as he stroked his chin. He'd stopped long enough to pull on his jeans, but his chest was bare. "Because one of my associates at LOST seems to believe otherwise. And your bank, well, I think the accountants there believe otherwise, too."

"Asher?" Bailey shook her head. "What are you talking about?"

"Didn't have the chance to tell you before," he murmured. "But I got Gabe to do a little digging into the shrink's finances . . ."

He'd done what?

"What?" Paul's voice sounded as if he were choking.

Asher shrugged, as if digging into a person's financial history was the normal course of business for him. "You recently received a very large advance from a New York publisher, didn't you?"

What?

Paul's mouth flapped open, closed, flapped open again. "How do you know that?"

"I know because LOST has quite a few helpful resources." Asher's head cocked as he studied the other man. "You're writing a story on serial killers . . . or rather, on the victims that *survive* a serial killer's attack. Those precious few that live to tell their dark tales."

Bailey's heart took on a double-time rhythm and her stomach seemed to bottom out. "You're writing about me? How can you do that? What I told you in our meetings was confidential!" She'd told him about her nightmares, about her inability to connect physically with anyone, about the guilt that gnawed and gnawed at her because she thought she'd let the other victim die.

Paul drew himself up, as if insulted. "I am absolutely aware of HIPAA laws. I would not violate any patient confidentiality. But if people choose to volunteer, if they want to *help* others by sharing their stories . . . how is that wrong?"

His voice reeked of sincerity. Of perfect justification. And he made her temples throb.

"I was hoping," Paul confessed quietly, "that you would soon realize that part of *your* healing process involved helping others, too. It would come full circle with your therapy, of course. You give to other wounded individuals, you tell them your story, and in doing so, you heal not just yourself . . . but everyone who—"

"Right, Doc," Asher cut in curtly. "So you *do* want her for the book."

"I am only taking *volunteers* for my book," Paul gritted back. "I merely wanted to give Bailey the option of participating. After all, she's the one who told me, time and time again, about her need to balance life's scales."

Balance the scales. Get rid of the guilt. "You manipulating asshole," Bailey spat.

Paul backed up a step.

"I'm not doing your book. Forget it."

"Bailey!" Now Paul appeared distraught. "We can help others. Teach them how to be stronger and how to overcome life's everyday obstacles."

Asher's laughter was rough. "I don't think a serial-killer attack counts in the 'everyday obstacle' column, Doc."

No, not even close.

Paul's cheeks flushed. "You and Carla Drake—the two of you would be perfect for the book. Two different women. Two different coping strategies."

"How do *you* know how Carla coped?" Asher wanted to know.

Paul waved that away. "She must have coped. Otherwise, she would have had a breakdown over the last few months. The mind can be a very fragile thing, especially after such a traumatic ordeal." Now his head swung toward Asher. "I would think you, of all people, understood the aftereffects of a situation like this one."

Asher's brows climbed.

"The news included a segment on your past." Paul's voice dropped sympathetically. "Asher Young. The name actually clicked for me as soon as the reporter said it, but then the guy showed a clip of you and your sister being led into a hospital after your own abduction. You had to kill the two men who held you, correct? What that must have done to your young mind—"

A muscle jerked along Asher's jaw. His eyes glinted with fury.

"Get out," Bailey snapped, surging forward. *Hell— just what all had been in that news story?* "You need to leave, now." And to think, she'd turned to this guy for help during her darkest time.

I was seeing him long before the Death Angel came into my life. Paul was supposed to help me deal with the loss of my parents. He was supposed to help me get back to normal.

She didn't even know what normal was any longer. Bailey stared into Paul's eyes and said, very clearly, "We're done, and you need to get out of my house."

"But I could include Asher and Ana's story in my book!"

He *hadn't* just said that.

She shook her head, denying it but . . . he had.

"You think you've just hit some kind of pay dirt." Asher stared at him with hard, glinting eyes. "Right?"

"The fact that the two of you . . ." Paul's gaze darted between Asher and Bailey. "That you've come together—it's classic survivor instinct. Look for someone else who is damaged, see the same weakness and try to—"

Asher's hand locked around Paul's shoulder. "Bailey isn't fucking damaged, and if you think I'm weak or that *she* is"—now his laughter held a cold, almost evil note—"then you are sorely mistaken."

Paul blinked quickly. "I—I meant . . . I meant you were responding to the pain and—"

"I don't give a shit what you meant. Bailey said leave, so I'm throwing your ass out now." And he steered the shrink right out the door.

"Bailey!"

"I think our sessions are over," Bailey said, shaking her head. "Good-bye, Dr. Leigh." Asher came back inside, standing just behind her. Bailey held Paul's shocked gaze for an instant more, then she slammed the door shut in his face.

A book?

What an asshole. Slamming that door had felt so incredibly good.

"You okay?" Asher asked her.

No, she wasn't even close to okay. "I told him . . . things." Secrets. Confessions. "Now all that will wind up in a book? I've already been on display enough for the world."

If possible, Asher's face tightened even more. "Fuck him. He *can't* write anything about you, Bailey. If he tries, we'll sue his ass."

"I thought I could trust him."

Asher pulled her closer. "Don't worry. I'll make sure nothing happens."

If only things were really that simple.

A GOLD MINE. He was seriously sitting on a freaking gold mine, and Bailey thought he was going to walk away?

Paul Leigh slammed his car door and hurried toward the elevator. His footsteps echoed in the parking garage.

Bailey Jones. Carla Drake. And now . . . Ana and Asher Young. Like gifts from God. His book was going to be packed with survival stories. Brutal firsthand accounts that would shock and transform readers. He could already see this book as a damn bestseller. It was time for him to make his mark on the world. All of his years of careful research, all of his painstaking experiments. *This will be the culmination for me.*

He'd studied serial killers. Watched victims. Learned and put himself right in firsthand situations so that he could fully *experience* the emotional traumas. No one understood serial killers and their victims the way he did. No fucking one.

And she thought he was going to walk away from that story?

Hell the fuck no. Bailey Jones did not get him, not at all. Pity. He'd done so much for her. All that she had—all of her strength—it was his doing.

The bitch wasn't even grateful.

She *would* participate in the book. They all would. He'd make them.

His thumb pressed into the button near the elevator, his mind spinning. He could fix this situation. Bring Bailey around. He'd always been good at handling her.

He'd messed up at her house. Been overeager. It was the news story. It had put him on edge.

I'll do better next time. I know how to work Bailey. How to get her to do exactly what I need . . .

The elevator doors slid open. He walked inside, his head down as he thought—

And the knife went straight into his side. He could feel the cut, feel the skin and muscles give way, and the pain came immediately—a cold burn, not a hot one. Shock flooded through him and he looked up. "Wh-what—"

"Hello, Dr. Leigh." The knife slid out of him.

He just stared, numbly. Behind him, he heard the elevator doors close.

"You think you understand serial killers, don't you? You think you are so fucking smart and strong. An unstoppable force."

Paul's hand had risen to cover his bleeding side. The blood pumped out so fast.

The knife hit him again. He hadn't even tried to deflect the attack. He'd been—

Numb. Shocked. This can't be happening. Not to me. Not me.

"But seeing the experience from someone else's eyes isn't the same as *living* through an attack."

The knife made a *slushing* sound as it slid from his body.

And finally—finally he tried to attack. Paul grabbed for the knife, but it sliced down in a fast chop and the tips of his fingers—

"Ahh!" Paul screamed.

His attacker laughed. "You're so pathetic. It's different when you don't have the power, isn't it? When you aren't in total control."

He'd lost part of his fucking fingers!

"I do thank you for all your help, Doctor. Got to say, I learned a lot from you."

No, no, he had to stop this. The knife was coming at him again. He could talk, he could make the killer understand—

I can help you.

The blade of the knife sliced across his throat. Blood flew out, hitting his attacker, hitting the walls of that elevator, spraying wide around Paul as he fell to his knees.

"But you know what?"

His face slammed into the floor. He tried to speak but only managed a weak gurgle.

"You're not going to survive a serial killer's attack.

You're going to die, right here, choking on your own blood."

The elevator doors dinged. Had they gone anywhere? Were they still on the bottom floor?

And why was it so cold?

"Hope you enjoy hell, Dr. Leigh. Maybe you can psychoanalyze all the damned souls down there."

THE KEYS JINGLED in the killer's bloody hands. The parking garage was completely deserted—the only vehicle there was Leigh's fancy BMW SUV, waiting to be taken. It wasn't as if the asshole shrink needed the ride any longer. He wasn't going anywhere, but he'd sure make for a good picture when the authorities finally *did* find his demented ass.

Using the remote—a remote that had been in Leigh's fingers right before they were chopped off—the killer unlocked the BMW and had its lights flashing. A prime, lush interior waited—an interior that was about to get smeared with Leigh's blood. Seemed fitting.

It was a good thing the SUV had dark, tinted windows. That tint was perfect for hiding blood-spattered clothes. A quick twist of the radio and music was pumping, blasting into the interior of that high-end ride.

A few moments later . . . the BMW slid out of that parking garage.

And the killer headed for the next target.

CHAPTER TWELVE

ASHER HADN'T COME BACK TO HER BEDROOM. Bailey lay in bed, her gaze on the ceiling, her mind locked completely on him.

After Paul had left, so had Asher. He'd made sure that she locked her doors—like she was going to *ever* leave them unlocked again in her life—and he'd left strict instructions for her to call him if she so much as got even a little bit scared.

Then he'd left her. He'd said that he had to check in with Ana and the sheriff, that she needed to stay away from the station because it would still be swarming with reporters.

That had been an hour ago.

She hadn't heard the roar of his motorcycle returning. And sleep—hell, yes, sleep was elusive. Even more so than normal.

So why am I even trying?

Bailey threw off the covers and climbed from the bed. She'd just go take a peek outside her window. Make sure everything looked okay out there.

As she tiptoed toward her blinds, she felt *exactly* like

some hapless heroine in a horror movie. If she saw a suspicious shadow out there, no way would she venture out. She'd be dialing nine-one-one as fast as humanly possible.

But when Bailey looked out the window, she didn't see anyone suspicious. Her street looked empty, and the streetlights put out a warm, cheerful glow. There was no car parked in the shadows, with a mystery driver just watching her house.

No reporters in sight at all.

Asher, when will you get back?

Bailey pushed the blinds into place once more. She had to get a grip. Since when did she *need* someone at her place? She'd been on her own—and fine—for months. Years, really, since her parents had died when she was just eighteen. A car accident that had taken them from her too fast.

Don't think about that accident. Don't. Don't think about . . .

The fact that she had been with them. That she hadn't been able to help them. *That it was my fault.*

Her phone rang, the moody beat of the music making her jump as she hurried toward her nightstand. She grabbed the phone and her shoulders relaxed when she saw Asher's name on the screen. "Hello?"

"I'm finishing up at the station now," he told her, the sound of his deep voice actually making her feel warm. "Accelerants were definitely used at the shop. Fire marshal thinks everything was in place well *before* we ever arrived."

"Why destroy her own shop?" *And who had that mystery guy been?* Lurking, watching upstairs . . .

"Maybe there was something in there she didn't want us to see."

Like the paintings? Bailey closed her eyes, and confessed, "I don't remember her being in the room with me."

"What?"

Her eyes opened. Bailey cleared her throat and paced back toward her window. "She had that painting of me, from the cabin. But I don't remember seeing her, not in my room . . ." Her words trailed away. *Maybe the Death Angel brought her in while I was passed out?*

"There's something you need to know," Asher said. "Wyatt has been digging into Carla's past."

She'd expected as much.

"Carla doesn't just paint canvases. She's also a licensed tattoo artist."

The mark on Bailey's shoulder seemed to burn. "I—I didn't see any tattoos at her shop." No tattoos. No tattoo equipment.

"Maybe that's because we didn't get the chance to look for them." Voices rose and fell in the background. "She got that license over five years ago, Bailey. And Wyatt spoke to one of her old bosses—she definitely had her own tattoo equipment."

She peered out the blinds once more. A black BMW SUV had just turned onto her street. *That's Dr. Leigh's car.* She'd seen it before, when he'd been on her doorstep, trying to get her cooperation for that damn book. The street lamps fell onto the vehicle, then it slid into shadows as the driver slowly pulled forward.

"No tattoo equipment was ever found at the cabin." Asher's voice had turned musing. "Perhaps it wasn't there because she kept it someplace else."

Her temples were throbbing. The BMW was gone. It had driven all the way down her street. *Maybe it wasn't Leigh. I'm sure lots of other people have the same vehicle.* "What are you saying?"

"I'm saying that you hired me to help you find a missing victim. Well, we found her. Only this *victim* tried to kill us both today, and now we see that she's a tattoo artist . . . and someone had to put that tattoo on you and on the other women."

"It wasn't Carla." She started to back away from the window. But then she saw the flash of more headlights. Now, another car was on her road. *Suddenly, this road sure is busy.* She tried to focus on Asher. *He thinks Carla is involved in the killings? Is that what he's getting at?* "She was hurt that night. He was *hurting* her."

"Are you sure?" Now his voice roughened. "Think about what you saw in that cabin, sweetheart. Really think about it. Did you *see* him hurting her?"

The new vehicle had rolled to a stop just in front of Bailey's house. "Someone's here." And it was a Jeep she recognized. "I think it's Spawn, again." When would he leave her alone?

"Don't open the door."

Like she needed to be told that. She had no intention of talking to the reporter.

"I'm finishing up here, and then I'm coming home."

Home. Her breath caught. She wanted to tell him to hurry. To get his ass there right then, but she just said, "Be safe."

"You, too, sweetheart. And let that jerkoff stand outside until I get there. *I'll* deal with him."

"I can fight my own battles." Spawn had pushed open

his door, but he wasn't getting out. Her eyes narrowed as she eased closer to the window. The lights in her room were turned off, so she didn't think that he'd be able to see her.

"Maybe I like fighting them with you." A pause. She didn't hear voices behind him any longer. Had he left the station? "And forget what that asshole said before. You aren't weak. You don't escape a serial killer by being *weak*."

Spawn was finally getting out of his vehicle. The car's interior light was on and it spilled onto him as he clamped his hands around the driver's side door. He slumped forward, his head going down.

Alarm flared within her. "I think something's wrong with Spawn."

"Yeah, he's a dick. That's his main problem."

"No." He'd pushed away from the Jeep's door. Took a step toward her. Why did his clothes look so dark? Were they wet?

Spawn staggered, nearly fell.

"I think he's hurt!"

"Stay inside."

But Spawn had just fallen face-first onto the sidewalk, and he wasn't getting up.

"He's probably drunk," Asher said. "I'll check him out when I get there. Stay *inside*."

"I don't think he's drunk." Headlights lit up the road once more. She glanced toward the streetlight just as it fell on that BMW. *Leigh?* "We need to check on him."

"Bailey—"

Spawn didn't seem to even be breathing as he lay in a

slumped mass on her sidewalk. Bailey bit her lip, then she turned from the window.

This is exactly what a horror heroine would do. Such a bad freaking move.

Only Bailey stopped to grab the gun that she kept hidden under her bed. She loaded it, checked that baby, and *then* she ran for the front door. She had her phone—still on—in her pocket and the gun gripped in her hand when she ran outside. "Spawn!" Bailey yelled. She'd paused just long enough to turn on her porch light.

"H-help . . ." His voice was weak, pain-filled.

Bright illumination from her light flooded onto him. Now she could see the blood on his hands. *Oh, my God.* Bailey's left hand yanked up her phone.

"Bailey! Bailey, dammit, talk to me!" Asher was yelling.

"Spawn's bleeding. He's hurt, I don't know how bad yet. Get an ambulance out here."

Asher swore, but, hopefully, he'd stop that swearing and get them help, ASAP. She rushed forward and put her phone down on the sidewalk, but Bailey didn't let go of her gun. "Spawn, what happened?"

He let out another ragged groan and tried to roll over. Her left hand curled around him and she helped him to turn. *Oh, shit. That is a lot of blood.*

"Crazy bitch . . ." Spawn muttered.

Seriously, he was calling her a bitch right then? When she was trying to help his sorry ass?

"Bitch . . . Carla . . . she stabbed me . . ." His hand lowered to his side. Bailey saw the cut in his shirt and the blood that still pulsed from the wound. "Took my c-camera . . . left me to d-die . . ."

"You aren't dying." Though he looked like hell. "An ambulance is on its way." She really hoped. "You're going to be all—"

The revving of a vehicle's engine caught her attention. Her head jerked up. The BMW was still there.

Who in the hell revs a BMW? And if that was Dr. Leigh in that ride, then why wasn't he coming to help?

The engine growled again. She couldn't see past the tinted windows. Someone was in that SUV, pushing down the accelerator again and again because they wanted to catch her attention.

Bailey started to rise.

Spawn's hand flew out and curled around her wrist, stopping her. "Sh-she's . . . insane. Whatever he—he did in that cabin . . . *that woman is crazy.*"

He did the same things to me. "Stay calm," Bailey said, even though the last thing she felt was calm.

"T-took my f-fucking camera!" His breath heaved out. He hadn't even seemed to notice the BMW.

Bailey couldn't look away from it.

Because someone else had come onto her street a few nights back, someone who'd revved a car's engine . . .

And then came at me and Asher.

"I needed th-those pictures!"

"And I need you to stay quiet."

The BMW's driver's side door began to open.

Bailey lunged to her feet and she brought up her gun. "Who are you?" she yelled. *"Who are you?"*

The door jerked closed. The engine revved again.

Loud and angry, and then the vehicle shot away from the curb, tires squealing and the scent of burning rubber trailing in its wake. Bailey ran into the street, her eyes on the car, mentally repeating the tag number again and again and again.

The BMW didn't slow at the stop sign. It whipped to the right and thundered away. Bailey stood there, in the middle of the street, her gun still gripped in her hand.

Spawn let out another ragged groan. "M-my camera . . ."

Like she cared about his camera right then. Bailey ran back to him. She put her hand on his side. "How long has this been bleeding?"

He hissed out a breath. "Off and . . . fuck . . . on. Started again . . . in the car . . ."

"Why didn't you go to the hospital? Why come here?" He needed a doctor, not her.

Another low hiss of his breath. "Thought she'd . . . come for you . . . too . . ."

Bailey glanced back down her street. And a cold fist seemed to squeeze her heart. *Maybe she did.* Maybe that hadn't been Dr. Leigh in the vehicle.

She stayed there with him, her gun close, until she heard the distinct growl of Asher's motorcycle. She recognized that heavy sound instantly, hearing it long before she saw the one beam of his headlight turn onto her road. "Asher's here," she whispered.

"Don't let h-him . . ." Spawn's voice was weaker. "Kick my ass."

"Then don't do anything stupid, and he won't." She squeezed his hand.

She could hear the wail of a siren, coming closer in

the distance. "The ambulance will be here soon. We'll get you stitched up."

His gaze was on her. "You . . . have to be c-careful . . ."

Bailey nodded. "I am."

"Bailey!" Asher had braked his motorcycle and he was running toward her.

"No," Spawn whispered. "Be careful . . . with him."

BAILEY HAD BLOOD on her clothes, again.

Asher's eyes narrowed as his gaze raked over her. The reporter had been taken away, loaded into the back of an ambulance, and rushed to the nearest hospital.

Wyatt was at the scene, and Ana was lingering close by. *The damn gang is all together.*

"He *told* you that Carla Drake stabbed him?" Wyatt demanded.

Bailey nodded. She'd put her gun back inside before Wyatt had pulled up. The guy probably had no clue that sweet Bailey Jones had been armed and—from the look of her—more than ready to fire moments before. "He kept saying she'd stabbed him and taken his camera." A faint smile curved her lips. "He seemed more upset about the camera than anything else."

"Fuck." Wyatt squeezed the bridge of his nose. "What is this woman doing? First the explosion, now the attack on Spawn . . ."

"He thought she might come after me." Her hands balled into fists. She wore a pair of loose shorts and a T-shirt, and Asher saw her shiver. "Spawn thought he was protecting me by coming here."

Asher didn't buy it. Spawn was hardly the protective type, and being a hero? *He's the last guy I'd expect.*

Asher slid out of his coat and wrapped it around Bailey's shoulders.

"No, I could get blood on it—"

"I don't care. I don't want you cold."

She gave him a quick smile.

That smile . . . shit, it did things to him. Even in the middle of that madness, Bailey got to him.

Deputy Ben ran toward the group. "Got a hit on that tag number!" He seemed out of breath. "Dr. Paul Leigh. He's got a practice up in Asheville and a home here in Brevard . . ."

"He's my shrink," Bailey said.

"He's her *ex*-shrink," Asher added. "The asshole was here earlier, trying to get permission to use Bailey's story in his book. He wanted her and Carla to talk with him."

"Maybe that's why he came back?" Wyatt seemed to consider this. "He wanted to talk more, but when he saw Spawn sprawled on the ground . . ."

"Wouldn't a shrink try to jump in and *help* someone who was wounded?" It was Ana who spoke. "A psychiatrist has an MD. I would think a guy like that would rush to assist a downed man."

"Only the driver of this car was just sitting out there, revving his engine." Bailey licked her lips. "He only left when I approached him."

When she'd . . . Asher's eyes closed. "Bailey . . ."

"Get an APB out, right now," Wyatt said. "I'll be taking a team to the shrink's house, but just in case he's still running on the streets, I want him found." His hands were on his hips. "I got some questions for the doctor."

"So do I," Asher stated. *If he was out here, skulking in his car tonight . . . then maybe he was here before, too.* They still didn't know who'd nearly run them down just a few nights back, but with the way this case had taken a 180 straight to hell, Asher didn't think they could ignore any details.

Is everything related? Is it all tied to the Death Angel?

Everything . . . tied to a dead man. A man who'd been buried without any real identity. Just the moniker of a monster.

"Get in line," Wyatt told him flatly. "Shit . . . a dead girl, an attacked reporter, and a burning building. All within the first twenty-four hours of my new job." He turned away. "This is a fucking nightmare."

A nightmare that was just going to get worse.

Asher knew that Wyatt wanted someone to answer for the crimes. He didn't want to face the same intense scrutiny that had driven the previous sheriff to—literally—run from his post.

When Wyatt walked away, Ana closed in on them. Her gaze swept over Bailey. "You okay?"

Bailey nodded. "Fine."

She didn't sound fine.

Bailey swiped her palm over her shorts and then offered her hand to Ana. "I'm Bailey, by the way. We didn't, um, officially meet before."

Ana shook her hand. "Ana." Her gaze seemed worried as she stared at Bailey. "We can get you out of town, you know. LOST has connections all over the place. We can get you in a safe house until—"

"Until you catch Carla? Or is it Dr. Paul Leigh?" She pulled her hand back. "I guess I don't know which one of them I'm supposed to fear now."

Ana raised one brow. His sister had always been able to do that—lift just the *one* brow, all schoolteacher style. "I'd say it's wise to fear them both. At least until we can get answers."

"I don't want to sit around and wait." Bailey focused on Asher. "If Wyatt is going to Paul's house, then I say we go and check out his office. His office is the guy's inner sanctum, always has been. So if he's looking for a safe place to crash, he might have gone there, not to his house."

Asher had thought the same thing. He nodded toward his bike. "How about we take a little ride?"

"Love to. Give me two minutes to change, and I am ready to go." Then she ran into her house.

Ana waited a moment, probably to make sure that Bailey was gone, before she gave a low whistle. "You sure that's wise? Taking her with you like that?"

"Leaving her damn sure isn't an option." He'd gone to the station for an hour and raced back, frantic to get to her side once more. "Besides, Bailey knows this guy. She can help me."

"Don't bullshit me. You aren't taking her with you because of any *help*."

"Ana . . ."

"You think I don't see right through you? This is *me*. And we don't have secrets between us." She paused. "At least, we don't usually have them."

The front door flew open and Bailey hurried down

the steps. She flashed Asher a wide smile. "See? I said I'd be fast." She hurried toward his motorcycle. Asher started to follow her, but Ana grabbed his elbow.

"Seriously, Ash, what in the hell are you doing?" she whispered as her fingers dug into his skin. "That woman should be put in a safe house. Locked up and—"

"I have been locked up." Bailey had frozen just a few feet away.

Mental note. Bailey has damn good hearing.

"I've been tied up, locked away, and it's something I never want to experience again."

"Bailey . . ." Asher began, trying to keep his voice gentle. "That's not what Ana meant."

"I know what she meant. A safe house." Her smile broke his heart. "Haven't you noticed it yet, Asher? I've been in my own prison—my own safe house—for months. And I'll go crazy if I have to stay there much longer." She inclined her head toward him. "I want to help. I want to find this guy. I want to stop being afraid and take my life back. Once upon a time, I was the woman who fought a killer."

You still are that woman.

"I'm not going to be the woman who lives in fear any longer." Then she marched toward his bike, threw one leg over the seat, and straddled that baby like a pro. She grabbed the helmet and glanced back at him once more. "You coming?"

I think I could love that woman.

A fast, reckless, and incredibly dangerous thought.

Ana's hand still gripped his elbow. "Oh, hell," she said, voice even softer than before. "It's too late, isn't it?"

Too late to pull away from Bailey? Yes, it was.

He stalked toward the bike. "You know how to drive a motorcycle?"

"Had a license for years." Her hand trailed lightly over the handlebars. "My dad used to own a bike similar to this one. Nothing like riding it on the open road."

"You are full of surprises."

"You have no idea."

He wanted to know. He wanted to know everything about her.

"But it's your bike," Bailey said as she slid back, making room for him. "So you drive. I'll give you directions to Paul's office."

He eased onto the motorcycle, and then Bailey pressed close behind him. Her arms wrapped around his waist and he felt the light crush of her breasts against his back. Asher had the bike revving to life and when he started to take off, he told her, "Hold tighter."

She did.

The bike spun around, and they got the hell away from the scene.

ANA WATCHED ASHER vanish into the night. Typical Asher, going too fast and heading straight into danger.

Only this time, it wasn't a physical danger . . .

Oh, Ash. I heard the way your voice changed when you talked to her. I saw the way you looked at her.

For the first time in years, her brother was on the verge of losing his control. He always held himself so carefully in check, never allowed for any emotional entanglements because he didn't want weakness . . .

But he was in too deep with Bailey Jones. She could even see why those two had connected. Survivors, both with bloody pasts. They probably understood each other.

Or maybe . . . maybe Bailey *thought* she understood Asher.

You don't. I don't even understand him. I just know that he can be dangerous.

After all, a girl never forgot the sight of her brother killing to protect her.

Killing . . . and smiling.

"Where did they go?"

Ah, that would be Wyatt. The stand-up sheriff who'd also looked at Bailey with a little too much emotion in his eyes. Ana made a point of noticing stuff like that. She was no profiler, nothing at all like Sarah Jacobs, the crazy-on-target lady who profiled killers at LOST, but Bailey could read folks pretty well. She looked for undercurrents between people, little signs of emotion.

Because, in Bailey's experience, emotion was always key. Most crimes weren't committed coldly, no matter what the news wanted people to believe.

Cold-blooded murder? Not a thing. Passion was involved. Emotions.

The men who'd taken her and Asher had certainly been about emotions. They'd *laughed* while Ana bled. They'd loved the pain they inflicted. Sick, twisted emotions and—

"Where did your brother go?" Wyatt asked again. His hands were on his hips once more. Was that supposed to be one of his power stances? How adorable.

"I suspect they went to track down the not-so-good doctor Paul Leigh."

His eyes became slits. "You suspect?"

She rolled one shoulder in a careless shrug. *Suspect. Know. What difference does it make?* "Asher wanted to question this guy. I think he believes if you get to Leigh first, then he won't have his chance."

"This is an official investigation." Now he looked even angrier. "LOST has no kind of jurisdiction here. He needs to stay out of my way."

"LOST has a pretty good record when it comes to closing cases." She gave him a wide smile. "And as far as jurisdiction is concerned, a little bird told me that the FBI will be swooping in soon here. Seems they didn't like the news coverage and they want to make sure a serial killer isn't hunting in the area once more."

"A little bird?" He seemed to be choking a bit on those words.

She gave another half-shrug. "A bird, a LOST agent who happens to be former FBI . . . whatever you want to call it." Dean Bannon had been the LOST agent in question. While he might not work for the Bureau any longer, he still had a few reliable sources there—sources who'd tipped him off about agents who were fast-tracking their way to little Brevard. "If you don't move quickly," Ana warned him, "you may find yourself sidelined."

He yelled for Deputy Ben. The guy came running. Ana began to back away. She had some leads of her own to—

Wyatt's hand curled around her wrist. "Where do you think you're going?"

"Away from here?" She let her smile widen a bit more. Men were easy. Smiles often confused or disarmed them. She knew what she looked like. Delicate. Not a threat.

So wrong.

Many men had made the mistake of underestimating her. She liked for them to make that mistake. *It makes things so much easier for me. So go ahead, underestimate away.*

"What are you holding back?" Wyatt asked her.

Her eyes widened. "I have no idea what you're talking about."

He swore. "Yeah, you do." But then he jogged to the waiting patrol car. Obviously, the hunt was on for Dr. Leigh. His siren blasted as he and Deputy Ben drove away.

Ana squared her shoulders. She had her own stop to make . . . a little side trip back to the sheriff's station where she intended to charm her way into a look at the old Death Angel case files. LOST's profiler would be there first thing in the morning, and Ana couldn't wait to see if Sarah had any new insight into the serial killer. Maybe they'd compare notes.

CHAPTER THIRTEEN

ASHER BRAKED THE MOTORCYCLE AND SHOVED down the kickstand. The bike's snarling engine echoed in the empty parking garage. His gaze slowly trekked around the scene, noting all the dark corners and shadows.

Asher killed the engine.

"He's not here," Bailey said, voice tight. "Maybe Wyatt will have better luck."

Maybe. Or maybe the guy was in the wind. But if Paul Leigh was gone . . . *Then let's find out why the hell he's acting so weird.* And in Asher's mind, stalking a patient—yes, that shit definitely counted as weird.

Asher glanced over his shoulder at her. "How do you feel about a little B&E?"

"Breaking and entering?" She had on her helmet, but the visor was up and she looked so damn cute. "Are you serious?"

"Dead serious." Because he wanted in Leigh's office. That tell-all book? Asher suspected the guy had already started writing it, and he'd like to see just how many of those pages were filled with information from Bailey's life.

Bailey took off her helmet, frowning at him. "I've never broken into anything."

Why did that not surprise him? His fingers curled under her chin, and he just had to lean forward and press a quick kiss to her lips. "Sweetheart, if I don't get in that office now, Wyatt will come swooping in." Wyatt, or the FBI. Ana had already warned him that the Bureau gang was closing in. "If I want access to Leigh's files, then I need to get them now."

Her gaze searched his. "You mean *my* files, don't you?"

"Yes." Because he didn't want that guy using anything of Bailey's in that book.

Her gaze slid toward the elevator. "So we're not really breaking and entering . . . we're just taking what belongs to me."

If that was how she wanted to think of it . . . sure. Asher kissed her again. This time, he let the kiss linger just a bit. He was such a bad influence on her. "Simple retrieval mission," Asher murmured against her mouth. "I've done this dozens of times."

He stood near the motorcycle and offered his hand to her. Bailey put her helmet down on the seat but frowned up at him. "You've broken into an office dozens of times?"

"Enemy camps. Isolated foreign offices . . ." He shrugged. "Trust me, those were much harder to access than this place." A deserted office building would be a piece of cake. They'd be in and out in five minutes.

She put her hand in his and rose. "A retrieval mission." Bailey blew out a rough breath. "Okay, let's go retrieve."

Hell, yes. He brought her hand to his lips and kissed her knuckles. Then they were heading toward the elevator. Her steps were fast, and Asher saw Bailey glance over her shoulder a few times.

Obviously, she was a woman used to staying on the *right* side of the law. And Asher normally toed the line, too, especially since joining LOST, but . . .

But I can't let Leigh hurt her. I need to see his notes.

He pressed the button for the elevator. There was a soft *ding* just a moment later, and the two doors slid open.

"Oh my God!" Bailey jerked her hand away from his. She started to step forward.

Asher grabbed her, locking his hand around her waist. "Sweetheart, *no.*" The stench had his nose twitching. *Blood. Death.*

Blood on the elevator's walls. Blood on the mirrored glass. Blood on the floor.

And Dr. Paul Leigh lay sprawled on the floor, his head turned to the side, a long gash where his throat should have been.

"We have to help him!" Bailey cried out.

"There's no help that we can give him." One look, and Asher knew the guy was dead. His skin had already taken on that chalky color that came from death. Leigh's body was still, the blood starting to congeal around him.

He's been dead awhile. No way was this guy in front of Bailey's house, revving up his car less than an hour ago.

But Leigh's killer very well may have been there. *Did you kill the doc then take his ride? Were you coming for*

Bailey, only she was armed and ready for you? Fuck, but he didn't like this mess. And Bailey was still straining, trying to get free to help the dead man. "Sweetheart, we can't contaminate the scene," Asher said.

"Asher!" She yanked at his arm.

"The killer could have left evidence behind." He pulled her out of the elevator. The doors slid closed once more. "We have to get a crime scene team up here, stat."

Bailey had gone stark white. She shuddered against him.

"Sweetheart?"

She nodded. "Call Wyatt. I—I'm okay."

He eased his hold on her. Bailey slipped away from him. She put her hand up, supporting herself on the nearby wall.

"You're not going to faint, are you?" he asked as he fished out his phone.

"No." Her eyes closed. "I'm just trying not to vomit all over you."

"Good. Keep trying that."

Her eyes flew open.

He put the phone to his ear. Wyatt answered with a furious, "You found the bastard, didn't you?"

Asher thought of the blood-spattered elevator. "Oh, yeah, I found him."

"Where the hell are you?"

"His office. And—"

"Don't question him until I arrive, got it?" Wyatt's bluster cut through Asher's words. "Just keep him there."

"Trust me, the guy isn't going anyplace." Asher exhaled. "Leigh is dead. His throat has been slashed wide open."

Silence. *"Son of a bitch."*

Asher had rather thought the same thing.

"You're not still in the building, are you?" Wyatt threw at him.

Yeah, they were.

"The killer could be there! Get Bailey out! Get her safe! Get—"

"Leigh has been dead awhile, and from the look of things, the killer is long gone." He eyed Bailey with worry. She was taking deep breaths and still looking too green. But she wasn't vomiting. Good for them both. "I think he killed Leigh and then took his car, because the doc's body is here but his ride is missing."

And that killer went to Bailey's house.

"Stay with her," Wyatt ordered. "Every second, you got me?" His siren wailed in the background.

Like Asher needed to be told that shit. *No, I'm just going to walk away and leave Baily on her own to deal with this hell.* The fuck he'd ever do that. He shoved the phone back into his pocket and put his hand on Bailey's shoulder. "You okay?"

"No, I am really tired of death." She drew in a ragged breath and turned toward him. "I'm even more tired of finding bloody bodies."

Speaking of that damn body . . . "I'm going to open the elevator again."

"What? You said we couldn't contaminate anything!"

"I'm not." He didn't plan to touch anything. But he thought he'd seen . . . "I just need to look at something, okay?"

"Fine. Do it," she muttered. "Just . . . be fast, okay? I so don't have the stomach for this. I would make a shitty horror-movie star."

So said the woman who'd already survived a serial-killer attack. She kind of *was* horror-movie material.

He pressed the button on the elevator. *Ding.* The doors slid open.

The poor bastard was still sprawled on the floor and, if possible, the stench in there was even worse.

Asher leaned forward, craning his head. The killer had jerked down the back of Leigh's shirt—the fancy button-down was stained with his blood, but it looked as if part of the material had been cut away on his shoulder and—

I see you.

"Angel wings are on his shoulder," Asher said. Dark, deep lines and curves. Only this wasn't like the sloppy job he'd seen on Hannah Finch. This design was oddly compelling, and . . .

It looks exactly like Bailey's tattoo.

"The Death Angel never attacked men," Bailey said as her shoulder brushed against his arm. He looked down at her. Her lips were trembling, but her eyes were on Leigh's prone body. "That wasn't his MO."

"Since everyone says the Death Angel is in a grave some place, I think it's safe to say his rules aren't in effect any longer." The new killer was doing things *his* way.

They backed up a step and the elevator doors closed.

Bailey's shoulders slumped.

"Wyatt will be here soon," Asher said. "He'll have a team with him. They'll investigate this whole building and maybe we'll get lucky and they'll find a link to the killer."

"Maybe."

His jaw locked. "Leigh wasn't targeted by chance. He's connected to you too intimately for that."

Her hands twisted. "I—I know."

"We still need to see those files."

Her head whipped up. "What? You think we're breaking into his office? *Now?*"

"I think the authorities will be here soon. If we want to see those files, we have to move, and move fast."

She swallowed. Her shoulders rolled back. "You aren't going without me."

"No, sweetheart, I didn't plan on going anyplace without you." Once more, he offered his hand to her.

Her fingers curled with his. He felt them tremble.

"We'll take the stairs," Asher said.

"Uh, hell, yes, we will. *No elevator.* I may never want to take an elevator again."

Then they were pushing open the door to the stairs. They hurried up three flights until Bailey told him to stop. "This is his floor." Her voice seemed to echo in the stairwell.

Asher opened the door and the thick carpeting swallowed the sounds of their footsteps as they advanced. Only they hadn't gone too far when Asher realized . . .

Someone else wanted to see Dr. Leigh's notes, too.

Because the door to Dr. Leigh's office swung open. A fancy glass pane had been to the right of that door—and the pane was smashed now, shattered into a hundred pieces on the floor.

Shatter the glass, then just unlock the door. Not the most low-key of break-in techniques, but obviously, the previous intruder hadn't cared about being low-key.

Is that what happened to Dr. Leigh? Did he walk into

the elevator and straight into the person who'd just broken into his office?

"Why come in here?" Bailey asked as they crept forward. She tiptoed around the glass.

"Leigh was the self-proclaimed serial-killer expert," Asher said. "And I saw the news clips about him—he said he knew the Death Angel best." *Probably based on what he learned from you, sweetheart. He used you to build himself up and to create a profile for the Death Angel.*

Leigh hadn't been involved with the original investigation at all. Some fancy suit from the FBI had done the profile back then.

Wonder how Leigh's profile matches up with the Bureau guy's?

He eased through the open door, being careful not to touch the wood or the knob. Bailey followed his movements exactly, slipping inside ever so carefully. They walked through the small reception area. The door to Leigh's inner office was open, too—and inside, the place was chaos.

Papers were scattered everywhere. Files overturned. A computer smashed.

Asher gave a low whistle. "Definitely looking for something." And from the way the lamp had been thrown against the wall . . . *definitely pissed.*

"We aren't going to be accessing his files on that," Bailey said as she frowned at the smashed computer.

No, they wouldn't. But maybe LOST could get their techs to retrieve the data on it, provided Wyatt was in the mood to cooperate with his team.

And the filing cabinets were empty. The manila

folders were tossed everywhere. Every patient record that the guy had—they were all scattered around the office.

Scattered . . . but maybe that's to throw us off. In this chaos, how would we know if a file was missing?

"That one is mine," Bailey said as she stooped over a file that had been thrown near the trash. Sure enough, her name was neatly typed on the white label. She picked it up before Asher could caution her and started flipping through the material there. "'Delusional. Possible dissociative disorder'?" Her words seemed strangled. "'Can't handle the trauma so she's created a second victim. Guilt ridden . . . guilt that is still possibly tied to—'"

Bailey stopped reading.

"Bailey?"

"This is bullshit." She slammed the file closed. "And no one else is seeing this." She squeezed the file to her chest.

"He was wrong about you," Asher said slowly. "You know that. We found the missing victim."

She gave a jerky nod.

"He was wrong," Asher said again. "You're not delusional. You're not crazy."

"Damn straight I'm not." Her chin notched up in the air. "We've got my file—let's get out of here."

Fine. He started to walk forward. The toe of his boot pushed against another file . . . He glanced down automatically.

Carla Drake.

"I—I think I hear sirens," Bailey whispered.

Asher scooped up that file. *Empty.* Had the doc made

the file, hopefully, *anticipating* that he could woo Carla into his care? Into contributing to his book?

Or . . .

Was she a patient? Had she been seeing Dr. Leigh, too?

"Asher, let's go."

His gaze scanned that office once more. The files were everywhere. Maybe the paperwork that belonged in Carla's file was scattered on the floor, but he didn't have time to retrieve it, not then.

Because yeah, he did hear sirens. Probably not Wyatt, not coming that fast. The guy must have called for other units to come in.

Asher and Bailey hurried out of the office and back down the stairs. When they reached the parking garage, he took the file from her and shoved it into one of the motorcycle's saddlebags.

Her fingers caught his. "We're taking evidence." She bit her lip. "Asher . . ."

He squeezed her hand. "It's all right." What did she think? That he wouldn't bend the law for her?

He'd do a whole lot more than snatch up a file.

For Bailey, I'm realizing that I might do just about anything.

He was still holding her hand when the first patrol car rushed up to the scene.

RICHARD SPAWN CRACKED open his eyes. The light was too damn bright. An antiseptic smell burned his nose and he let out a ragged groan.

"Sir? Sir, are you in pain?"

He turned his head and saw a pretty little blonde leaning over him. Concern darkened her eyes. "You've just come out of surgery. Everything is going to be fine."

Hardly. That little bitch had stabbed him. *And* taken his camera. He had to find her.

That camera was his life.

"I'm going to increase your pain medication, just a bit . . ." She fiddled with his IV line, and a cold surge seemed to seep through his veins.

Hell, yes, that's the ticket. He smiled at her.

She patted his arm. "Just get some rest. You'll be good as new in no time. No major organs were damaged, and your vitals are stable now. You were a very lucky man." She turned to leave. He enjoyed the sway of her ass.

The door shut behind her.

Richard closed his eyes. Lucky? Maybe. He could spin this story. Say that he'd been the victim of a deranged attack. Say that Carla Drake was a menace. After all, hadn't she torched that building in Asheville?

Yeah, yeah, Carla was trouble.

He was the victim.

His breathing evened out.

I just need my damn camera back.

His eyes started to close. He started to let that sweet morphine take him away when . . .

"Authorities are still on the hunt for Carla Drake, a person of interest in an ongoing investigation here in Transylvania County."

The TV in his room was on. The nurse must have forgotten to turn it off when she left.

His gaze focused on the television screen, on the reporter with the too-perfect teeth who was delivering the story. *I know that bastard.* He and Dave Barren had once worked at the same station. Only Dave had risen up the ranks at double-time speed . . .

And Richard had gotten pushed to the tabloids.

"This county has faced the terror of a serial killer before." Dave gazed soulfully out of the TV. "Will they be able to survive again?"

I don't know, you little bastard. Let's just see. Freaking Dave Barren . . . *He's trying to take my story.*

Richard yanked out the IV.

CARLA DRAKE WATCHED the authorities swarm the nondescript office building. She hunched into the shadows, not wanting any of those swirling police lights to fall onto her.

As she stood there, she saw Bailey Jones walk outside. The guy—Asher—was right with her. Was he *always* at her side? Like some kind of freaking guard dog?

She needed to get Bailey away from that guy. That was the trick. To get Bailey alone. This whole mess was getting worse by the second, and Carla knew she had to take control back.

Before anything else happened.

She looked down at her fingers. Rock steady. And she'd gotten the blood off. Finally.

But her face was being blasted on every news channel. She was being hunted, like some kind of animal.

This isn't what I wanted. I just . . . I wanted the pain to stop. I wanted to escape. To put it all behind me.

She'd stayed in the shadows for so long. She'd minded her own business. Why hadn't Bailey just left her alone?

It was all Bailey's fault.

Bailey Fucking Jones.

Asher put his arm around Bailey's shoulders.

Move number one would be getting those two apart. Move number two . . . *Bailey, you and I aren't done.* Time for them to have a chat.

Time to bury the past. *Because I can't live like this any longer.*

WYATT MARCHED OUT of the parking garage fifteen minutes later, glaring at Asher and Bailey. Bailey's temples pounded as she stared at him.

"That isn't pen ink on his shoulder."

She blinked. She certainly hadn't expected—

"It's not a fresh tattoo, either." Wyatt crossed his arms over his chest. "That tattoo is an exact copy of yours, Bailey. An exact match to the tattoos that all of the Death Angel's victims had."

"You're sure it's not fresh?" Bailey asked, shaking her head.

"No. Hell, no, it's not fresh. No scabbing, no redness. It's healed damn fine. So what I want to know is . . . why in the hell did your shrink have that tat?"

"*That's* what you want to know?" Bailey rubbed at the back of her neck, trying to loosen the knots there. "Don't you want to know who killed him? Why?"

"The killer yanked down his shirt. The killer *wanted* us to see that tat. So I think the *why* is pretty obvious." Wyatt's jaw had locked down—hard. "It's still all about the Death Angel. Even in the ground, he is screwing with us. The guy is freaking *worm food,* and I'm dealing with this shit."

"You need to dig up the body." Asher's words were low, grim.

Wyatt jerked toward him. "What?"

"Whatever remains were pulled out of that cabin on the night you found Bailey, you need to have them exhumed."

"There was damn little left!"

"Yeah, but there was still *something*. Your ME couldn't figure out who the guy was, so give LOST a shot."

Wyatt rocked forward onto the balls of his feet. "Because LOST is just so on top of things? Way better than the FBI and a bunch of hick deputies?"

"Wyatt . . ." Bailey began.

"Actually, what I'm saying"—and Asher's voice was still mild—"is that our forensic anthropologist, Victoria Palmer, *is* the best in the nation. The dead speak to her, and if you want to see what the Death Angel might have to say . . . then let her look at those remains. I can have Viki here in hours. If there is any way possible for her to figure out that man's identity, she'll do it."

That sounded like one fine plan to Bailey. "We need her," she said, and there was no missing the emotion in her voice.

"What we need," Wyatt rasped, the faint lines around his eyes deepening, "is to find Carla Drake. *That* woman is a danger. You think I didn't put the pieces together with her, too? She could be the killer! Maybe she had some kind of psychotic break after her attack—that shit happens."

Bailey flinched.

"She sat in my office, as cool as you please, and gave

me no clue about all she'd been through. That woman is a manipulator. I want her in custody. She nearly killed you both and she *stabbed* Richard Spawn." He huffed out a breath. "And one of my deputies just found her name on a file up on Leigh's office. If she was his patient, hell . . . don't you see? It all ties together. *She's* the copycat."

She knew Asher suspected the other woman, too. Hadn't he said as much right before Spawn had appeared, bleeding out, at her house?

But . . .

"There's no need to dig up the dead." Wyatt seemed so certain. "My team is going to focus on bringing in Carla Drake. I want her in custody long before the FBI arrives."

Asher glanced down at his watch. "I'd say you only have a few hours to get that job done."

Wyatt stormed away.

Bailey blew out a rough breath. "Dammit! We do need Viki!" She focused on Asher. "Shouldn't he want closure, too? If your teammate really is that good—"

"She is," he said simply.

"Then maybe we can finally end that mystery. Figure out *why* that jerk went crazy and took us." She rubbed her arms, chilled. "It never seemed random to me. That's what Wyatt said, that the Death Angel had just grabbed victims that were convenient. But it didn't feel that way. It felt personal. *Like he targeted me. Like he wanted me to suffer.*"

"Bailey . . ."

Her gaze shot up to his.

"Let's go home," Asher said. His voice was so gentle,

it nearly broke her heart. "Wyatt isn't going to let us in on the investigation tonight. Sarah will be arriving tomorrow—and I'll make a call, telling Viki to come this way, too."

She nodded.

His knuckles brushed lightly over her cheek.

"You are safe," Asher said.

Her heart pounded too fast.

"You are not going to suffer, not ever again." He tucked a lock of Bailey's hair behind her ear. "I would not let that happen."

Neither would I. When she'd been in that cabin, Bailey had learned that life could come down to a pretty simple motto.

Fight or die.

She'd fought before. She'd do it again.

They got on the motorcycle. She wrapped her arms tightly around Asher's body. And the rumble of the engine was oddly reassuring as they shot away from that tomb-like garage. The wind whipped against her face. She hugged his body, taking his warmth and trying to banish the image of Paul's body from her mind.

All of that blood.

And his throat . . .

She thought of her scars. Of the way she'd been sewn back together in the hospital. How she'd stared at her reflection in the bathroom mirror and thought that she looked like Frankenstein's monster.

She hugged him tighter.

Asheville was soon behind them and the darkness of the mountains stretched up ahead. The stars glittered overhead. The twisting, turning road was empty. The motorcycle hugged all those curves. Slid into them so easily.

The bike vibrated beneath her. Fear wanted to push through her, but she remembered Asher's words.

You are not going to suffer, not ever again.

Bright lights flashed behind them. Still in the distance, but they glinted off the mirror on the side of his handlebars.

She looked back, instinctively.

The lights disappeared. The driver must have eased into a curve, or one of the dips created by the mountains. The road didn't just snake to the left and the right. It went up and down, a roller coaster ride.

The lights appeared again.

The other vehicle was coming closer.

Faster?

"Asher," Bailey whispered, then stopped. It was just another car. Driving on the same road. That didn't mean anything.

But . . .

She looked back once more.

The lights were gone.

She turned to the front. Her home wasn't that far away. They'd be back there soon enough. Asher's hands gripped the handlebars so easily, and he controlled the bike perfectly as they drove down those winding roads. The minutes slid past. The wind whipped against her.

And—

The lights flashed on again, glinting in the mirror. Only the lights weren't far away this time. They were right behind her. Blinding. Too bright.

The motorcycle weaved for just a second, but Asher instantly brought it under control.

Bailey looked back—

There was growling all around her. The snarls of an engine. The motorcycle. And the big, dark SUV behind her.

The BMW?

She couldn't tell—the lights were too blinding. The other vehicle was just a mass back there and *it was surging toward them.*

Bailey screamed and the motorcycle lurched forward at the same instant, barely missing a hard hit from the SUV.

"Hold on," Asher told her.

Yes, yes, that was *precisely* what she intended to keep doing.

He revved the motorcycle and they blasted forward fast. But the SUV behind them just kept coming. *Coming and coming and coming . . .*

She was looking over her shoulder, fear nearly choking her. She could feel the heat from the SUV's engine. It was going so damn fast.

"Can't outrun it," Asher said.

Why not?

"But I'll outmaneuver the son of a bitch."

Do it! Do it!

Then he slid right over the double white lines. The SUV followed them, but when Asher zigged and zagged—there was no way the SUV could match his maneuverability.

Another curve loomed up ahead, and just as they were about to reach it—

Another car. This one coming toward them. Asher jerked the motorcycle back into the right lane as the other vehicle gave a long, loud honk. He'd had to slow to take that curve, it was too tight and dangerous, and—

The SUV clipped the back of the motorcycle. The bike spun then, twisting and twisting, and it slid toward the side of the road.

Only there *was* no side there. Just a drop. A scream tore from Bailey as she felt her body being thrown from the motorcycle. She tried to hold on to Asher, but it was no use.

She was tossed into the air. For an instant, she could actually hear the wind whistling around her. Blowing through her ears, blowing—

She hit the ground.

Asher.

And the SUV . . . it was still coming . . .

CHAPTER FOURTEEN

ASHER'S HAND GRIPPED THE OLD TREE ROOT. Fucking hell, but that had been close. He hadn't managed to clear the motorcycle before it hurtled toward that drop—and he'd gone over the edge. At the last moment, he'd grabbed on to the twisting root—one that shot out from the side of the incline—and he'd saved himself from a plummet to a brutally rough death.

His breath sawed from his lungs as he began to hoist himself up. Something was dripping into his left eye, and from the pain he felt in his forehead, he figured that wetness was blood. Scratches covered his body and his left wrist hurt like hell.

But the pain didn't matter.

Getting back up to the top? Finding Bailey? *She* mattered. "Bailey!" He roared her name. "Bailey, I'm coming." She hadn't gone over. He knew that. He'd tried to grab her, but when they'd been hit, she'd flown away from him.

She was wearing her helmet. She's fine. She's fine.

Only . . . was she?

Because he didn't know where the SUV had gone.

They'd passed another car—the one that had been honking and had forced him back into his lane—but that car . . . had it kept driving? Did the driver even realize that they'd been hit by the SUV?

"Bailey!" He roared her name louder as the twisting root seemed to give way a bit beneath his grip. Oh, hell, no, he wasn't falling. Bailey needed him, and he would *not* let her down. His feet dug in and he heaved himself up. He crawled over the edge and then pushed to his feet.

The SUV was gone. Another car, compact, a convertible with the top down, had stopped about ten yards away.

"Bailey!" Asher shouted again.

"She's here!"

His head snapped to the right. A man was there, leaning over Bailey's prone body. For an instant, Asher's heart just stopped. She seemed so small. So fragile. So broken as she lay on the ground.

The man backed away from her. "I was afraid to touch her! What if she broke her neck or her spine or—"

Asher ran to Bailey and sank to his knees beside her. "Sweetheart?" She still had on her helmet. Her eyes were closed and she was breathing—he could see the light rise and fall of her chest. The convertible's headlights illuminated the scene.

"I called an ambulance," the guy said quickly. "That SUV that hit you—shit, it just tore out of here! I mean, man, I don't know what kind of game you two were playing, but that ain't safe on these roads—"

"No game," Asher bit out. "He was chasing us all the way. Trying to hit us." And he had.

Or . . . *she* had. Just who had been driving that SUV?

His fingers pressed to Bailey's throat. Her pulse beat in a strong and steady rhythm. "Sweetheart . . ."

"Buddy, are *you* all right?" The guy was obviously worried. "It looked like you went right over the side. I thought for sure you were gone."

Like he would leave Bailey.

She gave a low, ragged groan, and her eyelids flickered open. "Ash . . . er?"

He caught her hand in his. "Right here."

She started to sit up.

"No, baby, wait—"

But she was already up and groaning more. "What—*oh my God*. The SUV!" Then she was grabbing him. "Where is it? Where did it go?"

"Probably got as far from here as it could," their would-be rescuer said as he shuffled closer. "I mean, basically that shit was a hit-and-run. Guy must've been drunk."

Not drunk. Very carefully, Asher took off Bailey's helmet. The woman had jumped to her feet but she was weaving a bit. "Where do you hurt?"

"I don't think he was drunk." Bailey was staring at their rescuer. "I think he wanted to kill us."

Asher's gaze slid to the right. His motorcycle was somewhere down at the bottom of that drop. His bike— and Bailey's case files.

Shit.

"My head hurts and my back aches." Bailey touched Asher's shoulder. "But it's bumps and bruises. I'm fine."

No, what they both were was *lucky*. "Did you see the other driver?" Asher asked the man who was shifting nervously beside them. "Get any kind of glimpse of that person at all?"

"No, no, it was too dark and the guy never slowed down." He whistled. "These damn mountain roads are treacherous enough without crap like that. I mean, how much closer to death can you come?"

Asher stared down at Bailey.

I don't want to find out.

IT WAS CLOSE to two A.M. before Bailey and Asher finally made it to her house. They'd had to stay at the scene, talk to a furious Wyatt again, get examined by the EMTs . . .

And then they'd had to get a ride home in Deputy Ben's patrol car. They were getting way too intimately acquainted with that particular vehicle.

"Uh, are you sure you two are all right?" Ben asked, glancing back at them once he'd parked the patrol car in her driveway. "Maybe you should go to the hospital tonight."

Bailey's whole body ached, but a hospital visit was the last thing she wanted. Her bed? To crash? *Yes, please.* "The EMTs said we were fine." She would *not* think about the drop that had taken Asher's bike.

And had nearly taken him.

"Okay, if you're *sure*." He hurried out of the car and made his way to the back. He opened the door for her. When Bailey slid out, he leaned in close and said, "I'm sorry all of this is happening to you."

For some reason, his words made tears gather in her eyes.

"Doesn't seem fair," Ben continued gruffly. "You

survived. That should mean you're free and clear now, but someone is messing with you."

Yes, yes . . . someone was. "Thank you, Ben." She'd met him a few weeks after she'd been released from the hospital. Ben was the deputy that Wyatt had often sent around to run a patrol through her neighborhood. He'd been new to the area, but friendly. Always kind.

Asher followed her out of the car. "Thanks for the ride, Deputy," he said, offering his hand to Ben.

Ben gave him a hard shake. "Wyatt wants me to patrol until dawn, and I will. If I see anything suspicious, you will know about it right away."

They headed toward the house. When Bailey reached her porch steps, she glanced back. Ben was watching them, his head cocked to the side. She gave him a little wave and he inclined his head toward her.

Bailey unlocked her door. All three locks. She and Asher headed inside.

She paused a moment, realizing that something seemed . . . off.

Ben's vehicle cranked up outside. She heard the heavy vibration of his engine . . .

Something is off . . . something that I don't hear.

She didn't hear the steady beep of her alarm. Whenever she entered the house, the alarm should have started beeping until she went to reset it.

But the alarm *was* off. When she looked over, she didn't see the ready red light. Instead, she saw the green one . . . indicating that the alarm was—

Asher grabbed Bailey and pushed her behind him.

"Don't!" A woman's sharp voice cried out. "Please, don't freak out!"

Too late. I am so freaked.

"How the hell did you get in here?" Asher demanded. His hands were fisted at his sides as he watched the woman who crept from Bailey's hallway.

The woman who was Carla Drake.

Carla shifted from her left foot to her right. "I . . . I know a little bit about electronics. Had a boyfriend once who used to install security systems. He told me how to get around them." She looked down at the floor. Her hands were behind her back. "Actually . . ." Now her voice turned bitter. "He taught me how to break into houses, too. Only one day he got caught and sent to prison, and I walked away." Sorrow flashed across her face. "Tim wasn't made for prison. He died just a month into serving his time."

Asher took a step toward her. "Sheriff Wyatt is looking for you now."

Bailey saw the other woman's head whip up. "It's out of control."

Breaking into my house definitely qualifies as out of control.

Carla focused her gaze on Bailey. "I just need you to listen to me, okay? Listen to my side of things."

"You tried to kill us at your shop," Bailey said. Was Ben gone? If she ran outside, could she flag him down?

"I just wanted you to leave me alone. When Wyatt called me in . . . I knew my secret was about to come out. I—I'd planned to disappear. The fire seemed like the way to go. After all, it worked last time . . ." She took a tentative step forward.

"Stop right the fuck there!" Asher barked.

Carla flinched.

"Show me your hands. *Now.*"

Why was the woman hiding her hands behind her back? *Don't have a knife, don't—*

Carla brought her left hand around to the front and—she was holding a camera?

The little bitch . . . took my camera.

"I'm sorry about the fire. I—I thought you were both out. That it was safe. I never meant for you to be hurt." Tears trickled down Carla's face. "I just wanted to be left alone! I don't want to be in the news. I see what they do to people—I don't want that! Don't want to be followed every moment. Or—or stalked, like she was." She lifted the camera toward Bailey. "Did you know he was watching you? All those times?"

Bailey's stomach knotted. "What are you talking about?"

Carla took another step toward her.

Asher immediately tensed.

"I'm not going to hurt her—not either of you!" Carla nearly yelled. "That's not why I'm here." She gave a wild, bitter laugh. "She saved me. You get that, right? Maybe she doesn't remember everything, but I do." She gripped the camera tightly. Tears tracked down her cheeks. "I was screaming for help. He was above me, wearing that stupid black mask. I couldn't get free and he was saying that *no one* would ever come for me. That I would die there, with him."

Bailey edged closer to the other woman.

Carla stared into her eyes. "You came flying into the room. You just—you just attacked him. You didn't know me. You knew *nothing* about me. You heard me screaming and you came." She shook her head, as if still trying to understand that. "He grabbed you. I saw him throw you to the floor. Your head hit so hard. I heard the thunk. I wondered if you'd died right then, but then I saw you still trying to fight him. His hands went to your throat."

Bailey felt Asher's stare on her.

"I could have done something then," Carla continued, her voice dropping. "Grabbed for his knife. Jumped on *him* from behind. I—I didn't. Instead, I ran. I ran right out of that cabin, and I left you there. I didn't look back. I—I saw the light in the distance. I recognized the damn area . . . I'd been there enough when I was younger. I saw the light and I ran and I ran until I got to my grandfather's cabin." Her lips pressed together. "I thought he'd help me, but he was *dead*. Dead in that cabin. I don't even know how long he'd been that way! That stupid freak the Death Angel had grabbed me on my way to visit him—I was so fucking close!—and I hadn't realized until then that my grandfather was *gone*." A sob shook her frame. "He was dead, and I was alone out there. With *nothing*."

The woman's pain was palpable. "Carla . . ." Bailey went toward her.

Asher grabbed her arm. "Bailey . . ." A warning was in his eyes and in his voice. *"Don't trust her."*

Couldn't Asher see that she was in pain?

"I left you," Carla said again, the words ragged. "I'd been gone so long when I thought about you again. When I realized . . . *she died in my place*."

A shiver slid over Bailey.

Asher's hold tightened on her.

"I wasn't going to let anyone else die," Carla said,

determination making her shoulders snap up. "I got the supplies from my grandfather's place. Once upon a time, he had a job with the fire department in Asheville. Was even an arson investigator for a while." She shook her head, as if banishing a memory. "I knew what to do. He'd *told me*. All about accelerants. Fire triangles. Shit . . . growing up, the guy was obsessed with fire. So there was nothing I didn't know." She huffed out a breath. "I went back to the Death Angel's cabin and I . . ." Her eyes closed. "I'm so sorry, Bailey. So sorry."

"Why?" Asher demanded. "What else did you do to her? I mean, you'd left her already. Was there something fucking else?"

"Asher," Bailey warned. "Stop."

Carla's tears fell harder. "I saw him throw you into the grave."

Oh, God.

"I thought you were dead then. I swear, I did. Or I—I would have tried to get you out. But you weren't moving and he just tossed you in . . ." She took a frantic step toward Bailey, the camera still gripped in her hands. "That was when I snuck back in the cabin. He was busy with you—"

"He was fucking burying her," Asher snarled.

"I went back inside." Carla's voice had gone small. Whispery. "I set the place to burn. I—I waited until he came inside, and then I hit him from behind. I knocked him out and he *burned* with that terrible cabin."

And Bailey had woken up in that grave. "If you hadn't stopped him, he would have come back and buried me alive." Had he done that to his other victims? Tossed them in the ground and covered them up while they were still breathing?

Please, no. Don't let them have suffered that way.

"I knew what it would look like . . ." Carla licked her lips. "You were the hero, I was the coward. The one who left. I knew what the news would do to me, so I didn't say a word. I ran . . . as far and as fast as I could, and I hoped that no one would ever find out what I'd done."

Bailey's chest was so tight it hurt to breathe. "You were a victim, too."

Carla cocked her head. "Was I? Because I killed that night. I killed him, and . . . when I ran the first time, I thought for sure I'd killed you, too." If possible, her voice dropped even more as she hoarsely said, "So what does that make me?"

"I don't know what it makes either of us." Bailey pulled free of Asher and put her hand on Carla's thin shoulder. "Survivors?"

Mascara smudges stained Carla's cheeks. "How can you even touch me? After what I did to you?"

"Because it wasn't a normal situation. It was life or death and it was hell and it was *insane*. I can't judge you for that—"

"The guilt is eating me alive."

"Carla—"

"I never understood, not until now," Carla said, shaking her head frantically. "Now I know what it's like." She thrust the camera at Bailey. "So I'm making things right."

Bailey took the camera, frowning.

"You're on that camera. Richard Spawn's camera. So

many shots of you. And I—I don't think you always knew when he was photographing you."

Bailey pressed the button to turn on the camera. Asher was at her side, staring down at the images as she began to scroll through them.

"Some are just of—of your house. I recognized them right away because . . . I've been by here before. Probably a dozen times. Never got the courage to come inside."

She saw the shots of her home. Her house . . . with Asher's bike parked outside. A scene that appeared to have been taken at night.

Bailey pressed the button once more.

Her house . . . she and Asher were on the steps. Heading inside. She recognized the outfit she had on—clothes from the first night she and Asher had met. The night when . . .

"He was the asshole who tried to run us over," Asher snarled.

She hit the button to scroll through the pictures, faster and faster . . .

And she saw a parking garage. The parking garage she'd been in at the LOST building.

Asher was with her in that pic. Leaning in close. They almost looked like lovers. *Even though we weren't, not then.*

Not then.

"He was stalking you," Asher said. "The son of a bitch."

She hit the button again. Again.

More photos. Photos from weeks ago. Months ago. Photos of her at the supermarket. At the library. Photos of her going into Dr. Leigh's building.

He was there, all that time, watching me. Always watching, and I didn't even know it.

"I think he's dangerous," Carla whispered. "He came at me . . . he grabbed me, and I reacted. I just . . . I needed to stop him. I *had* to stop him." Her eyes were big, tear-filled. "I know Wyatt will probably toss me in jail. That's fine. I get that but . . . but you needed to be warned. That reporter is *dangerous,* and I'm afraid that he's after you."

RICHARD SPAWN SLIPPED from the hospital. He had to put his hand to the wall because the damn drugs were still in his system. The morphine had given him a nice, sweet ride for a time, but he had to get back to business.

Lying up in a bed wasn't his style. Not when there was more to be done.

Too much more.

So he took a minute to gather his strength and maybe he staggered a bit when he cleared those emergency room doors, but no one tried to stop him. Car crash victims were being rushed inside. Everyone was swarming around them. That trauma scene gave him the perfect time to get out.

He sucked in a deep breath of that cold night air and glanced around. The last time he'd seen his car, it had been at Bailey's place. The deputies had probably towed it somewhere, and shit, wasn't that a pain in the ass?

But he needed transport. He needed to get out of there and get back to work. The Death Angel copycat was a story too big to miss, and with the shit Carla Drake had pulled . . .

Maybe I'll just be the story this time.

Smiling, he pulled out his phone. He knew one reporter in the area who'd really want to hear what he had
to say. *One glory-hound bastard who won't be able to
resist.*

Richard Spawn wasn't done. Not by a long shot. He
put the phone to his ear and waited for the asshole he
needed to answer the phone. He propped up against a
car, wincing in pain.

Answer the damn phone. Answer—

"Hello?"

"Dave? It's Spawn. Look, man, I've got a story for
you. One you're gonna want to hear—"

"Doubt it," Dave Barren drawled. "Your sorry ass
hasn't scooped me in years."

Bastard. "Oh, yeah? Come to the Montgomery Hospital, and I will blow your mind with what I know
about Carla Drake."

Silence. *Dumbass, just come on.*

"You're lucky," Dave finally said with a long and
too-loud sigh. "I happen to be close. Be there in fifteen
minutes."

Hell, yes.

I am still in this thing.

DEPUTY BEN LOADED Carla Drake into the back of his
patrol car. He was oddly gentle with her, asking again
and again, "Ma'am, are you okay back there? Ma'am,
do you need anything?"

Wyatt paced near the car. "Shit, Ben, this isn't some
fucking field trip! The woman is an arsonist!"

Ben stiffened. He looked back at Wyatt. "She's also
a victim."

Victims could be dangerous, too. Asher knew that all too well. He stood near the other men, his body still heavy with tension. It was such a fucking long night—*would it never end?* They'd called Wyatt, told him all about Spawn . . .

But the reporter was in the wind. The guy had seemingly vanished from the hospital. None of the staff remembered seeing him leave. They'd just found his empty bed.

And now Carla was being taken into custody. She'd fallen silent, her skin too pale, her eyes appearing almost dead.

"Do you think . . ." Wyatt muttered, "that you and Bailey can manage to make it until dawn without more hell coming your way?"

It wasn't a promise he was ready to make. "Not like we're the ones looking for trouble."

Wyatt raked a hand over his face. "It just keeps finding you, right. I got that." He glanced toward the patrol car. "What's your take on her?"

Bailey was inside the house, and he was glad. He'd wanted Bailey away from the other woman. "I don't trust her, not for a second."

"Hell."

"She *left* Bailey to die up there, you know that."

"I do." His hand fell. "But I also saw the number that the Death Angel pulled on those other women. So I figure Carla Drake had to be out of her mind with fear when she ran."

"I'm sure that's what any good lawyer will say about all her actions." The cover-up, the fire, the attack on Spawn . . .

"Post-traumatic stress." Wyatt nodded. "She probably needed as much therapy as—" He broke off, looking uncomfortable.

But Asher knew what the guy had been about to say. *As much therapy as Bailey.* The guy needed to stop worrying about Bailey. "Maybe Carla Drake *got* that therapy," Asher said. "And that's why her name was in Leigh's office."

Once more, Wyatt turned to look at Carla. Deputy Ben had leaned in to check on her again. "You think she could be a killer."

"I think she left Bailey to die. I think she stabbed a reporter, and I think she's not the damsel in distress that she seems to be." He glanced back at the house. "Bailey looks at her and feels empathy. I look at her—"

"And you see a threat."

Hell, yes, he did. And he saw dots that he could connect . . . dots that did not lead down a good path. His gaze returned to the sheriff. "How long was she in that cabin with the Death Angel? She is a tattoo artist—shit, isn't that something right there? All of the victims had tats. Did she have one, too?"

Wyatt hesitated. "I don't know."

"People are not always who they seem to be," Asher said flatly. "I sure as hell wish you would let our profiler take a turn with her. Let Sarah talk to Carla when she arrives."

Wyatt hesitated, but after a long, tense moment, he gave a grim nod. "Fine. I want to know the truth, too." He straightened his shoulders. "I'll use the profiler . . . and the forensic anthropologist you told me about before."

Asher blinked in surprise. Talk about a complete 180.

"You think I *want* to have killers running loose here? I need to make this area safe, and if LOST can help, then I'm going to stop being a dick about it and use your resources." He turned away from Asher. "Get some sleep. Try *not* to nearly die again before dawn."

"Can't make any promises on that," Asher called after him.

The sheriff threw up a middle finger and climbed into the car. Deputy Ben hurried to join him.

Asher stood outside a moment longer, watching their car drive away. The night air had turned colder, so much colder, and the chill swept over his skin. He heard the door squeak open behind him and then the soft pad of Bailey's feet on the steps. He turned to face her.

She stood on the edge of the porch, her arms wrapped around her stomach. The porch light fell behind her. She stared at him in silence for a moment, then said, "It's really been one hell of a night."

Serious understatement.

He walked to her. Slowly. He climbed the steps. Curled his finger under her chin. And Asher leaned forward and kissed her as gently as he could.

Hell of a night. But she's safe. And that's all that matters. He kept having flashes of her on that dark mountain road. Her body sprawled, her eyes closed. "Let's go inside."

She nodded.

He brushed a kiss over her lips once more.

When they went inside, he locked the door and heard her reset the alarm.

"It's an illusion, isn't it?" Bailey asked him.

He lifted his brows.

"The alarm. The safety here. Carla got right inside. No trouble at all. If she could get to me, then I guess anyone could." A shiver slid over her. "All this time, I thought this house was my haven. But it was a prison, too, and I'm seeing that now."

He headed closer to her.

"How long did it take you," Bailey asked him, "to get back to living a normal life?"

"I don't really know what normal is." He shrugged. "And I figure it has to be overrated anyway."

Her lips curled. "I want to believe her."

"I know you do."

"I want to think that she . . . she's like me. She was scared and lost and now she's finding her way back."

He waited.

"But I tried to remember more about that night, just like you said. I tried to remember what he was doing to her and . . . I don't think he used his knife on her. When I came into that room, he was leaning over her. His hands were on the bed. But . . . *no knife.*"

"Bailey . . ."

"And there was someone else in her shop. I *saw* him, but she's acting as if she set that fire all by herself."

Yes, she was.

"Lies. Truth. How can you tell the difference?"

Especially when someone was very, very good at lying. *I think Carla is good at telling lies.*

"I see it in your eyes when you look at her," Bailey continued. "I know you think she's not a victim. You think she was in on it all, don't you?"

He weighed his words. Thought about being tactful. *Screw it. She doesn't need protecting or coddling. Bailey needs truth.* "Her grandfather's cabin was right there. She was a tattoo artist." He gave a bitter laugh. "Fuck, yeah, I do think she was involved. I think she might have even been helping him all along."

Bailey paled. "She was screaming that night."

Are you sure about that?

"I don't want you to doubt me. Not you, Asher. *Not you.*"

He caught her hand in his. Pressed a kiss to her knuckles. "Wyatt gave the go-ahead for Sarah to talk with her. If Carla is holding back secrets, Sarah is the one who can figure them out."

"Sarah . . . you said she knew killers."

"Yes."

"But what about victims? Does she understand them? Because maybe *you're* wrong, Asher. And I'm right. Just like I was before. Maybe Carla needs help and not another prison."

CARLA DRAKE PULLED in a slow breath. It wasn't her first time in the back of a patrol car. If only. But she'd had far too many run-ins with cops during her life.

The young deputy, Ben, had been so nice. His hands had been gentle when he cuffed her, his voice soft.

Ben was driving now, keeping his eyes focused straight ahead, but Wyatt kept glancing back at her, frowning. She figured he was the kind of guy who didn't appreciate it when someone pulled one over on him. Too bad.

She was a pro when it came to manipulation. She'd had to be.

How else would I have survived? It wasn't as if she'd ever lived some fairy-tale life.

"Got to say . . ." Wyatt finally spoke, breaking some of the stark tension in the car. "I'm mighty curious. Do you have a black tattoo of angel wings on your shoulder, too?"

She swallowed. "No, I don't." She had eleven tattoos, exactly eleven. And not a single one of them was of angel wings. "I guess the Death Angel just didn't get time to mark me." Such a lie—she carried plenty of marks from him. They were just beneath the skin, where no one else could see them.

"How long were you with him?" Wyatt asked her.

Ben just kept right on focusing on that road.

"Too long," Carla muttered.

"How long?"

She leaned back in her seat. "Maybe I should get a lawyer." She figured there was no *maybe* about it. She was in deep, and she didn't want to drown. "So I think I'll just shut up until I have that legal representation, okay?"

He grunted. "Asher Young thinks you're a killer."

The car accelerated a bit.

"Know what I think?" Wyatt asked her.

I don't really care. You're not overly important to me. Nothing really seemed that important any longer.

"I think he's right."

Asshole. You don't want to see just how bad I can be.

THEY DROVE PAST a deputy's car, and Richard hunched down in the passenger seat of Dave's vehicle. "Shit! Those fuckers are everywhere!"

Dave laughed. "Dude, what's your problem? You scared of cops now?" He drummed his fingers on the steering wheel. "I mean, shit, you got another restraining order on you or something? I remember what happened to you in Miami, when you got too close to that pop star. Her bodyguards thrashed your ass when they found you hiding in her house."

Richard's hands clenched into fists. "I was just getting a shot."

"You were breaking and entering." Dave turned into a small motel's parking lot, one that was right on the edge of Brevard. "And I've heard you've been pulling some questionable shit with Bailey Jones, too." He flicked the ignition switch, turning the car off. "When are you ever gonna learn, man? You push too hard, and you get burned." But then Dave gave a low laugh. "Though I did have to drag your ass out of a hospital parking lot. So maybe you *did* get burned already."

"You always were a jackass," Richard snapped at him.

"A jackass who gets better stories than you . . . and doesn't have a wall of restraining orders. I think your problem, man, your problem is that you can't stay objective. You always fall for the ladies on the other end of your lens. You can't do that. Don't see them as people. They're just objects. A paycheck."

Richard growled at him.

"Now about that scoop . . ." Dave tapped his fingers on the steering wheel. "It had better be worth dragging my ass out of bed at this time of night."

"It's worth it, all right," Richard fired back at him.

"Then tell me."

"Carla Drake." He said her name quickly, nodding.

"She's the one who stabbed me. That bitch put a knife in my side."

And Dave laughed harder. "That . . . that woman on the run? The other Death Angel victim?" More laughter.

Rage pulsed in Richard.

"Were you stalking her, too? Shit, Spawn, you have to get control of yourself. No, no, wait—*you'll* be my story." And he reached into the backseat and pulled out his camera. "Bet you didn't think I even still carried one, did you? I can take some shots." He smirked. "But I'm still better than you." He popped off the lens cap and started snapping pictures. The flash lit up the car, and Richard lifted his hands automatically, trying to cover his eyes.

"The washed-up hack who got too close to his stories . . ." Dave taunted. "Attacked by the victims he hounded."

Richard fumbled, managed to unlock the door and then grab the handle. He nearly fell out of the car.

Dave's taunting laughter followed him. No, *Dave* followed him. The guy had come out of the car and was still snapping pics.

"You make me so fucking sick," Dave said. "I'm a real journalist. You're a tabloid paparazzi wannabe. You *think* you've got some scoop? Bullshit. I should have known better than to buy your lie."

"Stop it," Richard rasped.

"Got another story to tell me? More news to make that hospital pickup worth my time?"

"Yeah, yeah, I do . . ." Richard told him. He shoved his hand down into the borrowed hospital coat that he wore. A coat he'd stolen on his way out of that place. *I didn't just take the coat . . .*

Dave paused, the camera raised near his eye. "Don't keep me in suspense."

Richard lurched toward him. The parking lot was empty and the rage beat in his head. "I know who killed Hannah Finch."

"Yeah, we all know. Some Death Angel wannabe fool. Some dickless jerk who thought he'd grab attention by copying—"

Richard yanked out the scalpel that had been in his coat pocket. It sliced right across Dave's throat, sending a spray of red into the air. "I killed her."

Dave was choking, sputtering, and falling to the ground.

"Shit," Richard snapped. The guy was *loud*. No wonder the Death Angel had preferred that cabin. People needed to die in isolation. Then no one else would hear them. He bent down and clamped his hand over Dave's mouth, hoping no one in that motel had heard the guy.

Dave bucked beneath him. His blood was *everywhere*.

Nausea rose in Richard, but it wasn't as bad as it had been before, with Hannah. And when Dave stopped bucking, that sweet blast of power poured right through Richard's veins.

Hell the fuck yes.

He lifted his hand, and then he saw the camera, just lying there, covered in blood. "I hope you didn't break it, you jackass," he said, grabbing for it. His fingers swiped at the blood and he checked the lens.

Perfect.

He focused on Dave. Snapped a shot. "I know just what this image needs . . ." He rose and went back to the car. Dave's bag was still in the backseat. He rifled through it, found a pen, clicked the top . . .

And knew he'd be getting some seriously perfect pictures.

CHAPTER FIFTEEN

I WILL FUCKING . . . KILL YOU."
   The words yanked Bailey from sleep. Her eyes flew open and she realized—
I'm on top of Asher again.

Because they'd slept together. Just slept. They'd collapsed in her bed after the night from hell, and during those restless hours of sleep, she'd curled on top of him again.

Now his hands were tight around her waist, his fingers biting into her skin. And his voice—

"You will hurt. You will scream. Fucking . . . kill you."

Her heart slammed into her chest. "Asher, wake up."

"You won't hurt her again. Never. Fucking . . . kill you."

"Asher." He was scaring her. Not because of his words but because of the pain she heard in them. He wasn't talking to her, she knew that. He was in a dream, a nightmare. But Bailey had lived through too many of her own tortured dreams, and she didn't want him lost in that pain.

He's back in time, back in that terrible memory of

when he was taken. "Asher, wake up!" Now she was nearly shouting. Or as close to shouting as it was possible for her damaged voice to get.

His eyes flew open. For an instant, he stared almost blindly at her, as if he didn't know her, as if he'd never seen her before.

And his hold didn't ease.

"Asher, you're safe." She leaned forward and pressed a quick kiss to his lips. "You're with me. Your sister is safe. You both got out okay."

A shudder worked along his frame. And he groaned. "Bailey . . ."

She kissed him again, so carefully, wanting to comfort and soothe.

His hands weren't so tight on her anymore. His fingers caressed her skin, as if trying to take away any pain he'd given her.

"So sorry," he rasped against her mouth. "This is why . . . shit, why I don't usually stay with a lover . . ."

She pushed up on her elbows. "Because you have flashbacks?"

"Because I don't want to *hurt* anyone." So rough and angry. "Sweetheart, did I hurt you?"

"No, no, of course you didn't."

But he shook his head. "There is no *of course* about it." Then, still being so careful, he slowly lifted her up and put her down on the other side of the bed.

She didn't like that. Didn't like him *moving* her away. Bailey grabbed the sheet and pulled it up to her neck. "Asher?"

He rolled from the bed. He was wearing his sweats again, and she saw the hard, taut muscles of his back as

he paced toward her window. "Bailey . . . I hurt someone before."

That stark confession hung between them.

She shook her head, denying what he'd said. "The
men who took you deserved—"

"*She* didn't deserve it."

The breath she sucked in seemed to chill her lungs.

"I got stuck in a stupid nightmare, flashback, or whatever the hell you want to call it. She reached for me in
the night, and I . . . pushed her back."

"You pushed her?" Who? Who was he talking about?

His eyes squeezed shut. "I pushed her too damn hard.
I didn't even know it was her. I was caught up—I was
back *there*. She was trying to shake me awake, and
I reacted—I shoved her back, and when she came at
me again, I grabbed her, pulled up my hand, and I was
inches away from hitting her when I realized what the
fuck I was doing."

Oh my God.

"She ran the hell out of there and didn't look back."

He wasn't looking at *her* right then, and Bailey
needed Asher to see her. "How old were you?"

"Eighteen. Two weeks later, I enlisted. I had to do
something with all the rage inside. It was spilling out,
onto everyone near me."

"Asher."

His shoulders stiffened.

"Asher, look at me."

Slowly, he turned to face her.

"And you never spent the night with another lover
again? You're telling me this happened when you were
eighteen, back with a lover that long ago?"

"I never stayed the full night. Not until you."

Oh, wow.

"It was easy enough to leave when I was on deployments. Didn't exactly have stable relationships then."

She inched toward the edge of the bed, and Bailey kept her sheet up.

"In the military, I learned not to sleep too deeply. You always needed one eye open, and the shit I was doing then—it kept my mind busy. The flashbacks stopped. I even started to think . . . after all this time . . . maybe I'm better. That's why I risked it with you . . . but I shouldn't ever put you at risk."

"It was *one* nightmare, Asher. Just one."

"All it takes is one time to hurt someone." His gaze was tormented. "I'd never want to hurt you."

"You *didn't*. All that's happening in this town now— it's stirring up your past, that's all. So you remembered. You didn't hit me. You didn't hurt me. I'm fine."

His jaw tightened, and Asher marched toward her. He reached for the sheet and pulled it from her in a quick move.

"Asher!"

"You have red marks on your hips." Pain whispered in his voice. "I did that."

"I'm sure I've left far worse marks on you during sex."

"This wasn't during sex! And I *never* want to hurt you!" He dropped the sheet on the floor. "I'm such a fucking fool. Wanting what I can't have. What I shouldn't have. Because no matter what I pretend, I'm not good enough. I'm dangerous. Being a SEAL didn't make me better . . . it just taught me how to kill easier.

How to be a stronger weapon." His hands had fisted. "I am *no* good for you."

He spun and headed for the door.

She sat on that bed, wearing an old oversized college T-shirt. Her eyes narrowed on his muscled back. "Liar."

He stopped.

"You think I don't understand you? You think I don't see what's really happening here?"

His hands rose and gripped the door frame.

"You're scared." That gave her hope. "Because for the first time in forever . . . you want to stay the night with someone. With *me*."

"Bailey . . ."

"And you are afraid you'll hurt me. I do get that. And guess what? I'm afraid I'll hurt you, too."

He whipped back toward her.

"I have nightmares. Flashbacks. Sometimes I even get up and walk around the house in my sleep."

He swallowed. "Not the same—"

"Isn't it? When I was in the hospital, a nurse came at me when I was waking up. She was just checking my vitals but I—I didn't know that. I saw a stranger and I freaked." Her laugh held a slightly wild edge. That was okay, she felt wild. Wild and raw and as if she were fighting for something very, very precious. Something that she couldn't let slip away.

I'm fighting for him. I'm fighting for us.

"I broke her wrist."

He took a step toward her.

"I felt like shit after I did it. She was screaming. I was screaming, and I knew I'd done something terrible."

"You didn't mean it!" Another fast step toward her. "You were traumatized! You were—"

She climbed from the bed. Her toes curled into the hardwood. "So were you, Asher. *You* were a victim, too, and sometimes, victims strike out."

Every muscle in his body seemed to have gone tight. "I don't want to strike at you."

"You didn't today. You were calling out in your sleep. I tried to wake you up. Next time, I'll do it a different way."

"There can't be a next time. *I can't hurt you.*"

"Shutting me out will hurt me." Her chin was up. "I'm not some woman who likes pain or abuse, so get that shit straight. That isn't who you are. You're a protector. I knew it from the first. So you made a mistake when you were eighteen. I am so sorry that happened. I'm sorry that you ever hurt." Didn't he get that? She wanted to take his pain away, too.

"I am not that girl," Bailey continued, fighting to keep her emotions under check. "And you are not the same person you were then." She had to go to him. Bailey rushed across the floor and wrapped her hands around his arms. She felt the steely power of his muscles beneath her touch. "I feel safe with you. I *am* safe with you. And we can work through anything together."

"Bailey—"

"Do you trust me?"

"Yes." Ragged.

"Good. Then trust me to know my own mind. I wouldn't stay with a monster. With some man who hurt me. You aren't that kind of man. You're good. *You are good,*" she said again when he shook his head, her voice angry. "And we can work through anything, if we're together."

"I want you."

She smiled at him, feeling those words pierce right through her. "I want you, too." Not for a moment, not for an hour. Longer, so much longer than just a night.

"What if . . ." His head lowered toward her. "Bailey, what the fuck will we do if I love you?"

He said the words almost as if they were an accusation. As if she'd committed some terrible crime by making him even think of love. Her poor, lost Asher. He'd killed before for family that he loved. And . . .

"I would do anything for you," Asher said. "This isn't about you being a client. This isn't about any case. It is about you. About me needing to make sure you are protected."

"Do you think I would do any less for you?" He had to stop seeing what he'd done as some kind of twisted crime. He'd taken a life . . . to save a life. "You think I wouldn't kill to protect you? In an instant, I would do it."

And she pushed onto her toes and kissed him. She needed Asher to see—she wasn't afraid. He had to get past that bullshit fear he had. The two of them together—they had a chance for something special. She wasn't going to let that chance escape.

She'd fight for him. He'd better fight for her.

His hands curled around her body and he brought her in closer. Held her against his bare chest and his mouth opened on hers. Bailey's tongue swept past his lips. When he gave a ragged groan, that sound just turned her on.

Want me. Need me. Don't give a fuck about anything else.

The world was full of enough fear. She'd rather have something else.

She'd rather have him.

She could feel his arousal growing. His sweats didn't exactly provide him with a lot of coverage, and the hard heat of his length pushed against her.

"Bailey . . ." he whispered against her mouth. "What am I supposed to do with you?"

She had a few ideas.

She kissed his chest. Licked his nipple. He'd taken such care with her during their lovemaking, making her go wild. She figured this was her turn to show him that he could let go completely. She wanted him to know she could handle everything he had to give her.

So she bit his nipple. A light nip. Her hands slid down his abs. Freaking insane abs. She licked, she kissed, she gave him another quick bite.

"Aw, baby," he said, voice deeper than before. "You don't have to—"

"I don't *have* to do anything," Bailey stressed as she let her nails slide over his belly button, then down, down . . . "But there are some things I *want* to do." A lot of things. With him. Only him. She looked up and gave him a smile that felt wicked. "Maybe I've been saving up."

His jaw was rock hard. "I need you . . . so much, Bailey Jones."

"Let's see if we can make you need me even more."

And she pushed down his sweats. The long, heavy length of his shaft thrust toward her. Her fingers curled around him, pumping that cock, feeling the heat in her hand. She loved the way he thickened even more beneath her touch. Her thumb stroked the broad head, and when a light bead of moisture wet her skin, Bailey sank to her knees before him.

She took his cock into her mouth.

"Bailey!"

Her tongue stroked over him. She sucked on him, enjoying the surge of power she felt as she pleasured him. *I'll make that need go even higher. You won't fear anything but not having me.*

His hands curled around her shoulders.

"Sweetheart . . ." The one word was guttural.

Her hand was around the base of his shaft, controlling the thrusts of his erection. She eased back, just licking the head, and Asher shuddered. "No, Bailey, too much—"

Was there such a thing with them?

But then he moved fast, lifting her up and carrying her to the bed. He put her down quickly and she gave a little bounce on the mattress. Bailey almost laughed but her lashes lifted and she saw the fierce intensity in Asher's gaze.

Her laughter froze in her chest. She lifted her arms toward him, and he sank onto the bed with her, wrapping her up tight, holding her close.

He yanked down her panties a few moments later. She was wet and more than ready, and when Asher thrust into her, they both gasped with pleasure.

This. This is what I want. What I crave.

They rolled on the bed. She was on top of him now, her knees digging into the mattress as she rose and fell above him. The slow glide of his cock into her was pure heaven.

Their hands threaded together. They just seemed to fit.

Her heartbeat raced, her breath heaved out, and her hips moved, faster and faster as her release bore down on her.

When she came, Bailey leaned forward and kissed him. The orgasm ripped through her, surging so hard that she thought she might just collapse on top of him.

But Asher pulled her close. Held her. His hips surged into her once more and he shouted her name.

She was smiling as her eyes opened. Smiling when she saw the pleasure on his face. The same raw, wild pleasure that she felt.

It had never been this way with another lover.

And Bailey knew . . . it never would be again.

A FUCKING WALK of shame. That was what he was doing right then.

Royce Donnelley pulled the motel room door shut behind him. It was early, barely six A.M., and hopefully no one would witness him leaving that shit hole.

He'd drunk far too much last night. Mostly because he'd been pissed at Bailey. Bailey . . . who'd moved the hell on from him. That stupid news story—talking all about Asher Young as if the guy were some kind of hero.

Asher the Asshole was getting a ton of glory and fame.

That should be me. He was the one who deserved the attention, not Asher. And Asher had no damn business being with Bailey.

She's still beautiful. I bet the scars have faded so much more now.

Bailey had always been different from the other girls.

Royce looked back at the closed motel room door. He'd spent the night with some blonde—hell if he could remember her name. He'd thought she was fucking gorgeous during the night but when the rising sun had fallen through those broken blinds, his beer goggles had come off fast.

Now I need to get out of here. Before someone I know sees my ass.

He hunched his shoulders and hurried toward the parking lot. His car was there, sticking out like a sore thumb. The fancy BMW gleamed in the morning light.

I have got to get out of here.

His steps quickened even more . . .

And then the smell hit him. Rotten, horrible, strong enough to make him gag. Shit, shit, shit but he was *not* going to come to another one of these motels again. He hated bringing the women back to his place because then it was harder to kick their asses out.

And once they know where I live, they always show up again.

But this stench . . . Royce covered his mouth with his hand and slogged forward. He went around the back of his vehicle and then—

Saw the blood. The body. The man who'd just been tossed there, dropped right next to his precious new BMW.

For a moment, Royce couldn't move. He stared at that guy, sick, oddly fascinated. *My first dead body. So this is what it's like. A body . . .*

Oh, fuck.

He was going to have to report this. He'd have to call the authorities. They'd want to know why he'd been at the motel, who he'd been with. Shit, this wasn't going to look good for him.

Maybe I can call in an anonymous tip. I mean, that guy is dead. It's not like an ambulance has to rush to his rescue. It's obvious he's fucking gone.

He pulled the keys out of his pocket. Yeah, yeah, an anonymous tip. That was the ticket. Exactly what he needed to do.

Then a woman screamed, from right behind him.

He yelled, too, and spun around. The blonde was there, with mascara streaked under her eyes, with her hair shooting in a dozen directions, and her dress from last night falling off her right shoulder.

"What did you do?" she screamed at him.

What? Like he'd *done* this shit?

Then she whirled away and ran, screaming at the top of her lungs. And nearly every single door at the motel flew open.

And all eyes locked on him.

Son of a bitch.

"Someone, help!" he said, hoping he sounded appropriately concerned. "A man has been killed!"

CHAPTER SIXTEEN

ASHER FIGURED IT WAS TIME FOR INTRODUCTIONS. "Sheriff Wyatt Bliss, I'd like for you to meet Dr. Sarah Jacobs and Dr. Victoria Palmer, associates of mine from LOST who have agreed to help with the current investigation."

Wyatt stood up from behind his desk. The guy's face appeared haggard, as if he hadn't slept a single bit last night. He hurried around the desk, offering his hand first to Victoria—"Ma'am"—and then to Sarah. "Heard a lot about you both."

Sarah gave her slow, measured smile. "Please don't believe everything that you hear."

Sarah was a bit of an enigma to Asher. The woman played her cards very, very close to the vest. She was cool and controlled and the way she knew her killers— *downright scary.*

As for Victoria . . . she was more open. She smiled more, and lately, she'd been laughing more, too. She worked with the dead because she wanted to give them justice; he understood that about her.

But Sarah . . .

Hell, maybe I just haven't gotten too close to her be-

cause I'm afraid the lady will profile me. He knew it was a fear that many at LOST possessed.

"I know better than to do that," Wyatt said, exhaling. His uniform was rumpled but his badge gleamed. He glanced over at Asher, frowning. "Where's Bailey?"

The guy's voice still did it. Still hitched a bit when he said her name. He really needed to stop doing that shit. "She's talking with Deputy Ben." Actually, he thought she was trying to get the scoop on Carla from the fellow. When he and Bailey had arrived at the station, they'd quickly learned that Carla was in lockup, being held in the back.

Wyatt nodded. He blew out a long breath. "The FBI will be here in . . ." He looked at his watch. "One hour. I've been told I control this case for one more hour, and only that long, so . . ." He rolled back his shoulders. "Dr. Jacobs, you are welcome to go in and try talking with Carla Drake. Be advised that she has requested a lawyer and that you need to fully identify yourself to her. She may say *nothing* at all to you . . ."

"She may," Sarah agreed with a slow nod.

"But I want *someone* to try and make a run at her while there is still time." He leaned against his desk. "As for getting the Death Angel's remains exhumed, that's going to take time. I'll pull all the strings I have on that, but until I get news, Dr. Palmer, you are welcome to go and have a one-on-one chat with our ME, Dr. Moore. Maybe Moore can give you something to use there." His gaze slid toward Asher. "See? This is me, cooperating, because I don't feel like playing political shit. I feel like stopping this madness before anyone else gets—"

A knock on his office door cut through Wyatt's words. Frowning, he straightened away from his desk just as Deputy Ben poked his head inside.

"Sorry, Sheriff," Ben said quickly. "But we just got a report of a body found at the Jensen Motel. Guy's throat was slashed, from ear to ear."

Wyatt's eyes closed briefly. "Not another one."

"I can come with you to the scene," Victoria said quickly.

Right—dead bodies—totally her area of expertise.

Wyatt's gaze zeroed in on her. "Yeah, yeah, come with me." He turned his head toward Asher. "I trust that you're going to keep staying close to Bailey."

Hell, yes, he was.

"Right. Okay." Wyatt marched back around his desk and took out his gun. "Let's get moving then, Dr. Palmer."

WHEN BEN RUSHED away to talk with Wyatt, Bailey used that time to slip down the now unguarded hallway that led to the holding cell. Only one prisoner was back there.

Carla Drake.

She was curled up on the cot, her body facing the stone wall. Her black hair trailed behind her on the old pillow. She looked defeated and so very small as she lay huddled in the fetal position.

Bailey's fingers curled around the bars. "Carla?"

The other woman stiffened. "They locked me up. I—I knew they would but . . ." If possible, her body curled in even more. "There's something about being a prisoner again. I—I can't take it."

Bailey's heart hurt for the other woman.

"I'm sorry," Carla whispered hoarsely. "So incredibly sorry for what I did to you."

"You were terrified." Her hands tightened on the bars. "I swear, I understand."

Carla glanced over her shoulder. "No, you don't."

"Ms. Jones!" Ben's horrified voice had her jumping. "You shouldn't be back here!" He locked his hands around her shoulders and then stopped, as if uncertain of what to do.

Bailey pulled away from him. "Does she have to be locked up like this?"

Ben looked miserable. "Sheriff's orders." He bit his lip. "You can't be back here," he said again, voice softer, sadder.

"I know. I just—" *Wanted to make sure she was okay.*

"Go, Ms. Jones," Ben told her firmly.

Bailey squared her shoulders and stepped away from the bars. That was when she noticed the other woman, Sarah. Asher had introduced them, briefly, when Sarah and Victoria first arrived—they'd all met up right outside of the police station.

Bailey felt nervousness surge through her as she once again met Sarah's gaze. *Why do I feel this way with her?* Everyone knew about Sarah's father, Murphy the Monster. Sarah Jacobs had grown up with him, had *learned* about killers from him.

Was that why Bailey felt so tense when she was near her?

Or . . .

Am I afraid of what she'll see in me?

Sarah gave Bailey a small, fleeting smile. There was sympathy in Sarah's eyes. The same sympathy she saw when so many people looked at her.

Everyone still sees a victim.

She was more than that. Bailey peered back at Carla. They both were.

"Ms. Drake," Ben called. "There's someone here to see you."

Carla was staring at the wall again. "Is it a lawyer?"

"No, no, he's coming in real soon. This is Dr. Sarah Jacobs, and if you don't want to talk to her—"

But at Sarah's name, Carla had rolled over. Her gaze locked on Sarah, and a moment later, she jumped to her feet and hurried toward the bars. "I've heard of you."

"And I'd like to learn more about you," Sarah said simply.

Carla licked her lips. "I'll talk to her. Only her. I want everyone else to leave."

Well, that was something. Bailey sure hadn't expected Carla's quick agreement to a chat with Sarah. Ben put a light hand on her shoulder. "Come this way with me, Ms. Jones."

She let him lead her away from the holding cell, but Bailey glanced back once more. She sure wished she could hear what Carla had to say to Dr. Sarah Jacobs.

"Ms. Jones . . ." Ben sighed. "There's something you need to know. I got called away because another body was found."

Her eyes widened.

"And the guy who found the body? It was your ex, Royce Donnelley."

CARLA STARED INTO Sarah's eyes. She'd thought about this woman before. Her story had made an impression on Carla years ago. As a teen, Sarah had turned in her own father. She'd lived with a killer for years, but managed to escape. *To walk away.*

I did that, too.

"What was it like?" Carla asked her, tilting her head to better see Sarah through the bars. "Living with him all those years? Knowing that he was killing all that time?"

"Guilt ate at me constantly," Sarah told her after only a small hesitation. "Even as a child, I hated what he did."

Hated it but . . .

"Tried to kill myself. Tried to stop him." Sarah sighed. "And I failed at both attempts."

For a minute, Carla couldn't breathe. Her lungs had gone too tight. "I didn't know—"

"Most people don't know about the suicide attempt. That didn't make the headlines."

"Why are you telling me?"

"Because I want you to trust me. So I'm telling you my secrets . . ."

"And you think I'll tell you mine." *Think again.* It wasn't going to work that way for her. Carla was focused on one thing . . . survival. She was living for herself now. She kept being torn, conflicted about Bailey. But in the end, she'd done the right thing, hadn't she?

I gave her the camera.

So maybe that would even the scales between them. Now she could move on. *I can look after myself.*

Only . . .

I'm thinking too much in here. Remembering too much. Feeling too much. And she needed that all to *stop.*

Sarah was dressed in black dress pants and a light, soft-looking sweater. Her hair was styled perfectly, her makeup minimal. She looked elegant. She looked professional. She hardly looked like the child of a serial killer.

"What happened the first time you saw him kill?" Carla asked her.

Sarah's eyelids flickered. "I . . . heard him the first time. Heard her, actually. Her screams."

Carla flinched.

"But he told me it was just a bad dream. I believed him. After all, he was my father. His job was to protect me and keep me safe. And he'd never lied to me before."

"Not that you knew about," Carla muttered.

"Right. Not that I knew about." Sarah's voice was soft, almost gentle.

Carla inched a bit closer to the cell's bars. "Did you ever think you'd be like him?"

"Only every day."

Oh, hell, but this woman was good. "You're better than he was."

"He?"

"I saw a shrink." Her lips twisted. "I thought it might help me. That the guilt would stop eating me up if I just talked to someone . . ." Her words trailed away. "It didn't help. *He* didn't help. He just made everything worse. He made *me* worse, and that shouldn't have happened."

"The shrink you saw . . . was it Dr. Leigh?"

"Surprised he hasn't come in here," Carla muttered.

"He can't come. He's dead."

Carla's lips parted. She let her eyes widen.

"He was found killed last night. One of my associates, Asher Young, actually found the body."

"Asher and Bailey."

Sarah's eyes had narrowed. "Yes."

Tread carefully. "They . . . they always seem to be together." She licked her lips. "I guess it's good that she has someone like that—someone there to be with her."

"How do you feel about Bailey?"

I want to kill her. I want her to forgive me. I just want her to vanish. Looking at Bailey . . . hurts.

Because Bailey had done the one thing that no one else had *ever* done.

She was going to die for me. She fought . . . for me.

And everything changed then.

"Asher noticed that Dr. Leigh had a tattoo," Sarah said. "Black angel wings. An old tattoo, from the looks of things."

"An old tat of those wings?" Carla thought about that. "Why the hell would he have that?" Her heartbeat kicked up but her voice stayed calm.

"Maybe because he was obsessed with the crimes. He was penning a tell-all book on serial killers. Perhaps that tat was his way of paying homage to the killer."

She nodded. "Yeah, maybe. Twisted as fuck, though." A bead of sweat slid down her back.

"Or maybe . . ." Sarah's voice was still mild. Easy. "Maybe he *knew* the Death Angel. From what I've gathered so far, it seems Dr. Leigh has long been interested in the work of serial killers."

Carla was missing something. "Did you know him? Leigh, I mean?"

"I did," Sarah said, surprising her. "He tried—on more than one occasion—to get me to participate in some of his studies. He even wanted me to make arrangements to get him access to my father."

"Your father . . ." Now this was scary shit. "He escaped prison, didn't he? I heard that maybe he died in a fire, but no one knows for sure. Maybe he got out . . ."

Sarah's eyelids flickered. "You do know a lot about me."

Carla shrugged. "I read the papers. Follow the news. Same as everyone else."

Sarah nodded. "My father did escape. And, yes, there was a fire."

"He died?"

"A fire . . ." Sarah continued as her head cocked to the left. "Just like there was a fire at the Death Angel's cabin."

Carla's heart slammed into her chest. *Stay cool.* "I did that. I wanted to make him go away." Her head leaned closer to Sarah. "Did you do it, too? Did you want to make your father go away?" Because the details had been sketchy and—

"My father tried to save me. He was a twisted, sick man, but in his way, he cared for me. And no, I didn't do it to make him go away. I wanted my father in prison. I didn't want to watch him burn."

Silence.

Carla's breathing hitched. *Oh, shit, oh, shit . . .*

"Is there anything else that you'd like to ask me about, Carla?" Sarah asked her softly.

"I—I'm tired. I don't really want to talk anymore." Her shoulders hunched and she turned away.

"I'd like to ask you one more question," Sarah said.

Carla gave a grudging nod.

"When did you give Dr. Leigh that tattoo? Was it before or after you became his patient?"

For an instant, Carla's mind went completely blank. *I took the papers from that file. I destroyed the computer. No one knows. No one . . .* She tried to figure out what to say and then, when the silence stretched too long, she realized . . .

Not saying anything . . . that's the answer Sarah wanted.

She risked a desperate glance at Sarah.

"That's what I thought," Sarah murmured.

Hell. Her jaw clenched as she gritted out, "I want a lawyer."

"Good. You definitely need one."

"ARE YOU ALL right, Ms. Jones?" Ben asked her.

"I'm fine." She gave him a weak smile. "And how many times do I have to tell you . . . you can just call me Bailey."

He nodded. "Sorry, I . . . you shouldn't have been in there with her."

"I know." Her hands twisted. "That's not going to get you in trouble, is it?"

"I don't think so. But . . . don't do it again, okay? Don't—"

The main door to the station opened and two reporters rushed in. Their cameramen were right on their heels.

"Hell. I told them to all stay outside." Ben pushed her toward Wyatt's office. "Go in there while I take care of these guys."

She hurried toward the office, but before she could go inside, Asher was there. "Broke the rules, huh?" he murmured.

"Guilty." But at least she didn't flush while she said it.

He opened the door for her. "You heard about the new body?"

"And about the fact that Royce found it." Of all people . . . Royce.

He followed her inside the office. She hurried toward Wyatt's window and peered outside. "It's like a feeding frenzy." And once those reporters got news of the latest victim, they'd be swarming even more. Or maybe they already *had* gotten the news, and that was why two had burst inside the police station.

"It's not adding up," Asher told her.

Frowning, Bailey turned toward him. "What isn't?"

"Every damn thing about this case." He started to pace. "I feel almost as if we're getting hit from multiple sides. There's the killer who went after Hannah. Who left that camera on our doorstep. Then there's the SUV that keeps coming after us—an SUV that just seemingly vanished."

She wrapped her arms around her stomach. "It will turn up. There's an all-points bulletin out for that thing."

"I get the feeling that SUV could be at the bottom of a ravine someplace."

The way Asher's motorcycle was? Bailey flinched.

"I have to know," Asher said softly.

She licked her lips. "Know what?"

But he stalked toward her. "Bailey, they have a crew en route to get my motorcycle. Someone may find those files that were in the saddlebag. *Your* files. I need to know why you wanted them to stay hidden—I need to know so I can protect you. Back you up. *Take care of you.*"

She whirled to stare out of the window. "You like me."

"What?" His hand curled around her shoulder and he forced her to turn back and face him. "Trust me, sweetheart, *like* doesn't quite cover it."

"I like the way you look at me," she whispered. "The way you see me, and not anything else."

"I will always see you."

She wanted to believe that. "I was actually a patient of Dr. Leigh's even . . . before the abduction." Most people thought that she'd started seeing him after, to deal with all the trauma, but . . . no. *Before.* "My parents died when I was eighteen, and I'd been a patient of his, on and off, since then."

"I'm sorry about your parents," he told her softly. "I'm sorry, it's—"

"It was my fault." Stark. Painful. So cutting.

"What?"

"My fault they died. The guilt . . ." She shook her head. "Oh, my God, but the guilt would not stop, no matter what I did. It ate at me." Six months after her parents had died, she'd already lost thirty pounds. She'd been sick, heart and soul sick, and she'd let everything go.

Nearly myself.

"I was in the car when they had the accident. I was so stupid." *A careless kid.* "I'd been drinking at a party. I shouldn't have done it. I *know* I shouldn't, but I'd just graduated and I wanted to celebrate. I'd never had alcohol before, and I drank too much. I got so sick . . ." Her eyes squeezed shut. "I called them to come and get me. They did. *They always did things like that for me.* My dad didn't yell. My mom just told me to sit tight. And I sat out on that porch, vomit on my clothes, and I waited for them. They were coming to save me, again."

His fingers squeezed her shoulder.

"They arrived within thirty minutes. I climbed into the backseat. It had started to rain." The story was coming out, rapid-fire now. She'd never forget the patter of the rainfall and the slow slide of the windshield wipers. "We were almost home, going around one of those long, twisting curves, and my mom lost control." A tear slid down her cheek. "She'd looked back at me. One minute, she was asking me if I was all right, and the next . . . she was screaming. *I* was screaming. The car flew off the road and slammed into a tree."

He pulled her into his arms. Held her tight. "That was an accident. Just a terrible—"

"We were all still alive. At first."

"Bailey . . ."

"My dad was pinned. My mom . . . part of the tree had gone through the windshield and into her chest. But she was alive. Talking. I wasn't hurt at all." Her laughter hurt her throat. Such bitter, tortured laughter. "I tried to get them out, but the metal was twisted and none of our phones worked. I told them I would walk to town and get help. That I would be back for them, I *promised that I would be back for them*."

He was silent.

And she couldn't stop the words, not anymore. "I'd walked for maybe ten minutes when I heard the explosion."

"Jesus Christ."

"Sometimes, I can remember smelling the gas. At least . . . I think I can. I had to know gas was leaking, right? I mean . . . I must have known. I must have smelled it at the scene, but I left anyway." That was one of the things that tormented her. "The car ignited. They *burned* to death, and when I got back, all I saw was the flames."

"It wasn't your fault."

"I left." That was the simple fact. "I could have tried harder. I could have found a crowbar—we kept one in the trunk, I just . . . I forgot about it. I could have used it and I could have gotten my dad's door open. I could have *saved* him. I could have saved them both." Each word hurt her. "But I didn't. I walked away. They died."

He pushed her back. She thought he was going to thrust her away but he tightly gripped her shoulders and stared into her eyes. "That's it, isn't it, Bailey? That's why you couldn't leave Carla. Why you still don't blame her for anything that happened at that cabin."

"Asher—"

"You literally *couldn't* leave her, could you? You already carried a lifetime of guilt and it wouldn't let you out of that cabin."

The door flew open behind him. "Asher!" Sarah's voice was excited. "We have got to talk. You aren't going to believe—" She broke off, apparently taking note of the scene before her. "Is everything okay in here?"

No.

To Sarah, it probably looked as if Asher were in the middle of shaking Bailey. His hands were wrapped tightly around her shoulders and Bailey felt the wetness of her tears on her cheeks. "It's not what it looks like," she managed to say.

Asher's right hand rose and he carefully wiped away her tears. "It wasn't your fault." His words were said clearly. Firmly. "Your parents died in an accident, and if you *had* stayed there instead of trying to get help, you could have died, too."

Or I could have saved them.

"You think I haven't second-guessed myself? You think the guilt doesn't nearly choke me some days?" He never looked away from her as he spoke. "Why didn't I break loose from my ropes sooner? Why didn't I save Ana *sooner?* Why didn't I manage to convince those twisted bastards to hurt me, and not her?"

She could hear the ticking of the clock on Wyatt's desk.

"You can't change the past, and if you use it to beat yourself up again and again"—his fingers tucked a lock of her hair behind her ear—"then, baby, all you get are new scars. New pain. And, eventually, you have to let that pain go or it destroys you."

"Have you let the pain go?" Bailey asked him.

"There's something else I'm holding tight to right now instead," Asher told her.

Me. He's holding on to me. Her lips trembled as she stared up at him.

"Um . . . okay . . ." Sarah cleared her throat. "Obviously, you two are working through some . . . big . . . issues right now. And normally, I'd leave you to that."

Bailey and Asher both turned toward Sarah.

"But you need to know about that woman in there." She jerked her thumb over her shoulder. "Carla Drake is *not* who you think she is."

"She was the other victim," Bailey said, shaking her head. "I thought you knew—"

"I'd stake my professional reputation on the notion that Carla Drake was a participant in the Death Angel's crimes."

Bailey's jaw dropped. But Asher didn't even jerk in surprise.

"The tattoos," Asher said.

Sarah nodded. "I'd say they were her work. That would be why the authorities could never track down the tats—she wasn't working in the business any longer, but she still had her machines. She did the work. They were looking for a male tattoo artist, so she slipped right by their radar."

"She was screaming," Bailey said. "She killed him. She—"

"Her questions were wrong." Sarah said this with a sad smile. "I'm sorry to tell you, Bailey, I know you thought she was . . . like you. But she isn't."

"'Her questions were wrong'?" Bailey repeated. "I don't know what that means."

"She's fascinated by my father. Not repelled. Not just curious. She knows all about him."

"Most people know about Murphy," Asher said.

"This is different. *She's* different. I believe she was

involved with the Death Angel, intimately. I think he was the controlling force in their relationship. He manipulated her. Used her. She *saw* what was happening. She saw him kill—"

"How can you know that?" Bailey asked, her heart squeezing in her chest "You can't just talk to someone and *know*—"

"She wanted to know what it was like the first time I saw my father kill."

Bailey blinked. Okay, that was morbid, but . . .

"Not the typical question I get asked, especially by a crime *victim*. But Carla had a few other questions. She wanted to know if I killed my father. If that stopped the guilt for me . . ."

Bailey glanced back at Asher. "Carla has already confessed to killing the Death Angel."

"Confessed, yes, Asher told me that." Sarah tapped her foot on the floor. "But why hasn't she said more about him? What he looked like? I mean . . . you may not remember because he was choking you into unconsciousness the only time you saw his face."

Bailey flinched.

"Sorry," Sarah muttered. "I get . . . I'm better with killers. I say the wrong things with victims." She cleared her throat and Bailey's gaze slid back to her. "You don't remember, but I think she does. And she's deliberately withheld that information. *Why?* To protect him somehow?"

"There's no reason to protect a dead man," Bailey said.

"Exactly." Sarah's eyes gleamed. "You only protect the living. You protect the living . . . *and human nature is always to protect yourself.*"

CHAPTER SEVENTEEN

THEY DIDN'T BEAT THE NEWS CREWS TO THE little motel. Wyatt swore when he saw the flock of TV vans—and he knew they'd probably already snapped plenty of footage. *Shots of the dead man. To blast all over TV.*

"They have no conscience," he muttered. "None at all."

Beside him, Victoria Palmer shifted a bit in her seat. "They think they're doing their jobs."

He turned off the ignition. "Bullshit. They think they're getting a scoop. *If it bleeds for them, it leads.*" He knew the old press motto.

He jumped out of the car. He'd already called the ME, and the black van pulled up right behind him. Two other deputies were there, too, and with a curt gesture from Wyatt, they ran to push the reporters back.

The dead guy hadn't even been covered up. Yeah, okay, maybe someone had been trying to preserve evidence or—

Or maybe it just made for better news to show the guy all bloody.

"So glad you're here," Royce Donnelley announced

dramatically. A blonde woman in a rumpled cocktail dress stood behind him. "This poor man needs justice!"

Wyatt rolled his eyes. Royce was such an asshole. Why Bailey had ever dated the man, he had no clue. But Royce had sure left her fast enough when she needed him the most.

Ran right out, didn't you?

What a stellar guy.

Wyatt knelt near the body, aware of Victoria close behind him. A wave of surprise had him glancing back at her. "I know this man. He's a reporter. Dave Barren." Wyatt had talked to the guy just yesterday, giving him a brief sound bite for his six o'clock report.

Maybe someone didn't like your story, Dave.

"The Death Angel is killing again," Royce said, voice deep and carrying easily to the reporters. "Don't you see the tattoo on him?"

A tattoo that was already smudged. A tattoo that was also a real shitty job, much like the one that had been on Hannah Finch.

He rose, peering around the lot. Where the hell was the desk clerk? If there was a dead guy in the parking lot, the freaking desk clerk should have been out there.

I want to find Dave's car. But right then, the vehicle catching his attention most . . . "That your BMW, Royce?" Wyatt asked him.

"Well, yeah, but . . ."

"Want to tell me where you were last night?"

Royce backed up a step. The blonde woman put a protective—and possessive—hand around him. "He was with me," she said, her voice nasal. "We hooked up at Ballers around six, and then we came here." Her smile stretched. "All night."

Jesus save me. "Someone tried to run Bailey Jones off the road last night." He tapped his thigh. "The driver was in a vehicle very similar to that one."

Both Royce and Leigh drove BMW SUVs. He already had an APB out for Leigh's vehicle. He figured it had to turn up, sooner or later.

Hopefully, sooner. Before someone else gets hurt.

But the fact that Royce drove the same make and model car—only his was a dark blue and Leigh's had been black—that made him wonder . . .

Had Bailey's ex-lover gotten pissed enough to come at her last night? And he was just using the woman in the sagging dress as an alibi? It would have been easy enough to slip away from a sleeping partner and then come back to the motel. "You sure he was here with you *all* night?" Wyatt asked the woman.

She blinked and the scent of booze drifted to him as she staggered a little closer. "I . . . think so."

Bullshit. He was betting she remembered very little from the night before.

Before Wyatt could push her harder, Royce surged toward him. "Is Bailey okay?" Royce asked, his eyes widening with worry. "Can I see her? Does she need me?"

Idiot. Bailey hardly needed the guy who'd been screwing the flavor of the night. He turned away—and saw Ana Young standing in back of the crowd.

Ana Young was a woman you didn't miss easily. Actually, he thought she was pretty fucking unforgettable.

The ME had brought his bag forward and was bending to examine the body. Victoria watched him for a moment, then sidled closer to Wyatt. "Want me to tell you what I know?"

Uh, hell, yes. He nodded, but directed her back toward his car and away from some of those eavesdropping reporters. He noticed that Ana started making her way toward them.

"I know your killer is a male, probably around five foot nine, maybe five foot ten, and he's left-handed."

Wait, what? She knew that already?

"It's based on the victim's wounds," she said, shrugging. "A right-handed killer would have slashed the vic's throat from the left to the right. That's the normal angle of attack for a righty."

He glanced back at the body.

"But you can see . . . the depth of the wound is deepest on the *right* side, then it slashes back and is most shallow on the left side, indicating that we are after a left-handed killer."

Had Hannah's wound done the same thing? He couldn't remember, but he would make damn sure Victoria had access to that body ASAP. *Yes, she'd told me about five sentences and I'm impressed by her.* Maybe he was easy to impress or maybe she was just a hell of a lot more on her game than Dr. Moore.

"And the way the wound is located there . . ." Victoria added with a nod toward the body. "It's not angling up, or down, but is rather straight on . . . telling me there wasn't a large difference in height between the killer and the victim."

She was good.

"The blood-spray pattern indicates that a vehicle must have been here." She pointed toward the empty parking space. "See the spatter? It's missing a huge chunk. So I'd say there was a car here, and the killer just hopped in it and drove away. Based on the appearance of the body and the lividity that I see, that was several hours ago. Definitely would have still been dark then, so no one else would have even noticed the blood stains on the car." She tapped her chin. "But in the bright light of day . . . unless the killer has cleaned the car off . . . folks will sure start noticing now."

CARLA DRAKE FOCUSED on keeping her breathing nice and easy. She'd known that she'd be locked up. Going to Bailey Jones, giving her the photos—she'd had to do it.

There was nowhere else for me to run.

With Bailey Jones . . . she'd had two options.

Option one . . . *Kill her.* Bailey's death would have permanently gotten her out of Carla's life. Only . . . when she'd gone after Bailey, when she'd taken that SUV and slammed into the back of Asher Young's motorcycle . . . she'd felt no pleasure.

The guilt was just worse. So much worse.

She eased out a slow breath.

But it wasn't worse when I killed him. No, when she'd gone after the manipulative bastard who'd ruined her life, she'd felt good. Strong. *Vindicated.* Her eyes squeezed shut.

Two options. Kill Bailey Jones . . . or help her.

So she'd tried to help. She'd given her the camera, even though it meant giving up her freedom. But being in that cage . . . being trapped . . .

This is what they all went through. I let it happen.

She opened her eyes. Stared at her hands. She could

almost see the blood there. Did others see it, too? Carla thought that, maybe, Sarah had.

Smart Sarah Jacobs.

She knows what it's like. She knows what I'm like.

Talking with Sarah Jacobs had been a huge mistake.

But the worst mistake I ever made? It was stepping foot inside the office of Dr. Paul Leigh. And I made that mistake five years ago. Five long years.

He'd been in her head since then. The great doctor. The one who wanted to *help* victims.

Such a load of shit.

She heard the shuffle of footsteps coming toward her. Carla lay on the cot, pretending to be asleep. If that was Sarah again, she'd just go right on pretending.

"Are you okay, ma'am?" It was Ben's voice. Gentle. Careful. Always so careful.

She curled in a little tighter.

"Ma'am?" And then she heard the jingle of his keys. He was putting them into the lock. The metal groaned when the door opened.

She still didn't move.

Where can I go? I'd always be hunted. There's no point . . . Will this guilt ever end? How do I escape?

Ben put his hand on her shoulder. "Ma'am . . . what can I do to help you?"

She sucked in a deep breath and did the only thing she could. Carla rolled over toward him, knowing that tears were in her eyes. "I'm sorry," she whispered.

He frowned at her.

And she saw that he was still wearing his gun. That it was low on his hips. Right there for her . . . so very close . . .

Her hand flew out toward it. She grabbed the handle—
His fingers closed around hers. Their eyes locked.

She knew she wouldn't get out of there. Not alive. And, maybe, maybe that was the way things were supposed to be.

Maybe that was the way the guilt would finally end.

THE BLAST SEEMED to thunder through the whole police station. Asher immediately ran for Wyatt's door, yanking it open and rushing toward the holding area.

He knew the gun blast had come from back there. Knew that—

Gunfire blasted again—the fast retort of a bullet—and a woman's pain-filled scream.

Sarah and Bailey were right behind him when he ran down the narrow corridor. Another deputy from the station was in front of him—just steps in front of him—and Asher heard the guy swear when he caught sight of the figures in the small cell.

Carla and Deputy Ben. They were both on the floor. Both bloody.

Both shot?

Ben still had the gun in his shaking hand.

And Carla—she was propped up against the cot. The front of her shirt was soaked with blood. Had the second bullet hit her?

Ben dropped his gun and grabbed for Carla. "Help me!" Ben yelled. "Somebody *please* help me!" He put his hands on her wound and blood pumped up from between his fingers.

The cell door swung open again and Asher rushed

inside. Bailey was there, too, and Asher heard Sarah calling for help—for an ambulance.

Carla's head slowly turned toward Bailey. "No . . . guilt . . ."

"Carla, don't talk," Bailey said, her voice breaking. "Save your strength."

Not talking wasn't going to help her. Asher knew it. Based on that wound, hell, the bullet had been fired at almost point-blank range.

"Sh-she grabbed for my gun," Ben stammered. "Sh-shot me. We fought for the weapon and it went off." He was still pressing his fingers to her chest.

"I . . . was in the car . . ." Carla whispered, her eyes on Bailey. "S-sorry . . . for that."

"What car?" Bailey asked. But Asher saw by her expression—*she knew.*

"Mad at . . . you . . ." Carla said. "But more . . . mad at him."

Him.

Her body jerked, shuddered.

"Jesus!" Ben cried. "There's so much blood!" He gave a frantic shake of his head. "She shouldn't have done that! Why did she do that? I wasn't going to hurt her! I wasn't going to—"

Sarah shoved him back. She yanked open Carla's shirt, getting a look at the damage. Her gaze flew to Asher's. They both knew . . .

She only has moments.

"I . . . I did kill him." Carla's voice was even softer now. Barely a breath. "F-finally did it . . ." She smiled, a bare curl of her lips. "N-never saw m-me . . . c-coming . . ."

Asher saw it happen. The moment when she passed.

The pain faded from Carla's face. Her eyes seemed to glaze over. One moment, she was staring at Bailey, and the next . . . Carla's eyes were still wide open, but she wasn't staring at anything.

Gone.

So fucking fast. An instant of time.

"No!" Ben yelled. He tried to shove Sarah and Asher back. "No, she can't do this! I didn't mean to—*she can't do this! She can't die!*"

She had. She was gone. And when Ben finally got to her, pushing on her bloody chest, still trying to save her life, her body just rocked, just moved with the force of his hands.

"Please, no," Ben said, and he had tears in his eyes. "Don't do this."

Asher slowly backed away. Ben was bleeding from a hit he'd taken in his side. The guy would need to go to the hospital. Get checked out.

But Ben didn't seem to even be aware of his own injury. He was still pressing on Carla's chest. Trying to get her to come back.

His first kill?

The young deputy's body shook. "I—I just wanted to help her . . . I thought she knew . . . she *knew* . . . I was there to help her."

Carla didn't need help, not anymore.

Asher watched as Bailey put her hand on Ben's shoulder.

AN AMBULANCE ARRIVED to take Ben to the hospital. He climbed into the back, his expression so confused and lost.

Carla's body had been covered in the cell. She'd be transported away soon, too.

"I can't believe this fucking shit happened," Wyatt said as he stood at Asher's side. "She went for his fucking gun? Why? Did she have some kind of death wish?"

"I think she was afraid," Sarah said, voice carrying only to them.

"Afraid of what? Going to jail because of what she did to Spawn?" Wyatt shook his head. "A deal could have been worked out. I *told* her that last night. She could talk, tell everything she knew about the Death Angel, and we'd work something out."

The FBI had just pulled up at the station. They'd rolled up in their typical black SUVs. The doors opened. Agents in suits stepped out.

Bailey was silent as she watched Ben's ambulance drive away. Asher put his arm around her shoulders. He knew she was taking Carla's death hard.

She wanted to find the other survivor for so long. And she did . . . just to see Carla die.

And how was she taking the news that Carla had been in on the murders? Did she believe Sarah?

Does she believe me?

"I don't think Carla Drake wanted to tell anyone anything else about the Death Angel," Sarah said.

"Why the hell not?" Wyatt asked. "He's dead. Putting a name on those remains would have marked the case as closed. It wasn't as if she owed the bastard anything."

No, she *shouldn't* have owed him anything.

"Before those suits get up here," Sarah murmured, "I

have a question for you, Sheriff. Both Carla and Bailey had patient files with Dr. Leigh, correct?"

"There were files there, yeah, but—"

"What about the other victims? Were they also being treated by him?"

Asher felt Bailey's jerk of surprise.

"I don't . . . I haven't been through all the case files."

"The FBI is going to take over those files." Asher saw the agents gauging the throng of reporters. No doubt, they'd be holding a big press conference soon. That was their deal. Establish the chain of command early on—by getting in front of every camera they could find. "We need to know that information, right the hell now."

"Why—why would all the victims be seeing Leigh?" Wyatt asked as they all backed into the station. They hurried toward the small area that had been designated for evidence. "You think he was involved in some way?"

Bailey was too pale. Too quiet. Her gaze flickered from Wyatt to Sarah.

"I think victims are chosen for a reason." Sarah would know—too well—how killers picked their victims. "I think a pattern exists and we have to find it. We know—right now—that both Carla and Bailey had ties to Leigh."

"But Dr. Leigh didn't know she was the other victim," Bailey said, her voice little more than a rasp. "He didn't know . . . not until the end . . . that's when he came to my house, wanting to do a story. He said all along that I was wrong, dissociative, that—"

"Maybe he lied to you." Sarah's expression was grim. "Maybe he was a very, very good liar."

Wyatt gave a quick start of surprise. "Carla . . . she told me something like that." He shook his head, hard. "She *told* me that she lied all the time. I thought she was just bullshitting, trying to look tough . . ."

Asher thought—in that instance—that she'd been telling the truth.

Wyatt had picked up a big-ass box of folders—and the box was marked LEIGH FILES. He started thumbing through them.

"Maybe Leigh *did* know about Carla," Sarah continued. "Maybe he knew a lot more than you believed."

"Fuck. Here's one." Wyatt held up a folder. "Jamie Holiday. She was the second victim taken."

Asher wanted that file. "What does it say in there?"

Wyatt hesitated. "Like I can show this to you. Patient rules—"

"Come on . . . *now* you're going to throw rules at me? The FBI will be inside any minute. *What does the file say?"* Asher demanded.

Wyatt scanned the details. "Guilt complex. Her . . . her best friend drowned when they were sixteen. Jamie was swimming with her. She made it back to shore but the friend . . . she was never found."

Bailey backed up a step.

Asher's eyes narrowed as he considered all the angles with this case. "Carla said that she had a boyfriend once who taught her about breaking and entering."

A furrow appeared between Wyatt's brows. "Yeah, okay, so?"

"Cops got called to one of the break-ins. Carla slipped away, but the guy was busted. He died in jail." *And Carla had just died that way, too.*

"A pattern," Sarah said, nodding. "It's there. No one saw it before."

"Yeah, well." Wyatt slapped the folder down on the desk. "I don't see it *now*. So these two women might have seen Dr. Leigh, so Bailey saw him, too. It doesn't mean—"

"I left my parents to die." Bailey's voice was that of a lost child. "We all left someone . . . and the guilt was destroying us."

Death angels. They'd survived but had the killer thought they were supposed to die?

Wyatt stared down at the files. "If the other victims are in here . . ."

"If they had a similar experience, that's our link." Sarah started to pace. "We need to check those files. We need to see just why those other women—"

Footsteps. Raised voices.

Shit.

Asher turned and sure enough, the FBI agents were closing in. The agent in front, an older man with a bald head and slight paunch, frowned at them. "Sheriff Bliss?"

There isn't going to be time to look at those files, not now.

"I'm Agent Henry Franco, and I'll be taking point on this investigation from now on."

FRANCO HAD KICKED their asses out, pronto. But the guy had shown them one courtesy—instead of being fed to that frenzy of reporters out front, Franco had let them use the back door.

He'd also allowed Sarah to stay in the station. So, that was something. One point in their favor. Sarah's name tended to still impress the FBI brass, so when someone was looking to break a case and build the perfect profile . . . her help wouldn't be refused.

But Franco didn't want Bailey anywhere near the investigation. And I wasn't about to stay there without her.

She was silent as they crept toward her car. Far too silent. She was still shaken from Carla's death, and Asher didn't know what to say in order to comfort her. Maybe there wasn't anything that he *could* say.

They walked past another car, one that had also been parked in the shadows, away from the crowd. A blue Honda with dark red dirt stains on the side—

Asher stilled. He glanced back at the blue vehicle, noting the way those stains slid over the door. A pattern there, and it didn't look like the heavier material of dirt. It looked like—

Snap.

A flash went off right beside them, startling Asher for a moment. He blinked quickly and then—

A gun was pointed at him.

Richard Spawn—that fucking dick—had a camera dangling from a strap around his neck and the fat fingers of his left hand grasped a gun. Spawn smiled at him. And at Bailey. "Knew you'd come out, sooner or later."

"Spawn . . ." Asher snarled. "Put down the damn gun."

"Can't do that. Got to get my exclusive first." He licked his lips. "Bailey, come here."

Asher shook his head. "Bailey, do not move."

Spawn's eyes turned to slits. "Bailey, if you don't get that sweet ass here in the next five seconds, I'll shoot your boyfriend. Right in the heart. How long do you think it will take him to die?" He had the gun aimed right at Asher's chest.

After Carla, dammit, she *knew* how long it would take. "Bailey . . ." Asher rasped but it was too late. She'd already lunged toward Spawn. Traded her life . . . *for mine.*

Spawn grabbed her—fast and hard—and put that gun right under her chin. Then he smiled. "I did my research on you, Asher. I know just how to control you."

You are a dead man, Spawn. "Since when do reporters grab victims like this?" Asher demanded as he took a lunging step toward them. "What in the hell are you doing?"

"I'm not reporting on the news any longer," Spawn said, his smile stretching. "I'm making it. And by the time I'm done tonight, I'll have the fucking best story ever."

Asher shook his head. "You're crazy."

Spawn jabbed the gun harder against the underside of Bailey's jaw. "How do you feel about sweet Bailey Jones?"

Asher's gaze slid to Bailey's face. Her expression was blank. Not afraid. Not angry. Just . . . empty.

"How do you *feel* about her?" Spawn asked again, voice roughened. "You seemed to lock onto her pretty fast. So that got me to thinking . . . maybe you care for her."

"I do," Asher gritted out. He more than cared.

"Let's find out how much," Spawn taunted. He backed up, with Bailey in front of him, the gun still shoved under her chin. But his right hand thrust down into his pocket and he pulled out a small key ring.

He pressed a button and the trunk popped open. "Get in," Spawn said, jerking his head toward the open trunk.

Asher didn't move.

"Want to see how much damage a bullet will do to her from this angle? I bet it will go through her jaw, maybe come out her cheekbone. Or maybe . . . maybe it will go straight through her brain."

Bailey didn't make a sound.

"Get in the trunk," Spawn ordered. "Or I start hurting her. I start *killing* her, and that shit will be on you."

Asher looked into Bailey's eyes. Such gorgeous eyes. And he smiled at her. "It's going to be okay, Bailey."

She shook her head. "Don't," she whispered.

But he headed toward that open trunk. He climbed inside.

"Asher!"

"It will be okay." The trunk slammed closed a moment later, sealing him in darkness.

Asher didn't breathe for an instant, and then . . .

Then his hand slid down to his ankle. To the sheath that waited there. And he palmed the knife in his hand.

This scene won't fucking end like before. I won't watch while someone I love is hurt. Bailey won't be hurt. Not while I'm near.

His fingers tightened around the knife.

CHAPTER EIGHTEEN

Spawn shoved Bailey into the blue vehicle. "You drive," he snapped. "The better for me to keep the gun on you."

She cranked the car. His left hand held a steady grip on the gun.

"Figure since the lover is in the back," Spawn added tauntingly, "you won't do anything stupid like try to wreck the ride. Wouldn't want to hurt him, right?"

No, she didn't want to hurt him. Not ever. That was why she'd gone to Spawn, because she couldn't bear the idea of Asher being shot.

Only look where we are now.

"Keep to the back roads. We're heading out to a familiar spot. Got it ready last night. Had to find someplace to stay low after that bastard Dave turned on me."

She didn't know who the bastard Dave was. Her hands were tight around the steering wheel as she drove forward.

"We're going back to the cabin," Spawn told her, in case she hadn't figured out what he was talking about.

I figured it out, asshole.

"Seems fitting, right? The survivor dies at the scene of the infamous crimes."

He's going to kill me and Asher. Her foot eased up on the accelerator.

The gun jabbed into her side. "Speed the fuck up! Because I can always shoot your ass now and dump your bleeding body in the backseat. You can get to the cabin by being conscious or unconscious—the choice is *yours*."

Her foot pressed down on the accelerator again. "Why are you doing this?"

"Why? *Why?* Because I'm going to have the power this time. I'm going to be the one in the limelight. Not just chasing stories anymore, I'll make them." He laughed. "Figured out how to do that with the pretty redhead."

Dear God, he means Hannah.

"I was out in the woods, after tailing you and that jackass in the trunk . . . and there she was. Just put right in my path like some kind of freaking sign. Everyone was already forgetting the Death Angel, see. No one wanted to buy my stories, so I thought . . . I'll just make them all remember again."

Nausea rolled in her stomach.

"Turn right at the fork," he muttered.

This isn't a damn Sunday drive, bastard!

But she turned right.

"I didn't expect the rush." He was talking and talking and making her crazy. "I mean, I always wondered why the Death Angel did it, but I didn't understand, you know? Not until her blood was on me. Not until I stared down at her still body. Then I realized . . . *I did that.* I killed her. I took away her life." He laughed. "And it felt really fucking good."

You are so sick.

"I took pictures of her—because that's what the Death Angel did, right? And it was what I did, too. When I took those pictures, *I became* him. I saw the world through his eyes."

The Death Angel is dead. He doesn't see anything anymore.

"I didn't know how long it would be before someone found her body, so I figure I'd plant the camera at your place. I wanted you to know the Death Angel was back."

"You're not the Death Angel." She risked a glance in the rearview mirror. Was Asher okay back there?

"Got to admit, though, you nearly screwed things to hell and back for me when you found the cabin *before* you found the camera. But, hell . . . how was I supposed to know you would go to the cabin?" he muttered. "Couldn't believe that shit. I mean, I used that cabin because I'd found a note about it in one of Leigh's files."

Her head jerked toward him. *Leigh's files?* The car swerved.

"Eyes on the fucking road!"

"What files? What are you talking about?"

"Who do you think hooked Leigh up with the book deal?" Now he sounded boastful. "*I did.* That was *our* deal. We were going to blow the Death Angel story wide open."

She shook her head. "I don't understand."

"No, you wouldn't." He laughed again, the sound so taunting. "You never had a clue, did you? Leigh and his obsession with serial killers. Why do you think he *was* so obsessed?"

Her sweaty palms slid over the steering wheel.

"Because he was one," Spawn whispered.

"No." She shook her head. "That's not possible. He was—he was my shrink. He was helping me."

"Yes . . . he was. He was helping you all." More laughter. Grating laughter. "I figured that shit out. *Me.* Because I am the best damn reporter in the business. I don't care what that hack Dave said."

Who the hell is Dave?

"Turn left," he barked.

She turned left. Took the turn too hard and the car bounced.

"I put the victims together. I paid a bribe to Bliss— dumb fucking Bliss. A little money went into his palm, and he gave me copies of the Death Angel case files."

Wyatt had given him the case files?

"I pored over those files. I knew I could find a key in them, if I looked hard enough, and then . . . then I saw it."

Her lips felt numb. "A pattern. With the victims." Exactly as Sarah had said.

"Damn straight. I knew they meant something. I knew—"

Sarah was right. "We were all patients of Dr. Leigh's." *That* was what he'd discovered when he reviewed the files Wyatt had given him.

"Guilt complexes. Every single fucking one of you. So Leigh made his own experiment. Least, that's what he told me. He put you in the most extreme situation. He gave you a chance . . . save yourself or save someone else."

Help me! Please, help me!

"If you made the right choice, Leigh figured your guilt would finally end. And if that happened, he said he meant to let the victim go."

Her whole body was shaking. It was so hard to steer. And tears tracked down her cheeks.

"If you saved yourself . . ." The muzzle of the gun shoved harder into her. "Then you didn't deserve to live. The guilt was yours to bear, and death was all you'd get."

The Death Angel. "No." She didn't want to believe it. Something else had happened. Someone had just . . . just stolen Leigh's files. "He never . . . he never believed me about the other victim."

The Death Angel died in the fire.

"You made the right choice, so I asked him why he still tried to kill you." Now Spawn's voice had turned musing.

"Why?" Her lips were numb. *Can't believe this. Can't . . .*

But why would Spawn lie now?

He plans to kill me. Why lie to someone you planned to kill?

"You saw his face. So he didn't have a choice." He laughed. "Funny thing about that . . . I think *he* felt guilty because he had to change his precious rules. His experiment failed, not because of a victim not making the wrong choice . . . but because his damn mask fell off."

She remembered grabbing that mask. Yanking it hard. Looking up—

Her temples seemed to explode with pain.

"Good thing he was your shrink, right?" Spawn mused. "When you actually managed to survive, he was still safe because he could make sure that you remembered *only* what he wanted. He got to twist and turn the facts and make you remember the night the way *he* wanted you to see it."

I grabbed the mask. I tried to scream. I looked up and saw—

"Turn right up ahead. We don't have far to go now . . ."

ANA YOUNG TOOK one look at the men in the fancy black suits and knew the FBI agents had arrived. She barely contained an eye roll. Sure, Sarah got along with these guys pretty well, but Ana had never been on what she'd call friendly terms with them.

Mostly because when she'd been a kid, FBI agents had treated her brother like a criminal. They'd separated Ana from Asher. They'd questioned him, again and again.

She'd been the victim who'd been swarmed with hospital care, nurses, the one handled with kid gloves.

But Asher . . .

Because he'd only had one wound—that scar on his chin—they'd grilled him. For hours and hours. One dumb son of a bitch had even suggested that Asher might have been involved in the crimes.

I was the victim. He was the killer. She knew exactly what the agents had seen when they looked at her and her twin.

Her gaze swept around the station. Sarah was in there, huddled over some files and a big gray box. Viki was there, too. Talking on the phone with someone— maybe checking in with LOST? But Ana didn't see Asher or Bailey.

She swung around, intending to head back out and face that crowd of reporters.

"He took her home," Wyatt said.

He'd just come out of a nearby office.

"Your brother," he continued with a faint nod. "He took Bailey home. Things got a little . . . intense here, and I think they needed that break." His lips twisted. "Even if it was a break ordered by the Bureau."

Her gaze sharpened on him. "Define *intense*."

His hand rose and his fingers fiddled with his shiny sheriff's star. "Carla Drake is dead. I have a deputy on the way to surgery, and I've pretty much been informed by the governor that my job is *over*." He gave a mocking laugh. "Shortest time a sheriff ever served in this county. I broke the record."

Her lips parted to respond, but then her phone rang, vibrating in her pocket. She knew that familiar blues beat. Asher loved blues, so she'd programmed that ringtone just for him. "Excuse me, would you?"

Wyatt took off his star and put it on the counter. "Sure. Why not?"

She pulled out her phone. "Asher? Where are you? And what in the hell happened to Carla—"

"Track my phone."

"What?" She could barely hear him. The connection seemed so distorted.

"Spawn. Richard—" The line cut in, out. In. "Had a gun."

Her hand tightened around the phone. "Who had a gun?"

Wyatt whirled toward her.

"Spawn. Got me—" Static crackled. "In trunk."

What. The. Hell.

"He has a gun—" Once more, the line cut in. Out.

"Asher?"

"On Bailey."

Static crackled.

"Come help—" And the line died.

For a moment, she just stared at Wyatt. He stared back. "What's happening?" Wyatt asked, voice gentle, careful.

She looked at her phone. For an instant, the station vanished. She was back in that old, stinking warehouse. Her brother was in front of her. Staring at her with tears in his eyes.

Asher.

"Trace his phone." Her words flew out. "That reporter—Spawn—he pulled a gun on Asher and Bailey. He's got Asher in the trunk." *But I'm guessing the fool forgot to take Asher's phone and that's how he was able to call me.* And if she knew her brother . . . he'd have at least one weapon hidden on his body.

Asher never went anywhere unprepared. Neither did she. "Get that trace!" They could triangulate the signal and find her brother. They'd lost the call but she knew he'd call back. She knew—

The phone rang.

Blues. Sweet, sweet blues.

Hell, yes.

Wyatt grabbed his star.

THEY PULLED OFF the road and into one of the small parking lots that hikers used. The same lot that she and Asher had used when they came out for their first trip to the Death Angel's cabin.

"Your boyfriend thought he was such a badass when he met me out here," Spawn said. "I knew I should have run him down that first night. But he dodged too fast, and I didn't want to risk going back then."

She turned off the car. After all, there was no other place to go. "That was you . . . you were the one watching the house." But she'd already known that—thanks to the camera Carla had brought to her.

The sun was setting, casting a red glow over the car. "I was always watching you."

Carla was right.

"I mean, Dr. Leigh thought you should get to live. As long as you didn't remember the truth, everything was fine. He even had you believing you had some sort of dissociative episode going on. Smart fuck made you think you were crazy. Used hypnosis and some other shit. Bragged about it to me. Said he could control you completely."

I hate you, Spawn. "No, he didn't have total control. That's why I went to LOST."

His twisted smile faded. "That's when I knew I had to end you, sweet Bailey. Finish the chain. Dr. Leigh didn't agree. He'd let you go. Let Carla go—hell, he had that woman so twisted and damaged that she didn't even know which way was up."

Bailey licked bone-dry lips. *What can I use as a weapon? How do we get away?*

"I warned him that she was about to break, too. But the woman was like his fucking pet project. He said he was going to help her vanish. Didn't realize what he meant by that, not until I heard about the fire at her shop. Guessing he helped her out with that . . ."

The man I saw upstairs. The shadow moving around . . . the man in the mask . . .

Dr. Leigh? Her temples pounded. She saw shadows where she should see a man's face.

"I wanted to know how deep in the game she really was. Leigh would never tell me, not for certain. I think she was the first one, though."

Game? It hadn't been a game. It had been life. It had been death. It had been hell on earth.

"Because she'd let her lover get arrested . . ." The pieces were starting to fit.

"How the hell do you know about that?"

"Carla told me."

He blinked, seemed actually surprised. "You're lucky that crazy bitch didn't kill you. She killed Leigh, you know. Sliced his throat right open. Figure it had to be her, after all. She and I . . . we were the only ones who knew what he'd done."

The drumming of her heartbeat was too loud.

"Maybe she got tired of following his orders," Spawn mused. "Or maybe she realized the only way she'd be free was if he died. Because I know he wasn't going to let her go. He needed her, after all. Like the bastard told me, every successful experiment must have a control subject."

Experiment. Game. Rage built within her.

"But it's good that she eliminated Leigh. He was the old Death Angel. I am the new one. The guy was just lying low, not doing a damn thing. That doesn't make news."

Her heart raced so fast. Did he hear that desperate beat?

"*I* make news."

And he was going to make news again. Going to have her and Asher become his latest victims.

"Get out of the car," Spawn ordered her. "Loverboy is waiting."

Bailey didn't move. "You'll just torture us. Kill us."

He shrugged. "But maybe . . . maybe you'll over-power me. I mean, isn't that what you've been thinking all along? That you'll overpower me? That you'll some-how manage to get away? Save Asher?" He pointed the gun right between her eyes. "That you'll be the hero again? Brave Bailey Jones. She did it once more. She escaped the Death Angel for a second time."

"You aren't the Death Angel."

"And *you* aren't brave. You're just a lost little girl who's about to go for another walk in the woods. And we're going to see how loud you can scream this time." He glared at her. "Open the door, Bailey. Get your ass out."

She opened the door. Got out. Stood near the car. He followed her, moving slowly, crawling over the seat and maneuvering around the steering wheel. "Good girl," he mocked and he yanked her close to his body. "We're gonna check on the boyfriend now. I figure he'll play ball. He has to, right? Bet he can't bear the thought of watching another woman get tortured right before his eyes."

I can't let that happen. I can't let Asher live through that hell again.

"He'll kill you," she told Spawn.

"Doubt it. Not with my finger so close to the trigger . . . and the gun so close to your pretty head."

And it was close. Right under her chin. One wrong move, and it would blow.

But . . .

I can't let him hurt Asher. Wasn't that the reason she'd followed Spawn's command the first time? Why she'd let herself be taken by him?

To protect Asher. To buy them a few more minutes so that they could try to think of a way to escape.

Spawn had been right, on that count. But he was wrong about so many other things.

I'm not lost and I'm not afraid. For Asher, she could face any pain. She was between him and Spawn, and she was going to stay between them.

You won't hurt him. I won't let you.

"Push the trunk button," Spawn ordered. "Time to play."

Bailey had the keys in her hand. She made a show of lifting her hand, aiming it at the back of the vehicle. She pushed the button to release the trunk.

The gun moved beneath her chin, just a bit, as Spawn repositioned himself to better view the back of the vehicle.

He thinks Asher might come out and attack. He wants to be ready.

But . . . Spawn was waiting for the attack to come from Asher.

I won't make Asher face his nightmare. I can't do that to him.

The trunk was almost open.

Bailey sucked in a deep breath, and then she slammed her elbow back—back as hard as she could into Spawn's right side. She felt the give of skin and stitches beneath her hit and Spawn bellowed in pain.

That's right, bastard. I remember exactly where Carla stabbed you.

She lurched forward, out of his grasp, running for the back of that trunk. "Asher, run! Get away!"

He fired.

The bullet slammed into her, and Bailey hit the ground.

WYATT WAS DRIVING hell fast, but that wasn't good enough for Ana. She needed him to go faster.

"They've stopped." It was Sarah's voice, floating through the Bluetooth connection. "Signal is triangulated as best as we can get it. Straight ahead five miles. Turn right."

"That leads to the Mills Hiking Trail." Wyatt slammed his hand against the steering wheel. "Spawn is taking them right back to the Death Angel's cabin."

"You giving this intel to our FBI buddies?" Ana asked as she glanced back at the black SUV that trailed behind them.

She'd told everyone at the station what was happening—and now the cavalry was coming in force. The FBI had insisted on being part of that cavalry, and she hadn't been able to refuse. *I just need to get my brother back.*

LOST had used its resources to track Asher. Because that little sheriff's office? It hadn't been equipped for a mission like this one—not with time being of the extreme essence.

So Sarah had gotten on the phone with LOST. The organization had pulled some powerful strings . . .

And my brother is five miles ahead.

"I'm giving them the intel," Sarah promised. Then her voice hardened. "You be safe out there, Ana, understand?"

The only thing she understood was that her brother needed her. "It's going to be too much like before," Ana heard herself murmur. "If Spawn is threatening Bailey . . . I don't know what Asher will do."

"That's why you're going to be there for him. You guard his back." Sarah was firm. "And watch your own."

"I got her back," Wyatt said. "Don't worry about that." His siren wasn't on. They were going in silent, so as not to alert Spawn.

Spawn—the slimy reporter she'd seen skulking around the town? How had that guy gotten involved in this mess?

And could they stop him, before he hurt someone else?

WHEN HE HEARD the gunshot, Asher leapt out of the trunk with a roar. He raced around the back of the car, the knife gripped in his right fist, but he made sure to keep his hand behind his leg so Spawn wouldn't see his weapon. He was going to get the drop on that bastard and—

Bailey was on the ground.

He froze.

His Bailey was on the ground.

For a moment, all Asher could do was stare at her. She seemed so still. So incredibly, terribly still. "Bailey?" Her name came from him, hoarse, painful.

"Ah!" Spawn screamed. "What did the bitch do? I told her . . . just open the trunk! She wasn't the fucking hero! I told her that!"

Bailey was on the ground.

And he could see the blood on her back. "No . . ." Asher broke from his stupor and ran toward her.

"Stop!" Spawn yelled. "You fucking stop!"

Asher didn't stop.

A bullet blasted into his left shoulder. He barely felt the burn.

"Get the fuck away from her!" Spawn yelled. "This isn't how it works! I'll shoot you in the head! Right between your damn eyes if you take another step—"

Asher took another step. Another. He *ran* to Bailey and the bullets flew at him. Another hit his arm. One burned right past his cheek. He didn't care. He didn't stop until he was beside Bailey. He put his hand to her throat and his fingers were shaking.

Be alive. Be alive, sweetheart. You have to be alive for me.

His blood dripped onto her as his fingers pressed to

her throat. Then he felt it. The lightest, faintest beat of her heart.

Then Spawn pushed the gun against his temple.

"You don't listen well, do you?"

Asher looked up. Bailey was alive. She hadn't stirred at all when he touched her and there was far too much blood.

She needs help. I have to get her help.

"Get away from Bailey. Stand up. Or die now."

Asher stared into that sick fool's eyes. "I don't leave Bailey."

"You will die!"

"I don't leave Bailey." Because this wasn't a game. Wasn't some choice—his life or hers. For him . . . there was only Bailey. She belonged to him, completely and totally, just as he belonged to her. And he would do *anything* for Bailey.

Even give up his life.

But I'd rather take his. Asher felt tension coil in his body as he prepared to attack.

"You don't leave her?" Spawn spat. "What kind of crap line is that? Let me guess . . . *because you love her.*"

"Yes." Simple. True. He did love Bailey Jones. Maybe he'd loved her from the first instant he'd looked into her green eyes. Love at first sight wasn't supposed to be real, right?

But Bailey was real. What he felt for her was real.

And he didn't care *when* it had happened. All that mattered to him was that it *had* happened. He'd fallen in love with Bailey Jones.

And he'd die for her in a heartbeat.

"I wanted to kill you both at the cabin. It was *supposed* to be at the cabin! I even started to dig a new grave for her last night, but I guess . . . I guess this can work just fine—"

Before Spawn could finish his threat, Asher leapt up. With one hand, he knocked away Spawn's gun. With the other hand . . . he brought up his knife. And he drove that knife straight into Spawn's throat. *"Your turn,"* Asher snarled at him.

Spawn's eyes doubled in size, and his hands flew up. Frantically, he tried to grab for the knife.

Asher drove it in deeper and wrenched it to the side.

Then two vehicles hurtled into the little lot. One was a patrol car. Another a dark SUV. They screeched to a stop and gravel flew beneath their tires.

Wyatt jumped from the patrol car. "Step away from him, Asher!"

Smiling, Asher did. He lifted his hands.

And Spawn fell to the ground. He was gasping and gagging and choking, and Asher turned away from him. He went back to Bailey.

His Bailey.

Footsteps rushed toward him.

Two FBI agents were there, surrounding Spawn. Trying to help him. "Forget him," Asher snarled. "Bailey is what matters. We have to get her to a hospital!"

He reached for her, wanting to scoop her into his arms, and then he realized . . .

The bullet. The bullet went in right near her spine.

Ana's hands grabbed his before he could touch Bailey. He looked up at his sister, and when she flinched, he knew she saw the terror on his face. In the field, he'd had a teammate who'd gotten shot in the back. The man had been paralyzed and he'd died before any help could get to their remote location.

Not Bailey. Not my Bailey.

"What happened?" Wyatt asked.

"Get Bailey help." He pulled his hands from Ana's. He curled his body over Bailey's. "Get her help." Terror clawed at his insides, nearly ripping him apart. He knew what had happened. Bailey had tried to get away from Spawn. Only instead of running for the woods, for cover . . .

She ran toward the trunk. Toward me. She came to me.

And she'd been shot. Spawn had shot her in the back. Just gunned her down.

His fingers flexed. He wanted to kill that bastard all over again. And he knew that Spawn *was* dead. Sure, he was still gasping. Still twitching, but he wouldn't make it off that mountain.

Would Bailey?

"I love you," Asher whispered to her. "Please, baby, just hold on. Everything is going to be okay, I swear it."

He didn't want to think of his life without her in it. Bailey had *become* his whole world, in just a few short days. *I love you.*

He stayed there, with her, numb to everything else until he heard the whirr of a helicopter's blades. When the Life Flight crew rushed toward Bailey, Wyatt and Ana had to pull him away so the team could reach her.

And when that helicopter lifted off, Asher was right there with Bailey. As if he were going to let her fly away without him. His eyes were only on her, and in his mind, he kept repeating, *Don't leave. I love you. Stay with me. Please, Bailey, stay with me.*

ANA DIDN'T CRY, not until the helicopter had lifted off. Then she let the tears slide down her cheeks. She'd never seen her brother that way—and she hoped that she never would again.

"Did he even know that he was talking?" Wyatt asked, voice subdued. "When we were waiting on the chopper, did he realize—"

"No," Ana said briskly, breaking through his words. "He didn't." But Asher had been speaking, the whole time, and he'd broken her heart as he begged Bailey to stay with him, again and again.

Don't leave. I love you. Stay with me. Please, Bailey, stay with me.

"What's going to happen?" Wyatt asked. "Do you think . . ." His words trailed away.

Ana squared her shoulders. "I think Bailey is going to stay with my brother. *That's* what I think will happen." It was the only thing that could happen.

Because I don't know what he'd do without her.

Asher had spent years blocking himself off from other people, refusing to get close because he'd been afraid of that connection, but with Bailey, he hadn't been given a choice.

I guess that's what love is like. It takes over everything else. It overwhelms you.

It was a good thing Ana had never been in love. Because she never wanted the kind of pain she'd just heard in her brother's ragged voice.

She looked over her shoulder. Spawn hadn't been lifted out on that chopper—because he was dead. Her brother didn't play. When he attacked, he went straight for the kill.

She'd learned that lesson when she was fourteen. Spawn had taken that same lesson to his grave. "Get me to the hospital," she told Wyatt. "I want to be there when Bailey wakes up."

And she wouldn't say . . .

I have to be there in case she doesn't. Because if Bailey dies, then I think Asher may just break apart.

CHAPTER NINETEEN

THE SURGERY HAD ALREADY TAKEN SEVEN hours. Seven of the longest damn hours that Asher had ever lived. He paced in the waiting room. Paced and paced and stared at the operating room doors. When they'd arrived at the hospital, Bailey had immediately been wheeled to surgery. The nurses had stopped him at the door. The nurses had forced him to get his own wounds tended, like he'd given a damn about those scrapes. The bullets that hit him hadn't come close to anything vital. A few stitches, and he'd been fucking fine.

I'm fine, but what about Bailey? He felt as if he were about to lose his damn mind.

Ana was there now. Watching him. Worrying. He wanted to reassure her, but he couldn't. His every thought was on Bailey, as if he were willing her to survive.

If I want it bad enough, it has to happen. And I want Bailey, more than anything.

Sarah was there, too, and so was Viki. Silent, watching. The place felt like a damn tomb, and Asher hated that. Bailey didn't belong in a tomb. Not in a tomb, not in a grave, not in a hospital. She deserved to be out there, living, free. No more prisons. No more pain. Nothing to hold her back, not ever again.

When he heard the *whoosh* of that operating room door swinging open, Asher whirled around. A doctor was there, a guy who looked haggard and tired and wore green scrubs. "Bailey's family?" he called.

Fuck, yes, that was him. Asher rushed forward. "Is she okay?"

"A very delicate surgery." The doctor exhaled slowly. "She's in recovery now and—"

"I need to see her." No, he had to see her. Right then. Because he was splintering apart on the inside. Barely hanging on to his sanity. He needed to make sure she was alive. Had to see her with his own eyes. Bailey. *His* Bailey.

"And who are you?" the doctor asked, frowning.

Hadn't he just indicated he was her family? Shit, fine, he'd lie. He was her fiancé, her husband. He was anyone he needed to be in order to get back there and *see* her.

Footsteps rushed up behind him. Asher didn't look back but he heard—

"I'm Sheriff Wyatt Bliss. I can vouch for this man. Let him see her. I think she'll need to see him as much as he needs her."

The doctor's gaze darted over Asher's shoulder. He probably saw the gleaming star on Wyatt's chest or maybe he just recognized the guy—small towns and all of that—but he nodded. "She's in ICU. The second bed on the right—"

Asher was already gone. He couldn't wait to hear

the rest. Bailey was alive. He had to get to her. His feet pounded over the gleaming tiles and he heard one nurse call out to him, urging him to slow down.

He didn't slow down. Didn't stop—not until he was in ICU and he could see Bailey, right behind the clear glass.

She was pale. Too pale. Machines beeped all around her. Her lashes were closed.

He opened the door. Crept inside. His own ragged breathing filled his ears.

And then . . .

Her lashes fluttered. He could see the green of her eyes, only it wasn't as bright as before. Muted. Tired.

He hurried toward her. He reached for her hand, but hesitated. He didn't want to hurt her. Not ever—

"Ash . . ."

At that whisper, he smiled at her, his heart nearly breaking. "I'm right here, sweetheart." The only place he wanted to be. With her. Carefully, his fingers linked with hers. He squeezed her hand.

She squeezed him back.

"Am I . . . okay?" Her voice was so weak. Strained. And her eyes were already drifting closed again.

"Better than okay," he promised her. Asher leaned forward and pressed a kiss to her temple. "You are fucking perfect." *And you always will be, to me.*

"Liar," she said so softly. "But I . . . still love you."

In that instant, his racing heartbeat stopped. For a moment, he didn't even hear the beep of the machines around her. He just heard those sweet words, echoing in his mind.

Love you.

"I love you, too," Asher told her, his voice sounding rough and battered.

But Bailey's lashes were closed. Her breathing seemed easy. Deep. And had the pallor faded some from her cheeks?

His fingers gently smoothed over her hand.

"Don't worry," a woman's voice said, coming from behind him.

He looked back and saw the blonde nurse who'd been urging him to slow down.

The nurse smiled at him. "She's going to be all right. The doctor told you about her condition, right?"

Asher tried to remember what the doctor had said, but came up blank. He'd just known that the surgery was over and Asher's first instinct had been to get to Bailey. To see her. To touch her.

"No spinal damage," the nurse said, giving a little nod. "Part of the bullet had fragmented so the doc took extra time to remove all the pieces. But no spinal injuries, no significant internal damage. Give that woman a few days to recover, and she'll be as good as new."

His shoulders dropped.

"Want me to bring you a chair?" She glanced back over her shoulder, then at him. "We're really not supposed to let family stay that long but . . . I think we can make an exception this time. Something tells me she needs you."

No, I need her.

Asher cleared his throat. "Yes, I'd like that chair.

Thank you." Because there truly was only one place that he wanted to be.

With Bailey.

"So you're being called a hero again."

Bailey blinked when her blinds were pulled open and the sunlight spilled onto her hospital bed—and right into her eyes. "Ah! Asher!"

He laughed. "Ah, what? You know today's the big day. You get sprung from the hospital." He came toward her, bent, and pressed a quick kiss to her lips. "The reporters are outside, all desperate to get a glimpse of the woman who survived an attack not just from one killer, but two."

She grabbed his hand. Held tight. "You're the one who stopped him."

His eyes gleamed. "And you're the one who took a bullet rather than let him torture us both. You think I didn't realize what you'd done?" He lifted their joined hands. Pressed a kiss to the back of her fingers.

"I wasn't going to let him use me against you."

His hold tightened on her hand. "I was scared out of my head when I saw you on that ground."

She tried to smile for him. "I'm okay, now."

And Spawn was gone. Dead and buried just as . . . just as the Death Angel was gone.

She'd told Wyatt and the Feds everything that Spawn had revealed to her. She knew that they'd been working to unlock the files on Leigh's computer. To recover the data that might prove either the truth of Spawn's statements . . . or show them for the lie that they were.

I don't think they were a lie. I think I've been caught in lies for a long time . . . and the truth is out now.

"I want you to be better than okay, sweetheart." Asher stared into her eyes. "I want you to be happy. I want you to laugh and mean it, and I never want to see shadows in your eyes again."

Her lashes lowered. She couldn't promise those things. Bailey was pretty sure her past would always haunt her. The attacks had left their mark.

Asher let go of her hand. His fingers slid under her chin and he tipped back her head. Her lashes lifted so she was gazing into his eyes once more.

"I want us both to be better than okay," he continued, voice roughening. "And I think we can be . . . together."

She wasn't hooked up to any more machines. A good thing because she was pretty sure her heart had just accelerated like mad and any machines would have recorded that crazy hike. "What are you saying?"

His face was so serious. "I love you."

Take a breath. Take another one. "I love you." And her smile flashed, she couldn't help it. It just came and—

"See?" Asher murmured. "No shadows in your eyes." He leaned forward and pressed a soft kiss to her lips. "I want to be with you, Bailey. Today. Tomorrow. As many days as you'll let me."

I want you always.

He eased back, sitting on the edge of her hospital bed. "I get that we're still new, but what I feel for you, I *know* it's real."

She'd never felt this way for another man.

"I'll give you time—as much time as you need—to

see that we can work together. We can be happy. I can move here. I can quit LOST—"

"No." She absolutely didn't want him leaving LOST. LOST mattered. The work he did . . . it mattered. And maybe . . . maybe she could even help there, too. She'd survived hell—she'd like to help others there do the same.

She could understand the victims. Their pain. Maybe at LOST she could make a difference for someone else.

Maybe it was time to leave all of her past and look to the future.

Maybe I already am looking at my future.

"One day at a time," Bailey said, nodding. "How about we try that and see where it takes us?" But she already knew where she'd be going—to spend the rest of her life with him.

A rap sounded at the door. It squeaked open and . . . "May I come in?" Wyatt's voice. "Um, it's me . . . and Ana."

Asher stared into Bailey's eyes. "I love you," he said again, almost as if he just wanted to hear those words once more.

She wanted to hear them forever, so she smiled at him.

"Yeah, come on in," Asher called.

Wyatt strolled inside, his gaze worried until it locked on her. Then she saw the relief sweep over his features. "Looking good, Bailey."

She felt good. Sure, the stitches pulled a bit, but she was out of her hospital gown and in comfy sweats for her trip home.

"I have a car waiting *away* from the reporters," Ana

told her, giving a quick nod. "You don't need to face the throng out front."

But, for some reason . . . Bailey wasn't afraid of that throng. She wasn't sure that she was afraid of anything right then.

I have Asher. We made it through the dark. I want to see what comes next.

"The Feds managed to retrieve the data on Leigh's computer." Wyatt had his hat in his hands and he was twisting the brim. "Spawn was telling the truth. Leigh . . . shit, he wrote it all down. Like he was doing an experiment and documenting everything. Even told us who the poor bastard was who died in that fire."

Asher reached for her hand again.

Bailey stared up at Wyatt, trying to connect all the pieces of the puzzle. "But Carla said *she* killed the Death Angel. That she went back inside and knocked him out—"

"She lied," Ana said flatly. "That guy was a fellow named Jim Valler. He was a patient of Leigh's, too, one who suffered from a guilt complex just like the rest of you. When he was in college, his roommate died in a hazing incident. From what we can tell, Jim was the one who gave him the alcohol. Jim left school after that . . . seemed to vanish from the whole world after his friend was buried."

He hadn't vanished. He'd just become one of Leigh's patients.

"In his notes, Leigh said that Jim wasn't showing proper remorse. That he needed to be removed from the program. That night . . . with you . . . I think that was the end of the program," Wyatt said. "Leigh eliminated all loose ends. Or at least, he tried to."

"But Carla—"

"She was patient one," Ana said. "Sarah said she thinks Carla was the trigger patient for him. They had an . . . intimate relationship. Probably a manipulative one. Sarah built a profile on them both. She thinks Carla was terrified of Leigh—"

If she'd seen him kill, yeah, that made sense.

"But she was emotionally tied to him. So she worked with him in the 'tests' that he performed."

Asher's body tensed beside her. "Those weren't fucking tests. They were torture segments."

"Carla was the one who tattooed the victims. Sarah and the Feds think she also tattooed Leigh. That he wanted the mark as proof of his work."

And she'd gone to therapy with that guy? *Shit. Shit. Shit!* Her skin crawled.

"The crime teams retrieved fingerprints from Dr. Leigh's crime scene." Wyatt kept twisting the brim of the hat. "They found the prints *inside* the elevator, right on the buttons. Prints that belonged to Carla Drake."

So, in the end, Carla did kill the Death Angel. Just as she'd said as she lay dying in that cell. "In the end . . . finally did it . . . killed him."

"And we also found the BMW that tried to run you down," Wyatt added. "It was parked two blocks away from your house, in the garage of a home that was for sale. The place was vacant, so no one even noticed the BMW until the real estate agent came in for a showing."

Bailey's chest seemed to burn. "So much death." Guilt and blood and death. A cycle that seemed to have no end.

But it is ending. It's ending now. I survived. Asher survived. And I won't live my life always looking back. I won't feel guilt for the victim I didn't save.

She would focus on living. Loving. *I'll do what Asher said. I'll learn to smile more. To laugh.*

She could do it. *They* could do it.

Wyatt headed toward the bed. He paused near Asher and offered his hand. "I know we didn't get off on the right foot . . ."

Asher rose.

". . . but I appreciate your help. And LOST can damn well come back here anytime."

Asher shook his hand. "You are not nearly the prick that I thought you were."

Wyatt laughed. Then he looked at Bailey. "I'm always here, if you need me."

"Thank you."

He put his hat back on. "Okay, well, I'll keep the reporters busy out front. You guys slip away." He marched for the door.

Ana stared at them. Her gaze drifted from Asher to Bailey, then back. "You two were willing to die for each other."

Yes.

"Don't do that shit again." Ana glared at them both. "Got it?"

Bailey nodded.

"Good." Ana's glare dissolved into a smile. "Welcome to the family, Bailey." Then she came forward and wrapped Bailey in a hug. After a stunned moment, Bailey hugged her back.

Family.

Yes, she had one now. One that she would hold tightly. One that she would always protect.

And always love.

EPILOGUE

S O MAYBE SHE WAS CRYING. AGAIN. ANA HURRIED
down the hospital corridor and she swiped away
the tears that wanted to trickle down her cheeks.
At least no one was around to watch her break down
this way. A good thing. She had a rule about breaking
down in public—no one should *ever* see her cry.

"Ana."

Dammit.

Wyatt was there, frowning at her. "You okay?"

Her spine snapped right up. "Perfect." Better than
perfect.

He edged closer. "You look like—"

"Weren't you supposed to be taking care of the reporters out front?"

He shrugged. "On my way. But I . . . I wanted to say
good-bye to you first. I heard that you were heading
back to Atlanta tonight."

Yes. "Gabe has a new case for me."

"Right." He looked away. "Well, if you're ever in
town again and you want to get a bite to eat or . . .
well . . ." His cheeks flushed a bit. "You let me know."

The sheriff was asking her out. She blinked. "I'll do

that," Ana said softly. She wasn't about to reject the guy, at least not right then. Cold-hearted rejection wasn't her style. And the sheriff was a *good* guy. Mostly good, anyway.

He smiled at her. Then hurried off.

She watched him leave, her eyes dry now.

Yeah, he was a *good* guy, and that was his problem. Why the two of them would never have more than a casual dinner and a friendship.

Ana didn't do so well with good men. They didn't understand the darkness inside of her, a darkness that had been created from pain and torture and death. She wasn't one of those good girls who dreamed of a white picket fence and a happily-ever-after ending.

She'd been changed long ago, marked.

And now . . . now she had a very particular *type* of guy that she enjoyed.

The badder, the better.

Don't miss the next thrilling and sexy LOST novel from *New York Times* and *USA Today* bestselling author Cynthia Eden

WRECKED

Coming Spring 2017
Read on for a sneak peek . . .

CHAPTER ONE

THE KNIFE SLICED INTO HER SKIN. IT CUT DEEP, and the pain was white-hot. Ana Young locked her teeth together and stared straight ahead ... straight into her brother's horrified eyes. He was tied in the chair across from her, yanking and twisting against his ropes as he tried to break free.

But he couldn't escape. Neither could she.

But she could stay silent.

Asher ... her twin wasn't silent. He was screaming. *"Let my sister go! Stop it! Stop, please! Don't hurt her!"*

Asher didn't get it. The man with the knife ... he enjoyed hurting her.

Another slice. Even deeper this time. Ana licked her lip and tasted blood. The first slice had been to her face. Only her attacker had paused after that.

Let's save her pretty face for later.

And the knife had gone into her body, again and again. She tried to keep her eyes open. Tried to keep looking at Asher. When the end came, she wanted his face to be the last thing that she saw. She wanted Asher to know that she hadn't been afraid. That she was strong.

Another slice of that knife and she could feel tears sliding down her cheeks. The pain was wrecking her. Destroying the girl she'd been. Leaving someone else—some*thing* else in her place.

Don't fear the pain. Don't tense when the knife sinks into you. Look at Asher. Look at him.

"Let my sister go, you fucking bastard! You want to hurt someone? Hurt me, not Ana! Let her go!"

Ana's eyes were sagging shut. Asher's voice was fading. It suddenly seemed so distant. Odd, since he was just a few feet away. They'd put them close together so Asher would be able to see every cut perfectly.

Was she dying? Ana didn't want to go out like this. Tied up, trapped. Some sick bastard's toy.

She didn't want to go out like this . . .

Her eyes closed.

And part of her died.

The good part.

"Ana?" A hard hand closed over her shoulder. Ana jerked at the touch and the dream—more like twisted memory—vanished in an instant. She jumped to her feet, whirling around, and Ana found her boss, Gabe Spencer, frowning at her.

Way to make a killer impression on the big boss, Ana.

She shoved back her hair, lifted her chin, and straightened her spine. Not that straightening her spine did much. When you were all of five feet two inches, it was often hard to look intimidating. She wasn't the kind of woman who wore high heels—they just slowed her down when she was chasing criminals—so Ana had long grown accustomed to tipping back her chin and staring at the world with her go-to-hell gaze.

Only it wasn't exactly appropriate to use that gaze on the big boss.

Like it's appropriate to be caught sleeping at the office by him, either.

Ana cleared her throat. "Hi, Gabe. I was . . . brainstorming on the new case." She smiled at him. The smile was one of her secret weapons. Slow and disarming, that smile had saved her ass more times than she could count. In her line of work, some people erroneously thought that looking delicate was a weakness. Not so . . . Ana used her deceptively delicate appearance every single chance that she had.

But Gabe—former SEAL and now big, bad man in charge of LOST—well, he didn't exactly look disarmed. His bright blue stare swept over her, and a faint furrow appeared between his brows. "Did you pull another all-nighter?"

Maybe.

"Ana . . ." He sighed out her name. "I hired you because I *know* you're good. Your track record speaks for itself. You don't have to burn yourself out because you're trying to tear through the old case files at LOST and prove something to me."

Gabe was a good guy. He wasn't chewing her ass out for the on-the-job nap. He understood exactly what she'd been doing.

So Ana let her guard drop, just a bit, with him. After all, she'd known Gabe for years. They'd been friends long before she'd finally let him lure her into joining the LOST team. Gabe knew her secrets. Well, most of them. There were some secrets that even Ana's twin brother, Asher, didn't know.

And I plan to keep things that way.

"There are just so many of them," Ana said, glancing over at her desk and the files that were spread out there. "All those people . . . still missing. All those families . . . just hoping that their kids will come home. Husbands, looking for wives. Mothers, looking for their daughters. Friends, looking for—" She broke off, her lips pressing together. "I just want to help them."

And that was why she'd finally given in and joined LOST.

The Last Option Search Team was Gabe's baby. Years ago, his sister had vanished, and when the local authorities hadn't been able to find her, Gabe had joined the search. Unfortunately, he'd found his sister too late. He'd buried her instead of returning her home, and after that terrible tragedy, Gabe had made it his mission to help other families. The agents who worked at LOST were truly the last option for so many. People turned to LOST when their hope was gone. When the FBI and the cops and everyone else said the case was dead . . . LOST kept looking.

And the agents at LOST had been showing amazing results. Hell, within the last year, they'd even stopped two serial killers. They'd saved victims, not just found bodies. They were making a huge difference in the world.

And I want to be part of that difference.

So maybe she'd been burning the midnight oil as she reviewed case files. One in particular kept nagging at her. Cathy Wise. The girl had just been thirteen when she vanished.

And I was fourteen when I was abducted. Only Ana had gotten to go home again.

Cathy . . . hadn't. Not yet.

"I get personally involved," Ana confessed. "I know I should probably hold back but . . ." *But I can see myself in these cases. We have to help the victims.*

"No." Gabe's voice was soft. "We need to be involved, Ana. We need to care. It motivates us to get the job done." He inclined his head toward the files. "But you can't let the job consume you. As hard as we try, there will always be other cases. Others who go missing."

Her stomach twisted because she knew he was right. Every day, someone new vanished. Every day, a life was destroyed.

"That's why I'm in your office now," Gabe added. A faint smile curved his lips and his eyes glinted. "Not just because I wanted to interrupt your nap time."

Trust me, with the dream I was having . . . I'm glad you did interrupt.

"We have a new case. "

Ana took a quick step toward him.

But Gabe lifted a hand. "Before you get too excited, this case comes with some strings."

Strings? What was that supposed to mean? She was over her probationary period at LOST. She'd been handling cases on her own for weeks now.

"You'll have a partner on this one."

Well, yes, that was standard LOST procedure. *Always have someone watching your ass.* That was a Gabe Spencer directive that had come down on day one.

"He's . . . not with LOST."

Okay, now she was curious. "Then who is he with?"

"The FBI."

She tensed. A natural reaction for her. She didn't tend to like the Feds. With her past, with the way she'd seen the Feds tear into people's lives . . . *I don't exactly play nicely with them.*

"He's the one who brought us the case, Ana. Come in, talk with him, and just listen to what he has to say." Gabe paused. "And you should know that the agent asked to work with you, specifically."

Oh, hell, no. She did *not* like where this was going. Her inner alarms were definitely ringing. "What's this FBI agent's name?" The knot in her stomach twisted tighter even as she started a mental chant of *don't be Cash Knox. Don't be Cash Knox. Don't be—*

"FBI agent Cash Knox."

Of course. Because she truly did have some of the worst luck in the world.

"There a problem?" Gabe asked, squinting a bit at her.

Oh, jeez. Ana hoped she hadn't flinched or made some kind of horrible, pained face when he mentioned the FBI agent's name. "No, no problem at all." She pasted a big smile on her face.

"Agent Knox said that he'd worked with you before."

Worked with me. Had sex with me. Let's not go over all the gory details right now.

"But," Gabe continued carefully, as he inclined his dark head toward her, "this case . . . it's not going to be an easy one."

Fine with her. "I don't like easy."

He nodded, looking pleased, and Ana knew she'd given the right answer. "Then come into my office," Gabe said, "and I'll tell you everything. Agent Knox is waiting for us."

Right. She rolled back her shoulders. "Lead the way." *While I get my shit together.* Because she hadn't seen Cash in years . . . two years and a month, to be exact. She hadn't laid eyes on the guy since she'd left him sleeping after a night of great sex. She'd slipped away and hadn't looked back.

Because Cash is like Gabe . . . one of the "good" guys. And good guys weren't meant for her. Ana shoved a lock of hair behind her ear, grabbed her rather beat-up jacket from the back of her chair, and she hurriedly followed Gabe out of her office.

As they walked down that hallway, she glanced out of the window bank to her right. The bustling city of Atlanta was definitely alive and well . . . even though it was only a little after eight A.M. Gabe had been right about her all-nighter. She'd pulled another one because staying at home, having her demons torment her—well, it wasn't an option she wanted. So she'd escaped into work.

I thought if I couldn't help myself, maybe I could help someone else. Someone like Cathy Wise.

They passed Gabe's assistant, and Melody gave Ana

a quick, friendly wave. Ana waved back even as her gaze darted to Gabe's closed door. Cash was in there. How was she supposed to handle this?

Act as if nothing ever happened. She could do that. Cash would be all business, and so would she. Besides, it wasn't as if a good guy like Cash would cause trouble. Maybe he didn't even remember their night together. They'd both been drinking, thanks to the big celebration. Ana had brought in one of the FBI's ten most wanted, a sadistic asshole named Bernie Tate who'd enjoyed kidnapping and murdering women in their early twenties. He'd taken three victims by the time he was stopped.

And I was the one who stopped him.

She was still fucking proud of that fact.

Gabe opened the door to his office and held it, waiting for her to walk inside. Ana schooled her features, made sure her steps were slow and steady, and she marched in to face her past.

FBI special agent Cash Knox was turned away from her. He stood in front of the large windows in Gabe's office, and Cash's stare was on the city below. But, as soon as she crossed the threshold into the office, his body stiffened and his head turned in her direction.

Cash's gaze met hers. She'd forgotten just how intense his green eyes were. Forgotten that his face wasn't exactly handsome. Instead, it was rugged, a face with an edge that had made her think of danger the first time she'd seen him. Cash's jaw was hard, square, and currently clenched. His cheekbones were high, and a faint dimple notched the middle of his chin. A line of dark stubble coated his jaw. Cash kept his hair cut almost ruthlessly short; that look hadn't changed in the last two years. The guy's hair was so thick that if he let it grow, she was sure it would be something to see . . . sexy.

But that wasn't his style. An FBI agent who toed the line didn't have too-long hair. *And I'm guessing that stubble isn't part of his normal appearance, either.* It looked as if she wasn't the only one who'd pulled an all-nighter.

Cash stalked toward her. He had on a suit—a well-cut coat and basic black pants. She thought of that suit as FBI business time. His badge gleamed on his hip and when he shifted his arm, she saw the bulk of his holster.

Gabe followed Ana into the office and shut the door behind him.

"Ana Young," Cash said, his voice as deep as she remembered. "It's been a long time." He offered his hand to her.

And she was a professional, so she just gave him a small smile and took that hand. "Has it?" She released her hold after touching him what she figured was a good-manners length of time. Maybe her fingers tingled from the contact. Maybe she just imagined the tingle.

"It has," Cash agreed, dipping his head toward her. "Two years, to be exact."

No, it's been two years and one month. Not that either of us should know that.

Cash lowered his hand back to his side. "The last time I saw you . . ." Cash began.

Do not finish that sentence. The last time he'd seen her, she'd been naked. And on top of him.

"The last time I saw you," Cash repeated, his jaw hardening, "you'd just done the job that several dozen FBI agents hadn't been able to accomplish. You'd found Bernie Tate and you'd brought him into federal custody."

Her eyelids flickered. "It was my job. I was a bounty hunter." Actually, she could admit with pride that she'd been the best freaking bounty hunter in the whole United States. "And there was quite a reward on his head." But the reward hadn't mattered to her; it never did. She'd wanted to get that monster off the streets so that he wouldn't hurt anyone else.

And she had. Bernie was currently rotting in a maximum-security hold in Virginia—Wingate Penitentiary. A place reputed to be a real hell on earth.

"I need you to do that job again," Cash said.

Now she blinked in surprise. "Excuse me?"

Gabe walked around her and headed toward his desk. "Seems there was an . . . incident late last night." He eased into his chair and the leather gave a long groan beneath him. "Since you were pulling an all-nighter at the office, I'm guessing you missed the news."

Ana glanced between Gabe and Cash. "What news?"

"Bernie Tate was being transferred," Cash explained grimly. "But during that transfer, the prison van was intercepted. Bernie Tate escaped."

"You are kidding me." He'd better be kidding.

"I wish that were the case," Cash told her. "Trust me, I do . . . but he's gone. And I need you to find him."

"Before he kills again." She started to pace. She did that—when she was pissed, when she was scared, when she was trying to figure out what the hell to do next. "I can't believe this! The guy should have been locked away for the rest of his life! He shouldn't be out! How the hell did this happen?" She thought of his victims . . .

She still remembered them all.

Brenda George, twenty-two, a nursing student who'd been stabbed twenty-two times . . . the perfect number to match her age.

Kennedy Crenshaw, twenty-four, a young mother who'd still been alive when the cops found her . . . only she'd died an hour later, her body littered with stab wounds.

Janice Burrell, twenty-eight, a divorcée who'd made the mistake of hooking up with Bernie at a bar. He'd stabbed her so many times . . . her blood had covered the walls of the motel room that she'd been found inside.

"He'd said there were more victims," Cash murmured. "So the FBI worked out a deal to have him moved to a different prison, provided the guy talked and told us where those bodies were hidden."

Her eyes squeezed together. "You got played. Bernie wasn't the kind of guy who hid his kills. He wanted everyone to know what he was doing. He was *proud* of his crimes."

"I agree," Cash said, surprising her.

Her eyes opened and locked on him.

"But my boss didn't listen to me." The faint lines on either side of his mouth deepened. "Now we're in a serious clusterfuck situation. The media is freaking. We've got manhunts going in the area, and we need to get Bernie Tate back into custody, fucking yesterday."

Gabe tapped his fingers on the top of his desk. "I explained to the agent here that LOST doesn't normally hunt down criminals." His expression tightened as he studied Cash. "Our goal is to help the victims."

Cash raked a hand over his hair. "And I told your boss that if we don't stop Bernie, there *will* be more victims. It's only a matter of time."

Ana swiped her tongue over her top lip, feeling the old scar that raised the skin there. "Agent Knox is right. Bernie Tate isn't going to just disappear quietly into the sunset. He *will* start hunting again, and he'll take down as many innocent people as he can." She strode toward the windows. "Especially since he's been in prison," Ana mused. "He's been away from the blood for too long. He liked the blood, liked the thrill he got from hurting women." She could see people walking down on the street below. Men and women, going about their normal lives. Having no idea . . .

Danger is everywhere.

"You caught him before, Ana," Cash said, his voice roughening with intensity. "I think you can do it again. I got the all-clear from my boss to pull you in on this. The FBI wants Bernie back in custody, as quickly and as quietly as possible." There was a pause. "I need you, Ana."

She spun around. Her gaze jerked toward him. There was something in his eyes . . .

Cash exhaled on a long breath. "As I told your boss . . . the FBI is willing to offer certain incentives for your cooperation on this case."

"What kind of incentives?"

Gabe gave a low laugh. "The you-scratch-my-back-and-I'll-scratch-yours variety."

"The FBI is promising help on future LOST cases," Cash elaborated. "The FBI and LOST have crossed paths plenty of times, and sometimes that intersection has proven . . . painful."

That's an understatement.

"We're offering support to LOST. We're offering whatever damn deal it takes," Cash added grimly. "We just need you on board in the hunt for Bernie."

"The FBI certainly seems desperate," Gabe said.

Yes, Ana had just been thinking the same thing.

"Don't have much faith in your ability to bring the guy in, huh?" Gabe asked as he cocked his head to study Cash.

Anger flashed in Cash's eyes. "Let's cut the bullshit, shall we?"

Let's do that. She'd never had a lot of patience for bullshit.

Cash pointed at Ana. "She's the best tracker there is. I still don't know how the hell she found him before, but time is of the fucking essence. Bernie Tate is missing, and the FBI wants him brought back in. If Ana does the job, the FBI will owe LOST."

Definitely an I'll-scratch-yours favor.

"What do you think, Ana?" Gabe asked, drawing her gaze once more. "You joined LOST to find the victims, not to clean up messes left by the FBI. So if you don't want to take the case, you don't have to do it."

Cash growled.

Goose bumps rose on her arms.

Gabe rose to his feet. "Ana's choice," he said simply. "I told you I'd give you the chance to lay out the case for her, and I have. What happens next is completely up to Ana."

Her heartbeat drummed steadily in her chest. She thought of the files on her desk. The *victims* that needed her help.

And she thought of the women who could die if Bernie Tate was left to run free.

"May I talk to Ana alone?" Cash asked, his voice still rough.

Surprise flashed on Gabe's face. "Don't really know why you'd need to do that. Whatever you have to say to Ana can certainly be said to me, too." Now he slid from around his desk and walked to Ana's side. His arm brushed her shoulder. "I've known Ana for a very long time, and like I told you before, she has my utmost respect. That's why the choice is hers. If she wants this case, LOST will fully support her. If not . . ."

Cash's gaze slid between her and Gabe. His green stare hardened. He opened his mouth to speak—

"I'd like a moment with him," Ana said quickly. *Because I'm not sure what Cash may say next.*

Gabe's eyes slowly slid over her face. Whatever he saw there . . . well, it had him nodding. "Getting kicked out of my own office, huh?" A rueful smile curved his lips. "That's a new one."

She was so not winning points with him today. "Gabe . . ."

His hand brushed over her shoulder. "I'll be outside. I need to talk with my assistant, anyway. And . . . Ana . . ."

"Yes?"

"*You* make the choice."

He nodded toward Cash and slowly exited the room. Ana didn't realize she'd been holding her breath, not until the door closed behind him.

Then . . .

She became aware of just how thick and heavy the silence was in that office. She could also feel the weight of Cash's stare. She made herself look back at him.

"You seem . . . close to your boss."

Her eyes narrowed. *You'd better watch your step, Special Agent.* "Gabe is a good man. He wants to help the victims out there."

Cash swore. "And Bernie Tate isn't a victim."

"No, he isn't." Her hands twisted together. "But if Bernie isn't brought back into custody, there *will* be more dead women left in his wake. We both know that's true."

He stepped toward her. "Then you're going to help me? You could have just said so—"

"There are conditions." And she hadn't wanted to discuss these conditions in front of Gabe.

"Name them."

"One . . . I want honesty from you."

His eyelids flickered. "Are you saying I've lied to you before?"

"I'm saying that the FBI doesn't always play by the rules. If I'm working with you, if you're my partner on this, then I need to know I can trust you. I need to know that you'll have my back."

"I will." He sounded so sincere.

She wanted to believe him. "I'll need access to every

bit of intel you have on Bernie, even the confidential material, so don't think of holding back."

He nodded. "Done."

Okay, so far, so good. Time for the last condition. "You don't mention our past."

A muscle flexed along his jaw. "Want to run that by me again?"

"I don't think I need to do that." She lifted a brow. "I'm absolutely certain you know what I'm talking about. There will *not* be a repeat performance. If we're hunting Bernie, that's all we're doing. We'll stay professional, and the past will stay exactly where it belongs . . . dead and buried."

His gaze slid toward the closed office door. "You don't want the boss knowing about us."

"I don't want *anyone* knowing my personal business. If you have a problem with that—"

"Easy, Ana," he said, his voice going a bit soft when he said her name. Soft . . . raspy . . . the way he'd said it that long-ago night. "Despite what you think, I've never been the type to kiss and tell. Our past is our business, no one else's."

"Good." She gave a brisk nod. "Then it should stay that way." Ana offered her hand to him. "I think we have a deal."

Once more, his hand closed around hers.

And, dammit, his touch *did* make her skin tingle. She'd offered her hand to him again just so she could see, and unfortunately . . .

The attraction is still there. I touch him and my body reacts. I look at him and I need.

But sometimes, Ana's needs could go very, very dark. *Cash doesn't know about that part of me. He won't ever know.* Because this case was strictly business. And now they had a deal.

Time to hunt a killer . . . before he took another life.

BERNIE TATE GROANED as his eyes opened. He expected to see the old, sagging cot above him. His cellmate's ass would be dragging low over him, but . . .

No, I'm not in that hellhole. Not anymore.

His memory came rushing back to him. He'd been on the transport bus, the only prisoner. The guard had cuffed his hands but left his feet loose. Stupid mistake.

Bernie had waited for the perfect opportunity. Waited for his chance at freedom . . .

He smiled. *That chance had come.*

There was no fucking sagging cot above him. There was just the rough wood of a cabin. He could smell the scent of a fire burning somewhere close by, probably in the other room. His partner had sure done one fucking fine job of getting his ass to freedom.

Bernie sat up and swung his legs off the narrow bed. He shot to his feet, his stomach growling to remind him that he hadn't eaten since before he'd boarded that transport bus. Maybe his partner had a meal waiting in the cabin for him. Bernie smiled as he took a few fast steps toward the door.

Then Bernie tripped and he slammed, face-first, into the wooden floor.

"What the fucking hell?" Bernie snarled as he shoved himself up. He was in good shape—he'd made a damn point of staying in shape. Trapped in that prison, all he'd been able to do was work out. Exercise had kept him sane. Exercise . . . and his plans.

He had so many fine plans.

Goal one . . . find the bitch who got me locked up. Make her pay. Make her bleed. Make her scream.

But . . .

Bernie grabbed for his ankle. There was some kind of shackle on him. A cuff that locked around his left ankle and trailed back to the narrow bed. He grabbed the chain and yanked it and the whole fucking bed jerked toward him because the other side of that chain was locked around the foot of the bed.

The door squeaked behind him. His head jerked and his body twisted as he glared at the asshole in the doorway. "Is this some kind of joke?" Bernie shouted. "Get this thing off me!"

Then . . . then Bernie saw the knife. Glinting.

"No joke, Bernie." His partner stepped closer. The knife lifted. "It's time for you to pay."

What? No, no, this wasn't happening. He was free! He'd gotten away from that rat-hole prison. Away from the guards. He was free—

The knife sliced down toward him. Bernie lifted his hands, trying to shield his face.

The blade drove straight through his left hand and Bernie screamed.

"See," his partner whispered. "Payback."